BLESSING . . . OR CURSE?

"How long have you possessed this . . . gift?" Teleri asked.

"Gift?" the young man asked indignantly. "God above! You think I regard this thing as a gift? A good man is dying because of this—this creature living inside of me, and you think this is something I sought? This curse comes over me, and I have no control over it whatever."

Child of Saturn
Book One of
THE GREEN LION TRILOGY

KING & KINGDOM OF
YNYS CELYDONN

CHILD OF SATURN

TERESA EDGERTON

ACE BOOKS, NEW YORK

This book is an Ace original
edition, and has never been
previously published.

CHILD OF SATURN

An Ace Book/published by arrangement with
the author

PRINTING HISTORY
Ace edition/March 1989

ISBN: 0-441-10401-0

Ace Books are published by The Berkley Publishing Group,
200 Madison Avenue, New York, NY 10016.
The name "ACE" and the "A" logo are trademarks
belonging to Charter Communications, Inc.

PRINTED IN THE UNITED STATES OF AMERICA

10 9 8 7 6 5 4 3 2

Ace Books by Teresa Edgerton

THE GREEN LION TRILOGY

CHILD OF SATURN
THE MOON IN HIDING
THE WORK OF THE SUN

A GUIDE TO THE PRONUNCIATION OF THE NAMES OF PRINCIPAL CHARACTERS AND PLACES MENTIONED IN THE GREEN LION

Generally speaking:
c and *g* are always hard.
f is pronounced like *v* in English.
ff is just *f*.
ll is the Welsh *ll*.
dd is a soft *th*.
Vowels are usually the same as in Welsh, except where the names look Irish, or where I decided to pronounce them differently.
With no exceptions I can think of, the accent is on the penultimate (second to the last) syllable.

Specifically:

Teleri ni Pendaren (tel-AIR-ee nee Pen-DARE-en)

Ceilyn mac Cuel (KAY-lin mac KILL)

Cynwas fab Anwas (KIN-wass vab AN-wass)

Sidonwy (Sid-ON-wee)

Caer Cadwy (Kair KAD-wee or Kair Ka-DO-ee)

Camboglanna (Kam-bog-LON-nah)

Diaspad (Dee-AH-spad)

Calchas fab Corfil (KAL-kass vab KOR-vill)

Fflergant fab Maelgwyn (FLUR-gant vab MEL-gwin)

Tryffin (TRIF-in)

Garanwyn (Gar-RAN-win)

Gwenlliant (approximately Gwen-HLLEE-ant)

Glastyn (GLASS-tin)

Tir Gwyngelli (Tear Gwin-GELL-ee)

Mochdreff (MOCK-dreff)

Rhianedd (Hree-ANN-eth)

Cadifor (Kad-EE-vor)

Llochafor (Hllock-AH-vor)

Daire mac Forgoll (DARE-eh mac FOR-goal)

Derry (the way you think it is pronounced)

Morc (Mork)

Prescelli (Press-KELL-ee)

Caer Celcynnon (Kair Kel-KIN-non)

Manogan fab Menai (Mann-OH-gan vab MEN-ee)

*Not withstanding any of the above, the Celydonian language is not intended to represent any authentic Celtic tongue or dialect, known or unknown, either P or Q, nor any possible or conceivable variation thereupon.

CONTENTS

0.

The Mercury of the Philosophers

The wizard Glastyn disappeared one day, from the King's grand castle at Caer Cadwy. He had been a restless man, given to abrupt departures and unheralded arrivals; he loved to come on people unexpectedly, and delighted in all manner of disguise. Every traveler who came to the castle or stopped in the town below had some tale to tell of him: how he had been spotted at a fair in Walgan, garbed as a traveling herbalist, or in the brown robes of an itinerant friar, begging his bread along the dusty southern roads, or again—this time disguised as no one but himself—riding his old piebald pony on the outskirts of the forest Coill Dorcha.

Those who claimed to know him best confidently expected him to reappear at any time. But an entire season passed, and then another, and fewer tales of chance encounters found their way back to Caer Cadwy. At last, they ceased to come at all, and even the most hopeful were forced to admit that Glastyn was not coming back.

He left behind him: a whimsical, inconsistent king; an order of jaded, disillusioned knights; and a realm slipping slowly back into the chaos from which he, Glastyn, had rescued it some fifty years before. Two other things of some significance he left behind him: the Clach Ghealach and Teleri ni Pendaren.

A man of many diverse talents, Glastyn had been an Alchemist of some reputation, and was therefore accustomed to working with outwardly unpromising materials—which *might* explain why he had chosen for his apprentice and successor such an unprepossessing little waif as Teleri ni Pendaren.

For the Mercury of the Philosophers (so the Sages inform us) is a common substance, little regarded and seldom recognized, except by the wisest of the Wise. Its nature (they go on to say) is cold and moist, "a dull metalline species," "the child of saturn, of mean estate," "the water that wets not"—but enough. Let it merely be stated that much of the same could be said of Teleri.

She was short, slight, and colorless, with grey eyes and a quantity of fine fly-away hair the color of wood ash. She had so far revealed no great aptitude for wizardry beyond a species of semi-magical invisibility that owed as much to her size and her coloring, to her ability to move swiftly and silently, or to will herself to absolute stillness at the same time that she *imagined* herself elsewhere, as it did to any sorcery. Yet it served her well in place of the real thing, so long as nobody looked directly at her.

Three years after the wizard vanished, she remained the same: still small, silent, and colorless. She tended his garden, dusted the books in his abandoned tower laboratory, and continued her own studies in the arts magical. On occasion, she assisted Brother Gildas, the Royal Physician. She rarely practiced even the minor magics that Glastyn had taught her. She lived alone and seldom spoke to anyone. And she seemed unlikely ever to transmute herself from Apprentice to Wizard, or even from Child to Woman.

So Teleri was at the age of eighteen, the winter that the Princess Diaspad returned to Caer Cadwy—Diaspad, with her heart full of malice and her brain full of schemes by which she hoped to set her despicable young son on the throne of Celydonn.

But Nature, like the Alchemist, continually strives for perfection. She was simply taking her time over Teleri.

1.

A Storm Over Camboglanna

It was late in the year for rain, but the weather (like so much else) could no longer be depended upon. An unexpected warm spell at the beginning of winter brought a whole swarm of violent storms snarling up out of the south, and the snows of November melted rapidly under the driving rains of December. Then the long grey road winding through the brown hills of Camboglanna melted, too, until all was a treacherous quagmire of mud and gravel.

To the messenger from Mochdreff, urging his exhausted steed onward through the storm, the icy rain felt like splinters of glass, penetrating the wool and leather of his cloak and tunic, piercing him to the bone. He cursed hoarsely under his breath, hating the cold, hating the wet, aching with fatigue, despising this unwelcoming land and everything in it.

This land of low hills and shallow valleys, of farms and fences and thatched villages. No, he did not like this undulating, crowded country—so different from his own Mochdreff—but it was the unnatural stillness of the land, more than any strangeness he could see, that had fathered the vague uneasiness that gnawed at the back of his mind.

The land did not speak to him; or if it did, it spoke no language he could understand. And soil so dumb, so smugly secretive, must be hiding something.

The messenger peered ahead through the slanting rain. On a hillside far to the south, he could just make out the sprawling outline of a castle: lofty towers amidst the ruins of an older fortification. Beneath Brynn Caer Cadwy crouched a tiny walled town, clinging to the castle's outer bastions as if in dread of the sea grinding her teeth on the rocks below.

With his destination in sight, the messenger felt his spirits rise. He did not expect a cordial welcome, here among the outlandish Camboglannach, but he was a stoical, uncomplaining man, and would be content with a roof over his head and a place to sit, somewhere near the fire maybe, while the storm tore itself to pieces in the darkness outside.

In the guardroom near the Main Gate, the rain and winds battering the castle were muffled to a distant drumming by the thick stone walls. The guards huddled companionably over a smoking peat fire, dicing and drinking, or more productively occupied: polishing a sword or an axe, replacing a few broken links in a mail shirt. The air lay heavily in the tiny room, thick with the rich, moist aromas of the burning peat and the goose grease they used to keep their armor from rusting in the damp air.

A pounding at the gate sent the idlers scrambling for their weapons. The Sergeant and two others pushed aside the horsehide that served them for a door and disappeared into the passage outside. A moment later, hinges creaked and oak timbers scraped across cobblestones as the gate swung open—then closed again with a mighty crash as the wind smashed it shut again.

The Sergeant returned to the inner room, accompanied by a stranger in a sodden crimson cloak. Ten years ago, even five, any stranger presenting himself unannounced at the gate could have expected a lengthy interrogation and confiscation of his weapons before he gained admittance. But years of peace and easy living had eroded discipline; the Captain allowed the messenger to strip off his leather gloves and warm his hands by the fire before demanding an explanation.

"My message is for the King alone," the stranger growled, pulling a letter out of his pouch and thrusting it rudely under the Captain's nose.

"Mochdreff, is it?" the Captain muttered, recognizing the boar's-head badge imprinted in the wax. "The Princess Diaspad?"

The other men, suddenly grown hostile, eyed the messenger suspiciously. What news but bad news could ever come out of Mochdreff?

They were wary of all "foreigners" these men of Camboglanna and the south, distrusting their neighbors: the Draighenach, the

Gorwynnach, the Rhiane[...]
Gwyngelli—all of whom[...]
regarding the Camboglann[...]
dour Mochdreffi.

As for the Princess Dias[...]
nurture, but she had been [...]
and had not increased her [...]

The messenger returned [...]
into his belt, and stalked ou[...]
followed, but the Captain [...]

"Let the man find his ow[...]
No stranger could possibly f[...]
levels of the castle; he cou[...]
anywhere near the King. If t[...]
a guide, then so much the [...]

As the men put down [...]
interrupted amusements, the [...]
been thinking. "And wouldn[...]
be visiting her step-brother—[...]
Rhianedd so conveniently out of he[...]

The two young lords from Rhianed[...]
Queen's brothers, Cadifor and Llochafor, [...]
to their estates in the northern highlands by a [...]
their pretension and their relentless maneuvering [...]
For themselves, they were not general favorites, but S[...]
Queen, was well-liked—at least by the common-folk—[...]
such an excess of devoted loyalty that some of it encompasse[...]
brothers as well.

"But coming all this way in weather so foul as this?" the Sergeant asked. That hardly sounded like the woman they all remembered, who was addicted to personal comfort and hated, above all, to get her feet wet.

"Reckon it up for yourself," said the Captain. "A little more than a month since the Rhianeddi lords left us, eight or nine days for the news to reach her in Mochdreff, a week, maybe, for the Princess and her household to prepare themselves for travel—and who knew then that the weather would be wet?—then a fortnight or more on the road with the wagons and all, and that man sent on ahead . . ."

hey were all certain of that. And
hat it was that she had come for.

habit of falling in love, suddenly,
icably. Typically, these infatuations
violent, burning themselves out in a day,

th Caer Cadwy, one summer spent visiting
is ancestors, and was instantly inspired to
ll its former glory and beyond. Much to his
more to the amazement of others, the passion
nd the love affair was to last all the days of his
e reconstruction and renovation of the castle,
sporadically (and with a splendid inconsistency of
gh the years.

he ruins on the lower terraces, the castle was vast,
e hill, level on level, until it reached the top and spilled
sides. When construction rendered any portion inacces-
nlivable, the inhabitants merely picked up their belongings
ed to another part of the castle. The folk of Caer Cadwy
heerfully nomadic existence.

e castle reflected the changing moods and sudden enthusiasms
the King. It was a palace of magnificent contradictions, a
oulous mixture of styles and periods: towers that began in
ndressed dry stone and ended in elegant turrets of fine ashlar
block; ancient ruins melded to modern flying buttresses, gothic
arches, and machicolated battlements; broad, pleasant courtyards
and tiny secret gardens; staircases and passages that led by lengthy
and meandering courses . . . nowhere.

Moreover, the King cherished a fondness for novelties and for
carving and statuary of all kinds—iron zoomorphs, stone gargoyles, brazen centaurs, nymphs, and satyrs—which appeared
throughout the castle in some startling juxtapositions. Even the
shrubs in Sidonwy's garden had been trimmed and sculpted to
resemble fabulous beasts of heraldry and legend. The visitor to
Caer Cadwy, wherever he went, inevitably developed a sense of
constant, hostile, observation.

And so it seemed to the messenger from Mochdreff, as he
threaded his way through the maze of the inner Keep, where (he

had grudgingly been informed) the private apartments of the King might currently be found.

Only a few scattered torches lit these corridors. The walls dripped moisture; the rooms he passed through were all unoccupied. The man from Mochdreff began to fear that he had lost his way. Either that, or the servant he had asked for directions had purposely misdirected him.

A sound, a light pattering of footsteps—the messenger whirled around to see who followed after him.

As far as he could see in the murky half light, the corridor stretched empty behind him. Perhaps the sound had existed only in his imagination, inspired by the scowling gargoyles and leering zoomorphs; perhaps he had only picked up his own echoing footfalls. He turned again and headed resolutely in what he hoped was the right direction.

Something small and colorless moved in the shadows. Teleri crept out of hiding and scurried away, in the direction the messenger had just come.

No ghosts walked the halls of Caer Cadwy, for Glastyn's spells had laid them all. Yet the castle was haunted, all the same, by the lonely little wraith the wizard left behind him. Dressed in somber grey, she was rarely seen as she wandered through the castle, listening at doors, peering out of alcoves and peekholes and hiding behind pillars, keeping a secret watch over the castle and its inhabitants.

Unconsciously, she slipped into one of her favorite games. No longer Teleri ni Pendaren, sometime apprentice to the great wizard Glastyn, she became the ill-fortuned Princess Goewin, fleeing her father's hall for a fateful assignation with her nameless lover, and the long corridor, a corridor no longer, became one of the perilous paths winding down the cliffs below Dinas Moren.

Around a bend in the path came the sound of approaching footsteps, the light, quick fall of slippered feet. For a moment, Teleri (or Goewin) wavered, uncertain as to time and place; then the instinct for concealment took over. Teleri stopped where she stood, pressed up against the damp stone wall, and effectively disappeared. Disappeared, that is, until another young woman, herself all but concealed by a long brown cloak, rounded the corner and nearly knocked Teleri over.

Something fell to the floor with a clatter like bones, and the newcomer furiously confronted the little sorceress. Her make-shift invisibility shattered by their brief contact, Teleri was helpless before that sudden blaze of anger.

The long cloak had fallen open, allowing Teleri a glimpse of the bright, tightly laced gown beneath; like the girl who wore it, the dress was eye-catching, if a trifle shabby. Teleri recognized the face within the brown hood: Prescelli, Queen Sidonwy's spiteful little handmaiden. Dark-eyed, sharp-featured, and intense, Prescelli had a courtesan's lush, sensuous body and the face of a starving child.

"Little sneak!" Prescelli hissed. "You've been spying on me, haven't you?"

Teleri shook her head, tried to shrink away into nothingness. "I have not. Why should I?"

Prescelli stooped to pick up the armful of broken wax tapers scattered across the floor by the collision. A strange burden for a girl whose allotment of *tallow* candles could not be so generous— and the King's private chapel, where the finest white tapers burned day and night, lay just around the corner.

Teleri tried to slip past, but a shrill protest from Prescelli stopped her. "Not so fast, you filthy little spy! I want a word with you."

"Sneak" and "spy"—those names had been hurled at Teleri before (and behind her back she had heard unkinder whispers: "witch," "half-wit," "changeling"); it was to avoid such ugly names and scenes that she cultivated the habit of invisibility. But she was unable to disappear now, so long as Prescelli's attention remained so intently fixed.

"If you tell anyone what you have seen—"

"I've seen nothing," Teleri breathed, edging sideways toward the corner and concealment. "There is nothing for me to tell."

"And if I ever catch you watching me again—" began Prescelli. But now she spoke to empty air. Teleri had seized her moment of inattention and disappeared into the dark corridor around the corner.

"There are three kinds of wisdom," said the wizard Glastyn. *"Three Parts of Wisdom, we say: the Wisdom of the Body; the Wisdom of the Soul, or Intellect; and the Wisdom of the Spirit—or the Heart. Men have spent entire lifetimes striving for only a third part of that wisdom. Indeed, it is a great thing if a man can call himself master of any of these, but the true Adept is master of all three."*

"You are an Adept," said the child, looking up from her book.

The old man smiled into his long white beard, but he furrowed his brow as though he were frowning and he spoke sternly. "You have come very far in your studies, then? You feel qualified to pronounce this one or that one an Adept?"

"It isn't that," said the child, who knew the wizard's ways and understood that he was not really scolding her. *"I read it in one of your books. It says in the triad:*

"The Three Great Fallen Adepts
    Cynfarch   Master of Ravens
    Gandwy   Dragon-Tamer
    Atlendor   the Old

    "(But Greater than any of these was
    Glastyn   Heart-of-the-Oak)."

"I see," said Glastyn, *"that you have made some attempt to memorize the triad, but you have forgotten half of it—and that the most important part:*

    "(Who fell again and again
        and rose.)

"The Mastery of Body, Soul, and Spirit is not a thing to be achieved once and then forgotten. The road the Adept must follow is treacherous and he must walk softly and with great prudence. He who forgets that is fallen indeed, and he alone is beyond redemption."

The child returned to her book. But after a short while she looked up again and asked, "Do you think that I will ever be an Adept?"

The wizard did not reply at once, apparently absorbed in his work: the purification of gold by the agency of antimony. "That remains to be seen," he said at last. "The Wisdom of the Body—you are learning something of that in your sessions with Brother Gildas. If you become a Physician, that is a fine and noble calling. The Wisdom of the Intellect—that is what the science of Wizardry strives, in part, to elucidate. I have hopes that you may, after the usual seven years of study, become a Wizard worthy of the name."

"And the Wisdom of the Heart?" the child asked, when he did not go on.

This time, Glastyn did frown. "There is an order to these things, and each must come in its proper season. As for the Wisdom of the Heart . . . I do not choose," he said, "that you should learn that just yet."

Teleri ran until she came to a thick oak door, which she pushed open and slipped through, into the dark passageway beyond. The air in the tunnel was damp and dead, the blackness ahead of her absolute, but Teleri never hesitated. She closed the door firmly behind her and plunged fearlessly into the dark.

This passage, built into the thick walls on the upper levels, led, by short ways and by long, to all inhabitable parts of the castle. Everyone knew that the tunnel existed, but only Teleri knew all the doors, trap-doors, and sliding panels that offered access. Few others resorted to the passageway, even as a short-cut, but Teleri liked the friendly concealing darkness, and the tunnel's geography was comfortably familiar.

She extended a hand, feeling along the wall: rough, irregular stone, harsh lumps where the mortar had squeezed out and not been smoothed away. A change in texture indicated that she was nearing her destination.

A little farther on, she touched wood, found a hidden catch, opened the door a crack, and slid through. She had entered the

Wizard's Tower by the back way, and now stood at the foot of the spiral staircase leading up to Glastyn's abandoned rooms and to his laboratory.

She ran up the steps, impatient to return to her studies, feeling no need for invisibility here. To her surprise, she found the door at the top of the stairs unlocked, standing slightly ajar. She ran a sensitive hand over the doorframe, checking the wards that protected the door against forced entry, relaxed when the familiar tingling indicated that they still held. The door had not been tampered with, nor would this be the first time that Teleri had forgotten to lock a door behind her.

She pushed the door open and stepped into the laboratory. As always, the air tasted of dust and tallow and bitter herbs. As she glanced around the room, a cold chill slithered down her spine and a faint sense of invasion prickled across her skin. Did her imagination play tricks on her, or had someone actually taken advantage of the unlocked door to enter the laboratory uninvited?

Teleri's uneasy gaze traveled over the crowded shelves that lined the room. Even the brightest sunlight could not dispel the shadows that lurked in the laboratory's odd corners and alcoves; now, by the light of a three-branched candlestick, the shadows had crept out of hiding and thrust their long inky fingers into every part of the room. The wizard's books and paraphernalia covered the shelves and filled the cabinets. Most lay under an undisturbed powder of fine dust: the intricate five- and six-pointed pentacles; the elemental elixirs glowing red, yellow, green, and black in glass jars; the bejeweled ceremonial daggers; and the silver aspergillum. A golden pentagram painted on the floor was scarred and faded. These were the tools of ceremonial magic, the art of the full Wizard, and Teleri never used them.

But the mortars and alembics, the green glass phials and flasks—the equipment of the Alchemist or Apothecary—were sparkling clean and in slightly better order. Teleri knew the uses of herbs and the preparation of medicines and she spent many hours grinding, mixing, and distilling them.

The customary disorder remained unchanged. If someone (the light-fingered Prescelli, for instance) had been in the room during Teleri's absence, she had taken nothing with her when she left.

Teleri took off her cloak, hung it on a peg by the door, and wandered over to the nearest bookshelf. She selected a thick volume bound in crimson leather, and carried it over to the massive wooden armchair by the fireplace.

Teleri curled up among the dusty purple velvet cushions. She ran uncertain fingers over the richly tooled cover of the book, wondering whether she would be able to open it. Although she knew all the names that sealed each of Glastyn's books, it often happened that she found one which simply refused to open at her command. This particular volume had always remained stubbornly shut, try as she might to unseal it, but today she had a feeling that the time was right.

''*Cynfelyn*,'' she whispered, and the spell binding the pages together released its hold. The cover flew open, landing in Teleri's lap and breathing decades of mildew into the laboratory. With a sigh of satisfaction, Teleri made a nest among the cushions, balanced the book on her knees, and bent her head over the closely written page.

It was in this manner that Teleri had continued her studies ever since Glastyn's disappearance. He had evidently planned everything in advance, and the books opened or did not open according to that prearranged plan. It was like Glastyn to find a way to manage things though he was no longer there.

But Glastyn had always known how to manipulate people and events. Some fifty years ago, he had first appeared out of the forest, bringing with him the long-sought heir to the Crown of Celydonn. Despite formidable opposition from the greater lords of the island kingdom, Glastyn had successfully placed young Anwas on the throne. Then, ready for some *real* work, he set out to master the Wild Magic.

The Wild Magic was all around: stirring sluggishly beneath the soil, riding on the restless winds, gathering in the air like storm clouds. Once, these same forces, running rampant, had torn the kingdom asunder. A mighty alliance of warlocks had risen to power, calling up monsters from the depths of the seething earth and out of the boiling lakes, toppling a dynasty of great kings.

But Glastyn knew the ways of the Wild Magic. He drove it back under the earth, where it lent fertility to the soil; sealed it in trees and rocks, which afterward were known to speak with deep, inhuman voices; he bound it with his own name and with the

King's. Then, while the land and the people gradually returned to some semblance of normality, Glastyn found more work for himself.

In a half century of service to the Crown, Glastyn had kept busy. He convinced Anwas's son, the young King Cynwas, to establish an order of knighthood dedicated to bringing peace and order to the strife-torn realm. He traveled extensively, attending christenings, weddings, tournaments, deathbeds—any event that brought the principal families of the realm together. Not a man, woman, or child among them but felt his firm hand shaping the future course of their lives.

Then, at the age of nearly a century, he took an apprentice, trained her for five years, impressed on her that it was her duty to take his place when the dire, mysterious fate which he had foreseen finally overtook him—and slipped out of the sight of men.

But the Wild Magic, though tamed, had not been banished. Since Glastyn's disappearance many disquieting signs had appeared, indicating that the bindings were gradually dissolving: the unpredictable weather; crops that withered, inexplicably, on the vine; strange hybrid creatures—neither man nor beast—that stalked the forests or came down out of the Coblynau Hills; grotesque, evil-smelling corpses that an outraged sea cast up on the island's rocky beaches. Once again, as soon as the sun set, people locked and bolted their doors, and except within the walled towns and castles few dared to venture out of doors at night. Even here, in smug, respectable Camboglanna, fear of witches and their craft was spreading.

And what role in all this could an imperfectly trained young sorceress hope to play?

Teleri, no longer a student but not yet a Wizard, not precisely a Witch, but something uncomfortably close, was a puzzling little paradox that the King, his servants, and the nobles gathered at his court preferred not to worry about. They left her, for the most part, strictly alone.

Left her to hours of solitary study, her mind echoing to ancient names and spells and the long rich history of the Isle of Celydonn, until the old tales became a part of her daytime imaginings as well as her dreams at night, and the shades of long-dead kings and heroes became, at last, more real to her than the bustling world of the castle around her. Yet she stayed on at Caer Cadwy, observing the lives of the people much as if they were all part of another story in one of Glastyn's old books. This, in obedience to Glastyn's command.

Because Glastyn, when he first took Teleri for his apprentice, had appointed her as sole guardian of the Clach Ghealach, and it was the Clach Ghealach that protected the King.

One of the legendary talismans of the ancient kings of Celydonn, the Clach Ghealach was a great moon-colored crystal set in Cynwas's massive crown of state. It warded the King, and all in his castle on Brynn Caer Cadwy, from nightmares and sendings, from the unseelie host and the creeping horrors, and all the restless spirits that walk in the night.

How Glastyn expected her to keep the Clach Ghealach safe, Teleri did not know. She was never permitted to touch either the crown or the stone, which were kept under lock and key in the King's treasure room. But the wizard had laid the task on her like a geas, and it would have taken a more competent sorceress than Teleri to break any geas of Glastyn's.

And that was why she was here now, whiling away the long rainy afternoon, studying a book of spells she never really intended to put to use. Lulled by the peace that enfolded the tower room, she had already forgotten her suspicions about Prescelli and the unlocked laboratory door.

"*The origin of that feud between the Mochdreffi and the Gwyngellach,*" *said Glastyn, "is said to be a Matter of Wild Pigs.*"

The child at his side absorbed this information soberly. "Were they talking swine?"

"*It is an entirely unsubstantiated rumor,*" *said the wizard, "that talking swine are occasionally born in Mochdreff.*"

The little girl was disappointed. "Is it just a fairy tale, then? You don't think that the old stories could possibly be true?"

"*On the contrary,*" *said Glastyn. "I think it very likely that they are.*"

2.

Dwarfs and Leopards

She came amidst a flurry of excitement, a flutter of curiosity, a buzz of speculation—all of which was exactly as she had planned it. The weather obligingly cleared, allowing her to arrive in style, and the Princess Diaspad came with gay satin banners and fluttering harlequin ribbons, acrobats in spangled blue and gold, jugglers, wild beasts, dwarf guardsmen in scarlet trappings and glittering silver mail, and a grinning yellow-haired giant, at least ten feet tall.

The Princess was nowhere to be seen, concealed inside the great gaudy palanquin that twelve laboring dwarfs carried up the hill; but word of her arrival spread quickly. By the time that the entire procession had passed through the outer gate, a noisy crowd had gathered in the lower courtyard, ogling her shaggy woodwoses and her lame giant, straining to catch a glimpse of the Princess herself.

A breathless page brought the news to a group of squires playing a friendly game of "Cyffle" in a circle by the kitchen fire. "She's here . . . in the lower courtyard, with an enormous party of the oddest people!"

Several boys, not directly involved in the game, excused themselves and headed for the door, but Fflergant fab Maelgwyn of Gwyngelli went on dealing the cards, just as though the interruption had never occurred.

"Aren't you the least bit curious?" asked another boy, Kilraen by name, glancing from blond, broad-shouldered Fflergant to Fflergant's younger brother, Tryffin, who appeared to be dozing in the golden firelight. "I would think that the pair of you, of all people . . ."

Fflergant picked up and examined his cards, tossed a small silver coin down on the sooty flagstones. "The question," he replied, with unaccustomed hauteur, "is whether or not we choose to dignify the occasion by attending. It happens that we don't."

"Well, that, at least, is refreshing," snickered Daire Ruadh mac Forgoll. "And honest, too—for a change!"

"I'm glad that you approve, Derry." Fflergant tossed a card after the silver coin.

Daire and the other boys followed suit. "Oh, I do," enthused Daire, perversely pretending to misunderstand.

"Yes, I really do," he repeated, raising his voice the better to be heard above the clatter and the racket of the scullions and kitchen boys cleaning up after the afternoon meal. "It's so encouraging to learn that you consider *someone* beneath your attention, even if it is the King's step-sister—my kinswoman—and her son."

The squires and pages—sons and grandsons of King Cynwas's vassal lords—worked in the kitchen, the Hall, and the stables, and at a variety of menial tasks elsewhere, as part of their early training, but they were spared the dirtier and more demeaning tasks and did not, as a rule, mix socially with the kitchen staff or the grooms. In a few years' time, these noble youths would all be knighted and leave the kitchen behind, but the turnspits and the scullions would still be there. Yet it was not strictly true that squires never socialized with the lower servants, for Fflergant and Tryffin, whose birth placed them almost as far beyond the other squires as those boys were removed from the kitchen and stableboys, were perfectly willing to strike up a friendly conversation with practically anyone.

"Though they do say," Daire drawled (finding that he had failed to get a rise out of Fflergant), "that your Uncle Manogan thought the Princess quite good enough for *him*, once upon a time."

"That he did. But there is never any accounting for another man's tastes," Fflergant replied with a shrug, which came as close as anyone had ever heard him come to disparaging a lady. Fflergant had been born under a geas (that supernatural prohibition that the Gwyngellach took as seriously as their interminable feuds) forbidding him to insult any woman, be she princess or peasant, and he carefully avoided doing so—though Daire had been trying to goad him into it for years.

Fflergant led with a King, Kilraen followed with a deuce, the boy next to him played an Ace, and Daire trumped with another to win the hand. Kilraen and the other lad dropped out of the game, but Fflergant and Daire continued.

Daire smiled sunnily, gathered up the parchment cards and a handful of small coins, and tried another shot. "I quite agree with you. Your uncle was once betrothed to a goat-girl, was he not?"

But if he had intended to annoy Fflergant, his shaft went wide. Fflergant looked amused, as if considering some private joke. "A goatherder's daughter—I believe that is how the story goes. A lovely girl with a voice like a lark. My uncle used to have quite a weakness for women with beautiful voices, so they say."

"So I have heard. And your *mother* has a charming voice—I believe I've heard that, too," smirked Daire.

Fflergant flushed and started to reply, but Tryffin opened his eyes and said, quite evenly, "She has at that. Our mother could charm the birds from the trees. But really, Derry, you can't deal those cards until Fflergant has cut them."

"He did cut them," said Daire sweetly. "It happens you didn't notice, dozing there by the fire."

"It happens that I did notice," said Tryffin, equally dulcet. Like his mother, he had a soft voice which, combined with the musical Gwyngellach lilt he had never abandoned, made every word he spoke alight on the ear like a blessing. "And I also saw you add a little something extra once you had them back."

"He didn't," protested Fflergant. He knew Daire for a cheat, but honestly believed he had been watching him carefully the whole time.

"If I am not mistaken," said Tryffin, "the top four cards include both Aces from the last hand—those for himself—and two low cards for you." He flipped over the cards in question: a deuce, an

Ace, a four, and another Ace. "Transparent, Derry. Even if I'd not seen you hide those cards in your handkerchief . . ."

Daire gifted him with his very best smile. "You can't blame me for trying."

"Oh aye, I think that I might," Tryffin replied, brown eyes perfectly expressionless. Certain nefarious practices of Daire's, his cheating among them, had so far been overlooked by the other lads, because challenges were not yet permitted them, brawling was strictly forbidden, and reporting one of their own to the Master of Squires violated their code of honor. Yet even Tryffin's monumental tolerance had its limits.

Daire glanced from Tryffin to Fflergant and back again, wondering, as he so often did, which of the two he hated more: Fflergant, who usually responded to his baiting in kind, or his brother, who never gave Daire the satisfaction of an angry response. Whichever it was, Daire hated them both with his entire writhing little soul.

Daire was willing to forgive Fflergant and Tryffin the blond, pink-cheeked, robust good looks which gave them both a disarmingly wholesome appearance they did not *entirely* deserve. Daire was a good-looking boy, too, and knew how to trade on his beauty: downy cheeks, smooth skin, apricot-colored hair, and eyes as blue as an August sky. He could almost forgive Tryffin and Fflergant those advantages of wealth and rank that the pair of them made such a point of taking for granted. But that unshakable, apparently unpretentious but magnificently condescending belief in their own transcendent superiority that was the birthright of a Prince of Tir Gwyngelli—that, Daire could never forgive.

He revenged himself with poisonous innuendo and petty harassment and by relieving Fflergant, by fair means or by foul, of some of that not-quite-forgivable wealth whenever the opportunity arose. Daire was the fifth son of a miserly Draighenach lord, and found that a life of luxury and vice put a considerable strain on his already slender purse. A little extra income gained cheating at cards or dice was always welcome.

But even an accomplished cheat like Daire had little chance of success while Tryffin fab Maelgwyn was watching him. Tryffin amused himself by playing the fool, the lazy, good-natured rustic, but Daire knew from sad experience that Tryffin was none of those things. Daire knew it, but somehow he was always forgetting.

Having been reminded, and unpleasantly, Daire stood up. "This has all been very agreeable! But I really must be going now. It would be unpardonably rude to stay here enjoying myself when I ought to be below, greeting my *kinswoman* properly."

"Kinswoman indeed!" snorted Kilraen, once Daire was out of earshot. "Neither Derry nor that cloddish brother of his has ever set eyes on her, yet Derry's been carrying on as though she were coming here expressly to visit him! What would you care to wager that he's not all over the woman at once, just because she might be willing to use her influence to advance him?"

Tryffin and Fflergant both declined the wager. They were generous with their money, as all the world knew, but not inclined to throw it away foolishly.

In Sidonwy's sunny bedchamber in the Mermaid Tower, the Queen's chattering attendants alternated between assisting her to dress and fluttering from one diamond-paned window to the next, in a vain attempt to catch a glimpse of the activity in the distant courtyard.

Sidonwy sat very stiff and straight in her high-backed chair, her distress evident to all. The girls were not unsympathetic to her plight, but it had been a dull winter so far, and they were more pleased than otherwise that the Princess Diaspad had arrived to stir things up. They commiserated with the Queen, but privately hoped that the Princess's visit would prove as exciting as it promised to be.

"I don't see why you should go down, if it upsets you so very much," said the stately Fand, as she deftly plaited the Queen's thick dark hair.

"If my lord welcomes her, then so must I," replied Sidonwy, steeling herself to greet as a sister the woman who had undoubtedly come to win what Sidonwy's brothers had lost.

"But why should he welcome her, after all these years? And after she defied him, too, by marrying Corfil of Mochdreff!" Fand's sister Finola said from her place by the window.

"The King's enthusiasm for quarreling with his family is only matched by the pleasure he takes in reconciliations." The Queen spoke from considerable experience. "Now his sister has written to him, bewailing her lot as a lonely widow, seeking the King's guidance in rearing her only son, and expressing a deep longing to see her 'dearest brother' again—all carefully calculated to exploit Cynwas's better nature.''

Everyone nodded and sighed. It was just the sort of sentimental appeal the King might be expected to believe in, when he was in the mood to believe in anything at all.

"But you do not believe any of it," said Fand.

"He does not know Diaspad as I do," replied Sidonwy. "Indeed, how could he? He followed Ysgafn's lead in all things when he was a boy, and would *not* call her sister. But I was her friend." And Diaspad had been her friend, until the day that Sidonwy's impending marriage to the King was first announced.

"But it was no choice of mine," Sidonwy had protested. *"Nobody asked me if I wanted to marry your step-brother."*

"Yes, but you do want him," Diaspad replied bitterly, *"Cynwas and everything that he can give you. You will be Queen of Celydonn and I, I will rot away in obscurity tied to that whining nobody, Corfil!"*

"But you chose him," Sidonwy retorted. *"You married Corfil over all our objections. You must have wanted him once."*

"I had no choice," Diaspad had replied. *"And you know perfectly well who it was that I wanted."*

Sidonwy sighed, remembering. "She was always so passionate in her loving and hating, but sentimental—never! At schemes and plots, there she excels, and she has come here now to secure a crown for her son, I have no doubt of that."

"But your kinsmen from Rhianedd and Gwyngelli will find a way to prevent her," said Megwen confidently. "They would never accept a Mochdreffi heir."

"If any openly oppose her," said the Queen, "the King will surely be moved to champion her. If any attempt to dictate his choice, he will surely do the opposite."

"But you and your Uncle Dyffryn may gently influence him," suggested Fand. And Sidonwy smiled wearily and said, "We can certainly try."

With her hair coiled and pinned in place, her fur-trimmed cloak sent for, the Queen stood and looked around her, asking, with an air of bewilderment, "But where is Ceilyn?"

"Not here when he is finally wanted—wouldn't you know?"

said Finola under her breath—quite unjustly, for that young man was far more likely to be present when he was not wanted than to be absent when he was needed.

"The South Tower, wasn't it?" Prescelli volunteered. "You wanted—"

"So I did," admitted Sidonwy. "Then, I suppose, we must go without him."

Down below, the curiosity of the crowd was about to be satisfied. A pallid youth, clad all in black, approached the palanquin and drew back the scarlet curtains. To the horror of the nearest bystanders, two sleek golden leopards poured through the opening and dropped to the ground. Then Calchas fab Corfil reached into the litter and helped his mother to alight.

"Welcome home," said the King, planting a kiss on his sister's artfully painted cheek. And "Welcome home," Sidonwy echoed dutifully, bestowing a cold kiss and keeping a wary eye on the big cats.

Like her son, Diaspad was arrayed all in black except for the heavy golden jewelry at her throat and wrists. A silken veil covered but did not conceal her brilliant hair. She had an arrogant, sensual face, arresting in its beauty, skin like marble, and eyes of a bitter acid green.

The curtains parted again; a hunchbacked dwarf woman emerged, dressed like the Princess down to the tiniest detail.

"Dear me," said the Earl Marshall (Fflergant's Uncle Manogan). "Leopards. Freaks. Wild Men. One hardly knows what to expect next. And they call *my* people barbarians!"

And Diaspad's half-brother, Ysgafn, who could scarcely imagine anyone less barbaric than his tall, elegant friend, smiled appreciatively and marveled that Manogan could discuss so lightly the woman he had loved so passionately twenty years before.

Up among the battlements, far removed from the crowded scene in the yard below, Teleri kept watch, drawn from her lonely tower by an uneasy sense that Caer Cadwy was somehow under attack.

From this distance, Teleri could distinguish little beyond a black gown, a pale profile, and hair an improbable shade of auburn. (Was her imagination playing tricks again, or had she really seen the tip of velvety black tail sliding under the Princess's train?) Diaspad adjusted her veil, shrouding herself in inky darkness, and the dwarf at her side did likewise.

A soft sound behind her caused Teleri to turn, expecting to see one of the guards assigned to walk the allures. Instead, Ceilyn mac Cuel crossed the wall and joined her at her vantage point.

Teleri averted her eyes, tried to make herself smaller and greyer than ever. It did no good; she felt his bright, nervous gaze flicker in her direction, then away again. Try as she might, she could never hide from Ceilyn.

He watched her constantly, yet coldly refused to meet her eyes whenever she glanced his way. She feared him, not only for his ability to penetrate her illusions but also for who and what he was: Gorwynnach, born of a people who considered even the most innocent magic suspect; the son of Cuel of Celcynnon whose piety and persecution of witches had earned him the name of fanatic even in the forests of the north.

Yet if Ceilyn intended to denounce her as a witch, he was taking his time about it. Five years he had watched Teleri, and never yet made good the threat she read in his eyes.

At the moment, the young knight's attention was on the lower yard. He leaned into the embrasure, his pose deceptively casual, but she read tension in every line of his slender, wiry body. His devotion to the Queen was well-known—a passion which burned so hot at times that it might, in another man, have provoked scandal—yet Teleri sensed something very different now. His frown deepened, his nostrils flared, as though assaulted by some vile odor. She looked down into the yard to see what had disturbed him.

The King and his sister strolled arm-in-arm, moving across the yard toward the Gamelyon Gate. The Queen came next, leaning on the Marshall's arm, followed by Ysgafn, while Calchas and the leopards trailed behind. As Diaspad and her son drew near, Teleri caught the unmistakable stench of Black Magic.

"Why, in God's name, were they allowed to pass through the gate bearing all of that?"

Teleri drew back. Though he watched her relentlessly, Ceilyn had never spoken to her before. And how had he been able, at a distance, to sense what nobody down in the courtyard had been able to recognize?

"Spells of protection," she answered faintly. "Essentially harmless."

Ceilyn's eyebrows rose sharply. "Harmless? You expect me to believe that vile thing around Calchas's neck is perfectly innocent?"

His eyes were sharper than hers. Although Teleri could detect a gleam of gold around Calchas's throat, she could scarcely make out the tiny objects dangling from the golden collar.

"I never said innocent," she protested. "Though it must have appeared so to the guards at the gate. I suppose they all looked the other way, just as everyone pretends not to see the little vervain charms that all the children wear, or the horseshoes and rowan tacked up over all the doors for luck.

"But innocent—no," she added softly. "What harm the Princess—or whoever made those things—inflicted on herself . . . I sense Necromancy there, and darker things as well."

"What things?"

Teleri shook her head, unwilling to say more. It was not always wise to admit knowledge of some things. He frowned again, perhaps guessing which direction her thoughts were moving.

"We have a common cause here, I think. Why should you fear me?"

Teleri took a step backward. "You watch me," she said softly, accusingly.

He did not bother to deny it, only shrugged his shoulders and turned back toward the embrasure. "You watch me. You watch everyone."

His gaze traveled back to the courtyard below, but the Princess and Calchas were no longer to be seen. "It's Diaspad ni Erim we should both be watching."

"I have come," said the lad to the maiden's father, "to ask for the hand of your daughter."

The old man was sitting on the slope of Brynn Prennifanc; he was so huge that it was difficult, from a distance, to tell which was the maiden's father and which was Prennifanc Hill. His hair and his beard were like two tangled thickets. A family of eagles had nested in his hair and a colony of rooks was nesting in his beard. His arms were like two sapling ash trees and his legs were as thick as full-grown oaks. For that reason, he was called Mael-Duir the Giant.

"The man who would marry my daughter," said Mael-Duir, "must be brother to the wolves. He must tame the falcon of Oenafwyn, which no man has ever captured. Nine times ninety heroes have tried and all of them have failed.

"The man who would marry my daughter must spend seven days under the sea herding Dylan's cattle, and three days in the Castle of Glass. Many men have entered there, but few have returned alive.

"There is a creature," said the giant, "that lives at the end of the world. It is neither bird nor beast, fish nor serpent, yet it is very like to all of them. The man who would marry my daughter must bring me that creature's heart."

"All these tasks I can easily accomplish," said the youth, "though you may think them difficult."

"God knows," said the giant, "you may do all that you say. Yet I have other tasks which it will be impossible for you to accomplish."

From The Black Book of Tregalen

3.

The Feast of Christmas or *Mistletoe and Holly*

The weather changed again, and Caer Cadwy lay under a fresh blanket of glittering snow. Days were cold and bright, nights clear and freezing. As Christmas and its twelve days of feasting and celebration approached, the castle and the town below it filled with a pleasant sense of anticipation.

All along the crooked cobblestone streets of Treledig peddlers hawked sugarplums, gilded gingerbread, and winter apples. Cynwas's servants descended on the town and returned to the castle bearing mysterious bundles and armfuls of fragrant greenery. Pine boughs snapped and exploded in all the castle fireplaces; stone gargoyles and brazen nymphs wore garlands of mistletoe and holly tied up with red or gold ribbons. In the bakehouse, the Cook and his army of assistants prepared spiced beef and Paris pies, filling the outer courtyard with the scent of cinnamon and cloves and the promise of puddings and marzipan subtleties to come.

On Christmas Eve, the monks left their tiny stone cells in the outer walls and moved through the castle in a long candlelight procession, caroling: "When Christ was born. . . ." Sweethearts exchanged embroidered gloves, pomanders, and other scented tokens. And everyone wore his or her new winter finery to Midnight Mass.

Below the castle, beyond the town, the winter landscape stretched bleak and empty. For miles and miles, not a living thing stirred except for an occasional slinking grey shadow. Game was scarce; the farmers had slaughtered most of their stock, and what remained stayed safe in barns and high paddocks; the wolves, driven by hunger, every day grew bolder.

On Christmas morning, a group of young men, knights and senior squires, gathered by the stables, listening to the breathless account of the two who had just come in.

"The biggest wolf I ever saw," said Kilraen. "He would have carried off one of the children, if we hadn't happened by at the right time."

"Gypsies, you said?" asked Gofan mac Gofynnion.

"Strolling entertainers. Mummers, jongleurs, magicians, *and* dancing girls. And they will all be here for the revels tonight."

Several young men made appreciative noises.

"That puts me in mind," said Iaen Og, with a lascivious grin, "of a girl I met once in Treledig. A dancing girl from—well, I don't remember where—but she had, without question, the—"

His story was interrupted by Ceilyn, who murmured an apology and withdrew from the group.

"Bloody little prig," said Kilraen, before Ceilyn was quite out of earshot. But kind-hearted Fergos fab Neol frowned reproachfully at the storyteller. "Couldn't that have waited? Or was that what you intended? You know that Ceilyn won't listen to indecent stories."

"It was a perfectly decent story!" protested Iaen (not altogether truthfully). "You could repeat it to your own grandmother. Between me and God, he's just too ready to assume the worst!"

"No fault of yours, anyway," said Kilraen. "Didn't you notice? He looked sick from the moment I mentioned those traveling players. As if a little harmless entertainment under Cynwas's roof would contaminate him!"

The Christmas Feast had sadly diminished. Once, and not so very long ago at that, Cynwas and his knights had come to their Christmas dinner vowing not to taste of a single dish until one of their number had recounted some new adventure, a quest was proposed, or some marvel appeared before them.

Adventures there had been, in those heroic days, quests and mysteries and miracles beyond counting: floating heads, bleeding lances, childlike phantoms of unearthly beauty, strains of ravishing music issuing from out of the very air—many of these, no doubt, the work of Glastyn, illusions meant to enchant the senses, stir the heart, and inspire the flagging enthusiasm of Cynwas and his select circle of heroes, spurring them on to ever greater glory. But the enchantment had been real, for all that, and the deeds it inspired (for all the artistic embellishments they would later acquire), those were real, too, and it was a sad sign of a decadent present that miracles were no longer expected, no longer even hoped for.

As on this Christmas, thought Ceilyn mac Cuel, *the first Christmas within memory when no candidate was judged worthy of the accolade and the festivities began without the traditional Midwinter Knightings.* This Christmas, when everyone sat down to dinner in the Hall with nothing but dinner on his mind.

Oh, to be sure, it was a splendid feast, in a merely gorgeous way. The Cook and his assistants had produced any number of exotic dishes: cockentrices, whole roast swans, gilded peacocks . . . to name but a few. Bright banners adorned the lofty Hall; firelight danced on vessels of silver, pewter, crystal, and gold. The King and his courtiers were just as fine as ever, in respect to parti-color silks and satins, velvets, furs, and sparkling jewels. There was even music, during and after the feast—more raucous than melodic, if the truth were told—thanks to the itinerant troupe which had arrived as promised: conjurers, fire-eaters, dancing beasts, real foreign dancing girls, and more. But the breathless sense of wonder, the expectation that some miracle, some revelation, was waiting just around the corner—the *magic* that had once been Christmas—all that was missing.

How had that happened? When had the change occurred? Standing in his customary favored position on the Queen's right, between and a little behind the gilded wooden thrones, Ceilyn shifted his weight from one leg to the other, tensed and relaxed his muscles in order to relieve the cramp without appearing to fidget, and tried to remember Christmas two years past, the day that he was knighted.

That day there had been solemn ceremonies and a tournament, and tales recited during the feast of the exploits of the men who had won their spurs before him. And it had all been carried out with . . . a certain faded grandeur, an echo of all that once had been, a feeling as everyone went through the motions that the ceremonies, the vows given and received, still meant something.

But now there was not even that.

Ceilyn looked around him, searching the crowd for familiar faces: the doughty warriors whose mighty deeds and selfless exploits had made them legends in their own lifetimes. Many, sadly, were missing: those who had died heroically in their prime, and others, like Maelgwyn of Gwyngelli and Gofynnion mac Gware, who had simply gone home to govern their own lands. But for the rest . . .

Rhodri fab Elifri was the King's architect, Dillus fab Dalldaff his Seneschal. Scilti mac Tearlach, that sometime terror from the north, was Master of Squires, teaching grubby little boys how to handle their swords so as to present less of a danger to their friends than to their opponents; Branach and his brother Dianach held minor posts at court.

As for Manogan and Ysgafn (the Earl Marshall and the Lord Constable respectively): Ysgafn spent more time each year on his own estates in Walgan, overseeing the planting, the harvest, and the lambing, leaving his deputies to recruit and drill the King's tiny standing army; and whatever it was that drove handsome, cynical Manogan fab Menai to perform his own duties with such commendable precision, it was not the unspoiled idealism of his youth.

But their day was long past, and this was a day for younger men, trained in combat, eager to be out and doing, young men like himself, just waiting for a chance to prove themselves.

So why, Ceilyn had one day plucked up the courage to ask some of the older knights, why were not the young men empowered, organized, and encouraged to act in the King's name—to what end had they been educated, trained, and knighted, if not as guardians of the King's peace? Surely they were meant for greater things than spending their days at court, looking decorative, and performing the most trivial tasks!

"Leave well enough alone, laddie," said Scilti. *"Only count yourself lucky that you weren't born into the times that we remember. It wasn't all adventure and damsels fainting at a fellow's feet, you know. It was sleeping on the cold ground and going without meals, yes, and men dying or ending their days as cripples. A gut full of steel hurts, in case you didn't know it."*

And: *"The enthusiasm of youth—it's simply amazing,"* yawned Manogan. *"Had they the beginnings of wisdom as well, they'd be simply delightful."*

Not (to be perfectly fair) that Ceilyn's years of training were entirely wasted. Personal service to his betters, along with all the courtly graces, had always been an important part of any noble youth's education. Ceilyn had been given responsibilities—despite his youth, despite his unpopularity in some quarters—that permitted him to put that part of his education to good use.

And the physical testing of a knight came not only in battle. To endure endless tedious ceremonies, to stand as he did now, for hours on end, in a hot, crowded, noisy room, though his head throbbed with the skirling of bagpipes and the racket of horn and drum, though his eyes grew heavy from lack of sleep—and despite all that, never show any sign of boredom, weariness, or discomfort —that took stamina and self-discipline.

As it also took discipline to maintain a reverent and courteous demeanor at all times in the presence of ladies—even when the ladies in question were a pack of wicked teasing girls, determined to humiliate him. As Fand, Finola, Seelie, Prescelli, and the rest were now.

The dancing girls had appeared before the thrones, undulating in a manner that was little short of indecent. Olive-skinned, long-eyed, and scantily clad, they gyrated, rippled, and twisted themselves into nearly impossible contortions—nothing so exotic had appeared at Caer Cadwy in years. The men and boys were delighted, the women deliciously horrified, but Sidonwy's hand-maidens, once their initial shock wore off, were much more interested in Ceilyn.

To bring a blush to Ceilyn's cheek without actually indulging in any overt impropriety themselves was a challenge of which these young ladies never wearied. For Ceilyn was known to be that rarest of curiosities: a twenty-year-old male virgin. That alone made him a tempting target, but add to that a tendency, when embarrassed or self-conscious, to color up like a blushing maiden, and the temptation to harrow up his soul frequently became irresistible.

As it certainly was now. The girls nudged each other, giggled, cast sly sidelong glances in his direction, and Ceilyn was doomed from the very beginning—if the writhing dancers were not enough to disconcert him, the commotion caused by the young ladies could not fail. That he knew, without looking, exactly what Finola and the others were about, only assured their eventual success. He vowed not to give them the satisfaction, kept his eyes fastened on the dancers, tried desperately to think of other things—all in vain. Just because he knew that the girls watched him, he felt a hot, betraying blush spread across his face.

Fervently, he wished to be elsewhere, anywhere but here watching these perspiring, half-naked women, surrounded by tittering, curious girls. If only he could think of some excuse, some errand to take him away for a while—

Something soft brushed up against him; his little pale-haired Rhianeddi cousin, Gwenlliant, tugged at his sleeve. "There isn't any wine," she whispered, almost as if she guessed his thought and sympathized with his predicament.

He smiled gratefully down at the child. She was too young and lacking in malice to enjoy making sport of him—and now she had given him the means of escape. "Bless you," he said, under his breath, and meant it.

Somewhere, there was a page or a squire who had cleared away the wine and the cups from the High Table along with the dinner. That boy would have cause to regret his carelessness, by and by, but Ceilyn was more concerned, just at the moment, with rectifying the error.

He whispered a word of explanation in Sidonwy's ear, asked Dillus for the key to the buttery, and bade Gwenlliant's brother, Garanwyn, to accompany him below. It would be unthinkable for the Queen's own Knight Equerry to fetch and carry when boys were available to do it for him.

A short flight of stairs led down to the cellars where Dillus kept the wines and the silver. Two hundred years ago, this part of the castle had been a prison; the ceilings were low and the doors stout. Garanwyn's torch did little to dissipate the dry, chilly gloom. Their footsteps echoed off the walls, but the noisy merriment above had all faded away.

Someone had left another torch smoking on the buttery wall. As Garanwyn disappeared behind an iron grating in search of cups and a flagon, Ceilyn leaned up against the cool stones and closed his eyes, savoring this rare moment of peace.

How, in God's name, was he ever going to live through another winter? The long nights and the freezing weather that kept everyone crowded together indoors; the malicious pranks born of boredom; the short tempers and the lack of privacy. And outside, the howling of the wind—and the wolves. He had watched a pair of them this evening, prowling outside the gate, smaller than the great rangy wolves he had known in the north, but just as lean, just as hungry.

"Cousin? Are you well?" Garanwyn's innocent question made Ceilyn jump.

"I am perfectly well. Why shouldn't I be?" he replied sharply. Almost immediately, he regretted his rudeness. Despite the difference in their ages, Garanwyn was one of his few friends at court; Ceilyn had no wish to alienate him. "I can't think where the malvoisie is kept, that's all."

Garanwyn indicated a barrel at the far end of the room.

"You have a good memory," Ceilyn said, to take the sting out of his earlier discourtesy.

"Oh, we all know where to find the malvoisie these days," said Garanwyn, blue eyes dancing with mischief. "There's not a lad hereabouts, young Nefyn included, who doesn't make it his particular business to know the exact location of the malvoisie!"

"Good," said Ceilyn, with rare forbearance. "Perhaps we will see better service, after this."

Two days ago, young Nefyn had earned a memorable tongue-lashing by bringing perry when Ceilyn had called for malvoisie. But Garanwyn knew, perfectly well, that the page had been scolded for carelessness, not for a faulty memory. Had Nefyn tasted the wine as Ceilyn proceeded to do now, he would have detected the difference at once.

With the flagon of wine, the tray, and two jeweled goblets for the King and the Queen, Ceilyn and Garanwyn left the cellar.

"Have you eaten yet?" Garanwyn asked, taking his life in his hands. "I didn't see much of you during dinner."

"I was busy. Gofan brought me something to eat—I've forgotten what it was." Ceilyn had made a point of being busy, to avoid as much of the feast as possible.

"I meant to wish you well," said Garanwyn, as they climbed the stairs. "And I lit a candle for you this morning in the chapel." The Rhianeddi were always lighting candles: to commemorate birthdays and other anniversaries, for ailing friends or relatives, in times of personal or family crisis. Candles, churchbells, and incense were their sovereign remedies against all the ills of the world.

"Thank you," said Ceilyn, as graciously as he could. He did not like to be reminded of his birthday, which was a constant source of embarrassment and was always remembered because of his name. Everyone behaved as though he had chosen the day deliberately, an act that somehow betrayed a bad attitude on his part. Just this morning, he had overheard Finola saying, *"Imagine being born on Christmas Day! Do you suppose he thinks that all the celebration is on his account?"*

Emerging from the cool darkness into the crowded Hall, they passed by the Princess Diaspad, who lounged in a silver chair with her dwarfs and her shaggy brown woodwoses gathered around her, all of them raptly watching a youth in the scarlet cape, green tunic, and golden bells of a conjurer, who entertained them with a dazzling display of sleight-of-hand. Golden balls appeared out of nowhere, silken scarves bloomed into bouquets of flowers, white doves were transformed into glittering rings and necklaces. Interested in spite of himself, Ceilyn stopped to watch.

"—probably not my place to say so," Garanwyn was saying. "You push yourself too hard, expect too much of yourself. You do your own work twice as well as anyone else could and then take responsibility for the rest of us, too. You're very like the giant in that old tale."

"What giant?" Ceilyn asked absently.

"You know . . . the one with all the impossible tasks. Only you expect to perform them all single-handed."

There really was something terribly appealing about the young magician, though Ceilyn could not have explained where the fascination lay. Perhaps it was his easy, almost mocking self-confidence, his deft way with all the tired old tricks, his bright knowing smile that seemed to say, "I could do better than this, you know. I could work *real* magic, if I'd a mind to." Moreover, there was an eerie familiarity—

"Ceilyn?" Garanwyn broke into his thoughts again. "Shall I go on with the wine?"

Ceilyn nodded. "Yes, of course. You *can* pour, I think?"

But where (he asked himself) had he seen the man before? Not recently, at Caer Cadwy; he would remember more clearly. *Not* at Caer Celcynnon, certainly—not in the lifetime of Cuel mac Cadellin. And yet . . . taking a closer look, the fellow might very well be Gorwynnach, even Celcynnon-bred.

A white dove fluttered overhead, landed on the youth's outstretched arm. A dove . . . an owl . . . a hawk, perhaps? Of course, Ceilyn had seen a hundred boys hunting with a hundred hawks. Surely one of them had resembled this fellow. Somewhere in Gorwynnion, maybe, where hair that particular shade of russet brown was often seen, and those clear hazel-green eyes. Celcynnon, especially, bred true to type.

Satisfied with that explanation, Ceilyn remained enthralled until the performance ended. Only when the balls and the scarves and the silk flowers had disappeared up the magician's sleeves, and the youth had made his bow and vanished into the crowd, did Ceilyn remember his errand and hasten to catch up with Garanwyn.

Later, back in his place on the dais, Ceilyn watched a mum-show accompanied by the harsh, insistent music of the shawm and tabor. The masks were crudely made and garishly painted, the dance and pantomime awkward. So clumsily was the story presented that Ceilyn found it impossible to follow. His attention began to wander—only to return with a shock when the music abruptly ended and the dancers parted, revealing in their midst a man-high shaggy grey wolf.

The girls screamed and Ceilyn jumped, too, but it took only an instant to realize that the "wolf" was only a man in skins and an extraordinarily convincing mask. The wolf was a popular feature of the winter pageant, appearing either as hero or villain; little wonder, then, that so much skill and attention had been lavished on that one mask. Undoubtedly, the play elicited the same reaction wherever it was presented.

The play continued on to a murky conclusion. When the wolf removed his mask, the face underneath was the face of the young conjurer. Catching Ceilyn's eye, he smiled broadly—a peculiarly intimate smile, it seemed to Ceilyn.

But he can't know me, Ceilyn told himself. *He can't know anything about me.*

Yet the image of the wolf and the magician lingered, was still on his mind, hours later, when he lay wide awake on his hard, narrow bed. Forcing the images out of his mind, Ceilyn willed himself to relax. For once, his hard, disciplined body refused to obey him, remaining tense and wakeful. When he closed his eyes, he saw again the magician's suggestive smile and a voice at the back of his mind seemed to say, "But of course this is all a masquerade. We could do better, you and I. We know all about *real* magic, don't we?'' Ceilyn opened his eyes and abandoned all hope of sleep.

The room was still, except for the slow, even breathing of Fergos and his other roommates. Perhaps it was that sound that kept him awake; his hearing could be painfully acute.

He sat up in bed and glanced around him. He could see the room clearly by the faint glow of starlight coming in through the window: his own bed, wool blankets and sheepskin covering rumpled by his uneasy tossing and turning, the other narrow beds and their sleeping occupants.

He threw off the bedcovers, swung both legs over the side of his pallet. He wore nothing but short linen breeches, and the frigid air felt pleasantly cool on his bare arms and chest. He picked up the clothes he had folded so neatly a few hours before, now lying in a tumbled heap at the foot of his bed. He pulled on hose, boots, a shirt and doublet. Purely by force of habit he threw a cloak over his shoulders and fastened the clasp. He always dressed warmly in cold weather, to avoid awkward questions, but he seldom felt the cold.

On the stairs outside, he kept his footfalls light, lest the sound of his low-heeled boots striking the steps disturb someone. Two flights down, he opened another door and stepped through, stooping to avoid the lintel.

This was the chapel where the boys and some of the men said morning and evening prayers. Someone—Garanwyn, probably— had lit a dozen white tapers and placed them on the altar among the holly and evergreens. The candles had burned low; one of them flickered and died. Ceilyn knelt before the altar, tried unsuccessfully to form a prayer.

Even here, even in this place dedicated to prayer and contemplation, there was no escaping the hideous, jeering faces. They swarmed around the altar, perched above the narrow windows and the low doorway, hovered near the ceiling. Angels, archangels, seraphim, and cherubim they were supposed to represent, but they more closely resembled the demons and earth spirits that adorned the secular regions of the castle. If any difference existed between them it was only this: that this heavenly choir was, if possible, more horrible, more watchful and menacing, than their demonic counterparts.

All save one: a lovely, peaceful face above the altar, that always reminded Ceilyn of his mother. How and why that one beautiful image appeared among so many others that were ugly and perverted, Ceilyn did not know. But the angel served as a kind of talisman; by concentrating on her, Ceilyn could almost always conjure up a vision of his mother, a sure antidote against doubt and despair.

For just a moment, he succeeded, and Merewyn's still, radiant face appeared above the glowing candles, just as he had seen it so many times before, each year at Caer Celcynnon when she lit the Christmas tapers.

And then he was in that other chapel, the cold stony little church at Celcynnon, watching his mother and her attendants decorate the altar. At Merewyn's heels walked a solemn little boy. Ceilyn knew that child—how could he not?—and he knew what the boy was thinking. Watching him, Ceilyn felt again the same wondering delight.

God's love was with Merewyn, and in Merewyn, and the little boy felt that love as a palpable warmth. "He loves you, too," she assured him, but Ceilyn was only certain of that when she was near, and especially here among the holy things where she loved to be. And Merewyn and her Gwyngellach women whispered of secrets, hinted at mysteries of which the holly, the ivy, and the mistletoe were but visible symbols—symbols which, for Ceilyn, held a peculiarly personal power, because it was for the holly he had been named.

But the lovely vision faded, to be replaced by another: the church grown dark again, stripped of all decorations. An older Ceilyn knelt there now on the hard stone floor, sick with guilt and shame, while a cruel voice recited his sins. Sometimes, the voice seemed to go on forever, castigating, condemning, conjuring up images every bit as solid and terrifying as Cynwas's stone grotesqueries: the faces of the damned in Hell, writhing and weeping in eternal torment.

The faces and the memories began to crowd him so closely that prayer became impossible. Ceilyn rose and left the chapel.

Out on the allures, out in the clean air, he paused a moment to look and listen. All around him, Caer Cadwy slept peacefully. He could detect no sound but the solitary footsteps of a guard walking his rounds. A clear sky stretched overhead; a pinched and starved little new moon hovered on the horizon.

A candle or lantern burned in a window at the top of the Keep. Drawn by that tiny promise of light and warmth, Ceilyn moved in that direction.

He climbed a crooked staircase, turned left and descended a short flight, followed a winding tunnel through to the innermost courtyard, ascended yet another stair—even keeping to the allures as much as possible, it was impossible to walk a straight line through Caer Cadwy.

He opened another door, walked down a narrow corridor. The door at the other end was locked and barred. He turned back, wondering just where he was going and why. Then the oppression which had threatened him for days completely enveloped him.

Even the very air was charged with violence. Answering, a familiar wildness stirred inside him.

Not here, Ceilyn thought. *Oh please, not now.* But it was here, and it was now, and the thing that had stalked him for days had finally caught up with him; there was no place he could hide. A trickle of cold sweat ran down his side; his heartbeat accelerated painfully, and breathing became difficult.

Dear God, he prayed, *don't let it happen again. How much longer must I atone? What have I done to bring this thing on me again?*

But soon he was beyond asking, beyond even caring. His skin crawled and his insides writhed and there was nothing to do but wait for the change and welcome it when it came.

Manogan fab Menai opened the door and stepped into the long corridor. He groped for the torch which ought to be in a bracket by the door, but found the iron ring empty.

Something rattled in the shadows ahead of him. ''Who's there?'' he asked.

No reply, but that dry scraping and a deep, heavy breathing. ''Who's there?'' Manogan repeated, flinging open the door.

The thin, watery light without did little to alleviate the darkness within, but now a pair of green-gold eyes glowed in the lightless corridor.

The beast in the shadows growled, a low, threatening rumble.

Very slowly, Manogan slid his sword from its scabbard, the long knife out of a leather sheath at his side. But the beast exploded into movement, was on him before he had any chance to fend it off.

Manogan felt himself falling backward, heard a sharp crack as his head hit the floor. Then sharp fangs tore at him and darkness swallowed him up.

And in the bright morning, before the day was an hour old, the Princess Goewin went walking down by the sea. There she saw the young man, lying upon the rocks where the little brown seals come to sun themselves.

"Surely this is the most beautiful youth that ever was born," said Goewin. "I will sit here beside him until he awakes, and I will ask him his name."

He slept all through the morning, but the Princess waited patiently.

"God be good to you," said the Princess, when he opened his eyes. "Tell me your name and how you came to be here."

"As God is my witness," said the young man, "I cannot tell you my name or how I came to be here. What land I was in before this is a mystery to me. I cannot tell you, Maiden, the place where I was born, and the name of my father is entirely unknown."

"It is a sad thing that you should say so," said Goewin. "For I would feign be your friend."

"Do not distrust me because of that," said the youth. "I do not know my name or how I came into this land, but this I do know and would swear it on my life: You are the Princess Goewin, and it is you that I love."

From GOEWIN AND ELLWY: The Death of Goewin

4.

A Conversation With the Green Lion

Long grey shadows stretched across the snowy courtyard. Pennons and banners fluttered green, gold, and scarlet in a damp morning breeze. The day promised to be clear, cold, and brilliant.

But to Teleri, crossing the yard with a hurried step, the crystalline light of early morning lent an awful clarity to everything: the remarkable beasts on the banners, the gargoyles and zoomorphs leering at her from the walls, the figure in green and gold sprawled out upon the snow in the middle of the yard.

Teleri quickened her steps, felt her stomach twist into a hard knot of dread—just as it had earlier that morning when Brother Gildas's urgent summons brought her to Manogan fab Menai's bedside.

A man lay unconscious in the snow, dead or injured. She bent down to determine which, recoiled as she recognized him: untidy brown hair, fine pale features—Ceilyn mac Cuel of Celcynnon.

His eyes were closed and blood stained his face and his clothes and his hands, but he breathed slowly and evenly, and, pale as he was, the color in his lips and the palms of his hands was good. It seemed he might only be sleeping. Whatever had happened to him, whatever he had done, Teleri wanted no part of it or him. She turned away, took a few steps, stopped, and looked back over her shoulder.

A green lion on one of the banners watched her, glaring at her with a fierce red eye, condemning her for cowardice.

But Ceilyn mac Cuel! she protested inwardly. *If it were any other man* . . . Helpless as he looked, still she feared him.

He might be seriously injured, snarled the lion. *Even dying.* And Gwyngelli's golden dragon and the brooding Rhianeddi ravens all chimed in: *If not, he'll be dead soon enough. Dead of exposure, sleeping in the snow.*

Teleri wrung her hands. Someone would find him before that happened. Already, she heard activity in the next courtyard.

But you are a physician, a serpent with the face of a beautiful woman reminded her. They surrounded her on all sides: Walgan's brown bear and Cuan's rainbow-hued cockatrice, the swan of Draighen, blue rams and scarlet tygers, knotted serpents, hideous gargoyles, and all the other impossible creatures—mocking, malicious, insistent. *If you run away now, what will you be?*

She knelt in the snow beside him, very gently touched his pale face: warm, though he had been lying in the cold and the damp, perhaps for a long time. Was he feverish? She spoke his name, and his eyes slowly opened.

He lay there a while longer, smiling drowsily up into her eyes, as though in some pleasant dream. Then his eyes focused on her face, and his expression changed to one of puzzlement. He struggled to sit up.

"What happened to you?" Teleri asked.

"I don't remember," he said, frowning, passing a hand over his forehead. Then: "May God forgive me . . . I think that I have killed a man."

The knot in Teleri's stomach tightened. *"Killed a man? Who have you killed?"*

Ceilyn shook his head. "It was dark and I couldn't . . . If I could just . . . Manogan. Oh God, it was Manogan fab Menai, the Earl Marshall!"

"Manogan fab Menai," she breathed, drawing back in surprise. "Are you certain of that?"

Perhaps he realized that he had said too much already, for he started to speak, changed his mind, and sat silently staring down at the ground. Teleri watched him, a wild surmise growing in her mind.

Were it not for the lion and the stone gargoyles, she would have walked away from him then and there, walked away and convinced herself that she had imagined the entire encounter. She gazed at the green lion reproachfully. *All these years, I've seen my death in this man's eyes.*

"I'm not certain of anything," Ceilyn said. "Perhaps I . . . Yes, that's it, I was drunk. I drank too much wine last night."

Dazed and disconcerted he might be, but Teleri knew that those clear, almost feverishly bright hazel eyes were not the eyes of a man who had spent the night in a drunken stupor. "You don't look as if you were the worse for wine."

"Now, what would you know about that?" he retorted. Then, perhaps remembering the courtesy due a lady, even so young and odd a lady as this one, he added stiffly, "I beg your pardon. I forgot you were a doctor of sorts." He rubbed his forehead again. "If you know a remedy for the headache, I believe I could use it."

Teleri stood up, brushed snow off her cloak and her full skirts. "I might know of something. You had best come inside with me." Hesitantly, she offered him her hand. "Can you walk? Is any of that blood yours?"

He muttered an unintelligible reply, rose unsteadily, and followed her across the yard to the foot of the Wizard's Tower. Teleri's door, set into the thickness of the wall, was scarcely five feet high, built low for defense like most of the doors in the older parts of the castle, but it matched her tiny stature. She pushed the door open and walked right through into her little bedchamber, but Ceilyn, following after her, had to bend at the waist and duck his head.

Teleri pulled flint and steel out of a pocket hidden in the folds of her skirt, and knelt by the low fireplace to rekindle her fire. Ceilyn remained by the door, surveying the room with a suspicious frown. What he had expected of the bedchamber of an apprentice sorceress he did not know—but probably not this bare, ordinary little room. A narrow bed, a clothes chest, a table and wash basin, a bucket of water and a three-legged stool on the hearth were the only amenities. The room was as plain and colorless as Teleri herself, except for the carvings over the fireplace and the scarlet coverlet splashed across her bed.

Curled up at the foot of the bed was a fat grey tabby, who raised her head, curled her lip, and spat at him.

"Pay her no heed," said Teleri. "She is—was—Glastyn's cat, and dislikes everyone else quite impartially. I think that she only stays on for the hunting."

Eyeing the tabby warily, Ceilyn crossed the room and seated himself on a stool by the fire. The cat sprang from the bed and stalked out the door. Teleri closed it softly behind her.

Teleri poured water from the bucket into the basin. While Ceilyn washed the blood from his face and hands, she searched among the bags and pouches suspended from her belt. Finding what she wanted, she took a wooden cup from the mantel, mixed a handful of white powder with water, and offered the cup to Ceilyn. He hesitated, then swallowed her potion down.

He wrapped his cloak around him again, but Teleri had already seen the dark blood on his doublet. "Will you let me take a look at your shoulder?"

He shook his head, held his cloak more closely around him. "It was only a scratch."

"Even a scratch can mortify if not properly treated," she said. "But if you would rather have Gildas . . ."

"I would rather be left entirely alone, if you really want to know. I beg your pardon . . . but you did ask."

"Yes," she said. "But I do wish that you had given me another answer."

He darted a longing look at the door. "I don't understand."

"I helped Brother Gildas to stitch Manogan back together," Teleri said. "He was horribly torn up, but he seems likely to live."

Ceilyn collapsed on the stool by the fire. "He is alive? I thought he was dead. I'm glad, of course, but . . . he ought to be dead."

"Can you tell me what happened?"

He took several deep breaths. "It was just—just a stupid quarrel. You know the kind of thing. We had both—it was Christmas, you know, and the spiced wine and the wassail kept going round and round. . . ."

"The Marshall said nothing about a quarrel. He said that he was attacked by an enormous grey wolf."

Ceilyn shook his head. "That can't be. A wolf in the castle? And he—when Manogan fell, he must have hit his head. He'll be suffering from delusions. There was . . . there was a wolf in the play at the revels last night."

Teleri knelt on the hearth beside him. "Manogan was weak, but perfectly lucid. I'd never seen anyone who had been savaged by a wolf before, but I can guess what it must be like. And I do know what damage a sword or a dagger can do." Her gaze traveled to the place where his swordbelt ought to be. "Where *are* your sword and dagger."

"I—in my bedchamber. Where else?"

"I see," she said. "You fought with the Marshall and left him there, presumably to die. You took your weapons back up to your room. And then—not bothering to wash off his blood or your own—you wandered outside to take a nap in the snow. Do I have that right?"

"It wasn't like that at all."

"How was it?" she asked.

"I *told* you," he said coldly. "I don't—perhaps I simply imagined the whole thing. Maybe I'm the one suffering from delusions."

"But the Marshall did very nearly die. You didn't imagine that." She touched him lightly on the shoulder. "Only a scratch, you said. But would there be so much as a scar remaining now?"

"What are you trying to say?"

"I think . . . that you are a shapechanger—a werewolf," she said.

He ran a shaking hand through his tangled hair, smiled disbelievingly. "You're joking, of course. That's absurd! This is Camboglanna—things like that just don't happen here."

"But you are from the north," she pointed out, "where such things are rather more common."

She studied his face in the flickering firelight, noticing, for the first time, all the tiny subtle differences that marked him. For a young man who led such an active life, much of it in the sun and air, his skin was remarkably fair and delicate. And his cheek, though he must have been out at least half the night, was as smooth as a girl's. Even lying in the snow, he had been warm to her touch. And she knew his reputation: stronger, faster, and more agile on the tourney field than men brawnier and more experienced, uncannily sharp senses which made him the terror of erring squires and pages. Whatever he was, he was not like any other man she had met before.

"Do you expect me to say nothing about this?" she asked. "Or did you intend to go to the King yourself?"

"Naturally, I will go to the King," he said. "And to the Marshall. I am willing to accept punishment for what I did."

"And you don't think—you don't suppose that they will notice the inconsistencies in your story and make some of the same guesses I did?"

Her question seemed to knock all the fight out of him. "What if I . . . just went away? What would you do then?"

"That would depend. Perhaps if I better understood exactly what happened last night," she said, "I would know what ought to be done. You must know that I'm not eager to run to the King with tales of shapechanging warlocks. Once people begin to ask questions . . ."

He thought that over for a minute, finally reached a decision. "Very well," he sighed. "But there isn't much to tell, and you've guessed most of it already. I met the Marshall quite by accident last night. As I chanced to be a wolf at the time, the encounter turned . . . unpleasant."

She took some time shaping the next question. "How long have you possessed this . . . gift?"

"Gift?" Ceilyn stiffened. "God above! You think I regard this thing as a gift? There's a man injured, possibly even dying—a good man, who never did me any harm—and you imagine this is something I sought? This *curse* comes over me, and I have no control over it whatever."

"I take it," she said, "that your peculiarity isn't known here, or among your people in Gorwynnion?"

"I think you must know as well as I do, what would happen if my family knew," he said. "It would break my mother's heart, and my father—if Cuel mac Cadellin knew, if he even suspected, he would condemn me to the stake and light the faggots with his own hands!"

"But you said—you aren't really a warlock. Not if this isn't something you *will* to happen."

"And what does that signify, pray tell?" he asked. "It is an evil thing, this curse of mine, and how could it have come about except through my own wickedness?"

"And are you," she asked wonderingly, "so very wicked as that?"

"You think that you know all about me, don't you?" he said. "Everyone thinks that they know, but they don't! You all imagine that I've set myself up as some sort of a saint, that I fancy myself better than anyone else. But don't you see—it's quite the opposite. Because of this curse, I have to try harder, allow myself few mistakes—and still I'm so much worse than any of them!"

"How?" she persisted. "How are you so much worse than anyone else?"

"In any number of ways," he said. The treacherous color rose in his face. "You wouldn't understand. You're a female, and innocent enough, I suppose, in your way; you have no idea what goes on in a man's mind, what he might be capable of, in thought if not in deed. The secret sins are very strong in me. And I have tried everything, every penance that ever I heard of: hairshirts, flagellation, walking barefoot in the snow . . . everything. But always at the end—for all my prayer and fasting, despite confession and absolution—still there is my abominable pride!"

"Well," said Teleri, "you do sound very bad, of course. But I don't believe that you are accursed at all. Perhaps I am not so well educated as you in matters of sin and salvation. But I do know something about magical gifts and how often—how woefully often—they are misunderstood or misdirected.''

"I thought that I told you," he said impatiently, "that I don't direct—I don't use or misuse this thing at all."

"I am scarcely astonished," she said. "How can you hope to master something, when you insist on misnaming it?"

"Now we have strayed into territory where *I'm* forced to admit ignorance," he said with a sigh. "You tell me—by what means can I master this thing, if not by prayer or penance?"

"I don't know." Teleri sat down on the edge of her bed. "But there is always power to be gained by giving something its proper name. And—as prayer and penance would seem to have failed you—what could you lose by trying some other way?"

"They didn't—they didn't absolutely fail me," he protested. "I did believe, for a time, that I had mastered it. You see, I had this idea: The best knights, the heroes in the old tales, were all capable of miraculous works. So I thought that I, in adhering to the same discipline and ideals, might also gain power . . . power to cure myself. And I did feel different, the very first time that I put on armor. Better, maybe. And in all the time that I've lived here at Caer Cadwy, last night was the first time that the—the weakness overcame me.''

"Then what would you accomplish by going away now?"

"Accomplish? But surely you see the danger. If it should happen again . . . I never know beforehand, you know. Even when it was happening all the time, I never knew. Oh, it did seem a bit worse during the winter, when food is scarce and the wolves—the real wolves—grow bolder. But it has occurred at other times, too. And now that it's all beginning again, now that I've actually tasted blood, there's no telling what might happen."

"But what does happen when you are a wolf?" Teleri asked.

He sprang to his feet, began pacing the flagstone floor. "I don't go about indulging a raging hunger for human flesh, if that's what you mean. Manogan was the first, the very first. He took one look at me—at the thing that I had become—and he drew his sword. Then I—''

"Then you, quite naturally, defended yourself," Teleri finished for him. "Not an unreasonable act for a wolf—or a man."

"But it was *my* fault," he insisted.

"How was it your fault?''

Ceilyn stiffened. "The problem would never have presented itself, if it weren't for my wretched, my obscene curse!"

"You could say that. But you might also say that this time you were the victim of Manogan fab Menai's peculiar luck."

He thought that over, apparently much struck by the idea. "It would be comforting for me to believe that. But even so, suppose that Manogan's luck turned on him again, or another man stumbled into bad luck? I would hate to be the instrument of his misfortune another time."

"But where do you propose to go," she asked, "that you can escape the promptings of fate—your own, or any other's?"

His erratic pacing slowed. "I don't know. Or perhaps I do. There are places to the north where few men go. I could—I could become a hermit somewhere in the wilderness." He looked into the glowing heart of the fire, and a vision of the White Martyrdom, the stern, simple life of the ascetic dwelling in the desert waste, rose up before him—a vision infinitely appealing. "Perhaps I wasn't far wrong after all," he said. "Perhaps I only chose the wrong surroundings to seek that purification and release I longed for. But if I were alone in the wild, far from the worldly pleasures of the court, the distractions and the temptations—"

"But can you—" Teleri hesitated to destroy that beguiling image. "Can you leave here so easily as that? A man like yourself with obligations and duties . . .?"

His radiance dimmed. "I'll have to disappear. You don't have to tell me how wretchedly dishonorable that will be, and what a poor beginning for the new life I have chosen. But better than concocting a lie, better than deceiving the Queen, who trusts me." He thought a moment longer. "I suppose the other men will be getting together some kind of a hunt, once the Marshall's story spreads. I'll ask leave to join them . . . not precisely a lie . . . then slip away when nobody is looking.

"Oh, they'll wonder when I don't come back—maybe even look for me a day or two. But I'll not be missed by many. And those few who will be affected, why, they are just the ones who would suffer if the truth ever came out."

"Perhaps they will forget you here," said Teleri. "But you will still remember. You can't run away from who and what you are."

"It may be that I can't," said Ceilyn. "But I am certainly going to try. Perhaps your advice is kindly meant. But you haven't lived with this thing, you can't possibly imagine what it is like.''

"No," said Teleri, conceding defeat. "I don't suppose that I can." She still thought that he had made the wrong decision, but she had no right—no reason, really—to ask him to stay.

The sky was dark and the wind was rising when Ceilyn led his chestnut gelding out of the stable. His eyes had gone dark and stormy, too; he found it more difficult than he had anticipated, to leave this place he had called home for five years.

The rest of the hunt had gone on before him. He had taken time to change his clothes, to dispose of his blood-stained cloak and doublet, to ask leave of the Queen. Now he must ride out alone. That made his departure and disappearance simpler, but somehow sadder.

He paused for a moment, glanced back at the Mermaid Tower, up toward the Queen's bedchamber window, hoping to catch a glimpse of a face, even a suggestion of movement. But there was nothing. She was not there. That made going simpler and sadder, too.

He vaulted into the saddle, looked over his shoulder one last time. Then he turned, and rode out the gate.

"You would do well, my father," said Menai, "to think carefully before you swear friendship with that man. Have not he and his people been our enemies since time out of mind? Is not Corrig, himself, known for treachery and deceit?"

"I am resolved," said Maelwas, "and there is no more to be said."

"So be it," said Menai. "But only promise me this: When you take his right hand in token of friendship, look you also to his left."

"Indeed, I will not do so," his father replied. "For it is not in my nature when I call a man 'brother' that I should trust him with anything less than my life."

And for years afterward, Menai fab Maelwas (usually the kindest and most compassionate of men) had few words to say about Corrig of Mochdreff or his own bizarre revenge; yet he would smile whenever Corrig's name was mentioned, and this is all that he would say:

"The rats and the boiling oil presented little problem; but as for the wild dogs and the spotted plague . . ."

From the Oral Tradition of Tir Gwyngelli

5.

The Owl and the Nightjar

January brought more snow and a cruelly cold New Year. The wind howled all night, a thin, rough-edged lament; a light, powdery snowfall continued day and night without ceasing, and the water froze solid in the castle ponds and fountains.

Garanwyn fab Cyndrywyn sat cross-legged on his bed in the long, drafty dormitory that housed the squires. He had bundled up in his cloak and all his blankets, and he was desperately trying not to think about food.

A silver goblet had vanished from the Hall, misplaced or stolen, no one knew which. Without a culprit on whom to place the blame, the Seneschal put all the boys on half-rations until the cup was found or replaced. Banished from the Hall and the Solar, the squires and pages spent their idle hours huddled around the kitchen fire or upstairs in the dormitory, as hungry and cross as young bears.

But *some* people (Garanwyn thought resentfully) found these privations easier to endure. Some folk were just such big, indolent oafs that none of it seemed to matter! Not hunger or cold or undeserved punishments, not mysterious attacks by wild beasts, that had everyone else on edge. Some people just did not seem to care at all. Garanwyn glared at his kinsman, Tryffin fab Maelgwyn, who lay on the next bed, wrapped up in his fur-lined cloak, to all appearances sleeping the (totally undeserved) sleep of the just.

But Tryffin could always sleep. No tossing or turning in the night for him, no pacing the floor, wrestling with the hideous pangs of hunger—oh no! Tryffin slept like a baby all night long and he could spend half the day sleeping as well. At least, he appeared to be napping. His eyes were closed and he had not moved a muscle in hours—but there was never any telling what really went on in that dark Gwyngellach mind of his.

The door opened and Fflergant walked into the room, shaking snow out of his hair and brushing it off his scarlet wool cloak. He cast a sour glance at his brother. "He's not really sleeping, you know. He only does that to annoy the rest of us."

"I suppose," Tryffin replied, without even opening his eyes, "you would rather I were awake and trying to provoke a quarrel?"

"Sleep, if you like," Fflergant said cordially. "There will be that much more for the rest of us."

Tryffin sat up, suddenly bright-eyed and eager. "You have it, then?"

Fflergant produced a small bundle from underneath his cloak, proceeded to untie it. "That's food!" Garanwyn exclaimed, as a cascade of nuts and dried fruits landed almost in his lap.

Fflergant offered him a wrinkled winter apple. "Is it, now? I confess, I had nearly forgotten the look of it." He sat down at the foot of Garanwyn's bed, tossed a piece of fruit to Tryffin, and selected one for himself.

Garanwyn eyed this unexpected bounty mistrustfully. "How did you come by this?"

"Not dishonestly, if that is what you mean. We bribed one of the servants," Tryffin explained around a mouthful of pear. "He was going into Treledig this afternoon, and we thought he might be willing to handle a little commission for us."

"Of course. I'm surprised that none of the other lads thought to do the same."

"As to that," said Fflergant, "I have a suspicion that some of them did. He had quite a number of little packages to sort through before he found ours. What's the matter?" he asked, as Garanwyn, far from falling hungrily on the food offered to him, continued to gaze at it wistfully.

"Do you think that we ought? I mean, we're supposed to be fasting until supper."

"Did you steal the silver cup?" Tryffin began sorting the fruit and nuts into three equal piles.

Garanwyn sighed. "Of course I didn't."

"Were you the one who mislaid it?"

"I can't have been," said Garanwyn. "I didn't serve at the High Table on the night the cup disappeared."

"Well, then?" Fflergant and Tryffin asked together.

"It's a question of honor," Garanwyn replied stiffly. "We're expected to accept the punishment given us—not try and circumvent it. We're supposed to be men of honor—not churls."

"As to that . . ." Fflergant shrugged his shoulders and swallowed a handful of raisins. ". . . being a howling savage myself, I wouldn't know. I leave the finer points of honor to you northern lads, who know all about it."

"I didn't mean to preach," said Garanwyn.

"Of course you didn't," Fflergant said indulgently. "You simply cannot help yourself. It's your early upbringing I don't doubt. Sometimes," he added provocatively, "you sound exactly like your cousin, Ceilyn mac Cuel."

"And what is the matter with our cousin, Ceilyn mac Cuel?" Garanwyn wanted to know.

Tryffin and Fflergant exchanged an amused glance. "And here I thought you would be flattered. You tell me—what *is* the matter with your cousin, Ceilyn mac Cuel?"

Garanwyn sighed; there was no denying that he had walked into that one with his eyes open. "Well, you can't blame our troubles on Ceilyn—not this time. If Ceilyn were here, the beastly cup would never have disappeared. The younger lads are unpardonably careless when he isn't here to keep an eye on them."

"Oh aye, no doubt," said Fflergant. "Nothing ever gets pinched or wasted or goes wrong when Ceilyn is here."

"Anyway," said Garanwyn, "nothing so valuable has ever disappeared before."

"So why isn't Ceilyn here, then, where he belongs? I don't recall asking him to go chasing halfway to Hell after the Earl Marshall's wolf!"

"Maybe not . . . but perhaps you should have done," said Garanwyn. "As it *was* your uncle the wolf attacked."

"Just supposing that it really is the wolf Ceilyn is after," Fflergant said, under his breath.

"And just what is that supposed to mean?"

Fflergant shook his head. "Only that Ceilyn is just as likely to be off somewhere abusing himself, doing one of his ghastly penances for some perfectly imaginary sin of his. It makes me sick to think—"

"You make *me* sick," Garanwyn sniffed. "You're always going on about family loyalty as if it were the One True Faith, and here you have no more respect for your own blood-kin than if he were—"

"Calchas fab Corfil?" Fflergant suggested maliciously.

Garanwyn flushed angrily. "And that's another thing. You always preach tolerance like a Gorwynnach extolling abstinence—but it is another matter entirely when your own prejudices come into it!"

"We do tolerate Calchas." Tryffin pried open a nut with the point of his dirk. "Your lad is still in one piece, isn't he?"

"Very well," Garanwyn said loftily. "I will admit that he hasn't been exactly pleasant, especially to the pair of you. But maybe you wouldn't be so agreeable either, if everyone treated you like—"

"An outsider?" Tryffin suggested. "A barbarian?"

"As though you didn't exploit that barbarian nonsense yourselves!" said Garanwyn. "It's always: Don't look at me, I'm just a savage from the Gwyngelli Hills. But no one would ever take you for Hillmen if you weren't constantly reminding us; you're both too big and blond. And for every little jest about blue paint and naked savages there are five or six bootlickers waiting to soothe your precious feelings, just because your father is the richest man in Celydonn and calls himself a king back in Tir Gwyngelli!''

Fflergant ground his teeth. ''If anyone tries to lick my boots, I'll kick his—''

''I never said that you cared for that sort of thing,'' Garanwyn interjected hastily. ''I only meant that you could afford to show a little compassion. Only think what it must be like for Calchas here. No friends or kinsmen close to his own age—except for Morc and Derry, who wouldn't be fit companions for a toad! And then there is that dreadful mother of his.''

''Some folk find her amusing. Cynwas seems to find her extravagances enormously diverting, and he's not the only one. But if Calchas fab Corfil is such a baby that he's afraid of his own mother, I don't see why it is your task to wipe his snotty little nose for him,'' Fflergant sneered.

''The King asked me to take Calchas under my wing—as you already know,'' snarled Garanwyn. What had begun as friendly teasing was rapidly turning into a full-fledged quarrel.

''And you were such a coward that you hadn't the courage to tell Cynwas that he had no right to ask you to take the part of the grandson of the man who murdered your own great-grandfather,'' Fflergant spat out.

Garanwyn's color changed from red to white. ''I am not a coward. I ought to knock your teeth right down your throat.'' He reached under his bed and pulled out his knee-high riding boots.

''You and whose cavalry?'' Fflergant sneered.

This was not a bad assessment of Garanwyn's chances. He was no weakling—no boy who was could last long as a squire or page. With the pallor of winter emphasizing his fair Rhianeddi coloring he looked delicate—and was quite the opposite. But he was no match for either of his brawny kinsmen, and he knew it.

He kicked off his unheeled calfskin shoes, pulled on his boots, one after the other. ''You believe that you are God's special benefaction to the rest of the world . . . don't you?''

Fflergant smiled smugly. ''Maybe I do. And maybe I am.''

Garanwyn stood up. ''Well, I think you are a pig!'' he said, and stalked out of the room.

A long silence followed, broken at last by Fflergant. "Before God, that was inexcusable!"

Tryffin nodded his agreement. He finished his own little cache of fruit and nuts and started on Garanwyn's.

"But I spoke out of turn as well. . . ."

"I'll not deny that."

Another lengthy silence. It was true that the Gwyngellach raised reverence for home and family almost to the status of a religion. The broad-minded Hillfolk accounted few sins unpardonable, but quarreling with a kinsman without good cause was among them— even if that kinsman had been born and reared in the north and was therefore prone to be insufferably self-righteous.

"Why do I say these things?"

"I reckon," said Tryffin, "you don't stop to think."

Fflergant glared at him. "I leave that to you, you're so good at it. Why didn't you stop me?"

Tryffin smiled sweetly. "Because Calchas fab Corfil fab Corrig isn't the only one who has to learn how to wipe his own snotty little nose."

Fflergant weighed, briefly, the merits of fratricide.

"Very well," he decided. "I deserved that."

He wandered over to the nearest window and gazed out. In the yard below, he spotted Garanwyn striding purposefully toward a flight of stairs leading down to the lower courtyard and the stables. "That young idiot is wearing his riding boots. You don't suppose he is going to go out riding alone and get himself eaten by wolves?"

"No one has seen a wolf since Christmas—and not for want of looking." Tryffin cleared away the last of the nut-shells and stretched out on his bed for another nap. "And if you want to go down and beg Garanwyn's pardon, why don't you just do it—and leave the wolves out of it?"

Fflergant hesitated by the door. "You can't sleep all day. A ride in the open air would do you good—give you a better appetite for supper when it finally comes."

Tryffin groaned. "Who's a coward now?"

"I intend to do my own apologizing," Fflergant said haughtily. "But I thought you might come along."

The only answer was a soft snore. Disgusted, Fflergant rummaged under his own bed, pulled his riding boots on, threw open the door, and clattered down the stairs. But the sound of a door slamming on the floor above brought him up short.

Tryffin appeared at the top of the steps, carrying his boots. "You're in the Devil's own hurry, aren't you?" he said.

In a corner of the outermost courtyard, between the new stables and the Main Gate, stood two long, low, ramshackle buildings, scarcely visible beneath a tangle of withered vines and the long icicles that hung from their eaves almost to the ground. One of these buildings still housed a number of animals: the plodding carthorses that carried the servants into Treledig on market days, Teleri's grey pony, Kelpie, and a few ancient geldings used by those of the squires and pages who had no riding horses of their own. The other building, the more dilapidated of the two, was occasionally used to store hay or grain during the dry summer months. Why the building still stood was a mystery, for the walls leaned crazily and the roof looked ready to collapse under its burden of ice and snow.

Inside the abandoned stable, a boy and a girl were playing. The boy, a sallow, dark-haired youth of about fifteen, well-wrapped up in sable furs and crimson velvet, had placed a smoking rushlight in a kind of bracket on the wall. A little pale winter sunlight filtered in through the holes in the thatch, but it was a dismal, chilly place they had chosen for their game. The girl—some five or six years younger than the boy, and dazzlingly fair of skin and hair—shivered, though she, too, had come out warmly dressed in layers of lambskin and wool.

"I don't like this game," she said. "It's not the way you said it would be. I want to go in now."

The children knelt on the frozen ground, among wisps of rotting straw and droppings from the owls that lived in the rafters. Their breath, whenever they spoke, made icy clouds on the frosty air.

"The sooner we begin," said the boy, shoving a crude doll fashioned out of straw, string, and hair into her hand, "the sooner we will be done. Just recite the piece I taught you. It won't take long."

"But I don't understand it," she said. "I don't know what it means. I don't see—"

"It's poetry, you little fool," the boy cut in impatiently. "You're not supposed to understand it."

"It can't be poetry," she said primly. "It's too ugly. Poetry is never ugly."

"And you know all about it, I suppose, Madam the Bard." His fingers bit cruelly into her wrist until she cried out in pain. "Say it," he commanded.

Reluctantly, the child began:

"I am the lightning that destroys
I am the vengeance of the gods
I am the Word in letters of flame
I am a howling on the wind

"I don't remember what comes next, Calchas."
"The owl and the nightjar," he prompted her.

"The owl and the nightjar know its name
The raven knows but speaks it not
The wolf and the roebuck alike flee from it
They will not know it or speak the Word
For it is a potent doom
And the end of all things."

In a stall on the other side of the wall, Garanwyn listened. At first, he had ignored the voices issuing from the abandoned stables. During the summer months when hay was stored there, it served as a trysting place for the romantically inclined, and this was not the first time he had heard whispers, giggles, or girlish protests on the far side of the wall. But when he recognized one of the voices he stopped saddling the old dappled gelding and strained his ears to hear more. The more that he heard, the sicker he felt.

"There is darkness at the root of it
There is pain and wailing at the heart of it
The body knows only despair and the death of all hope
My enemy must die."

The door at the far end of the stable creaked open, and two large figures appeared, silhouetted against the light: Fflergant and Tryffin.

"What do you want?" Garanwyn asked nastily, hoping, by his rudeness, to drive them away.

But Fflergant had come in a conciliating mood—and it was

nearly impossible to offend Tryffin. "We've come to make amends—I have, anyway," said Fflergant. "I said things that I shouldn't have, and I apologize."

The voices on the other side of the wall had fallen to a murmur, but Garanwyn had no way of knowing how much the other two could hear. "Apology accepted," he said, turning his back, pretending to tighten the girth on his saddle. "Is there anything else?" he asked coldly.

"We hoped you would allow us to go riding with you," said Fflergant.

The chant began again:

> "Let her heart be as a stone
> Let her eyes grow dark as night
> Let her blood burn in her veins
> And her—"

Garanwyn raised his own voice, in order to drown out the other. "I would rather go alone, thank you very much."

"If that is what you want," said Fflergant, more puzzled than offended. He began backing out of the stable, but Tryffin stopped him, gripping his shoulder. "Hark to that. Isn't that Gwenlliant?"

Garanwyn began to feel sick again. "It might be," he forced himself to say icily. "There were some children playing in there a while past. But you were just leaving, weren't you?"

An anguished cry split the air: "Calchas! She's *burning*!"

Garanwyn dropped the reins, pushed past his cousins, and ran for the door.

In the abandoned stable, the straw-dolly burned. It lay on the floor where Gwenlliant had cast it, filling the air with clouds of black smoke and a stench like something nine days dead.

Gwenlliant struggled frantically in Calchas's grasp. "You little fool," he hissed, trying vainly to silence her with a hand over her mouth. "You'll burn, too, if anyone hears you."

He did not hear the other boys explode through the door, was taken entirely by surprise when Garanwyn tore the sobbing little girl out of his arms and shoved him violently to the ground.

Garanwyn wrapped his arms around his sister, buried his face in her mist-colored hair. "No one will hurt you," he whispered. "Don't be afraid. I won't let anyone hurt you."

Behind him, Fflergant and Tryffin tried to stamp out the fire, but the greedy blue flames were not easily extinguished. In the end, Tryffin smothered them with an old grain sack he found in a corner.

"God of Heaven!" exclaimed Fflergant, waving his arms to dissipate the choking dark smoke. "It smells like someone has been burning dead cats!"

Garanwyn looked up. "Go away," he whispered hoarsely, still clutching the little girl protectively. "Can't you see . . . this is no concern of yours."

Tryffin bent down, gingerly picked up the charred remains of the doll. He examined the reeking bundle of straw, string, and hair, then silently handed it over to Fflergant.

"It wasn't her fault," Garanwyn mumbled. "He tricked her."

Calchas picked himself up off the floor, brushed the dirty straw off his velvet cloak. "She tricked me. She had me fooled, with her sweet face and her innocent ways—until she cast a spell over me and led me here against my will. But you have only to look at her to see the truth. The mark is on her for all to see. She's a witch-child."

"That's a lie," Garanwyn insisted. "That's a filthy lie."

"Of course it's a lie." Fflergant shoved Calchas up against a wall, so hard that he knocked the breath out of him.

Tryffin said, "You had better send her away. You won't want her to see this."

Garanwyn brushed the web-colored hair out of his sister's eyes, wiped her tears with a corner of his cloak. "Go inside, wash your face, find something to do, and don't say a word of this to anyone. Do you understand?" Gwenlliant nodded, and her brother gently pushed her toward the door.

"Keep your hands off me," Calchas was snarling. "You have no right to touch me. If you hit me again, I'll tell my—"

This time it was Tryffin who slammed him up against the wall. "Tell your mother? I think not. I really think not."

"What are you going to do to him?" Garanwyn asked, scarcely knowing what to expect while this uncharacteristically violent mood was on his cousins.

"Well, now, there's the question," said Tryffin grimly. "Where we come from, people don't care to rush into these things. We like to take our time and devise something really intricate. We're very imaginative, we Gwyngellach." He took Calchas's hand and methodically began breaking the fingers. Calchas screamed, struggled to pull away, and collapsed on the ground.

"You've been begging for this ever since you set foot through the gate," growled Fflergant. "Someone told you, maybe, that it was perfectly safe to insult us to our faces—true enough, for we're slow to take action when the offense is purely personal. But you touch our women or our children, that's another matter."

"But I didn't harm her," Calchas whimpered, writhing on the ground. "She took no harm from me."

"Maybe she did and maybe she didn't," said Tryffin. "There's no way of knowing if she's been hurt in some way that the scars don't show." He bent down, grabbed a handful of lank dark hair, and pulled Calchas up into a sitting position. "But I promise you this: If you ever come near her again, if you speak to her, or spread any lies about her—if you even look at her in a way that we don't care for—they're likely to find your ugly little head in one part of the castle and the rest of you scattered elsewhere. Do you understand?"

Calchas moaned a faint reply. Tryffin offered him a hand up. "You give us any trouble after this, and we'll eat your liver for breakfast, some fine morning."

Calchas ignored his offer of assistance. He scrambled to his feet, nursing the injured hand against his chest. But he gained a little confidence once he reached the comparative safety of the doorway. "You're a savage," he snarled weakly. "You're both savages."

Tryffin smiled, revealing an indecent number of perfect white teeth. "It's too late now to appease us with pretty compliments."

As soon as Calchas was gone, Tryffin and Garanwyn wordlessly scuffed out the pentacle and the other signs he had scratched on the earth, while Fflergant dismantled the doll. The straw and the knotted string he scattered on the ground, but the lock of hair, after a moment of thought, he wrapped in a piece of the sack and tucked into the front of his doublet.

"I think that you should tell us," Tryffin said, "everything that you know about this."

Garanwyn avoided his eyes. "I don't know what you mean."

"We think that you do," said Fflergant. "We think you should tell us why Calchas chose Gwenlliant to take part in this nasty little game of his."

"Spite and malice," Garanwyn mumbled. "You were right and I was wrong. These old feuds just won't die."

"It's no use," said Tryffin. "We already know. Do you think we could know your sister and you for as long as we have, and not know the truth?

"I mind the first time that I saw her," Tryffin went on, in his soft southern lilt. "At my grandfather's in Rhianedd, it was, and she visiting from Cadir Cynfarch—where they enjoy no such wards and protections as we do here at Caer Cadwy. A little bit of a thing, she was, and loaded down with all the trinkets and charms and bells her nurse had sewn onto her gown to keep the Good Folk from snatching her, or—"

"Our old nurse was a superstitious peasant woman," Garanwyn interrupted him. "She believed all kinds of nonsensical notions: that your father is the King of the Fairies, and that the Sidhe covet fair-haired children. And if you think that Calchas was telling the truth, why did you—"

"For the part that was a lie. Because the tiny bit of truth in his accusation made that lie more dangerous," said Tryffin. "You should know that we would never let any harm come to Gwenlliant. Isn't she kin to us, and as dear as either of our own sisters? And won't you just think—if she is in danger, if you have reason to believe that she is susceptible to . . . certain influences, then shouldn't we know about it, too, the better to protect her?"

"Well," said Garanwyn. "Maybe there is some truth in what you say. Oh, very well. I do have reason to believe that she is . . . susceptible, as you say. But she isn't a witch!"

"Certainly not."

"And she's not been possessed!"

"No," Fflergant said soothingly. "Your sister has obviously not been possessed. I never heard yet that possession by devils rendered little girls sweet and docile."

"And what we saw here—it's not something that Gwenlliant would think to do on her own."

"That is obvious as well," said Tryffin. "Someone here betrays more knowledge of magic than it's decent for anyone but a wizard to know. Certainly more than a child like Gwenlliant might pick up on her own. Then, too, considering the intended victim—"

"The victim?" Garanwyn said blankly.

For answer, Fflergant drew the lock of hair out of its place of concealment.

"Sweet Jesus and all the Saints!" breathed Garanwyn. He had not even looked at the doll before.

"Yes," said Fflergant. "I do believe we all know where we have seen hair this incredible shade before."

"But his own mother! That's—that's absolutely vile!"

"We all know that he is afraid of her," said Tryffin, leaning up against the flimsy wall, which creaked alarmingly under his weight. "Though now that I come to think of it, it seems strange that he should be. Oh, I'll admit that she is a formidable woman, and a lad owes respect to his own mother—but he's not a child, and if he doesn't care for her company, he needn't endure it. For all that Diaspad ni Erim styles herself Princess of Celydonn and Cynwas permits it, who is she really? The bastard or the step-daughter of the late King—depending on whose story you happen to believe— Corfil of Mochdreff's widow . . . but Calchas, filthy little beast that he is, is Lord of Mochdreff in his own right."

"But his mother governs in Mochdreff until he—no, she does not," Garanwyn corrected himself. "He can't be less than fifteen."

"The Mochdreffi come of age at twelve," said Tryffin. "Calchas has been Lord of Mochdreff in fact as well as name for at least three years, yet he scarcely behaves as though he were his own man."

"Are you suggesting that the Princess wields some *unnatural* influence over Calchas?" asked Fflergant.

"I don't know," said Tryffin. "But I will say this: There is something going on there that bears looking into."

"Damn it," said Tryffin, when the three boys were back in the other stable, unsaddling Garanwyn's horse. "It fits and it doesn't fit. It all falls together so neatly—and makes no sense at all."

"What?" said Garanwyn. "What makes no sense?"

"Everything. The arrival of the Princess, followed by the attack on Manogan, then the way that the mummers and the wolves all disappeared right after Christmas. It's been a strange winter altogether, and I'm not thinking of the weather. But what does it all mean?''

He frowned as another, more disturbing thought came to him. ''There's been another disappearance, too. Just think of this: If plots are afoot and witchcraft is a part of them, it might suit someone—I don't say the Princess Diaspad, but someone—it might suit their purposes very well, to be rid of the one person who sees too much and hears too much, is always there when you don't want him, and is so blindly devoted to Cynwas and Sidonwy that he could never be bought, or intimidated, or otherwise persuaded to ignore or forget anything he might see or hear.''

''Oh no!'' Garanwyn felt his heart sink as the meaning of Tryffin's words struck him full force. ''You are absolutely right. Oh, it is like Ceilyn, right enough, to keep after the beastly wolf long after any sensible man would have abandoned the chase. But it is *not* like him to play truant, or to neglect to send word to the Queen if anything delayed him. Why did we never think of that before?

''But where on Celydonn *is* Ceilyn? And what do you suppose your 'someone' has done to him?''

Ceilyn gazed at the wolf, and the wolf, an enormous silver-grey male, gazed calmly back at him. Ceilyn knew that the others were somewhere near; he could sense them all around him, pale shadows against the hard, glittering snow: The pack of southern wolves which had followed him for days. He no longer paid them any heed; hungry as they were, the wolves had not yet threatened to attack him. And it was clear, by now, that his business was with the old wolf, the great shaggy northern wolf who led the pack.

Tegillus snorted and side-stepped nervously. Only by remaining absolutely calm himself had Ceilyn been able to keep the big gelding under control. He fought down his own rising panic, patted a shivering chestnut flank, spoke as soothingly as he could.

The big wolf sat in the middle of the road. Whichever way Ceilyn turned, wherever he went, the old wolf was always there before him. Not threatening, not even barring his way—only waiting. Once, Ceilyn had pulled out his sword and brandished it, hoping to frighten the wolf away. But the beast only sat there, calmly watching him with those uncanny hazel-green eyes, while the little wolves circled at a distance, snuffling and whining, maddened by the scent of the man and the horse—they would have been on him in a minute, Ceilyn knew, were it not for the restraining influence of their leader.

For the first time in seven days, Ceilyn spoke to the wolf. "You have no right," he said. "You have no claim on me. Whoever or whatever you are. Not that I don't recognize you—I remember you well enough, though you wore another face the last time we met. But then, you probably expected that, too.

"You know everything I intend to do, even before I know it myself. Maybe you've planned everything out in advance. Perhaps you think that you've left me no choices at all."

A wind was rising, with an edge like a blade on it. The southern wolves drew near. Ceilyn refused to look at them, tried to ignore the insistent pressure of their hunger, his own hunger, and the *remembered taste of blood. And the big wolf continued to stare, unblinking, absolutely certain that he must have his own way at last.*

"But there is always one more choice," said Ceilyn, resting one hand on the hilt of his sword. "Always one last choice."

6.

Elderflower Wine

Gofan mac Gofynnion awoke in total darkness, only minutes, it seemed, since he had first closed his eyes. Someone sat on the edge of his bed, shaking him by the shoulder.

"What time is it?" Gofan asked drowsily.

"Not late. An hour or two until Matins." Kilraen's voice came out of the darkness. "But Ceilyn mac Cuel's just come home, looking like ten thousand years in Purgatory."

Gofan sat bolt upright, threw off his covers, and reached blindly for his shirt and hose. "Ceilyn? But where in—?"

"He didn't say, and no one had the courage to ask. You ask him, if you really want to know. Don't bother going down to the stable. He met Garanwyn downstairs and put him in charge of Tegillus. The poor beast looks nearly as bad as Ceilyn does."

Gofan dressed quickly in the dark. Upstairs in Ceilyn's bedchamber it was dark, too; the hearth was cold and the windows were shuttered and bolted against the wind and snow. Gofan listened, but detected no movement in the room.

"Ceilyn?" he whispered.

"I'm here."

Gofan fumbled in his pocket, drew out a stub of a candle. By the fireplace, he found flint and steel. He lit the candle and turned, shielding the flame against the draft from the door.

Ceilyn sat near the foot of his bed, struggling out of his riding boots. If he had looked grim and worn when he left the castle, nearly a fortnight ago, he was positively haggard now. Gofan knelt to assist him.

While Ceilyn undressed, Gofan found a towel and a basin of water and placed them on top of a clothes chest at the foot of the bed. He had learned, during twelve months of service as Ceilyn's squire-of-the-body, not to ask questions or expect explanations, but curiosity finally overcame discretion. "Where *were* you all this time?"

Ceilyn gazed blankly into the basin of water, did not answer immediately. "I believe that I went as far north as Loch Argadh."

"In search of the wolf?" Such foolhardy dedication seemed beyond even Ceilyn. "You were gone eleven days."

"Was it only eleven days?" Ceilyn looked up, frowning. "This is Epiphany? Isn't there an old story . . . between Christmas and Twelfth Night . . ."

He dipped his hands into the bowl, splashed icy water on his face and neck. The shock seemed to revive him. "The Queen—is she well?"

"Quite well. Though worried about you, of course. We all wondered—"

"You must send word that I'm here, and present my apologies," said Ceilyn, as he toweled himself off. His teeth chattered; Gofan had never seen him react to the cold so violently, had never (now that he came to think of it) seen Ceilyn display any weakness or vulnerability before. *He's been pushed to the very limits of endurance,* the boy thought.

Gofan removed the basin, opened the chest, and took out a change of linen. "News travels swiftly. She ought certainly to know by now."

Ceilyn stiffened, managed a facsimile of his old disapproving glare. "A matter of courtesy, Gofan."

"Yes, sir," the boy murmured, greatly relieved to hear Ceilyn sound so much like himself. "Will that be all?"

"Lay out a complete change of clothes before you go," Ceilyn replied, slipping into his shirt.

"You're going out?" Gofan could scarcely believe his ears.

"If that meets with your approval," said Ceilyn, in *exactly* his old manner.

Grateful, this once, for the warmth of his blue wool tunic and the fur-lined cyclas he belted over it, Ceilyn snuffed out the candle and softly closed the door behind him.

A luminous white mist had crawled in from the sea, then coiled itself, serpentlike, three times around the Wizard's Tower. Ceilyn knocked at Teleri's door. Receiving no answer, he tried the one next to it. That door was unlocked, so he pushed it open and stepped inside.

He stood in a narrow passageway, at the foot of a stone staircase. A torch on one wall illuminated the first few steps but the rest disappeared in darkness. His heart pounded and the blood sang in his ears as he climbed the winding stairs. The door at the top stood partly open, and a warm glow of candlelight spilled out onto the landing.

Teleri, in a long white nightdress and a faded tartan shawl, sat curled up in the wooden armchair, reading a book. Ceilyn hovered on the edge of her vision; after a long time he took a familiar shape in her mind. "Come in," she said.

Ceilyn hesitated on the threshold. He folded his arms, propped himself against the doorframe. "I have to ask. Did you send the wolves to bring me back?"

"I? The wolves? What power have I over the wolves?" she said.

He glared at her. "They never deserted me until this morning, when it was obvious I was coming back here."

Teleri closed her book. "I haven't the least idea what you are talking about."

She studied his face, shocked, as Gofan had been, to see such a change in him. So white and worn he was that she might never have recognized him, were it not for those strange, turbulent eyes, and his tight, defensive posture, even in exhaustion. "When did you last sleep?"

"Three or four days ago."

"And eat?"

"Yesterday, I think. Maybe the day before. I had to hunt. I didn't dare to stop at any of the farms along the way, for fear—I didn't know what I might do. Or become. No, don't bother," he said, as she started to leave her chair. "I'm well enough. But I need to talk to you."

Teleri sat back down. "You had better begin by telling me about the wolves."

Ceilyn uncrossed his arms, took a few wobbly steps, and sat on the floor at her feet. "I left Caer Cadwy with no clear idea where I was going," he began, in a weary monotone. "I don't remember when or how I thought of Coill Dorcha, but it seemed the perfect place to go. If I was spotted in that area, if word came back here . . . well, I wouldn't be the first man to disappear in those woods.

"All the way to Coill Dorcha, I was aware of the wolves. I could hear them, scent them, but mostly they kept out of sight. All but one of them: a big fellow about the size of a foal. His eyes—I told you there was a man disguised as a wolf at the Christmas revels?—this wolf had eyes like that man.

"All the time that I was heading north, the wolves followed me, but they never gave me any trouble. Until I came to the forest, and the big wolf was there waiting for me."

Teleri leaned forward in her chair. "Forbidding you to enter the forest?"

"It was more like—like he had summoned me there, like he was *expecting* something. I can't explain why I felt that way, but I—I reined up, backtracked a mile or two, and headed east for half a day. Then I turned north and tried to enter Coill Dorcha again. But the big wolf was waiting there, too, just within the margin of the forest, and the little wolves appeared in a circle around me. Tegillus and I broke through their circle and headed south and east again, hoping to enter Coill Dorcha the next day by another path. But it all happened exactly the same as before.

"This went on for days. I don't know how many. I rode north, I rode south, east, and west—the damnable wolf was always there between me and the forest. Finally, I decided to abandon that plan, and head for the Coblynau Hills instead."

Teleri frowned. "And the wolves followed you?"

Ceilyn nodded wearily. "For almost a day I thought we had shaken them. You know the region between Loch Argadh and Coill Dorcha? There is a road leading up to the foothills and the old copper mines. Tegillus and I followed that road for the better part of a day, and I'll swear there wasn't another living thing within miles—until we came to the foothills, and there he was again, sitting in the middle of the road, and the little wolves all around. It completely unnerved me. That creature wanted me—I was sure of that—but I wasn't about to do what he expected. I thought—the choice seemed clear: I could do what he wanted me to do, or I could die. So I decided to come back here, make my confession, and take my punishment.

"I know what you are about to say," he added, as Teleri opened her mouth to protest. "If I wanted to die, I might have chosen a better way, and spared my family the disgrace. The truth is . . . I wanted to meet my fate here, at home. I guess I was just tired of running. But on the way back, I started thinking. I remembered what you said to me—about giving things their proper names. I didn't understand it then, and I don't now, but you implied that I might gain some measure of control over this—this thing inside me, if I learned more about it. And remembering all that, I began to want to live again.

"Only I don't know where or how to begin to—to learn," he said. "Unless you will help me."

She put the book aside and slipped out of her chair. "I think I might be able to help you, a little. I have no easy answers for you now, but Glastyn's books may aid me."

Ceilyn stood, too. "You'll search them tonight—right now?" He moved in her direction, stumbled, and might have fallen had Teleri not put out a hand to steady him. It was only a brief, casual touch, but Ceilyn turned scarlet, and Teleri, suddenly acutely conscious that she was in her nightdress and that her feet were bare, drew back as if stung.

"I beg your pardon," said Ceilyn. "I didn't . . ."

"No, of course not," Teleri agreed breathlessly, because the very idea was absurd. Yet she could not bring herself to meet his eyes.

"You are tired and ought to rest," she said, rearranging the dusty purple cushions. "I will begin the search tonight, but you must promise to try and sleep."

Ceilyn collapsed among the pillows, protesting faintly. "I don't dare to sleep. There is no telling what I might be when I wake up again."

"I promise you, you can do no harm nor come to any in this room," she said, and stole a sidelong glance at his face. She saw nothing there now but pain, fear, and exhaustion. "There are potent protections here, and I know how to use them. Were that not so, I would never ask you to stay."

Ceilyn settled more comfortably in the chair. "You will tell me just as soon as you find anything—anything revealing?"

"I will tell you," she said. Already, his eyes had closed, his breathing slowed.

By the time she had crossed the room, selected another thick volume from the bookcase, and sat down on a bench by the fireplace, Ceilyn was fast asleep.

Total exhaustion, both physical and mental, makes an effective sleeping draught; Ceilyn did not wake until an hour after the bell tolled for morning prayers. He woke to a creaking of hinges as the laboratory door swung open.

Teleri appeared on the threshold, in the old grey kirtle and cloak. She carried a covered dish. Leaving the door slightly ajar, she crossed the floor on silent feet, evidently taking pains not to disturb him.

"What time is it?" he asked, yawning and stretching. "I ought to go to the Queen. I owe her an explanation."

"I sent word that you were ill this morning," she said, setting the dish down on the nearest table. "And I brought you some breakfast. I hope you don't mind."

She crossed to the vaulted fireplace, pulled the bench a little closer, then knelt on the hearth to rebuild her fire. Ceilyn leapt to his feet, ashamed to allow her to wait on him.

"Let me," he offered. "No, of course I don't mind. It was kind of you to bother."

She stood up, allowing him to arrange the logs and kindling in the great sooty maw of the fireplace. "No bother. I generally go down to the kitchen at odd hours to fetch my own meals." She carried the dish over to the bench and lifted the white napkin. A pungent whiff of goat cheese escaped, reminding Ceilyn that he was ravenously hungry.

When the fire was burning briskly, Ceilyn pulled out his bone-handled knife, sliced some bread and cheese, skewered them on the point of his dirk, and held them over the flames to toast. Out of a cabinet, Teleri produced a pot of honey, a full-bellied green glass bottle, and two clay cups. She poured a pale golden liquid into one cup and handed it to Ceilyn.

He sniffed it curiously, took a sip. "Elderflower wine, isn't it?

My mother always brought me some when I wasn't feeling well. Medicine, she said, but I think it was meant for a treat."

"Yes," said Teleri, as she sat down on the bench. "Though it does have some slight medicinal properties."

Ceilyn kept his seat on the hearth. He sensed a remoteness in Teleri's manner, that had not been there last night. Not as though she were angry or offended, but simply as if she had retreated to some distant place where he could not follow. To cover his own awkward sense of isolation, and because he had not taken much notice of his surroundings last night, he examined them now.

He did not like the looks of a grinning yellow skull nailed up over the door, or the glassy-eyed mummified crocodile hanging from the ceiling, or some of the apparatus cluttering the shelves. But the bundled herbs that hung from the rafters, the gleaming retorts and alembics, the furnace, the phials and flasks, all put him in mind of his mother's stillroom. He thought how pleasant it might have been, breakfasting together by the fire, if only he could make Teleri look his way.

The laboratory contained a vast number of books. Teleri had spread six or seven across the table; others were piled on the floor beside the chair or crammed into the shelves. A hundred? Maybe two hundred? In all his life, Ceilyn had never seen so many books. The monk who had taught him and his little brother, Celi, their letters had possessed maybe a dozen, his mother and his father between them perhaps half that number, and Ceilyn himself owned only one: a tiny illuminated prayer book, given to him one Christmas by Merewyn. It was almost incomprehensible to him that anyone should own, much less read, so many imposing volumes. Because his own experience with books had been so limited, he regarded them all with respect, even a little fear.

He swallowed a last bite of toasted bread and cheese, summoned up his courage. "Did you discover anything . . . significant last night?"

Teleri nodded. "I learned little that I didn't know before, but I found much to confirm those guesses I had already made."

"I would just as soon know the worst at once, if you don't mind."

She moved toward the table where she had left the open books, and Ceilyn followed after her. "There is nothing bad to tell you,

Ceilyn. All the same, it's not what you are expecting and perhaps you won't like it much." She drew one book closer, so that Ceilyn could read it, too.

An intricate diagram in faded brown and red ink covered most of the page: a lineage of the kings of Celydonn and their immediate descendents. Halfway down the page, he spotted one of his own ancestresses, the Princess Essylt.

The original genealogy ended abruptly several inches from the bottom of the page, with the name "Cynwal V," but someone had added two more names in a different hand and darker ink:

ANWAS II

CYNWAS

Ceilyn knew why those two names stood apart; the generations between Cynwal V and Anwas II were unknown. And because Anwas had no known brothers, uncles, or cousins, because Cynwas fab Anwas was childless, the succession remained undecided.

Though the great houses of Rhianedd, Gorwynnion, and Tir Gwyngelli all claimed Mother-Right through distant female ancestors, this meant only that the King might choose his successor, according to the ancient law, from literally dozens of claimants, according to his own whim. Because Cynwas had married his maternal cousin, Sidonwy ni Duach, and because of certain agreements between Anwas and old Drwst of Rhianedd, most people believed that Cynwas would favor the Rhianeddi claim and eventually name Sidonwy's eldest brother as his heir. But Cadifor fab Duach fab Drwst's position was far from secure.

Further complicating matters was the questionable status of Diaspad ni Erim—or Diaspad ni Anwas, as she chose to style herself—and the vexed question of her paternity and legitimacy. Anwas had never acknowledged her, not even after he married her mother, but Cynwas had called her "sister" ever since he first ascended the throne, and he allowed her precedence accordingly.

Teleri turned over several pages. When she found the page she wanted, she put a finger on one name near the bottom: Ceilyn Conyn Isfan.

"Ceilyn mac Cuel mac Cadellin mac Cei mac Cynan mac Cadir mac Tam mac Coll.'' She recited the generations softly, indicating each one with a slender finger. "You can see that your family tree intersects with Cynwas's at several points, and that you are descended from kings of Celydonn through all four grandparents and six of your great-grandparents—as well as kings and ruling princes of Rhianedd, Tir Gwyngelli, Draighen, and Gorwynnion.''

Ceilyn frowned, unimpressed by these glorious antecedents. "I knew all that already."

"Yes," said Teleri, with a sigh. "But don't you see? They were wonderworkers, some of those old kings. I don't have to tell you that—you spoke of knights and heroes before you left."

"But the knights in the old tales were granted special abilities by virtue of their valor and purity,'' said Ceilyn. "It was a sign of divine grace."

"But what of those heroes in the ancient tales, those kings and princes who worked their wonders in another age—a pagan age?"

"They were—they were good men, too, I suppose,'' Ceilyn replied. "Innocent, because they had not yet been given the opportunity to espouse the True Faith.''

"And the gifts they possessed were similarly innocent—were they not?"

"But the old gifts disappeared long ago," Ceilyn insisted. "I'm not the only man in Celydonn, not even the only one at Caer Cadwy, who can claim Blood Royal on both sides of the family. I could name you several others: Fflergant fab Maelgwyn and his brother, Tryffin; their uncle, Manogan fab Menai; my cousins Garanwyn and Gwenlliant; the King and Queen, of course. But they're all quite ordinary."

"Are *you* quite ordinary?"

Ceilyn sighed and shook his head. "My own peculiarity is not one of those lost gifts. The kings of Celydonn were never shapechangers.''

"Your ancestors had many extraordinary abilities—no one knows their full extent," said Teleri. "In the old days, when men divided this island into many kingdoms and principalities, all the kings and princes, even some of the lesser chieftains, were marked for greatness. A man had to prove himself extraordinary in some way, in order to rule. It is true that their gifts were not always magical. Some of them were poets, scholars, warriors; but many more were prophets, warlocks, and wizards. Cynfelyn the Emperor, Sceolan Flamingbeard, Cynfarch of the Ravens—not ordinary men, no indeed.

"I found nothing specific about the gifts of your people in Celcynnon, but those gifts must have been impressive. Only consider: Your clan is a small one, the lands you hold neither vast nor desirable, yet your forefathers married some of the highest born maidens in the realm. Why, do you suppose, did great kings and princes regard them as equals and give them their daughters?

"Also, there is this." She turned another page. The next one was beautifully illuminated, bordered with strange flowering vines and a whole menagerie of fantastic creatures capering among the foliage, all done in brilliant reds, greens, and blues, and embellished with gold leaf. "Here you will see the arms and badges of the greater and lesser lords of Ynys Celydonn, as well as other signs, symbols, and devices associated with each clan.

"You can see the dragon of Gwyngelli, the raven of Rhianedd, the brown bear of Walgan—you are familiar, of course, with the legends surrounding these devices. But look here: These are the ancient arms of Caer Celcynnon."

"*Vert, a wolf's head erased, Or,*" Ceilyn read. "And the crest, *a wreath of holly, proper.* Those were my grandfather's arms, but my father adopted the stag and the cross after they appeared to him in a vision.

"Yes, I see," he said. "You think that the wolf might have carried some significance, too, at some time in the past."

"In which case," Teleri said, "you may have *inherited* the powers of a shapechanger—and you aren't being punished for your sins at all."

"But surely all such powers manifesting themselves in the present age are works of the Devil," said Ceilyn, stubbornly clinging to the stern creed of his father and his grandfather. "It is different for you," he added quickly. "I understand that Wizardry is a science of the mind, requiring a strict discipline. That allows you to study and control magic without being corrupted by it. But those who traffic in the Wild Magic are no better than witches and warlocks."

This was a common prejudice, to equate the acquired discipline of the Wizard with White Magic, and the inherited powers of the natural magician with the Black Arts and heathen religions. Teleri knew better. Glastyn, for instance, had been as much White Warlock as Wizard, as much Herbalist, Seer, and Weatherworker as Alchemist, Astrologer, or Mage. Her own studies encompassed many arts and mysteries which the ignorant condemned without understanding.

She said nothing of this to Ceilyn. Despite his polite disclaimer, she knew that her age, inexperience, and sex rendered her claim to the title of Wizard suspect, and therefore left her open to accusation of the other. But if she could not tell him, still there was one way she might be able to help him to understand.

"Come with me," she said, reaching for her grey wool cloak, "and I will try to show you how wrong you are."

"The nature of iron is such," said the wizard Glastyn, *"that it congeals, conceals, and sublimates the spirit within the corporeal. Therefore, under the influence of Mars (or Iron) many things subtle, powerful, and remarkable cannot exist."*

7.

The Womb of the Earth

The gate was hidden behind a tangle of dark, snow-dappled branches; a brass lion holding an iron ring in his mouth served in place of a door knob. Teleri lifted the ring and pulled, and the gate grated open. Ceilyn peered curiously over her shoulder, to see what lay beyond.

Icicles hung like silver thorns on leafless rosebushes and around the rim of a wide brass sundial. There was a pond in a mossy stone basin, frozen as hard and as clear as glass, and an ugly little statue poised at the center under a cold mantling of snow. Two or three chilly brown hedgesparrows hopped around on the frozen ground. It was an unkempt little garden, blasted by winter, bleak but in no way threatening.

Teleri whispered her name and passed through the gateway. But Ceilyn, following immediately behind her, felt something snap shut in front of him, barring his way.

With the tips of his fingers, he explored the invisible gate within the archway—invisible, but as solid and unyielding as oak. He felt the timbers, the bolts holding them together, even the irregular grain of the wood. "I can't—there's something here; I can't get through."

Teleri sat down on her heels, dug a shallow hole in the snow. She touched the soil of the garden, whispered a Word, and the barrier melted away. "Try it now."

Ceilyn stepped into the garden, took a few steps more, then

stopped and stood still, utterly amazed.

The air was still but all the vines and branches quivered, as if in breathless expectation. He could hear sap singing in the leafless branches, feel life throbbing beneath his feet like some vast subterranean heartbeat, the blood in his veins—all pulsing to the same tellurian rhythm. He drew in his breath, and smiled, for sheer wonder.

Next to the pond stood a marble bench, perched on four feet like the forepaws of some huge predatory beast. Teleri sat down and patted the seat beside her, in invitation. Ceilyn crossed the garden, sat down beside her, and she smiled back at him in sudden sympathy.

Here in her own place she seemed different: warmer and sweeter, somehow. Among the frail, glittering icicles, she no longer appeared so pale and fragile herself. And here, where winter had robbed all else of color, some of her own returned to her. The cold brought a tinge of pink into her cheeks and her lips; her clear eyes reflected back some of the blue of the sky, and her long hair, hanging in a thick braid over one shoulder, turned to silver-gilt in the sunlight.

"This," said Ceilyn, glancing around him, "must be the greatest of all Glastyn's enchantments."

"And yet," said Teleri softly, "it is all a part of that very magic you have been taught to fear."

Ceilyn frowned, greatly puzzled. "That hardly seems possible."

"You know," said Teleri, "that Glastyn bound the Wild Magic. He could not unmake it—that would have been disastrous. Magic is as much a part of Ynys Celydonn as earth or stone; without it, the entire fabric might unravel, the island simply dissolve into nothingness. So he buried it deep and bound it lightly, so that men might know the benefits and not the dangers. And a little, a very tiny portion, he planted here, just below the surface. Within these walls, the Wild Magic runs exactly as it will.

"You demonstrated, once, that you recognized the stink of corruption. Do you detect it here?"

Ceilyn inhaled deeply. The air was full of old, dark, gritty scents: the odor of dead leaves, the breath of living soil—disintegration, yes, but with the promise of rebirth. Nothing here truly died. "No, but it might be—it could very well be—that I'm not infallible in that regard."

Teleri sighed. "Truly, if you won't believe the evidence of your own senses, I don't know what I could possibly say to convince you."

Ceilyn looked around him. The desire to believe what she told him, what everything he saw and felt here confirmed, was compelling. But his early upbringing, everything he had been taught all his life to believe, was strong, too. "Let us suppose that I believed you. That I agreed that the magic in this garden was innocent of good and evil alike, and that my own magic was similarly innocent. What would you tell me to do?"

Teleri hesitated. "I would say . . . go north again, in search of the wolves and, if they still wait for you, accept their invitation to join them. Living as a wolf, learning what that means, you might also learn the name you are seeking, the name that will give you mastery over both your natures."

Ceilyn scowled, not liking that advice at all.

"That is what I would tell you, if I thought that you would do it," said Teleri. "It is the best advice that I can give you. But it is not all."

Ceilyn brightened. "You mean . . . there might be another way?"

Teleri reached inside her cloak, brought something out from a hidden pocket: a slender bracelet wrought of some dark metal. "I didn't spend the entire night reading genealogies. I spent hours looking for this, because I had seen it among Glastyn's things before. I do not know its original purpose, but I know how it might be of use to you.

"In one book," she continued, "I came across a spell involving the use of iron, and I remembered something you told me before you left: that you felt somehow different the first time that you wore armor. Also, that your . . . gift or curse, whatever you choose to call it, had not manifested itself in the five years you have lived at Caer Cadwy. First as a squire and then as a knight—I suppose the occasions when you had no weapon or piece of harness, no iron or steel about you, were few and far between. But the night that you changed into a wolf you were unarmed, and perhaps more vulnerable than you knew."

She held the circle of iron a moment longer, turning over in her mind all that she knew of the powers of metals, their secret generation in the steamy womb of the earth, their descent in flames from the heavens, the age-old mysteries of the smith and the forge. "There are many things which cannot abide the touch of cold iron. For you, I believe, it inhibits the transformation from man to wolf."

This was a little better; the use of iron to combat baleful influences was universally accepted. Ceilyn took the bracelet. "And if I wear this—then I will never be without the touch of iron when I need it. But what are these signs I see engraved here?" he asked suspiciously.

"Signs of protection only," she assured him. "They will strengthen the power of the iron if need be. And see . . . when you put it on and close the clasp, it makes a perfect circle. There is power in that, too."

Already, Ceilyn thought that he could feel the benefit of the iron. His face lit with incredulous relief. "Can it really be so simple as that?"

"No," she said, "but this will serve for a time. But Ceilyn, you may keep the wolf from taking shape, but he will still be there inside you. Sooner or later, I think, he will demand that you put a name to him."

Ceilyn shrugged. "I will face that problem if and when I must. Surely, as long as the iron bracelet works, there will be no need."

The shadow on the sundial had shifted a long way since first they had entered the garden, and Ceilyn saw that it was nearly noon. He had spent the entire morning in idleness—and he still owed the Queen an explanation for his lengthy absence.

"You've been most kind," he said, standing up, growing suddenly formal.

She replied softly, "There's little enough I was able to do. In the end, I think, you must help yourself."

Then Siawn, son of Sarannon, rallied the King's Army. He knew that Cynwal the King was dead, crushed by Gandwy's dragon, but Siawn knew nothing of Sarannon's death, or that Sinnoch was dead as well. He was the only man living of all Cadwy's line.

(But Dechtire, the wife of Sinnoch, was at that time great with child, though it seemed doubtful, now, that she would live to bear her child. Nor was there any way of telling whether the babe would be a boy. But no infant could hold the kingdom together, or lead armies against the Warlock Lord—it was Siawn fab Sarannon who would have to be King.)

So Siawn took his army back to Caer Cadwy, which no army yet had taken by siege or by force; they called it the Fortress Impregnable. Siawn went back home to Caer Cadwy, and Gandwy and his army followed him.

And Gandwy had magical engines, and the walls of Caer Cadwy came tumbling down.

From The Great Book of St. Cybi

In the snowy ruins on Brynn Caer Cadwy's lower slopes, an ill-assorted party picked its way through the rubble: the Princess and her son, accompanied by the leopards, two of Diaspad's squat, ill-favored servants, and (lagging a bit behind) Pergrin the lame giant.

Calchas limped, too. Three of his fingers had been bound and splinted; a faded bruise along his jawline lent a touch of sickly color to his otherwise pallid features. Both Calchas and his mother had wrapped themselves up warmly in fur-lined cloaks, but the flimsy crimson livery worn by the servants afforded *them* scant protection against the biting cold. Nevertheless, it was Calchas who felt ill-used.

"If you want bones," he was complaining, "why don't you send Bron down to the graveyard some night?"

"Bones buried in consecrated ground never suit my purposes," replied his mother, lifting her heavy skirts to avoid catching them on the splintered rock and tangled growth. "And I want to be absolutely certain of getting exactly what I want."

Calchas snorted. "I can't see that the last charm you made for me did much good. Power over my enemies, you *said*, and look what happened."

"It was meant to bring confusion to your enemies—which is not quite the same thing," said the Princess. "And it won't do even that much, now that you've broken it."

In contrast to her hard, vivid features, her tone was soft and soothing. A thousand willful passions had left their mark on her face. Though witchcraft had enabled her to eradicate the ravages of time and depravity, and not a wrinkle or a blemish marred the smooth perfection of her skin, the scars burned there by her ferocious loves and hates went deeper and could not be erased. The face would always betray all the rage and bitterness of her past, but her low, sweet voice betrayed nothing.

"I don't quite understand, Dear Boy," continued Diaspad, "how you came to break the talisman. Scuffling with one of Manogan's nephews, was it?"

"Scuffling?" Calchas exclaimed indignantly. He neglected to watch where he was going and caught the edge of his cloak on a thorny branch. Impatiently, he pulled himself free, ripping the hem and shaking down a fine powdering of snow on the black velvet. "I was attacked! Oh, he pretended it was an accident—else I'd have complained to Uncle Cynwas—but I know better. That big ox isn't as clumsy as he likes to pretend. No, Tryffin fab Maelgwyn is not so stupid as he would have us believe—or so clever as he likes to think!"

"But why?" Diaspad wondered. "What reason had he to attack you?"

"Why?" said Calchas. "I wouldn't think you would have to ask why!"

"Still," said the Princess, "I find it hard to believe that big placid boy takes the ancient grudge so much to heart. And if you had insulted him personally . . . the Gwyngellach consider it demeaning to counter verbal abuse with physical violence. Though when they do become violent—are you certain there isn't something more involved here?''

''Well, he did say something, when he offered me a hand up,'' Calchas admitted cagily. ''Something about not liking the way that I looked at his cousin Gwenlliant. And *I* didn't like the way that he smiled when he said it.''

Diaspad frowned thoughtfully. ''I would be interested to know exactly what he meant by that.''

''How should I know?'' Calchas replied, aiming a kick at one of the dwarfs. But the dwarf, displaying a skill born of long practice, neatly evaded him. ''Between me and God, I ought to be able to look at a girl any way that I choose.

''As a matter of fact,'' he admitted, ''I did have some ideas—for later, naturally, when I am King and can have whoever I want. She's an appealing little thing. But her brother and her cousins have no way of knowing what I was thinking.''

''No, but the child might have sensed your intentions,'' said the Princess. ''I did tell you that Gwenlliant bears all the signs of a natural-born witch. You had best stay away from her—and her brother, too, if you can't make friends with him. They are tremendous favorites of the King and Queen, you know. You won't gain favor with my brother by quarreling with Garanwyn or molesting his little sister.

''Besides,'' she added, ''the girl has an ill-omened name.''

''She's trouble, that's certain,'' muttered Calchas. ''But it's Fflergant's and Tryffin's heads I'd really like, if you want to know!''

''I thought that I had explained to you, Darling, why I can't oblige you there,'' said Diaspad, nimbly skirting a pile of cracked and blackened stones. ''Not just yet. As princes of Tir Gwyngelli, they are, in some sense, bound to the land, and are therefore under the protection of the Lady. As long as I serve the Dark Mother, I dare not use the power I derive from that service against either of them.

''Later, when our plans here have prospered, I might strike a bargain elsewhere. But to do so now might cost me more than I am willing to pay.''

''I would think it worth the price, whatever that may be,'' protested Calchas. ''They stand as close to the throne as anyone, and they're bound to get in our way sooner or later.''

Diaspad shrugged. "That I very much doubt. As far as I can see, the Crown of Celydonn means next to nothing to Maelgwyn of Gwyngelli, or to his sons. Indeed, why should it? The way the Gwyngellach see these things, the King of Celydonn is a far lesser personage than the Lord of Tir Gwyngelli. Oh, Maelgwyn is willing to swear fealty and send his sons here for Cynwas to foster, but only as a gesture of friendship and good-will—otherwise meaningless. The Gwyngellach, as you know, delight in social fictions. If Cynwas likes to pretend that Maelgwyn is his vassal instead of his ally, then Maelgwyn—and his brother, and his sons—are all quite willing to indulge him. Anything to keep the poor fool happy, that's the way they see it. But Maelgwyn *rules* in Tir Gwyngelli, and Cynwas would never dream of interfering. And to be Lord of Tir Gwyngelli is the only title, of the only place, and the only people—as the Gwyngellach see it—that holds any real significance in the natural order of things."

"You seem to know a good deal about them," said Calchas, sounding bored. "Maelgwyn, and his brother, and his sons."

"I knew the Marshall rather well at one time," replied the Princess. "I knew Manogan fab Menai . . . very well indeed."

They came to the chosen place: the ruins of an ancient tower where, according to legend, the last defenders of the old fortress had met a bloody end. Here, buried in unhallowed ground, Diaspad hoped to find the mortal remains of those men.

She brushed the rime off a low stone wall and sat down, fastidiously arranging her dark cloak so that none of the folds lay in the damp snow. One of the tawny leopards climbed up beside her and stretched out in the cold winter sunlight. At Diaspad's signal, the dwarfs retrieved a pair of spades they had concealed in the vicinity the night before, and began digging through the rubble. The giant, an excellent sentry because of his height, stationed himself so that he had a clear view in every direction.

For his part, Calchas continued to sulk. He stood a little apart from the others, brooding on his manifold wrongs.

"My darling," said the Princess, all sweet conciliation, "you must know the price of the life of a prince of the blood."

"Another prince, I suppose," said Calchas, affecting disinterest.

''Yes, Darling, another prince. And if I were to bargain now, offering only what I could promise with complete certainty to be able to deliver up—who would that have to be?''

''Oh,'' said Calchas, sorry that he had brought up the subject. ''Yes, I see.'' For all his mother's lavish assurances that everything she did was for his sake and his sake alone, he did not believe a word of it. He was her puppet prince and knew it, the only means by which she, a woman, might further her ambitions.

And yet she *did* love him—the child of her bitterly unhappy youth, alternately abused and smothered with affection—he knew that, too, and somehow, that frightened him as much as the other.

''I knew that you would understand, my bright boy,'' said Diaspad. ''Later on, I promise you, we shall attend to your young friends. I have my own reckoning to settle, when the time is right.''

By now, the two dwarfs were hard at work. Over the past one hundred and fifty years enough earth had sifted in between the tumbled stones to cement them together almost as firmly as if they had been mortared. The two small men, their hands already numb and clumsy in the frigid air, found it no easy task to dig and pry the stones out.

''We shall have enough to do, now that we are settled in,'' said the Princess. ''Did you know, by the way, that someone else has been practicing magic under my brother's roof? Something rather petty and dirty, by the feel of it.''

Calchas felt his heart skip a beat. ''Gwenlliant?'' he suggested, determined to brazen it out until he knew exactly how much his mother knew or guessed. ''What about Glastyn's apprentice—the girl no one ever sees? I forget her name.''

Diaspad laughed. ''The little grey mouse? I doubt that she has the courage to stray down any forbidden pathways, that one. Besides, no pupil of Glastyn's would ever allow an open pentacle to bleed all her spells of their power. Whoever this is, his or her spells are all going awry. I only wish I knew who it might be.''

''Whatever for?'' Calchas asked weakly. ''Surely he . . . she presents no threat to us?''

''A threat? Certainly not!'' The Princess's laugh, like her voice, was very low, but a suggestion of a growl made her laughter far from pleasing. "But quite possibly a tool we might be able to use. Think of it: some poor soul who wants something badly enough to risk everything for it, someone who has a dangerous secret. Such a person might be vulnerable to persuasion, don't you think?"

Calchas's heartbeat steadied. She did not seem to suspect him as yet. He resolved to be more careful in the future. "But how will you ever find out who it is?" he asked, as casually as he could.

"Not difficult," replied his mother. "We already know two signs by which we may know this person: an unfulfilled desire and a guilty conscience. Envy and fear usually leave their mark."

Bron and the other dwarf had already tossed out a few splintered beams and some sharp pieces of broken crockery, also a skull and some long bones which they had piled at Diaspad's feet. Now Bron shook the last few particles of dirt from a tiny yellow fingerbone. Diaspad held out an eager hand. "Let me see that."

As the Princess took the fragment of bone, a shiver of pleasure passed over her. "Do you feel it?" Though her voice remained soft and pleasing, her avid face was terrible.

"I don't feel anything." Calchas bent over and scooped up the skull, turned it over and examined it curiously. Most of the back of the head was fractured or missing; what remained was a shade or two darker around the edges. Calchas grimaced and let the skull fall to the ground.

"This man died hard," said the Princess. "Resisting to the end, angry and blasphemous in his last moments. This will do very well." She nodded to the servants. "Try to put the stones back so that everything looks undisturbed.

"I think," she added briskly, "that the time has come, now that we are comfortably established here, to put our plans for my old playfellow and her two brothers into effect."

"Cadifor and Llochafor?" Calchas asked. "What need to interfere with either of them? From all one hears, they seem bent on engineering their own ruin, and don't need help from you or me. There they are: holding court in the north, living like kings, when they ought to be living as quietly and blamelessly as possible, at least until they are restored to favor."

"They rely on the good-will of their sister and the diplomacy of their uncle to smooth things over," said Diaspad, absently stroking the speckled head of the leopard at her side. "Failing that, they rely on Cynwas to experience another change of heart. A curious mixture of sentiment and irrational fears, my brother Cynwas. How many times in the past—times when Cadifor was politicking openly, times when he was meddling in matters he had much better have left alone—did the King's friends warn him that Cadifor was not to be trusted? And yet he would not hear a word against him, the friend of his youth, blood of his blood, brother of his thrice-beloved Queen. And *then,* at a time when Cadifor was actually behaving himself, attending solely to his own affairs, Cynwas takes it into his head to banish not only Cadifor but Llochafor as well, and no one knows precisely why.

"And then there is Sidonwy: dear, sweet, painfully honest Sidonwy" (here, there was a note of tender regret in Diaspad's voice, though whether it was real or feigned Calchas could not tell), "and her habit of saying exactly what she thinks and acting on the spur of the moment. In fact, she is so totally without guile that we ought to have no trouble convincing my brother that she's been lying and cheating him for years.

"And without Sidonwy to plead in his favor," Diaspad concluded, "Cadifor fab Duach hasn't a chance in Hell of being named as Cynwas's heir!"

"But what is the use of provoking another misunderstanding between the King and Queen?" asked Calchas. "It won't last. They've quarreled at least a dozen times since we came here, and always made it up again in the most maudlin way imaginable."

"They always make it up again," said the Princess, "because that old fox Dyffryn fab Drwst is on hand to play peacemaker. If Lord Dyffryn were not here to interfere, I feel certain that a more permanent misunderstanding could easily be arranged."

Calchas brightened. "Then you will have to arrange something nasty for dear old 'Uncle Dyffryn,' won't you?"

Diaspad smiled. "He is the grandfather of your two young friends, Fflergant and Tryffin, isn't he? And any unpleasantness we can arrange for him must touch them as well, one way or another.

"So you see, my precious one," she added, fondly stroking his hand, "Mother is going to provide you with a little amusement after all."

"Thank you, Mother," said her grateful son.

"I worry," said the old nursemaid, "about the Crown Prince's health. He eats so very little, and most of that sweets, that I fear he will make himself ill. Now, if I had a nice bit of red meat to tempt him with . . ."

"Red meat?" said Morfudd the Queen. "Red meat? Pray tell me what that has to do with anything. You tell me that my step-son is overfond of sugarplums."

"As to that," said the old woman, "he likes his red meat and his greens—when he can get them. But there's little of either to be had on Aderyn in the winter time, and most of that finds its way to the High Table. In the Nursery, it's salt herring three times a day, all winter long, and the poor little fellow doesn't care for that—not a bit!"

"Bring me my step-son," said the Queen, "and we will settle this, once and for all."

"They tell me," said Morfudd, when Cynwas stood before her, "that you are a spoiled brat and will not eat the food that is given you. We will have no more of that! You will eat the good salt herring, or you will eat nothing at all."

"Lady, Lady," protested the old nurse, "the Crown Prince is such a delicate little lad. If he will not eat, he will make himself ill. When I think of his poor moth—"

"Indeed," said Morfudd, who still hoped to produce a son of her own—a son who could never rule in Celydonn while Cynwas lived. "That would be a great pity. But the matter lies entirely with the Crown Prince. He may eat or he may starve, just as he chooses. Now take the boy away. I think he understands me."

"Oh yes," said Cynwas to his nurse, a short while later. "I understand my step-mother, never doubt it. It would amuse her to see me eat what I do not like—but it would please her better to see me starve.

"So put what you will before me, and I will eat it all. But when I am King of Celydonn . . . we'll see who eats salt herring!"

8.

A Bowl of Goldfish

Everyone walked warily on fish days. As a consequence of his early years spent on Ynys Aderyn and the steady diet of herring that had rendered his childhood hideous, the King had never acquired a taste for fish, no matter how imaginatively it was prepared. Indeed, many of his friends firmly believed that Cynwas had moved his court to the larger island simply to insure a steady supply of fresh meat. When (as on Fridays, and during Lent) red meat was forbidden, the King generally felt deprived, if not absolutely ill-used, and dinner at the High Table became a risky proposition. While a royal display of temper was not absolutely guaranteed, it took precious little to bring one on. It had been on a Friday, for instance, that a relatively innocent remark made by Cadifor fab Duach had so offended the King that Cynwas banished both of the Queen's brothers on the spot.

So it came about, one Friday in early January, that Cynwas's young attendants (their punishment recently lifted, though the cup had never been found) exerted themselves as they had never done before. Nevertheless, as course after course arrived, to be almost immediately removed, as the King rejected one elaborate dish after another, it became increasingly clear that an explosion of some sort was imminent.

Cynwas turned away, untasted, an elegant Pike Galentyne; he barely touched the Musclade of Minnows; he toyed with a dish of oysters stewed in ale, irritably rejected the Perch-in-Aspic, and indignantly declined the baked herring—in short, found nothing to please him but a dish of winter roots and chestnuts, which hardly sufficed to satisfy him. By the time that his pages presented the frogs and carp, the King had lost all interest in the meal, and he sat back in his chair, bored, out of sorts, and still hungry.

While one squire whisked away the golden plates, another youth hastened forward to offer the King a bowl of warm wash water. Something—perhaps a flash of color reflected in the silver basin—reminded Cynwas of a question he had been meaning to ask Lord Dyffryn.

"Well, Uncle," he said, laving his fingers in the rose-scented water, "I must confess that I am eager to inspect that fabulous new acquisition of yours. When are we to see it?"

Dyffryn looked up from his dish of saffroned eels. "I beg your pardon, Lord?"

The King dried his hands on the spotless white linen that a third squire presented to him. "The sidhe-stone from Gwyngelli. I have been told that it rivals even the Clach Ghealach and the legendary Clach Grian."

"As to size and clarity, perhaps," Dyffryn allowed modestly. "But otherwise it is quite an ordinary stone, possessing no warding properties as far as we know. But if you have a fancy to see it . . . of course I will send for it at once."

During all this, Diaspad sat dallying with her own dinner—a crystal bowl full of tiny golden carp. She pretended to take no interest in the conversation, though a tenuous plan was already taking shape in her mind.

The gem arrived at the same time as the cheese and sweet wafers that made up the last course. The jewel rested in an ornate silver casket. Dyffryn unlocked the box and took out the gem: a pale, iridescent blue sidhe-stone, about the size of a child's fist and practically flawless.

"Magnificent," breathed Cynwas.

"Perhaps you would like to examine it more closely?" said Dyffryn.

Cynwas inspected the stone enviously, and fell victim to one of his sudden, irrational infatuations. "A gem like this would look well in the Regalia."

Diaspad looked up from her dish for the first time. "May I see it?"

Cynwas placed the gemstone back in the box and passed it down the table. Diaspad lifted the lid and peered inside. "A truly wonderful stone," she drawled, fingering the gem. "Fit for a king indeed. But then . . . I had heard you keep great state, back home in Rhianedd."

"Unkind," said the Queen softly. "You do my uncle an injustice. He is a modest man and lives simply, as all who know him can attest."

''Indeed,'' said Diaspad sweetly. ''Would that the same could be said of *all* your kin.''

Sidonwy stiffened, but Dyffryn passed the remark off with apparent good humor. ''I fear it is something of a family failing, the love of finery, a delight in spectacle. But in this instance, I purchased the sidhe-stone as a gift for my wife. I hope that the extravagance of a fond husband—and one so newly wed—may easily be excused.''

''Certainly the extravagance may be easily understood, when the Lady herself is so worthy of the gift,'' said the King warmly. But he continued to eye the shimmering jewel with longing. ''Such a stone comes along only once in a lifetime. Yet what use would Fiona have for such a toy? Name a price, Uncle, and I will pay it. Then between us we shall find a more suitable gift to delight your Lady.''

Dyffryn considered this offer carefully. No one knew better than he the signs of a burgeoning obsession, how difficult Cynwas could be when denied, how extravagantly grateful when satisfied.

''As to that, Cousin,'' said Dyffryn silkily, ''I don't believe there should be any talk of buying and selling among kinsmen. But if it would please you—''

''What a charming idea,'' the Princess broke in. ''Truly inspired! A friendly wager—yes, that would be best. And my brother must offer a stake of equal value. You are quite right, Lord Dyffryn. So much more civilized than *buying and selling*, as though we were all tradesmen.''

Dyffryn stared at her, greatly abashed by this unexpected suggestion. He had intended something very different: a gift to the King, an excess of royal gratitude, a few well-chosen words on behalf of Dyffryn's other, exiled, nephews—perhaps even, eventually, a reconciliation.

But Cynwas swiftly took up Diaspad's suggestion, plainly delighted by it. ''An excellent diversion, to be sure! But what shall the contest be?''

Dyffryn thought quickly. Well, why not a wager after all? A hard-fought game, a royal victory (Dyffryn would see to that), and the King excited and elated by his success . . . yes, that might serve even better than the other.

''A game of chess?'' he suggested, then recognized his mistake as the King's face darkened. Cynwas loved the game but he played impulsively and generally lost. "Of course, if you are weary of chess—as I must confess I am myself—why, then, we might hazard the gem on a game of 'Tables' instead."

The King's face, always a faithful mirror of his emotions, cleared instantly. "That is an excellent idea, Uncle."

"Oh yes," purred the Princess Diaspad. She closed the casket and passed the box back to Dyffryn. "I have always considered 'Tables' an admirable game."

"Derry," said Diaspad, as she drew her young kinsman aside, directly after dinner. "You have professed yourself eager to be of service, and now there is a little something you can do for me." She whispered a few words in his ear, adding out loud: "Run up to your room and fetch them for me—there's a good boy."

Derry grinned and reached into his purse. "No need for that," he said smugly. "I have what you need right here. I had planned a little game later this evening, but since you need them . . ."

"What a charming boy you are, to be sure. So resourceful!" she said, patting his coppery curls approvingly. "Do you know?—if all goes well this evening, I might find other little tasks for you to do. Yes, I really might!"

"You have only to ask," said Derry. "I'd do almost anything."

"Yes," said the Princess, "I rather thought that you would."

"We have not yet determined," said the King to his uncle, as the two men, their attendants, and two pages bearing torches climbed a twisting stair in the Mermaid Tower, "what my own stake in the game shall be."

Dyffryn had already given the matter some thought. "There is a certain fine old book I have long coveted."

"The sixth-century Gospel—of course, I remember," said Cynwas, as they reached the top of the stairs and entered the Solar. The volume had once been one of his greatest treasures, but his interest in the book had long since waned. Forgetting, for the moment, his desire for the sidhe-stone, Cynwas was delighted at the opportunity to pass the once cherished Gospel on to his favorite uncle.

The Queen awaited them in the Solar: a large, pleasant chamber adjoining Sidonwy's private apartments, which boasted a fine fireplace at either end of the room, a polished wooden floor, and many arched windows offering a spectacular view of the courtyards below. A low table and several high-backed chairs stood near the larger fireplace, where two pages were laying out Cynwas's favorite inlaid game-board, ivory dice cups, and his best bone and ebony playing pieces.

The King and his uncle took seats on either side of the table, but the game did not begin at once. Dyffryn's grandsons brought in a flagon of wine and some jeweled goblets, and Ceilyn poured—for the King and Dyffryn; for the Queen, who sat nearest the fire, holding the silver jewel box in her lap; and for the Earl Marshall and the Lord Constable, whom Cynwas had invited to observe the game. Then Diaspad's servants caused another delay, when they noisily dragged her silver chair up the stairs and into the Solar, and ran about the room collecting velvet cushions and satin pillows which had to be arranged just so. . . . During all this, the Princess arrived, leaning on Derry's arm, and Calchas trailed along behind her, in shoes, hose, and doublet of such ornate cut and configuration that he presented a bizarre figure even in solid black.

"How in Celydonn," Fflergant whispered in Tryffin's ear, "does he contrive to walk in those shoes?" No one had thought to dismiss these two, so they had stationed themselves behind their grandfather, hoping to see most of the game before anyone remembered to send them away.

The Princess took her time settling down, but at last pronounced herself tolerably comfortable. Derry sat down on a cushion at her feet, and Calchas arranged himself on one arm of the silver chair and began idly tossing a handful of small coins.

"Shall we begin?" the King asked testily, impatient to get on with the game, eager to claim his prize.

"As it please you, Lord," said Dyffryn, and the game finally commenced.

It was evident from the beginning that the players were evenly matched. Both men knew the game well, neither took any unnecessary risks. So long as the dice played no favorites, it promised to be a long, slow battle.

An hour into the game, a careless throw by Dyffryn caused a

brief diversion. The dice tumbled off the board, rolled across the floor, and landed somewhere out of sight. An enthusiastic search followed.

In the end, Fflergant and Calchas both spotted the dice in a far corner of the room and dived for them at the same instant. Not a whit discommoded by his fantastically elongated footwear, Calchas was the quicker and more agile of the two, scooping up two of the dice while Fflergant scrambled for the third.

The boy from Gwyngelli snarled something under his breath, and Calchas, with uncharacteristic good grace, yielded the dice. Fflergant triumphantly returned the set of three to his grandfather, and the game began again.

Luck seemed to favor Dyffryn now; the ebony playing pieces advanced rapidly and to great advantage. Indeed, Dyffryn began to wonder how he would contrive to lose the game without appearing to do so deliberately.

Diaspad leaned over and whispered something in her stepbrother's ear. A tiny frown appeared between Cynwas's grey eyes. He shook his head in abrupt denial, and the Princess sat back in her chair. The game continued, but it seemed that the King had lost all pleasure in it.

Another lucky throw by Dyffryn only served to increase Cynwas's dejection. "You seem to have a talent for throwing double and triple sixes."

"I have certainly been fortunate this afternoon," Dyffryn agreed, with a resigned air, as he moved three of his pieces to an advantageous point.

Cynwas reached out, as if to pick up Dyffryn's dice . . . hesitated . . . withdrew his hand . . . and glanced up at his sister. Diaspad smiled and shrugged. With a sigh, the King picked up Dyffryn's dice and weighed them in the palm of his hand. "It would almost seem that two of these dice are *weighted*," he said disbelievingly.

A long frozen silence settled over the room, broken, at last, by the Queen. "You cannot possibly believe . . ."

"I would be very reluctant to think so," replied the King sincerely. He offered the suspiciously heavy dice to his sister for inspection, hoping she would be forced to declare them honest after all.

The Princess waved the dice away. "You must not ask me. Ask instead those two honorable gentlemen at your side. Their word will convince you where mine could not."

Manogan accepted the dice, tossed each one experimentally in his hand. His sleepy brown eyes rested, for a moment, on the Princess, before he passed judgment and handed the dice over to Ysgafn. "It might be so—it is impossible to say for certain."

Everyone waited breathlessly for Ysgafn to speak. "Two of them do feel a bit heavy," he admitted, "but as these are all your own dice, I don't see—"

"They are like my dice," said the King, comparing them to the three he had used. "Though perhaps the spots are just a little darker."

Cynwas looked at his uncle, a man he had loved and respected all of his life. "I am forced to conclude that *someone* has exchanged these dice for those I allowed you to use, and that the exchange took place sometime during the course of the game."

"It might be so," Dyffryn replied calmly, utterly secure in his innocence. "When the dice fell from the board and were lost, someone in this room might easily have found the opportunity to make an exchange." He glanced significantly in Diaspad's direction.

"And yet . . ." said the King, "your own grandson was the one who found and returned the dice."

All eyes turned to the hapless Fflergant. "I brought them back," he said, "but Calchas had his hands on them before I did."

Calchas examined his knuckles, cocked an eyebrow, and smiled nastily at Tryffin before replying. "That's a lie. I never touched them at all."

The healthy color in Fflergant's cheeks grew brighter still. "You know that you did!"

The King glanced around the room. "Did anyone see who it was that first picked up the dice?"

No one said a word. Fflergant looked to his brother, but Tryffin shook his head. Had he seen what happened, he would have spoken at once; since he had not, there was nothing he could say. The bane of Tryffin's existence (but never discussed outside the family) was a geas forbidding him to knowingly tell a lie. Though he could, and frequently did, obscure or evade the truth—often with no better excuse than a typically Gwyngellach desire to test the credulity of others—he had never told an outright lie in his life.

"I think," said Dyffryn, "that we are placing too much importance on something we had intended should serve us as a pleasant diversion. It was always my intention, Cousin, should the game go in my favor, to make you a gift of the sidhe-stone."

He put the key to the silver casket into Sidonwy's hand. She opened the box, looked inside, and gasped. "My dear Lord, I believe there has been a mistake. The box is empty."

Dyffryn leaned over and looked inside the casket. "But this is impossible!"

During the commotion which followed, the excited speculation among the onlookers, the futile search of the table, the Queen's chair, and the floor around it, one of Dyffryn's personal attendants —an old man who had served him for nearly half a century— approached and whispered a few words in Dyffryn's ear. "The sidhe-stone is *where?*" Dyffryn exclaimed.

The old man shuffled his feet before replying out loud. "On its way to your Lady, at Glynn Hyddwyn, my Lord, as you ordered it to be done directly after dinner."

Dyffryn's assurance began to crack. "*I* ordered this?"

"Yes, Lord," said the old man. "You *did* command me, and I carried out all your orders immediately: four men to escort the gem north, the jewel to be concealed on one of them for safekeeping, and no one to know of their departure until they were well on their way."

"My goodness," said Diaspad, in case anyone missed the implications, "you certainly were confident that the victory would be yours!"

"It's not true," said the Queen faintly. "It cannot be true."

"Indeed," said the King, pressing the back of his hand against his brow, as though his head ached, "if someone would present convincing evidence that it is *not* true, I would be grateful to hear it."

During all this, Ceilyn had been listening, but with only half of his attention. He had his own ideas about what had happened here, and awaited an opportunity to put them to the test.

When he thought that no one was watching him, he edged toward the table to inspect the dice more closely. He brushed his fingertips across the suspected pair; a touch convinced him that no magic had been used in weighting them. Though the dice were dishonest, they were innocent of enchantment. But the other die, the honest one that had tumbled to the floor at the same time as the two that had disappeared and then been replaced, that die felt unnaturally warm to his touch.

Ceilyn thought about that. He had seen a flash of silver pass from Calchas's hand to the Princess's lap at about the same time that Dyffryn cast his dice so carelessly. It put him in mind of something he had once seen Glastyn do: The wizard had moved a number of heavy boulders over a considerable distance, simply by manipulating a handful of pebbles. Ceilyn wondered if Calchas might have employed his silver coins in a similar fashion.

And he remembered something else, something he had once heard the wizard say: that the minds of servants and other simple folk were easily manipulated, not, as some people thought, because the lower orders lacked intelligence, but because they spent their entire lives taking orders from those they considered their betters, and were thereby rendered susceptible to suggestion. Thinking of this, Ceilyn took a long, careful look at Dyffryn's servant, and decided that the old man's gaze was oddly unfocused.

Ceilyn was suspicious, but there was nothing he could actually say or do. He could only watch helplessly as the King left the room, and offer Sidonwy a sympathetic arm to lean on when she, too, signaled her intention to depart.

Prescelli threaded her needle and attacked the hem once more. "Do hurry, Prescelli dear," said Seelie, "or we'll be late for morning prayers again."

It was the morning after the fateful game of "Tables," and Prescelli sat cross-legged on a ragged pile of blankets at the foot of her bed, clad only in her threadbare shift, mending a velvet gown so creased and shabby that it hardly seemed worth the effort to mend it again. "I *am* hurrying," she said, between clenched teeth.

Her sister, meanwhile, offered no assistance, nor did she think to loan Prescelli one of her own beautiful gowns. Seelie sat on the broad window seat, alternately braiding and unbraiding her soft golden curls, rearranging her spotless skirts and her long, fur-trimmed sleeves, only pausing, every now and then, to inspect her own pretty reflection in the small hand mirror that dangled from her girdle. There were many at Caer Cadwy who admired Seelie's fastidious honey-haired beauty, but none so ardently as did Seelie herself.

"I don't know how you do it," she trilled. "Yet another ripped hem! But then, you always were careless with your things, weren't you, Darling?"

Prescelli did not deign to reply. Whether or not she was careless with her things remained to be seen, since she had never, as far back as she could remember, possessed anything of value that was truly and exclusively her own. All her life, it had been Seelie's broken toys and outgrown ponies, Seelie's faded ribbons and draggled tippets, Seelie's old gowns and discarded trinkets. Now Prescelli had completed the pattern by falling in love with Seelie's intended husband, a strapping young fellow called Iaen Og.

"If you are in such a hurry," she said coldly, "pray don't allow me to detain you. I don't need *your* kind assistance to find my way down to the chapel, you know."

"But you're so forgetful, Dear," said Seelie. "You have missed morning prayers three times already this week. It looks so bad, and of course I feel responsible. . . ."

Prescelli stifled a bitter laugh. The thought of vain, empty-headed Seelie taking responsibility for her own actions, let *alone* anyone else's, was just too ludicrous. *And where were you, sister mine, when I needed you most, when I first arrived at court so ignorant, so eager to please? What were you doing, Seelie dearest, when I started bartering my body to buy affection, when I gave myself to all the wrong men, when I took to lying and stealing to gain all the things I couldn't get in any other way? Why, you were up in your bedchamber combing your hair, or trying on a new gown—no pretty sentiments or fine sisterly responsibility then, as I recall— leaving your precious little sister to blunder her way through the politics and the passions and the temptations of the court!*

But there was no point in saying any of this to Seelie. Seelie lived in a world of her own, completely oblivious. She accepted the privileges of a favored elder daughter as nothing more than her due, and she had far too lofty a sense of her own worth ever to fall into the kind of traps that had tripped up Prescelli. And that being so, what was the use of saying anything?

Instead, Prescelli swallowed her anger. "I'll finish up here soon and be down as quickly as I can. Please don't trouble yourself on my account. Please."

"Very well," said Seelie, rising dreamily to her feet and sauntering toward the door. "I'll be on my way. I do so hate to be tardy."

But once Seelie was safely out of the room, Prescelli began to move with admirable dispatch. She cast down the half-mended gown, threw open a clothes chest, and drew out another equally shabby gown, dressing herself and pinning up her long dark hair so swiftly that Seelie, had she been there to observe, would have been gratified.

Then, standing on tiptoe, she removed the torch from a bracket by the door. Prescelli had plans of her own this morning, but attending Mass with her sister and the other girls was not among them.

Instead, when she left her bedchamber, Prescelli turned away from the chapel and climbed a set of stairs to the top of the Mermaid Tower. She crossed the battlements, entered the Keep, and ran up another, creaking, staircase, to a part of the castle that had been unoccupied for years. She passed down a long, dark corridor, festooned with cobwebs and carpeted with a thick layer of soft grey dust except where her trailing skirts had already swept the floorboards clean. She continued on until she reached a suite of tiny, airless rooms. One of these rooms Prescelli had appropriated for her own uses, a fine and private place in which to practice forbidden spells.

Prescelli closed the door behind her, and placed her smoking torch in a ring above the make-shift altar she had previously erected in one corner of the room. On the crimson cloth draped over the altar, and on the floor to either side of the altar, and in niches all around the room, stood dozens of candles: fine white beeswax and humble tallow, some standing in proper holders, others in pools of their own congealed drippings—all of them stolen.

Prescelli had taken the better part of the winter assembling so many. She had filched them from private chapels and public rooms, hiding them under her bed until she smuggled them upstairs, a dozen at a time. Yet she did not begrudge the effort. For when they were all alight, all of them glowing golden in the dark, shuttered, stifling little room, what a fine sight they were! Like a coronation, or a Rhianeddi funeral—something splendid, anyway—but better, much better, because it was all for her own private benefit, a special secret to be shared with no one else, ever.

But today Prescelli could not spare the time it would take to light so many. Instead, she selected five of the tallest wax tapers, five with proper candlesticks to hold them, lit them one after another, and placed each one on a separate point of the pentagram she had previously drawn in chalk on the floor. Though Prescelli did not know it, the broken lines in the figure, where she had carelessly scuffed them out, had caused all her spells to go awry.

A flask of wine, a bowl of well water drawn up at midnight with appropriate ceremonies, a ring of base metal colored gold, and the missing silver goblet stood on the altar among the candles. Very carefully, so as not to spill any, Prescelli poured a little wine into the purloined goblet. Then, muttering the prescribed incantation, she dropped in the ring and added three drops of well water.

"It is only right," Prescelli's father told her, on the day that she left home, *"that Seelie should have the fine clothes and as grand a dowry as we can give her. She is the one who will make a great marriage and benefit us all. After she is wed, after she has won the hearts of all Iaen's noble relations, she may find it possible to arrange marriages for her younger sisters. It will be a lucky thing for you if she does,"* he had added cruelly, *"for as God is my witness, you will never find a husband on your looks alone!"*

But Prescelli did not want one of Iaen's kinsmen—noble or otherwise—did not want any marriage of Seelie's arranging. She wanted Iaen Og himself, and she was ready to go to any lengths necessary in order to get him.

Already, she had taken many risks: stealing the candles and the cup, sneaking into Glastyn's laboratory in the vain hope that she would be able to open his books. Finally, in desperation, she had pawned a piece of jewelry (not her own) and sought out a certain old woman with an evil reputation, who lived by the docks in Treledig. But all these risks meant nothing—or they would mean nothing if ever she could make her spells *work* and accomplish something for once in her life, entirely on her own, beholden to nobody!

Taking a deep breath to steady herself, Prescelli took her place at the center of the pentagram, screwing her eyes shut to aid her concentration. In order for this particular spell to succeed, she must first visualize the face of her True Love reflected on the surface of the wine. Alas, this proved to be more difficult than it sounded, and at this point in the spell Prescelli always came to grief. Oh, she had never yet failed to form a picture of Iaen Og in her mind, but as soon as she opened her eyes and looked into the cup the picture she had so faithfully depicted immediately faded.

But this time a picture did appear, and held for nearly a minute, a face she could perceive too dimly to recognize, though she knew at once that it was not the face she wanted to see. Those shadowed, haunted eyes bore no resemblance to the amiable blue-eyed gaze of Iaen Og.

With a cry of disappointment, Prescelli cast the cup aside, threw herself down on the dusty floor. The wine spread across the floorboards in a crimson flood, soaking into her rubbed-velvet skirt. A little cloud of dust and cobwebs rose up around her and settled on her dress and in her hair. Prescelli took no notice. So keen was her disappointment, her rage at her own impotence, that she beat her heels against the floor, lay her head on her knees, and burst into hot, angry, frustrated tears.

But she did not weep long. A sound outside the door, very like a stifled laugh, silenced her. She scrambled to her feet, hurled herself against the door, hoping to keep the intruder out. The door would not lock, the key lost, the bolt rusted and useless, but anyone who wanted to enter had best be ready for a struggle!

Minutes passed, and nothing happened. Finally, unable to endure the suspense any longer, she wiped her tears with a grimy hand and cautiously opened the door. As far as she could see in either direction, the corridor was empty. She listened for another moment, then stepped across the threshold.

"Well, Prescelli, imagine encountering you here!" an all-too-familiar voice said cheerfully, and something slithered out of the shadows.

"Derry Ruadh mac Forgoll!" Prescelli said breathlessly. "What are you doing here?"

Derry bestowed one of his better smiles on her. "That hardly matters. What are *you* doing here?—now, that's an interesting question."

Prescelli cast a forlorn glance at the door. Why had she never thought to plug the keyhole? "I don't know what you think you have seen—" she began.

"I've seen enough," he said. "More than enough to ruin you, Sweetheart. A love spell, was it? Yes, I thought so. And I can guess the intended victim. Not very pretty, Prescelli, not very pretty at all!"

Prescelli bit her lip in vexation. She and Derry had once been intimate, and she knew his twisted little soul well enough to fear him. She also knew better than to let him see how frightened she was. Derry could be especially vicious when he knew that he had the upper hand.

Perhaps it was as well that she could not see what a pitiful picture she presented, her face all tear-stained and dirty, her bright, tawdry gown dusty and wine-stained—or know how much Derry was enjoying her distress. "Come, now," she managed to say lightly, "I hardly think that even now I've actually shocked *you*. Still, you do seem to have me at a slight disadvantage, and I suppose you'll be wanting . . . some sort of compensation before you promise not to tell."

Derry laughed. He delicately removed a scrap of cobweb from her hair, traced, with his finger, the path of one tear down her cheek. "Still offering the same old thing? But nobody cares for shopworn goods, you know. And this isn't one of your little thefts—this is much, much worse. Besides, it isn't what *I* want that matters, for you have someone else to deal with now, someone who will ask more than I ever would."

"I don't understand," said Prescelli. "Morc . . . is it Morc that you want me to—?"

Derry snickered again. "No, Prescelli, someone more important than either Morc or I has an eye on you—though not, I fancy, in quite the manner to which you are accustomed!"

"Our ancestors," said Glastyn, "believed that the King and the Land were inseparably linked. 'As the King lives his life,' they used to say, 'so goes the realm.' Therefore, an illness which afflicts the King might engender a blight on the crops, and domestic strife within the royal household could easily lead to civil disorder."

"But that can't be true," said Teleri. "The King and Queen frequently disagree, yet the kingdom is at peace."

"The kingdom is at peace," said Glastyn, "but how long will it remain so? Then, too, there is the matter of the Wild Magic, and of the bindings."

"But it is the power inherent in your name which reinforces the bindings," said the little girl.

"The power in my name," said Glastyn, "and in the King's."

9.

Of Fire and Water

Mornings, the Queen and her young ladies spent in the Mermaid Tower, occupied with their spinning and mending, their fine embroidery, and their harp lessons. They had gathered in the Solar, in pursuit of these various occupations, on one particular day, about a month after the unfortunate incident of the sidhe-stone and the dice, when the King precipitously appeared among them.

"You had a letter this morning, I believe?" he asked, descending on Sidonwy, who sat embroidering by a window.

"I did indeed," the Queen replied evenly, refusing to be provoked by this highly irregular greeting.

"From your uncle, Lord Dyffryn?"

"From our uncle, yes," said Sidonwy, not so evenly as before. Lord Dyffryn had departed a fortnight ago, to join his wife and youngest daughters in Rhianedd. "He had traveled as far as

Ildathach, and was sadly disappointed in Conchobar's hospitality," she continued, a little too casually. "I hope he will write again from Glynn Hyddwyn, for I long to hear how Fiona and the new baby fare."

"Hmmph!" snorted the King. "No more than that?" Perhaps he felt a bit jealous because Dyffryn had written to Sidonwy and not to him, perhaps he was disappointed because his uncle said nothing to dispel the cloud of suspicion under which he had left Camboglanna. Whatever the reason, Cynwas decided, then and there, to take violent exception to the letter. "It is impertinent for him to write to you, and equally improper for you to reply."

At the first note of displeasure in the King's voice, the young ladies had followed the Queen's example, suddenly becoming completely and discreetly engrossed in their separate tasks. But this last pronouncement was too much for Sidonwy, who looked up from the white surcote on which she was embroidering Celydonn's leaping lion in green silk, and asked, "Not write to Dyffryn? Whyever not?"

"Your uncle," said the King haughtily, "left here in disgrace."

"He may indeed have fallen out of favor—the justice of that I will not dispute, though I might well do so," she retorted. "But he did not leave Caer Cadwy by your order, nor was he denied an audience before he left. If there has since been any talk of exile or disgrace, I have yet to hear it."

"Have you not?" growled the King, the more enraged because he knew that she spoke the truth. "Then hear me now: Dyffryn fab Drwst is banished, from my presence and from my home. Camboglanna is forbidden him, just as it is forbidden your brothers, and all communication between you and your kin at Glynn Hyddwyn must cease. I ought to have forbidden that from the very beginning," he added, "lest he pass on messages from those other traitors—"

"My brothers," said the Queen, in a low, furious voice, "are not traitors!"

"I have not named your brothers, Lady. But if the accusation seems apt . . ."

"It seems," said Sidonwy, plying her needle so vigorously and with so little care that the stitches would all have to be picked out and reworked later, "that you are determined to keep me and my kinsmen apart. That is unkind and unfair. My home has been full of your sister and her people all winter long, and the inconvenience to me has been considerable.''

''Once, she was your dearest friend,'' the King pointed out.

''My friend, until she alienated me by her disloyalty to you,'' the Queen retorted.

''I have long since forgotten any wrong she did me in the days of her youth and unwisdom,'' said Cynwas loftily. ''Besides, she keeps me amused. But perhaps,'' he went on, descending with a rush, ''it would please you better to be at Glynn Hyddwyn now, among those precious kinsmen, than here at Caer Cadwy with my sister and me.''

''Perhaps,'' said Sidonwy defiantly, ''it would.''

It seemed a trivial quarrel at the time, no different from a hundred other spats that had preceded it. But this time no reconciliation followed. For now there was no Lord Dyffryn, no kindly silver-haired uncle, to gracefully bring about that reconciliation. Now there was only the King's step-sister, green-eyed and malicious, to tease and provoke further hard words, to remind Cynwas, whenever he seemed to be weakening, that his dignity was at stake, that it was not his place to sue for forgiveness, that Sidonwy . . .

''But doesn't dear Sidonwy look well?'' the Princess gushed on more than one occasion. ''I cannot think when I have seen her so beautiful . . . so blooming. Well, perhaps she is a little thinner, as you say, but there is nothing surprising in that. Such a busy life as she leads: hunting and hawking all day long, now that the weather is fine, and dancing away the night.''

And Cynwas did not stop to consider that Sidonwy had never been one to pine or sigh. Outspoken she might be, when angry or disgusted, but her personal griefs and disappointments she always concealed by throwing herself into a flurry of feverish activity.

Not to be outdone, Cynwas did the same, embarking on an endless course of enforced gaiety, in the relentless pursuit of new amusements. The Princess Diaspad abetted him in this, for she had a positive genius for inventing original entertainments and adding bizarre twists to all his old pastimes. Masquerades, pageants, games of chance, elaborate practical jokes . . . her invention was inexhaustible.

Nor did the King alone fall under her spell. Fantastic new fashions, exotic dishes, elaborate mannerisms and affectations: She introduced them one after the other in rapid succession, and the sycophants, idlers, and pleasure-seekers of the court slavishly imitated her.

And it was all so very gay, the pace she set so frantic, that no one could afterward say exactly when and how it had all turned vicious and character assassination became the latest rage.

Of course, there had always been loose talk at Caer Cadwy, even in the "old days," but this was subtly different. Never before had the gossip been so deliciously daring, epigrams so witty and cruel, insinuations so pointed, or reputations so readily and recklessly ruined.

The principal victim of this new sport was the Queen, easy prey, now that the King had turned his back on her. She had few close friends among the powerful, and the love of the common-folk could not help her now. To make matters worse, Sidonwy's thoughtless behavior, her refusal to follow any of the good advice offered to her, soon offended many of those who might otherwise have supported her, with the result that the saner, more sensible element at court kept themselves rigidly aloof from both factions, declaring neither as the Queen's friends nor the Princess's.

And so she had no one to turn to, no sympathetic friend to offer her companionship and comfort, no one but her personal attendants —those youths and maidens whose livelihood depended on her continued favor—and one gentleman from Rhianedd, named Elidyr fab Esgeir.

Naturally, she found the greatest consolation in the company of Elidyr: a friend of exactly her own age and similar background, whom she had known since childhood. Elidyr was an unassuming gentleman, so bland and self-effacing that people rarely noticed him. Now, however, the court subjected his friendship with the Queen to the most minute scrutiny.

It did not take Diaspad and her gossipmongers long to magnify this innocent friendship almost beyond recognition. From childhood friends, the Queen and Elidyr rapidly advanced to childhood sweethearts. Then word spread of a secret betrothal, entered into just before Sidonwy's marriage to the King had been arranged. That the Princess had been Sidonwy's trusted confidante in those early years lent considerable credibility to these rumors, and therefore, indirectly, to the insinuation that followed: that Elidyr and the Queen were lovers still.

Even when Sidonwy recognized her danger, she was too stubbornly proud—and too desperately unhappy—to send Elidyr away. "I have done nothing to be ashamed of," she told everyone who would listen, "and God himself knows that we have never been alone together in our lives."

As for Elidyr, he knew what he ought to do, but he was a soft-hearted, weak-willed fellow, completely but not very wisely devoted to the Queen. Against his better judgment—and ignoring the passionate hatred he read in Ceilyn mac Cuel's eyes—he allowed her to persuade him to stay on.

One breezy morning in March, a large party gathered by the stable and the mews, preparing for a day spent hawking. Calchas was there, and Derry's brother Morc, and many more besides, but the King and the Princess, both of them avid sportsmen, had elected to stay behind, putting the finishing touches on a new divertissement to be presented that evening after supper.

Calchas stood a little apart from the crowd, trying to soothe his fidgeting, ill-tempered black stallion. A stallion was a rare sight at Caer Cadwy, though not unknown. The King kept several for stud, down in the meadows below the castle. For riding, however, the ladies preferred dainty little mares or intelligent, doe-eyed mules; the small pages and handmaidens rode stout ponies from Rhianedd and Aderyn, and Cynwas and his men chose geldings—sturdy, sleek, dependable beasts, ferocious but disciplined in the mock-battles of the tourney, yet gentle and safe among the ladies. But the Earl Marshall had once owned a savage chestnut stallion with a voracious appetite for stableboy, a beast who could be depended upon to make a dangerous and embarrassing display when anything female approached him. People still remembered Manogan's stallion, and spoke of him with awe.

While Calchas continued to devote his attention to the temperamental black, Morc purposefully descended on a group of young ladies who had gathered by the mews. They presented a pretty picture, in their brightly colored gowns and their long fluttering sleeves all beribboned and bedagged. Seelie and Megwen returned Morc's greeting civilly enough, but Fand and Finola pointedly ignored him: Fand, by suddenly becoming completely absorbed with the Queen's pretty blue peregrine, which she carried on her wrist; Finola, by turning her back and entering into a spirited conversation with one of the pages. They did not like Morc, who was rough and uncouth for all his rugged good looks, and the matter of a feud stood between them. He was the son of the Lord of Leth Scathach, they the nieces of Leth Skellig's Lord—Draighenach both of them, to be sure, but implacable in their mutual hostility.

But Morc, who felt no particular allegiance to his own faction (nor, to do him justice, any particular animosity to theirs), professed himself a great admirer of Fand's blue-eyed, raven-haired beauty, and he made a remarkably persistent suitor. Today, though Fand ignored his greeting and repeatedly refused his offers of assistance, his persistence finally won him a small concession: Fand permitted him to hold the peregrine for her, while Fflergant lifted her up into the saddle.

Sidonwy and Elidyr arrived at about that time. The Queen looked worn and drawn, in spite of her bright, artificial smile. Mounting her cream-colored mare, she dropped her gloves. Elidyr, all devoted solicitude, picked them up and handed them to her, managing to take her hand and kiss it in the process. Watching all this, Calchas and Morc exchanged a suggestive smile.

With her bucket in her hand, Teleri threaded her way through the outbuildings and the thatched cottages in the outer courtyard, past the wash house where the drably clad serving women (and one misshapen old dame in black and scarlet, more agile than any of them despite her humped back and twisted limbs) beat, and boiled, and wrung out the laundry. Here in the sunlit publicity of the outermost courtyard, where the castle craftsmen, the fletchers and chandlers, the blacksmiths, coopers, and wheelwrights, plied their trades, Teleri had never been able to achieve invisibility. Yet within this crowd of busy humanity, it was possible, if she moved quickly and met no one's eyes, to cloak herself in a featureless anonymity. Yet she lingered by the well, this morning, longer than was necessary, to watch the crowd by the stables.

Something was not right, something she felt, rather than saw or heard. She scanned the crowd, trying to locate the source of the problem.

She saw the usual milling about, heard the last-minute wagers and arrangements, the agitated bating of hawks and the impatient stamping of horses. . . . No, things were not exactly as usual, because everyone seemed a little *too* boisterous, too skittish, too disorganized. The peregrine passed from Fand's wrist to Finola's . . . was handed up to the Queen . . . over to Elidyr . . . back to Sidonwy. . . . No one seemed to know exactly where she belonged. Just watching all this, Teleri felt a cloud of confusion settle over her mind.

That cloud dispelled at the sight of Ceilyn leading Tegillus out of the stable and into the yard. Teleri did not want to meet Ceilyn, here or elsewhere, so she hastily filled her bucket and faded into the crowd of women clustered by the wash house. Then, safe and unnoticed in their midst, she stopped and stole another look at Ceilyn.

Hours later, as Teleri knelt among the tender green shoots in her garden, the sun suddenly disappeared and a thick fog came spilling in over the garden wall. Not an ordinary mist, drifting in from the west and the sea, but a curious clinging dampness out of the northeast. Teleri put aside her gardening tools and stood up. She tested the air, decided she did not like the feel of it. Yet the mist must be harmless, or how had it penetrated the castle's magical defenses, how entered into the enchanted garden? Then she thought of the hawking party, and of the Queen.

Leaving her tools behind on the dirt, Teleri ran to the gate. In the yard outside, the fog was already so dense she could not even see so far as the Wizard's Tower. She was forced to follow the wall until she found her own door, and once inside and away from the stifling mist, she needed a moment to catch her breath again.

Out of a cabinet above the fireplace, Teleri took a small ebony chest. She placed the chest at the foot of her bed and opened the lid. The crystal ball inside felt as cold as ice, even through its black velvet wrappings. And when she lifted the cloth, she discovered to her dismay that the mist had somehow entered into the crystal. She could see nothing inside but a churning white fog.

Teleri sat cross-legged on her bed, warming the crystal ball with her hands, trying to penetrate the mist. Her hands grew numb and her mind grew number. At last, unable to fight the compulsion any longer, she curled up on the scarlet counterpane and fell into a deep, dreamless sleep.

By the time Teleri awoke, an hour or two later, the mist in the courtyard had dissipated. Yet a certain apprehension lingered, an apprehension that was eventually confirmed: The hawking party returned in the late afternoon, hours after they were expected, and the Queen and Elidyr did not return with them.

Someone dispatched a messenger to inform the King of the Queen's disappearance, then the whole party waited nervously for Cynwas to appear and question them. As Teleri stood in the shadows by the stables, watching the milling and confused company, she felt a light touch on her elbow. Turning, she found Ceilyn there beside her. For weeks now, she had been avoiding him, ever since that morning they had spent together in the garden. She had acted on impulse, offering him her help, allowing him and his problems to disrupt her safe, solitary, predictable existence, an impulse she had since repented. Yet now that they finally met again, she felt unexpectedly pleased to see him. Then he smiled tentatively, and she turned away from the question in his eyes.

To cover that moment of awkwardness, Teleri asked the obvious question. "Where is the Queen?"

"I hoped that you could tell me," he said. "We lost her and Elidyr when the mist came down. We spent hours looking for them after it cleared, then we all came back here hoping they had simply turned back and arrived here ahead of us."

Teleri looked around her, uncomfortably aware that talking to Ceilyn made her blatantly visible to others. "Come with me," she said, slipping past him, into a secluded corner of the yard behind the wash house. She sat down on an overturned oak tub, and Ceilyn joined her there a moment later.

Teleri said: "They can't be lost. Not in open, familiar country. Not in broad daylight."

"Some of the others believe that they planned to slip away—an assignation or an elopement—and that the mist was just a convenient coincidence. It's not true," Ceilyn insisted fiercely. "God knows, she has been unhappy, and yes, she has been known to do ill-advised things, acting on impulse. But this . . ." Jealous of Elidyr Ceilyn might be, ready to wring the fellow's fool neck for allowing his name to be coupled with the Queen's, but he had never believed any of the rumors. ". . . She loves the King, for all you might wonder why sometimes, and she would never do any—"

"I am certain that you are right," said Teleri. "And that was no ordinary mist that separated Elidyr and the Queen from the rest of you. Didn't you notice? Didn't you sense something?"

"Yes, yes, it was all wrong, somehow, though I couldn't tell you—are you trying to tell me that someone actually conjured up that fog, in order to divide our party and spirit the Queen away?"

"Yes, I am," said Teleri. The clue that had eluded her earlier, the answer she had sought in the crystal, had finally come to her. She could picture the scene now, just as it had been that morning: the crowd of washerwomen, the lines of clean laundry—and Diaspad's hunchback serving woman, conspicuous in her gaudy scarlet, hovering over a kettle of steaming water. "I can guess how it was done, but not precisely why—for what could anyone gain by abducting the Queen now?"

"There is no telling what someone might imagine she stands to gain," said Ceilyn grimly. "Oh yes, so long as the Queen is out of favor, that suits the Princess Diaspad very well. But she must know, as well as you and I do, that just as soon as any real harm befell the Queen, the King would experience a complete change of heart. Still, there is no guessing how that woman's mind works, or what mischief she is capable of devising. We have to find Sidonwy at once!"

"Yes," said Teleri. "But how?"

"I think there might be a chance," said Ceilyn diffidently. "I found something that the Queen dropped, about the time that she disappeared, and I brought it back, hoping that you . . . Well, you do use things like this, sometimes, to help you find people, don't you?"

He pulled something out of his belt and handed it over: an elegant green kid glove, one of the pair that Sidonwy had carried earlier. The leather was lightly perfumed with ambergris and civet; the cuff bore the Queen's cipher worked in gold thread.

"This might be of use," Teleri admitted cautiously. "So personal a possession, so recently worn . . ."

Ceilyn looked relieved. "I ought to go back to the others," he said, rising to his feet. "But you will let me know . . . ?"

"Yes, of course," said Teleri absently, her thoughts already centered on the glove.

Back in her room, she found that the crystal had changed. The ball was clean again, shining with all its former light, except at the very heart of the crystal where the fog had concentrated in a tiny grey cloud, that turned and twisted, as if trying to conceal the even tinier shapes that Teleri could just perceive moving within it.

This time, she was determined to penetrate the fog, convinced that she knew who wandered at the heart of the mist, and that the glove was a valuable link. She sat on her bed as before, the crystal nestled in the palm of one hand, and the Queen's glove held in the other. She tried to think of Sidonwy, as she must have been when the mist first came down, and later, finding herself separated from her escort.

The fog had thinned and gradually disappeared, but the confusion, the mind-numbing sense of wandering from place to place without any real bearings, still lingered. Sidonwy was weary, so bone-achingly tired that she scarcely even noticed Elidyr anymore, had lost all sense of time since they had parted from the others. All her thoughts, all her hopes, were centered on the peregrine.

It had seemed so logical, when she and Elidyr first emerged from the mist back into the bright blue afternoon, so natural and right in their first euphoria at finding themselves free of the stifling terror of the fog, to fly the peregrine, to send her soaring triumphantly aloft, a living banner to rally the divided party. Only after the peregrine was actually in flight did Sidonwy remember her earlier misgivings, remember that the falcon, after behaving so strangely all afternoon, ought not to be flown at all.

By then, it was too late. The peregrine fought the air, a hundred feet up, bating wildly as though bound to the earth by some invisible tether. Sidonwy's heart missed a beat, at the thought that the falcon had somehow become entangled in her own jesses. If that were so, she might break a leg—or worse, a wing—or strangle *herself, in her furious struggles to work free. But no . . . Sidonwy saw with relief that the green leather jesses still dangled free.*

And then, quite suddenly, the peregrine had abandoned the struggle. No longer fighting whatever it was that hampered her, the falcon plummeted earthward, righted herself only inches above the ground, flipped over in mid-air, then soared skyward—this time in a new direction—apparently unhindered.

Naturally, Sidonwy and Elidyr had followed her, expecting that once the peregrine killed she would return to the glove. But the falcon did not kill, or return to Sidonwy, not all that long afternoon, not for all Sidonwy's and Elidyr's whistling and coaxing and luring. And every time that she tried to change her course, by even a degree to right or left, there was another struggle, the same wild bating and flapping, until the falcon allowed herself to be drawn back again, west by southwest, the only course permitted her.

And Sidonwy continued to follow, though the miles passed by in a featureless blur. First riding, then walking when the mare showed signs of fatigue, but always determined to regain the peregrine, though she perish in the attempt.

For the falcon was a haggard, taken and painstakingly trained by Cynwas himself, his joy and his treasure for an entire season, then impulsively presented to Sidonwy (and this while his passion for the bird still flamed hot), tendered as a peace-offering after some trifling quarrel. To lose the King's gift now, when it seemed there might never be peace between them again, was more than Sidonwy could bear.

Finally, the falcon settled. Stooping swiftly downward, she landed atop a crumbling vine-covered tower perched on a rugged precipice by the sea. And there she remained, for all their frantic efforts to lure her down.

The hawking party had congregated below the Keep, where the King stood listening to a dozen incoherent and contradictory accounts of the Queen's disappearance. Teleri skirted the crowd, crept up the steps, and stationed herself beside one of the weatherbeaten winged lions which guarded the doors, where she might see and hear everything without attracting any attention.

"Ceilyn mac Cuel," the King was saying. "Was it not your duty to guard the Queen?"

Ceilyn opened his mouth—no doubt prepared to take all blame on himself—when someone spoke up in his defense. "It wasn't Ceilyn's fault. She sent him away."

"But I was at fault," said Ceilyn, glaring at his would-be champion. "She scolded me for discourtesy to—to another member of the party, and she—"

The King brushed his explanation aside. "I want to know who, aside from Elidyr, *was* with the Queen when the mist overtook her."

Nobody seemed to know, and another round of denials and contradictory accounts followed. But Ceilyn chanced to look up and, spotting Teleri, slipped away from the crowd to join her beside the stone lion.

"It is true," he said, when Teleri told him all that she had learned from the crystal, "the peregrine was never quite right. But the place that you saw, the ruin . . . I can think of several places that might answer that description."

Indeed, a whole chain of watch-towers had once guarded the great Bay of Camboglanna, and though most had been destroyed during the dynastic wars some still remained in a largely ruinous state, and all of them within an afternoon's ride of Caer Cadwy.

Down below, Prescelli appeared on the scene, diffidently approaching the King and handing him what looked like a scorched scrap of paper. Everyone waited expectantly while Cynwas scrutinized the fragment. "Where did you come by this?" he asked sharply.

Ceilyn moved a little nearer, in order to get a better look at the writing. He rejoined Teleri a moment later. "Prescelli says that she found a fragment of a letter in the Queen's bedchamber. The message had mostly burned away, but two names remain: Elidyr (apparently his signature) and Dinas Trachmyr. Do you think that was the place that you saw—Dinas Trachmyr?"

Teleri nodded.

Ceilyn shook his head, utterly confused. "But it makes no sense.

If they planned an assignation—what of the mist and the peregrine?''

"For that matter, what need of a note?'' Teleri pointed out.

"You are absolutely right,'' said Ceilyn. "Why would Elidyr write to her? He sees her every day, and it would be childish, no, it would be utterly foolish, for the pair of them to pass incriminating notes between them, when a few whispered words would suffice. The letter is—it must be—a forgery.''

Teleri and Ceilyn both knew how easily a forgery might be accomplished. In an age when those who could write prided themselves on a clear, precise, uniform hand (in Elidyr's case, a beautiful old-fashioned uncial, still used in Rhianedd and the north), no man's hand or signature was unique. That was why elaborate wax seals were needed to establish the validity of official documents. Ceilyn, who had also been raised in the north, could, if pressed, render a decent imitation of Elidyr's hand, and he knew of at least a dozen others at court who could have done as well.

Down below, someone volunteered to lead a search party to Dinas Trachmyr, and a number of men agreed to go along.

"If they leave right now, they may find the Queen and Elidyr still at the tower,'' said Teleri. "Even if she is on her way home now . . . if they left anything to show that they were there at the tower, or if anything was planted in advance . . . As it is, the King is angry and suspicious, but what will he think if Sidonwy and Elidyr are found, anywhere between here and Dinas Trachmyr, alone together, with night coming on?''

"He will think the worst. Under the circumstances, he is bound to assume the worst. I only hope,'' he added grimly, "that Elidyr has better sense than to try and clear her name by himself. I am the one who ought to fight for her, if it comes to that. In the meantime . . . perhaps I had better go along with the others, in case I can offer her any aid.''

"There is something else you might do, if you go to Dinas Trachmyr,'' said Teleri, as Ceilyn started down the steps. He stopped and looked back at her hopefully. "You can see that the falcon is caught and brought back here. Bring her yourself, if at all possible. And whatever you do, don't let Calchas or Morc lay a hand on her.''

"And where," said the lad, "is the falcon to be found?"
"In the land of Oenafwyn: three days' journey if you follow the moon."
"And how," said the lad, "is the falcon to be taken?"
"There is no way for you to capture her, but to call her by name."

From The Black Book of Tregalen

10.

Chasing the Moon

The Queen and Elidyr met the search party about two miles from Dinas Trachmyr. Sidonwy was scarcely coherent, Elidyr uncharacteristically grim. Finally reaching the limits of bone-headed obedience, Elidyr had taken stock of the situation, realized the Queen's danger, and asserted himself for once in his life, threatening to carry her away from the ruined tower, by main force if necessary. "Either you will accompany me, dear Lady, with such dignity as befits you, or I shall drag you back to Caer Cadwy whether you will or no."

Once outside the influence of the peregrine and the spells and compulsions surrounding her, Sidonwy's mind began to clear, though her memories of the afternoon remained cloudy.

"I don't know . . . I can't remember," she said, when Ceilyn questioned her. Yet she remained fixated on the peregrine, begging Ceilyn to find the bird and bring her home again.

"I'll not return to Caer Cadwy without her," he vowed. And the Queen, reassured, allowed him to kiss her hand, and permitted the others to take her home.

Ceilyn watched until they were out of sight, then followed the curve of the bay until he reached Dinas Trachmyr. The peregrine had disappeared, had apparently found a place to perch unseen and settle down for the night.

Ceilyn looked around him for a suitable place to set up camp. Dark was rapidly descending, and the tower looked dark and forbidding painted against the gaudy sunset. Ruins of this kind, where men had died suddenly and violently, and no new tenants had come to exorcise the evil influences, were frequently haunted, but the surrounding countryside offered no other shelter. More important still, the tower boasted but one means of entry, through an arched doorway. Though the door was missing, the portal alone provided needed protection. There were things that walked in the dark hours, things that no man wanted to meet, and many of them could not cross over a threshold without an invitation. Between the tower ghosts and those other things—the night-walkers, the howlers, and the creeping horrors—Ceilyn felt more inclined to cast his lot in with the ghosts.

By the last fading light of sunset, he unsaddled Tegillus, left the chestnut grazing by the tower, and foraged for firewood. Three or four wind-blasted ash trees, clinging to the edge of the cliff, provided him with all the dead branches he might need.

Ceilyn selected two relatively straight sticks and piled the rest of the wood in a corner of the guardroom. He carried the sticks outside with him, examined the ivy growing on the wall, pulled out his dirk, and sawed off a two-foot length of the tough, sinewy vine. He sat down on the steps, stripped the leaves from the vine, then bound the two sticks together to form a rude cross. This, he balanced on the beam above the doorway.

Next, he led Tegillus up the stairs and made him as comfortable as possible in the guardroom. He always kept grain in one of his saddlebags, but the nearest drinkable water was in a stream half a mile distant. For that, they would both have to wait until morning.

Ceilyn built a small fire in the center of the room and set the rest of the wood aside to keep the fire going later. This, he did not so much for warmth as to keep the night things at bay. Then he unbuckled his swordbelt, drew out his sword and his dirk, and placed them on the ground within easy reach. Feeling a little safer for the triple protection of fire, cross, and cold iron, he wrapped up in his cloak and stretched out by the fire.

The floor was hard and uneven, the night as cold and damp as a sea-trow's kiss. A hollow feeling in his stomach reminded him that he had already missed two meals. He lay awake, tossing and turning for many hours before finally falling into a light, fitful doze.

He stood beneath a flowering appletree. He *was* in the garden, not dreaming at all—he could smell the damp earth, the blossoms on the bough. His mother smiled at him and said, "Eat of the fruit, why should you not? This is the garden of Our Lord who loves and would deny you nothing that you need."

But Cuel said: ". . . the sins of the fathers. You were conceived in sin . . . born in wedlock but conceived in sin. Marriage between second-cousins—it was a lawful union, you understand, but sin in the sight of God. I never meant to touch her, never meant to . . . mine the sin, mine the everlasting shame, but mine also the duty to purge you of all those vicious tendencies the flesh is heir to."

He heard a great wailing and a gnashing of teeth all around him, and saw the body of an old man in a bloody winding sheet with a great gaping wound in his thigh. No, all was darkness. Ceilyn sprawled face down on the chapel floor, felt the cold stones hard beneath him. "Father, please . . . ah God, I never did it, never did it. Yes, I looked at the girl, but not with lust, I swear to you, Father, I swear. . . ."

"My precious child, of course you did not," said his mother, so kindly, and offered him the apple—but it was not his mother, after all, but Sidonwy, offering him a chalice full to the brim . . . was it elderflower wine? She took him in her arms and he buried his face in her hair, long silky hair the color of wood ash, and he could rest there forever, safe and free from sin, if only it weren't for those wretched giggling girls!

They were there, of course; he was never able to escape them. Fand and Finola staring at him, covering their mouths to stifle their laughter . . . Megwen and Seelie, and Prescelli in one of those damned tight gowns with a rip in a seam, reciting that tired old joke: "Ceilyn mac Cuel? But my dear, you must know that Ceilyn is only interested in *married* ladies—his mother, the Queen, and the Virgin Mary." Like it was filthy, all of them sneering as though it were something of which he ought to be ashamed. What was really dirty . . .

"Please, Father, no! I only barely touched . . . stumbled and caught myself . . . and she too innocent to guess what I was—"

He woke, drenched in cold sweat. This would never do. He was a knight on his first quest, and must maintain absolute purity of mind as well as body. He must not, must not yield again. He rolled over, smashed his clenched fist into the wall again and again, until it was all battered and bloody. Then he gritted his teeth while the flesh painfully knit back together again. But the pain did not last nearly long enough. He curled up in a ball on the floor and waited for sunrise to deliver him.

Through a gap in one wall, Ceilyn watched a pale fugitive moon flee the crimson holocaust spreading across the eastern sky. When she slipped out of sight, he sat up and stretched his stiff and aching muscles.

Emerging from the ruin into the soft light of early morning, he led Tegillus down to the stream. Daylight, as always, had exorcised many of his demons; he felt his spirits rise. As he climbed back up the hill, a short while later, Ceilyn spotted a distant speck of blue-grey circling high overhead, against the brighter blue of the sky. Was it Sidonwy's peregrine? He thought so, because of the manner in which she flew: a dizzying series of close spirals, as if futilely resisting some mysterious force which drew her back, again and again, to Dinas Trachmyr.

When the bird finally seemed to break free of that influence, winging away in a southerly direction, Ceilyn left Tegillus grazing on the hill and followed on foot as swiftly as he could go. There was rough country in that direction: rocks and ravines, thickets and bogs, country which he could not hope to cover on horseback.

Much later, after losing the falcon and finding her again when her flight veered eastward, Ceilyn's enthusiasm for the chase began to wane. He had no idea of the miles he had traveled, how many hills and rocks he had scrambled over, bogs he had waded through, bushes and briars he had plunged into, unheeding. He only knew that he was tired, dirty, and hungry, and heartily sick of the whole business.

He blundered into yet another thicket, startling a bushy-tailed bagwyn into flight. He paused a moment to catch his breath and watch the silvery goatlike creature bound out of sight, reflecting wryly that he had about as much chance of catching the falcon as he had of taming the shy, elusive bagwyn.

For the peregrine was a haggard, taken and trained as a young adult rather than as a nestling; such birds, once lost, reverted to the wild very quickly. Even had she been an eyas, taken at an early age, she might still have refused to respond to his whistling and coaxing. Although Ceilyn had been raised, like all young men of his class, among horses, hawks, and hounds, animals never seemed to take to him. Perhaps they sensed some strangeness about him; perhaps they only responded to his own guilty fear. Whatever the reason, he found it virtually impossible to mount and control any horse save his own Tegillus, that he had hand-raised from a foal, and it had taken many months of devoted attentions and many offerings of choice tidbits saved from his own plate before he had finally won the grudging acceptance of the King's wolfhounds. As for birds: There was not a hawk or falcon at Caer Celcynnon or Caer Cadwy that could long abide his touch, no matter how ardently he wooed her. For a knight on a quest, he reflected bitterly, he seemed singularly ill-fitted for the task allotted him.

But the falcon, as far as he knew, had not yet killed and eaten. She, too, must eventually stop, eat, and rest; when she did, Ceilyn intended to be there.

Now she led him north, across acres of purple heather, through another patch of boggy ground, and finally toward a copse of oak trees. There she settled at last, high in an ancient oak, her jesses of green leather dangling tantalizingly, far beyond Ceilyn's reach. When he finally arrived at the foot of the tree, breathless, hot, and dusty, she ruffled her feathers, cocked her head, and glared at him with a dark, hostile eye.

He sat on a gnarled root and scowled back at her. He knew very well that it was no good blaming the falcon. The poor creature was obviously confused and frightened, probably under some vile enchantment perpetrated by the Queen's enemies. . . . Nevertheless, he was not the source of her troubles, and she had no business to look at him that way.

What was it, he wondered, that gave some people the ability to handle birds and beasts? Not just the ordinary ability, which he lacked, but that special talent granted only to a few? He remembered, in particular, one old man back in Gorwynnion, a falconer known throughout the north for his uncanny way with birds. The country-folk said that the bird had not been born that could refuse that old man when he called. There had even been some suspicion of witchcraft, but the man had led such an exemplary life that the talk soon died. Ceilyn had never actually met the falconer, but he believed that he had seen him once, at a distance.

Growing a bit drowsy in the dappled sunlight, he leaned back against the craggy oak, dreaming of a day long past, in the forests of Gorwynnion . . . whispering green leaves overhead, a single shaft of sunlight illuminating the clearing up ahead . . . a dissonant tinkling, as of hawkbells . . . and a ragged old man in green and scarlet patches like some fantastic figure out of a pantomime, summoning a wild owl. His shrill, oddly compelling call echoed in Ceilyn's mind; even remembered now, so many years later, it struck some deep, responsive chord.

Suddenly wide awake, Ceilyn wondered what would happen if he called the falcon as the old man had called the owl. He believed that he remembered the sound, the exact pitch and intonation, but he was not so certain that he could reproduce it.

He scrambled to his feet, determined to give it a try. He took the feathered lure he had been carrying tucked inside his shirt, and stationed himself several paces from the oak tree. He whirled the lure overhead, calling to the falcon again and again. His first attempts sounded nothing at all like the call he remembered, and only startled the peregrine into side-stepping nervously along the branch.

Then another memory came to him; he thought he could hear Teleri saying, *"There is always power to be gained by giving something its proper name."* He had only the dimmest idea what she meant by that. That wizards worked their wonders by intoning magic words and invoking names of power, everyone knew that; but Ceilyn thought that Teleri had meant something different. Like identifying the essential characteristics that made a thing what it was . . . what made a falcon a falcon, and not a sparrow, an owl, or even a goshawk.

A wizard would know that, or a falconer. Perhaps the peregrine knew, but she would never tell him. Or would she? The earth had spoken to him in Glastyn's garden—might not the falcon do so as well?

Closing his eyes, he filled his mind with the image of the

peregrine. He reached deep inside himself until he touched the old familiar wildness, but this time, instead of panicking and rejecting it, he held on to it. It was the only way, if a way existed, that he could hope to communicate with her.

What is your name, peregrine falcon? Seemingly out of nowhere (but surely he had heard the verse somewhere before?) the answer came:

> Keen-eye
> Dark-eye
> White-throat
> Speckled-breast
> Blue-wing
> Swift-my-flight
> Cleave-the-air
> Death-comes-suddenly
> Fierce is the pleasure
>   of the long, terrible plunge.

> What is my name?
> Fly-far
> Pilgrim-of-the-air
> Traveler-to-the-north
> Sickle-beak
> Talon-foot
> Hold-fast
>   Peregrine Falcon.

This time, when he opened his eyes and loosed the call, he knew that it was right.

All around him, the wood was very still and bright in the late afternoon sunlight. The peregrine fluttered up, seemed to hover for a breathless moment on the golden air . . . and then, just as gently as thistledown, the beautiful creature landed on Ceilyn's outstretched arm.

At that same time, a painful scene was taking place back at Caer Cadwy. The Queen had summoned Prescelli to her bedchamber and, amidst tears, recriminations, and excuses, told the girl that she would have to look elsewhere for employment.

In the anteroom outside, Sidonwy's other attendants had gathered, some out of sympathy, others merely for the sake of curiosity. When the door finally opened, and the tearful and defiant Prescelli stepped out, the other girls immediately surrounded her, demanding to know exactly what had happened.

"But Darling," said Seelie, when Prescelli had told her everything, "didn't you *tell* her? Didn't you say that you had no way of telling that the letter was not genuine? Didn't you say that you were just concerned for her safety, and gave the letter to the King in good faith?"

"Yes, I told her," Prescelli replied duly. "She simply did not believe me."

There was a short silence. "Well, go right ahead and say it," Prescelli hurled at them. "Why should she believe me? A liar and a thief like me? It was only a matter of time—"

"At least," Seelie said brightly, "you will already be home when I return to prepare for my wedding. You will be there on the day to wish me well. . . . That's some consolation, now, isn't it?"

Prescelli ground her teeth. "I can scarcely believe my good fortune."

"But what will you do now?" asked Finola.

Prescelli shrugged her shoulders. "I suppose that I will go upstairs and pack all my things."

Upstairs, in the room she had shared with Seelie and several other girls, Prescelli threw open her clothes chest and began sorting through her dresses and underclothing. Before long, the room was in a wild disarray.

She stopped and looked around her: at the rubbed velvets and shabby silks, the patched and mended linen shifts, and the motheaten furs. Scarcely worth the trouble, she thought, to pack up such a pitiful collection and carry it back to Ynys Carreg.

The door creaked open behind her, and Derry mac Forgoll sauntered into the room. "What are you doing here?" Prescelli demanded. "You're not allowed in these rooms!"

Derry ignored the question, closed the door, and bolted it behind him. "Been sent off, have you? But it is going to be all right, you know." He picked up one of her shifts, examined it, with evident amusement. "The Princess said that you wouldn't suffer for doing as she told you, and she is going to keep her word."

Prescelli snatched her underwear out of his hands. "And how does your precious Princess think she will convince the Queen to take me back, now that Sidonwy is already convinced that I am part of some wicked plot against her?"

"I meant that the Princess is willing to offer you a position in her own household," said Derry.

The shift fell from Prescelli's suddenly nerveless fingers, and she turned nearly as white as the linen. "Take service with—with the Princess?" she asked in horrified tones. "Oh, but I never . . ."

"Why not?" asked Derry. "Between me and God, Prescelli, you ought to be pleased! It is a damned sight better than being sent home in disgrace, and more to your advantage, just at the moment, than staying with the Queen."

"I don't see that," said Prescelli. "Oh, I admit that the Princess has everything her own way now. But the King and Queen will eventually reconcile—they always do—and where will the Princess Diaspad be then?

"Besides," she added, closing the clothes chest and sitting on the lid, "I've done one wicked thing because the Princess told me to, but I don't care to get involved in any more of her horrid schemes."

Derry laughed. "And when did you develop this delightfully moral attitude?"

"Whatever you think," Prescelli said, "I don't like to do things that hurt other people—people who have never harmed me."

"Maybe not, but you do them readily enough if you think you stand to gain something by it," said Derry.

"Only when there is no other way," she insisted, pulling out her hair pins, nervously unknotting her tangled locks. "I do have to take care of myself, you know. Nobody else ever does."

Derry deposited himself on one of the beds and smiled up at her, meltingly. "Why don't you come over here, Sweetheart, and see what I am able to do for you?"

"No thank you," said Prescelli coldly. "I would rather lie down with pigs. And that isn't my bed, supposing you are interested."

"Whose?" asked Derry, stretching out luxuriously on the fluffy eiderdown and silky sleeping furs. "Don't tell me—I can guess. Feather mattresses and all these lovely furs—who but the fair, pampered Seelie? But you, Dear, you wouldn't hesitate to take a tumble with her soon-to-be-wedded husband. Why so delicate about using her bed?''

Prescelli stared at him in silence. He certainly was a remarkably beautiful youth, and there had been a time when the sight of him lying on Seelie's bed, smiling up at her so provocatively, would have set her pulse racing. But that was before she became acquainted—intimately acquainted—with some of his more vicious habits. Now she could only wonder that she had ever been attracted to such a despicable little snake—not that going to bed with Derry had been entirely her own idea (there had been the small matter of a stolen brooch and Derry's proclivity for blackmail), still, she had been a willing victim in the beginning.

"Does she like it when you bed with other women?—the Princess, I mean.''

Derry's eyes narrowed dangerously, so that Prescelli added hastily, "I mean, I couldn't help noticing that the pair of you—well, it isn't supposed to be a secret, is it?''

"I would advise you," he said, "if you are going to serve the Princess, to start learning *not* to notice things. It will be much safer that way, believe me. You just keep your mouth shut and do exactly what she tells you to do—nothing more, nothing less.''

"Yes, but I haven't said that I will accept a position with the Princess," said Prescelli. "Supposing she actually offers me one.''

"You don't have much choice, do you? Here or on Ynys Carreg . . . If word ever gets out about your activities in that secret room of yours—''

"But the Princess promised!" Prescelli protested.

"She said: If you were a good girl and did exactly what she told you to do, no one would ever have to find out," replied Derry. "It is just that she hasn't finished telling you, yet, all that she wants you to do.''

The bells of Caer Cadwy chimed their evening call to Vespers, and the churchbells in the town below answered like an echo, as Ceilyn rode Tegillus up the hill to the castle. It had gradually dawned on him that he was returning, successful, from his very first quest. He bore the peregrine triumphantly, unhooded on his wrist. Though she had shown no disposition to fly away, he kept a firm grip on her jesses just in case.

He dismounted by the stables, handed Tegillus over to a groom, and looked around him. He spotted a grey skirt just disappearing behind one of the little half-timber cottages. Ceilyn followed, across the yard and around behind the mews, where he found Teleri waiting for him.

"You had difficulty catching her?" she asked, taking the falcon.

He felt his face grow hot under her cool grey gaze, grew suddenly acutely conscious of his dusty and disheveled condition. "Some difficulty, yes, but you said . . . That is, I had promised the Queen, so I had to bring her back."

Wordlessly, Teleri examined the tense and quivering peregrine. "Look at her leg," Ceilyn suggested. "I *felt* something there."

But Teleri had already located it: a silken bag, containing a handful of earth, what must be soil from Dinas Trachmyr. The bag had been tied with a scarlet cord, knotted nine times, then wound as many times around the falcon's left leg.

"I thought it might be something like this. The knots in the cord and the manner of the binding are responsible for the confusion everyone felt who handled the peregrine, and the bag of earth continually calls to its place of origin. A simple spell, but effective. Unfortunately, there is no way to discover who did this.

"Still," she added, handing over the falcon, "you should show all this to the King. He will draw his own conclusions—if he knows what to think at all—but at least it supports what the Queen already told him."

She glanced up at him, shyly. "It is amazing that she came to you, in such a state as this. You must possess a considerable talent for handling wild things."

And Ceilyn felt himself flushing again, this time with pleasure.

The night was clear with a thousand burning stars, but the moon remained in hiding. Ceilyn left the Queen's rooms, crossed the dark, deserted inner courtyard, circled around the Oriel Tower, and climbed a stair to the top of the walls.

A light breeze ruffled his hair, carrying the tang of the sea and a suggestion of something else. He paused and took a deep breath, trying to identify it. A soft patter of footsteps continued an instant longer, then stopped.

He turned and searched the darkness behind him. By one of the corner towers, he detected a lighter patch of grey and an unmistakable scent of herbs. He called Teleri's name, and she emerged, reluctantly, out of hiding.

"I was looking for you," he said.

She drifted a little closer. "What did the King say when you showed him the falcon?"

"As you predicted, he didn't seem to know what to think. He said he couldn't imagine why anyone would want to tamper with the Queen's peregrine."

"And there is no use telling him," said Teleri softly, "what he would rather not believe."

"And yet," said Ceilyn, "it seems obvious. Who else stands to gain so much if the breach with Rhianedd widens?"

"And who else," said Teleri, "came to Caer Cadwy armed with so much magic?"

Ceilyn nodded. "She is a witch, of course. But how could I tell him that? It's not the kind of thing that a man wants to believe about his own sister—and coming from me . . . he would put it all down to superstition and prejudice, Celcynnon on another witch-hunt. But you," he said, "you're Glastyn's chosen successor. If you told the King—"

Teleri took a step backward. "Oh no, I couldn't! I am as vulnerable as you. If she chose to counter my accusation with one of her own, it would be my word against hers—and who do you think the King would believe?"

They stared at each other in helpless silence.

"Still," said Ceilyn, "if you can't say anything, there must be something you could do to prevent her from causing any future trouble. You have magic of your own. You could—"

"Oh no." Teleri shook her head again. "There is very little that I could do. Just because I tried to help you before, because I tried to help the Queen today, you mustn't get the idea that I can or will set other things right here. It's not that I don't want to . . . but I'm not much of a sorceress, not really."

She turned to go, but he stepped in front of her, blocking her way. "But you've been studying magic for so many years. I don't understand—"

"No," she said, "you don't. The things I have been studying . . . the movements of the stars, the secret names of plants and animals, the Three Parts of Wisdom—of Body, Soul, and Spirit

. . . they are not worth much, so long as I lack the skill to use them properly. And I was just beginning the practical part of my education—just a few simple spells—when Glastyn went away. I've spent eight years studying magic—one more year than it takes to make a Wizard—but I dare not use any of it.

"It is as if . . . as if you had been watching other men use weapons during all the years you've been here, but never picked up a sword yourself. The control isn't there, the mental and physical reflexes, the trained responses. Only what I have learned is so much more dangerous—you could hardly imagine the dangers."

Ceilyn began helpfully. "When we were talking about my—my problem, you said—"

"That was different."

"Well, you know more about these things than I do. But I don't really see that it is. And it was good advice that you gave me."

"So good that you are willing to return it unused?" she asked. She wandered over to the parapet, stared out through one of the crenellations, past the crumbling ruins, across the gently rolling hills of Camboglanna. "Sometimes," she said softly, "I wish I were in Coill Dorcha with Glastyn . . . turned into a tree, or whatever it was that actually became of him."

Ceilyn joined her by the battlements. He leaned one elbow atop the nearest merlon, looked down at her a little wistfully. All shadow and silver in the starlight, she seemed very distant, very still. He had a sudden irrational urge to touch her, to hold on to her, before she retreated any further.

"There are plenty of trees in Coill Dorcha already—believe me, I have been there," he said. "And if Glastyn left you here instead of taking you with him, he must have had a reason."

She said absently, "He did have some idea of my taking his place as Court Wizard . . . but it just didn't happen that way."

"But he left you here. He must have expected something of you. Glastyn always had a reason," he insisted.

She drifted past him, toward the stairs. Growing exasperated, Ceilyn followed and reached out to stop her.

She stared, disbelievingly, at his hand on her arm. She was accustomed, as a physician, to touching when the need arose, but not at all accustomed to being touched.

"If you want to know what I think," he said angrily, "I think you are afraid to find out what you might be able to do."

He had been spinning fancies all evening, pleasant fantasies about quests and adventures and deeds of daring, but his plans would all be spoiled if Teleri refused to play the part he had assigned to her.

She tried to pull away, but he only tightened his grip. "There is nothing to find out," she insisted. "Making good-luck charms and helping Brother Gildas when he needs another pair of hands. Really, that is all that I am good for."

"Helping Brother Gildas," he said disdainfully. "And yet, you're a doctor yourself. I've seen you at work, you know: patching up someone after a tournament, bandaging a turnspit's hand when he burned it. You're a skilled physician in your own right, yet you continue to work in Gildas's shadow."

"In the shadows," she said tremulously, "that is where I feel the safest."

"Safe from what?" he asked. "I don't believe that it is magic you are afraid of—just everything else under the sun."

"Perhaps I am. But if I am—why should it matter to you?" She trembled violently, looked ready to burst into tears.

"I am sorry," he said, releasing her. "I didn't mean to frighten you. And it is true—I have no right to tell you what you ought to do."

"No," she said. "I do understand. You are concerned for the Queen. And I would help if I could. But you saw yesterday, there was nothing much I could do."

"God knows," said Ceilyn, "there would be few knights at Caer Cadwy if every man who failed to carry away the prize at his maiden tournament retired afterward in despair. And it seems to me that you acquitted yourself very well. It is true that we've failed to convince the King there is a plot against the Queen, but he's not so certain that Sidonwy meant to run off with Elidyr, either.

"The only problem is," he continued, as they moved to the top of the stairs and began to descend, "the Princess is not finished yet. No, I don't believe that the Queen is in any physical danger; it is enough for the Princess to keep them apart, to prevent Sidonwy from influencing the King on her brothers' behalf. But if the Queen died, or if there were a divorce, all Diaspad's plots could come to nothing. The King might remarry—his council would insist he remarry—and then there might be children."

They cut across Sidonwy's heraldic garden, walking among the sculptured lions, unicorns, and dragons. "But the Princess will go to any lengths to keep things exactly as they are now, no matter who suffers in the process, no matter what harm she causes elsewhere. And you are a wizard—or the next thing to it. You are supposed to value harmony, balance, and proportion."

"My power lies in seeing and foreseeing," she protested, stopping beneath one of the huge topiary lions. "I have no power to *act* effectively."

"Perhaps not, acting all on your own," he admitted. "But I could be of use to you. I am close to the Queen, I can go places, see and hear things, speak my mind and be heard where you cannot. And I would gladly serve you." Impulsively, he knelt at her feet. To any onlooker, watching from a distance, he might have appeared to be at the mercy of the springing beast above him. "You have only to command me—and I would swear any oath that you like."

She did not know whether to laugh or to cry, so astonished was she by his offer, so embarrassed by his manner of presenting it. "You are sworn to the Queen," she said weakly.

"I don't see any conflict. I've also sworn fealty to the King and pledged myself to the Crown and Kingdom of Celydonn. It's all the same, isn't it? Glastyn chose you for that same purpose. And working together, we could do great things."

Still, Teleri hesitated. He began to feel foolish, kneeling there in the dirt. To say nothing of the blow she had dealt his pride. He knew that he was not well-liked, but he also knew how much grudging respect he had won for himself; there wasn't a lady at Caer Cadwy, no matter what she might feel for him personally, who would not be gratified to have Ceilyn mac Cuel kneeling at her feet. No lady, that is, but this one.

"An oath can be a dangerous thing," she said. "I don't want to be responsible for yours."

"Very well," Ceilyn sighed, getting to his feet as gracefully as possible. "A promise—a simple promise, not a sacred oath—to help one another at need?"

"Yes," she said, because she could not think of another way to satisfy him. "If that is what you really want. And naturally, I will do whatever I can to aid the Queen.

"But don't expect too much of me," she added wistfully, "or you will surely be disappointed."

And Siawn died, not knowing that he was the last, and therefore named no man to succeed him.

And Dechtire, the wife of Sinnoch, being a widow bereft of all her kin, feared for the life of her unborn child. She went into the forest Coill Dorcha and was never seen again. Whether she and her child died soon after, or whether they prospered there among the outlaws, whether her son grew to manhood and fathered children of his own, no man can truly say.

And while the people continued to wonder what fate had befallen Dechtire and her child, the Lords of Rhianedd and Gorwynnion and Tir Gwyngelli each claimed Mother-Right and contended for the Crown. Their strife continued for generations.

Then out of the forest came Glastyn, when a hundred years had passed, bringing with him the boy he called Sinnoch's heir.

From The Great Book of St. Cybi

11.

Of Gold as Well as Baser Metals

Life at Caer Cadwy maintained a feverish pace. The rackety pursuit of pleasure, instigated by the Princess Diaspad, showed no signs of abating, and the new "Mochdreffian" fashions could be seen everywhere, though the mode sometimes changed from day to day, and even from hour to hour. Though Sidonwy finally sent Elidyr away and adopted a more sedate style of living for herself and her household, she inspired but few to follow her example. The castle was like a giant clock which someone had wound so tightly that it no longer kept the proper time.

On the first day of April, the King summoned his knights together in council. As custom dictated that Cynwas be the last to arrive, the Knights of the Order of the Lion of St. March gathered in the new council chamber well before the appointed hour. Due to a lack of seating, Ceilyn mac Cuel, Fergos fab Neol, and Iaen Og, the junior knights present, remained standing. Rather than send for another bench, Ceilyn stood with his back to a wall, arms folded across his chest, glaring at those men whose dress and politics offended him. An intricately dagged sleeve here, and a bejeweled belt there, a pair of slippers with toes elongated to preposterous lengths, a pourpoint in the newly popular shades of mulberry, tangerine, and crimson—all revealed a Mochdreffi influence.

Ceilyn, of course, eschewed these affectations; no slashes or patches or wildly clashing colors for him. He always dressed well—for anything else would be an insult to the Queen—but he never dressed extravagantly. He appeared today in his own colors: honest, serviceable Celcynnon green and gold.

Forced, by Ceilyn's example, to stand, Iaen and Fergos had stationed themselves by the door, and so were the first to hear Cynwas's approaching footsteps. A moment later, the King entered the room, and all who had been seated rose respectfully to their feet. Cynwas took his place at the head of the long oak table that ran the length of the room, and bade the others to be seated as well.

Without any preliminary ceremony, he plunged directly into the business of the council. "We are here to discuss candidates for the Order of the Lion of St. March, to be knighted at Easter. These are the names I would like you to consider." He handed a roll of parchment to Manogan.

The Marshall unfurled the scroll, quirked a questioning eyebrow when he read the names, but passed the list on without comment. Not so Ysgafn, who almost dropped the scroll in his surprise.

"Daire Ruadh mac Forgoll . . . and Morc, his brother!" the Constable exploded. "Who on earth was it that recommended these two?"

"These are my personal candidates," the King replied coldly.

An astonished and embarrassed silence followed this announcement, to be broken at last by Dillus. Five years ago—in what he later described as a moment of sheer and unmitigated stupidity—the Seneschal had accepted Morc as his squire-of-the-body. "If it please you, Lord, why was I not consulted before Morc's name was submitted?"

"I am consulting you now, Dillus," said the King testily. "Am I to understand that you have some objection?''

Dillus took a moment to reply, no doubt framing a suitably diplomatic response. ''Morc's progress . . . has not been altogether what it ought to be. It is my opinion that he is not entirely ready to be knighted.''

''The man is twenty-two years of age,'' said Cynwas, growing visibly more impatient. ''If you do not deem him worthy yet, when do you anticipate that he will be?''

Dillus shifted uncomfortably in his chair, fidgeted with the silver buttons on his pourpoint. He valued his post at court and was reluctant to jeopardize it, but he was a decent man, uncomfortable compromising his principles. ''Ah well, that's just it. I don't know that he will ever be ready, more is the pity.''

The King's irritation became even more pronounced. ''What, then, are we to do with him? We can scarcely expect him to spend the rest of his days in his present capacity—a young man of his birth and connections. What would you have me tell my s—his father and all his relations?''

''Ah well,'' said Dillus weakly, ''if his father is so eager to see Morc knighted, well, being a landed lord, Forgoll could do it himself. Or send Morc to Conchobar in Ildathach to have it done. They set great store by the Order of the Branch, up in Draighen. But as for admitting Morc to *our* order, I don't think that he is up to our standards.''

''Thank you,'' said the King, with icy formality. ''I will give your words due weight in making my final decision.'' He transferred his frigid grey stare to Rhodri fab Elifri. ''I suppose I should ask you . . . Is there anything you would like to say concerning Daire?''

Now it was Rhodri's turn to squirm in his chair. ''Derry does well when he makes the effort, but that isn't so often as it should be. And he is just a bit young, right now, though perhaps in a few more months . . .''

''I see,'' said the King. ''Yet younger men have been knighted— and over strong objections from this council—and afterward proved themselves more than worthy to sit here.'' His eyes rested, for a moment, on Ceilyn.

Ceilyn, who had so far said nothing at all, but had listened to everything with deep dismay.

"Ceilyn mac Cuel," said the King, "you usually have some-thing to say about each candidate. Have you nothing to say about these?"

Ceilyn shook his head. It was true that Morc was a boor and a bully, and had constantly to be reprimanded for mishandling serving girls, also true that Derry (not content with his own wickedness) had, by bragging and teasing and dropping sly hints, led many of the younger boys into vice—but the King already knew these things, and if he chose to ignore them, there was absolutely nothing to be gained by reminding him. "No, Lord," Ceilyn said quietly. "I don't think that I have."

Cynwas was as surprised as he was gratified. "Am I to understand that you *approve* my candidates?"

"No," said Ceilyn stiffly. "Only that I have nothing to add to the objections which have already been raised."

Surprisingly, the King did not take offense. For just an instant—looking at this boy who was everything that he had once hoped all his knights would be, and had long since discovered that they could not be—the King's resolve waivered. In Ceilyn's face, as in a mirror, Cynwas saw all of his own disappointments, all the compromises and disillusionments that had made him the man he was today: vain, sentimental, capricious, selfish and generous by turns, always longing to believe the best of a man, all too ready to suspect the worst.

He slumped down in his chair, scowled at Manogan and Ysgafn, Scilti, Dillus, Dianach, Rhodri, and the rest—the friends of his boyhood, the companions of his adventurous youth. On every face, he saw vanity, cupidity, and dissipation. Was there any man here who had lived up to his early promise, any man worthy to prate of standards, the sacred obligations of knighthood?

And he had already promised his step-sister that Morc and Derry would be knighted at Easter. He closed his eyes wearily. "We will proceed with the knightings as I had originally planned."

He was already rising, when Dianach fab Tallwch spoke up. "Lord, there is one name missing from the list. We agreed at Christmas that my squire Fflergant—"

"As to that," said the King, returning to his seat, "I have since changed my mind. I have come to entertain serious doubts about that young man's character."

"I don't quite see—" Dianach began.

"Can you deny," Cynwas interrupted him again, "that the boy is a notorious libertine?"

This charge was so unexpected and so grossly out of proportion that Dianach was taken by surprise. "A notorious—I'll not deny that the lad is popular with the ladies," he said. "But a libertine?"

It was true that any knight or candidate for knighthood was expected to deal honorably with all women, and the squires, during their time of service, were strictly enjoined to maintain a respectful distance—but that rule, of all rules, was the most laxly enforced. Had it not been so, there could have been no question of knighting either Morc or Derry.

"You know how boys will talk," Dianach began again. "It is altogether likely that Fflergant's exploits have been exaggerated . . . romanticized, you might say, by the other lads. Well, I'm not saying that there haven't been women, but that is to be expected with a good-looking boy like Fflergant. To say nothing of his birth and the fact that he will one day be as rich as . . ." Here Dianach paused, for the customary superlative was "as rich as the Lord of Gwyngelli." "Well, he *will* be Lord of Gwyngelli. Naturally, the women encourage him. But even at that—"

"Are you recommending that special consideration be given him on account of his birth?" Cynwas asked disapprovingly—just as though he had not recently made a similar suggestion on Morc's behalf. "If he is to be knighted for no better reason than that, I think that *he* might settle for a lesser order at his father's gift."

But Dianach was not yet ready to admit defeat. "Supposing I spoke to the lad, and he promised to mend his ways between now and . . . say, Midsummer. . . . Might he not be knighted then?"

"No," said the King. "I am inclined to think not." Purely as a formality, he added, "Will any other speak in Fflergant fab Maelgwyn's favor?"

All this time, the Earl Marshall had held his tongue. As Fflergant's uncle, and for the sake of fairness, he refrained from speaking in the boy's defense. But this was too much; he opened his mouth, was about to speak, when Ceilyn surprised them all by saying quietly, "I wish to speak for Fflergant."

Everyone turned to stare at him. In the two years that Ceilyn had been attending these councils, he had never been known to speak in *favor* of any candidate.

"In the course of my duties," he went on, "I've had ample opportunity to observe Fflergant. He is strong and he is quick, one of our finest young fighters. I have never seen him fail in honor or chivalry, and his generosity and his kindness can be attested to by all the younger boys and all the servants." He paused, began again. "And whatever amorous adventures Fflergant may have had in the past, I never heard yet that any woman took harm from him, or that he bragged or spread tales of his conquests afterward, or that . . ."

But the King was not listening, and Fflergant's sexual escapades —real or imagined—did not really interest him. He still believed that Fflergant had helped his grandfather to cheat at "Tables" and irrationally blamed the boy for all the trouble that had followed.

"This council is closed," he said, with such awful finality that no one had the courage to protest. Once he had taken his leave, however, everyone started to talk at once.

"Why didn't you speak out when Derry was named?" Fergos hissed in Ceilyn's ear. "It's not so long ago that you and I were both squires and forced to spend more time with Derry than either of us liked. You know what Derry is—why didn't you tell the King?"

"Why didn't you?" Ceilyn retorted.

Fergos shrugged. "Iaen and I are the youngest here—at least in point of seniority. I didn't think that he would listen."

"He was not particularly interested in my opinions, either—as you just witnessed," said Ceilyn bleakly. He started toward the door and Fergos trailed behind him.

"Poor Fflergant," said Fergos, as they passed through the door and walked down a corridor. "He will be sick about this for certain. One look at Dianach's face will tell him exactly what happened. Still, it was generous of you to speak up on his behalf."

"I don't know what you mean," Ceilyn replied coldly. "If I didn't think that he was worthy, I would never have said so."

Fergos only laughed, not in the least offended by Ceilyn's manner. "Now, don't get up on your high horse with me! I would be the last to accuse you of any favoritism. I only meant to say that Fflergant and Tryffin both give you about as much impudence as they can get by with. Another man might bear a grudge."

Ceilyn rarely explained himself to the other men or boys, but he was not averse to company right now, and welcomed any distraction to take his mind off that travesty of a Knight's Council. Besides, he rather liked Fergos, who was the closest thing to a friend among the other knights that Ceilyn possessed. He decided to make an exception.

"Fflergant and Tryffin have an idea that I single them out for some special persecution."

"You don't think that you are . . . a little harder on them than you are on any of the other lads?" Fergos asked, as Ceilyn opened another door and the two of them stepped out on the wall walk.

"Quite possibly I am," said Ceilyn. "I also keep a sharp eye on Gofan, and sometimes on Garanwyn, too. Not because I don't think they are worth much—quite the contrary. Of all the boys here, I think that Garanwyn, Gofan, Fflergant, and Tryffin are the most promising. And not just because they all happen to be kinsmen of mine—though that certainly makes me more eager to see them do their best.

"The fact is," Ceilyn continued, "despite what the King professes, despite their father's orders to the contrary, Fflergant and his brother do, sometimes, receive special treatment here, and not the sort they are accustomed to at home. It is all one big happy family in Tir Gwyngelli, and the sons of the Lord are everyone's fair-haired boys—but it goes both ways, and a prince of Gwyngelli never forgets his obligations to his people, not ever. The kind of attention they get here is considerably less wholesome." He glanced over his shoulder. "I don't know how much you know about the Gwyngellach."

Fergos shrugged. "Not very much. I suppose Tryffin and Fflergant are fair examples. You can't reckon by their Uncle Manogan—he's been here twenty years or more."

"They are an innocent people, really," said Ceilyn, as the two young knights entered the tower which housed the armory. "Very generous, very emotional, and amazingly fond of children—though they don't steal babies, as some folk say, and they stopped painting themselves blue several generations back.

"Likely it surprises you," he added, as they entered the room where the armor and the practice weapons were kept, "to hear my father's son speak in favor of the 'ungodly' Gwyngellach. But maybe you are forgetting who my mother is."

"Yes, of course," said Fergos. "Maelgwyn's cousin, isn't she?"

"It isn't true that you can't believe a word the Gwyngellach tell you," Ceilyn went on, stripping off his outer garments, donning the padded coat he wore under his armor. "Oh, they are great ones for the tall tale, and they will tell terrific lies in order to spare your feelings, but they won't lie for profit, or break their oaths, or bear false witness—that would be dishonorable. They have few arts and crafts, but excel at those they care to practice. You have seen examples of their metalwork, of course?"

"Oh yes," said Fergos, helping Ceilyn to slip into his coat of chainmail. "I've seen it. Tryffin and Fflergant were both weighted down with it—arm-rings and pectorals and I-don't-know-what—when they first arrived here. Really marvelous, though a mite old-fashioned for my tastes."

"Of course the raw material is abundant in Tir Gwyngelli," Ceilyn continued. "Even the peasants wear silver ornaments, so they say, and the mines yield ore of amazing purity, as well as fabulous gems. But that is not the end of it. They know secret processes by which they refine their silver and gold to an almost alchemical purity, and there are no metalsmiths anywhere to rival the goldsmiths of Gwyngelli. An arm-ring or a wrist-guard of Gwyngelli gold is worth three times a similar piece made elsewhere."

"But what, if I may ask," said Fergos, as he began to arm himself, "has all this to do with Fflergant and Tryffin?"

"It seems to me," said Ceilyn, "that not all the gold in Gwyngelli is to be found in the mines. Fflergant and his brother were very carefully raised according to the traditions of their own people, and they are fine examples of everything the Gwyngellach believe in, but then Maelgwyn sent them here to broaden their education." Ceilyn girded on his swordbelt, hitched up his mail, so that the belt took more of the weight.

"They have learned a great deal since they came here. Grown more civilized, by Camboglannach standards, for they have trimmed their hair and put aside most of their old-fashioned jewelry, along with their goatskin boots, acquired a good deal of court polish—no harm in any of that. But there are other things they might learn at Caer Cadwy: things like envy and discontent, and lying for gain, and the misuse of power and position."

"And you don't want to see their natural innocence spoiled . . .

their savage purity," said Fergos, the light beginning to dawn.

"That sounds condescending the way you say it," Ceilyn said, as he led the way down to the practice yard. "I don't think that I mean it that way. But don't you see—being half Gwyngellach myself, I know how to recognize real Gwyngelli gold when I see it, and I'll not stand by silently and watch while it is debased."

"So it is all for their own good, your interest in them," said Fergos, adjusting the straps on his shield. "But you are willing to let them assume the worst."

"What could I say?" Ceilyn asked. "Do you think they would welcome my interest—or curse my presumption? I never asked to be knighted ahead of the rest of you, to be put in charge of boys very nearly my own age, but everyone seems to think I arranged it that way."

"There is that," Fergos admitted. "But perhaps if you tried to explain how you feel—at least told them what really happened at the council . . . Otherwise, they will blame you for what happened today, Fflergant and his brother both. They will be certain that you spoke against him."

"They will believe what they choose to believe," said Ceilyn, never loath to martyr himself. "And the proceedings of the council are secret, as you very well know. I will not violate that secrecy to secure any man's favor."

Fergos drew his blunted practice sword. "Between me and God," he said, shaking his head, half amused, half admiring, "you really are a fanatic, Ceilyn mac Cuel!"

"Likely I am," said Ceilyn, as he drew out his own sword. "Yes, very likely I am."

. . . and after the Queen died, Anwas looked about him for a new love, and his eye fell on Morfudd, the wife of Erim. And Erim was an old man, and ailing.

And when Erim died, Anwas pledged himself to the widow. But he would not make Morfudd his wife until after she was delivered

*of Erim's child. And Morfudd professed to be satisfied, saying
secretly to her friends, "When the child is born, if it should be a
man child, then surely the King will acknowledge him."*

*And Morfudd was brought to bed and the child was born, and
mother and child prospered. But Morfudd, on being informed that
the babe was a lusty girl, and not a boy as she had hoped, gave such
a cry* (diaspad) *of anguish that the doctors and midwives came
running, convinced that she was in mortal agony.*

From The Life of Anwas *(attributed to Glastyn)*

Upstairs, in Diaspad's luxurious bedchamber, the two successful
candidates for knighthood, all unaware of the accolades about to
descend on them, were occupied, each in his own characteristic
fashion.

Morc slept on a tygerskin rug by the fireplace, all in an untidy
heap, an overturned flagon and an empty pewter goblet at his side
testifying to the fact that he was dead drunk as well as sound asleep.
Derry, on the other hand, was sulking, and sulking was one of the
things he did best. He had an idea that it made him irresistibly
attractive to women, but in this he was badly mistaken. Nor was the
Princess Diaspad like the other women with whom he had amused
himself in the past, the tavern girls and the little castle drudges. His
scowls did not frighten her into compliance, his sulks did not
inspire her to coax him into a better humor. Entirely unmoved, she
sat in her silver chair, graciously permitting Prescelli to brush and
arrange her luxuriant auburn hair.

Prescelli's new duties were usually of a humbler sort: mending
linens, emptying chamber pots, sweeping out the ashes, while the
little hunchback Brangwengwen and the other dwarf women dressed
Diaspad and assisted her toilet. Naturally, Prescelli resented this
state of affairs, but she knew better than to voice any objections. So
she held her tongue, but she gained some small satisfaction by
surreptitiously pinching the little hunchback black and blue whenever she came within reach.

Today, however, being unexpectedly promoted, Prescelli took special care over her work, hoping that the Princess would be pleased, and allow her to perform similar tasks in the future. She finished plaiting the Princess's hair, and pinned the braids in two thick coils over the ears. She reached for the box containing Diaspad's golden cauls—but the Princess put out a hand to stop her. "Not that box. Bring me the casket bound with the copper bands."

Prescelli mutely obeyed. Diaspad opened the little wooden coffer, drew out a length of braided silk embroidered with pearls and gold thread and tiny glinting gemstones. "This is for you, my dear."

"For me?" Prescelli touched the green silk tentatively. Never had she seen anything more beautiful or something she wanted more—so naturally she knew it could not really be meant for her.

Diaspad laughed musically. "Can't you guess what it is?"

"A love charm?" Prescelli breathed. "Oh, Lady, is it a love charm?"

"I promised you one, did I not?"

"Yes, oh yes, but that was weeks ago. I thought you had changed your mind."

The door opened and Brangwengwen entered the room, bearing a covered tray. As the Princess lifted the cover and sniffed at the contents, Prescelli winced. She did not like to watch Diaspad eat—the way that she always played with her food first, then picked it apart, piece by piece, before she took a single bite, and then, when she did eat, the sound of all those tiny bones crunching between her teeth made Prescelli absolutely queasy.

"You do understand," Diaspad said, "the power of a so-called love charm is somewhat limited. Oh, young Iaen will be obsessed with you, unable to eat, rest, or sleep until he secures your favors. But you are not to expect . . . well, I suppose the best word is tenderness. Passion, yes. Romance, of the hair-tearing, breast-beating sort, possibly. But no tenderness. There are some things, you see, that cannot be forced.

"You will need a lock of Iaen's hair," she added, placing the silken girdle in Prescelli's shaking hand. "When you have that, bring it to me, and I will show you what you must do."

"A lock of hair?" Prescelli experienced something vaguely

resembling a twinge of conscience. "Oh, but that—that sounds rather like—"

"Witchcraft? Black Magic?" Diaspad picked up a particularly tempting morsel and dangled it by the tail. "And your own pitiful attempts to snare Iaen for yourself . . . what were those, if not Witchcraft?"

"Well," said Prescelli uncertainly, "I don't think that they were, not really. I daresay I would be in trouble if word ever got out, because, lacking the proper training, I was meddling in things I ought to have left alone, but I never used hair, or bones, or blood . . . or called on spirits. . . . No, I don't think it was Witchcraft, properly speaking."

Diaspad reached out as if to take the braided silk back. "Yes, of course—you are as innocent as a babe and wouldn't want to sully that innocence with any such contrivance as this."

But Prescelli was unable to give the beautiful thing back. "I didn't say that," she protested, clutching the length of silk to her bosom. "I do want it, I really do. It was only for a moment, when I thought . . ."

The Princess graciously permitted her to keep the girdle. "There is just one thing," she said. "You may keep the charm and use it just as often as you please—but Iaen Og is only yours until June. He must leave for Ynys Carreg in time for the wedding, and he must marry your sister exactly as planned."

Prescelli could not suppress a cry of protest. "But why? I mean . . . why should you care who Iaen fab Iaen marries?"

"I don't," said the Princess. "But your people and Iaen's certainly do. A little gossip, a breath of scandal, that we can easily handle. But a broken alliance between two families would cause too many questions to be asked, and by people brighter than your Iaen.

"We don't need that sort of trouble. No, you don't need that sort of trouble, for I'll not deceive you: If questions are asked, I shall deny that the girdle came from me."

Prescelli held back her tears of disappointment. "Yes, I see," she said softly. "Until June, then. I will have to be content with that."

It is in the Alembic—our Castle of Glass—that the real work is accomplished, and fire and water truly united. For as it is in the Great World, that nothing of value can be accomplished without suffering and hardship, so it is in the Little World, and the Alchemist cannot complete the Work except with great difficulty and through the exercise of great patience. And so it is with the union of the Male and Female principles.

From a letter from the mage Atlendor, to his pupils at Findias

12.

An Exchange of Confidences

Within the castle upon Brynn Caer Cadwy there were many gates: gates between gardens, tilt-yards, and courts; gates between the inhabited parts of the castle and the ruins; gates of heavy oak, of copper and bronze, and gates of delicate wrought-iron lacework. There were gates standing perpetually open, gates that opened only at the proper password, and gates that remained permanently shut, the keys to unlock them lost, the bolts securing them rusted into place. But in all that vast rambling pile, only three gates connected Caer Cadwy to the world outside.

One of these was the Main Gate, situated at the top of the long dusty road winding up the northeast face of the hill, through which most visitors to the castle passed. The South Tower provided access, by means of a broad stone staircase, to the town below. And lastly, down in the western ruins, there was a sally port, seldom used and rarely remembered, that led, by means of a crooked, treacherous path, down to the beach and the glass-grey waters of the bay.

But the two great gatehouses provided more than ingress and egress. That which housed the Main Gate—a formidable structure with two guardtowers, a portcullis, murder holes, and every means of repelling invaders—also served as a barracks for the guards; and the South Tower currently housed those officers of the court whose previous rooms in the Keep or above the Hall were presently undergoing renovation. Among these, and the most recently evicted, was Manogan fab Menai, who spent the Monday after Easter moving his possessions from his old chambers to a suite of pleasant rooms near the top of the tower.

Naturally, the Marshall did not perform the physical labor himself. For that, he called on the servants and a troop of squires and pages. Among these were Garanwyn and Fflergant.

Now, on any other day, or under happier circumstances, a healthy, active boy like Fflergant might have welcomed this break in his daily routine, and would have been perfectly content manhandling chests and footstools, tables, benches, rolled-up tapestries and the like, up the spiral staircase all the day long. But it happened that Fflergant was in a vile mood this morning, and nothing could please him.

The younger boys made a point of avoiding him—all, that is, but Garanwyn, who felt that Fflergant had a perfect right to be moody on that particular morning, and was therefore disposed to listen patiently while his friend aired his wrongs.

"Too many steps," Fflergant kept muttering, as they climbed the stairs one last time, balancing a pile of rugs, featherbeds, and purple draperies. "A fine view, he said, but mark my words: He will tire of it soon. A man his age—forty if he is a day—climbing stairs like he was a damned mountain goat!"

"Well, I think it is a very nice set of rooms, and the Marshall ought to be perfectly happy here," said Garanwyn soothingly. "And it is hardly as if your uncle were feeble!"

"It's true," Fflergant grudgingly admitted, as they negotiated a final turn in the staircase and achieved the landing just outside Manogan's door. "I only hope that I am as fit in twenty years' time. Oh, all right!" he added, pushing open the door and letting down his end of the load in the middle of the antechamber. "I know that I am behaving like a pig! But I just—"

"I know what it is, and you can go ahead and *be* a pig, if it makes you feel better," Garanwyn offered cordially. Yesterday had been Easter and the knighting ceremony. *"It's not being passed over that hurts—at least not so much,''* Fflergant had said, when the names were announced a fortnight ago. *"There are many more knighted at twenty than there are at nineteen, and there's no shame in that. But to be passed over in favor of Derry mac Forgoll!''* Garanwyn reckoned it would take a day or two for Fflergant's customary high spirits to be restored to him.

"Yes, the rooms are well enough," Fflergant admitted, looking around him, beginning to feel ashamed of his ill-nature in the face of Garanwyn's patient good-will. He pulled open a pair of wooden shutters and leaned out the window. "As for the view . . . Well, will you kindly look at that! The standards of knighthood are coming down indeed, when even the great Ceilyn mac Cuel is no longer above dallying with mere serving girls!"

"Look where?" said Garanwyn, joining his cousin on the broad window sill. "What on earth are you talking about?"

"Over there," said Fflergant, gesturing in the general direction of Sidonwy's garden. "Isn't that your cousin Ceilyn talking to the little lass in the grey gown? Right under the Queen's window, too, for God and all the world to see—some people have no respect for the proprieties! And this isn't the first time I've seen the pair of them together, either."

"They are just talking," said Garanwyn. "It is possible for a man and a girl just to be talking, I think. No harm in talking to a girl. Besides," he added, taking another look, "that's not one of the serving girls, is it? That's Glastyn's Teleri."

"Good God! I believe you are right," exclaimed Fflergant, looking again in surprise. "I had forgotten that child was still among us."

"She's not a child," said Garanwyn thoughtfully. "She is years older than I am . . . more your age or Tryffin's. At least, she used to be. I suppose there is no telling about these things where wizards are concerned. But you say that you've seen them together before?"

"Once or twice," said Fflergant, as the humorous side of this unlikely friendship began to dawn on him. "And I always thought our Ceilyn so particular in his choice of friends." He laughed to see Garanwyn frown. "Holy Mother of God! You do think there is something between them, don't you?"

"Not what you are obviously thinking," Garanwyn said. "Rather the opposite. It just occurred to me that it would be just like

Ceilyn, when he finally decided to take some interest in a girl, to choose the most untouchable maiden he could find."

Down below, in the shade of a boxwood hedge where she and Ceilyn had stopped to talk, Teleri chanced to look up, just in time to meet Fflergant's curious gaze across the courtyard. Ceilyn saw the change and the stillness creep over her.

"What is it?"

"We are being watched," she said softly.

Ceilyn looked where she looked, glared up at Fflergant and Garanwyn, and stepped in front of Teleri, shielding her from their eyes. "I'll have to find more for them to do—they've nothing better to do with their time than sit there gawking!"

Yet it came to him that he ought not to be seen too often in her company. His first thought was a generous concern that he might inadvertently sully Teleri's name by appearing too attentive; the second—of which he was immediately ashamed—was that some taint of magic might attach to him. He went first hot then cold with embarrassment, looked away so that she would not guess what he was thinking, then realized that in doing so he had betrayed himself.

Teleri said nothing, only bent down to pick up the basket at her feet.

"I'll take that," he said roughly. Then, remembering his manners: "If I may."

He accompanied her across the yard, cursing himself, his awkwardness, and his damned transparent emotions. Yet perhaps Teleri guessed less than he feared. For when they came to the garden gate and he handed over her basket, she invited him in. Against his better judgment, he accepted her invitation.

Stepping through the gateway, Ceilyn stepped into summer. The garden was a riot of greenery, ranging from the pale silver- and grey-greens of chamomile and catnip to the dark glossy green of wild rose. Mullein, fennel, and purple foxglove already stood as high as Ceilyn's shoulder, and the roses, both red and white, were in full bloom. The statue in the pond, which was not—as Ceilyn had originally supposed—a loathsome monster, but a woman of heart-breaking beauty, had exchanged her winter mantle of snow for one of windblown rose petals.

Was it Ceilyn's imagination, or could he really hear the grass growing and the roots burrowing downward in their ceaseless quest for water? He could never decide how much was real here, how much skillful illusion. Even the air seemed different beyond the garden gate: not only scented by the fennel and the mint, but clearer and brighter. He felt a little dizzy whenever he took a deep breath.

"It changes," he said wonderingly, "every time that I come here."

"It changes," Teleri said matter-of-factly, "every hour and every day. As many times as I've seen her, she never shows me the same face twice."

Ceilyn handed over the basket, wondering whether she meant the garden or the statue. At that same moment, a long green tendril of ivy snaked down the wall and wrapped Teleri in a close, possessive embrace.

Very carefully, to avoid actually touching her, Ceilyn disentangled her. Yet when the vine finally released its grip, neither Ceilyn nor Teleri made any immediate attempt to move apart—for one sweet, dizzying moment, they felt passing between them the same silent sympathy they had shared here before. Then Teleri stepped out of the circle of his arms; the piercing sweetness faded, and was gone.

Teleri knelt down amidst the spiky catnip, drew a little bronze knife out of her belt, and set to work at once, seeming to forget Ceilyn's presence altogether. He was growing accustomed to her strange habits, her forgetfulness and the way that her thoughts wandered. Though he did not understand why she sometimes had difficulty focusing her attention on him for any length of time, he had learned that her periods of inattention passed swiftly, too.

Ceilyn watched her now, completely absorbed in her work, cutting out the old woody catnip in order to make room for new growth. He wondered what went on in her mind, what thoughts ebbed and flowed there like waves breaking on the shore. There were so many things he wanted to ask her—where she had lived and what she had been before Glastyn made her his apprentice. A foundling in the forest, like the late King Anwas? No, she had said something once about Ynys Aderyn, and that rocky little island had no forests. Perhaps Glastyn had found her, a baby in a basket, washed up on the beach like a piece of flotsam or jetsam. That seemed appropriate, somehow, and she never said anything about her family.

He sat down on the ground to watch her work. "Where do you go to when you disappear?" he asked suddenly. "I mean . . . I know that you don't go anywhere, really. I can usually tell when you are near by the sound of your breathing or the scent of herbs, and once I've located you, I can see you clearly enough. But where do you go . . . in your mind . . . when you want to hide?"

"It isn't always the same place," she said, sitting back on her heels. Her attention had come back to him naturally, just as he had known it would. "When I have time to think about it first and decide, I usually imagine myself here, or down by the sea. But when I have to do it suddenly, and go to the first place that comes into my mind, sometimes I find myself somewhere . . . less pleasant."

"Where?" he persisted, hoping that the answer might provide some insight into the riddle she represented.

"There is a mountain," said Teleri. "Somewhere very far away. At the top of the highest peak stands a castle of ice. The walls of the castle are high and the peaks of the mountain so sheer, from a distance they look so sharp you could cut yourself on them."

Ceilyn shuddered. "It sounds a terrible place."

"Oh no," said Teleri. "The castle is very beautiful, very peaceful. The walls are transparent and I can see for a thousand miles in every direction. But the chasm on the other side . . . that frightens me. Once, I stood on the very edge of the abyss, looking down and down. . . ."

She could see that her words had shaken him. "It is nothing to worry about, Ceilyn," she said softly. "It is nothing more than a game."

She moved across the garden and knelt among the chamomile. As always, she carefully observed all the proper rules when tending her herbs; were she to leave out any part of the ritual, the magical properties of the plant would be lost. So she always cut with her right hand and gathered with her left, and she used gardening tools of bronze, like her knife, or wood or some other harmless substance, because the touch of cold iron was forbidden. As she worked, she explained to the plant exactly what she was doing and why. There was no need, this time, to leave an offering for the earth, because the little clumps of chamomile she dug up would be transplanted to another part of the garden.

After a time, Teleri asked a question of her own. "Where were you yesterday? I heard . . . I overheard . . . that your absence at Mass and during the ceremonies afterward caused quite a stir. Especially as it was Easter."

Ceilyn stretched out on a sunny patch of grass by the pond. "I went to Mass in Treledig. After that . . . I didn't go anywhere. The truth is, I didn't want to be there for the ceremony, though it wasn't some grand gesture as everyone seems to think. I wish that I could do something, just once, without everyone noticing and ascribing some damnably self-righteous motive. I know how such a gesture would look coming from me, after so many of the others opposed my own knighting."

Teleri replanted the chamomile, treading each little clump into the ground. It was a masochistic herb, Glastyn had taught her, and the more one trod on it the better it thrived. "Because you were so young?" she asked.

"That was part of it. I was the youngest man ever to be created a knight at Caer Cadwy," said Ceilyn. "Though I made it on merit alone and not because of any political considerations. No, it was mostly because I was left-handed."

"Oh," said Teleri, "but that's all nonsense, you know. It's not unlucky, no matter what you have heard."

"Well, I was beginning to believe that it wasn't, and if you say otherwise . . . of course you ought to know," said Ceilyn, looking relieved. "But my father believes there is an uncleanliness in the left hand. He used to punish me for cutting my meat the wrong way, and he ordered the priest who taught my brother and me our letters to tie my left hand behind my back."

It occurred to Teleri, who never thought much about liking or disliking other people, that she would *not* like Ceilyn's father. "But of course it isn't unclean," she said. "I wouldn't use my left hand to gather medicines, if it were! And I can't believe that the King, after all his years with Glastyn, would accept such nonsense."

"Well, he didn't, of course," said Ceilyn. "But some of the other men did. When I think of all the resentment that I had to endure, and then everyone just meekly accepts Morc and

Derry . . .'' The very names were bitter on his tongue.

Truth to tell, he was growing tired of hearing himself complain. And it was all of a piece anyway. He could see the whole world falling apart around him, and nobody lifting a finger to stop it.

Like the castle above, the town of Treledig presented a mixture of the old and the new. This had come about wholly as a result of the town's natural growth from a tiny fishing village to a bustling port and trade center, and not, as in the case of the castle, through any whim of the King. But the labyrinthine cobblestone streets, the wandering alleys, the crazy-paved squares with their spouting fountains, the half-timber houses all crammed together or piled precariously on top of one another, had come together in a fashion as haphazard, fantastic, and confusing to the traveler as anything Cynwas himself might have conceived.

Moreover, that spirit of perversity that expressed itself so freely in the castle above had also infected the sculptors and sign-painters of the town. Among all the heroic statues in the squares, the mermaids and tritons in the fountains, the fish, fowl, and rampaging beasts on the signs and banners that identified the shops and stalls, one might search in vain for a friendly face. There were suspicious scowls in plenty, lascivious leers, smirks, sneers, bared teeth, rolling eyes, and faces marked by a weary resignation—but not one single simple open smile.

The people, however, were another matter entirely: prosperous and cheerful folk, perhaps a trifle self-important, yet considerably more open-minded than their neighbors in the villages and farms. For trade was the foundation of Treledig's prosperity, and trade, of necessity, fostered a more cosmopolitan outlook.

But Treledig also catered to the castle folk. And so it was, one particularly fine morning, that Queen Sidonwy, accompanied by her handmaidens, her pages, and Ceilyn, went down to Treledig to do a little shopping.

As they had many stops to make, the ladies elected to move from shop to shop on foot, which meant that the pages were required to lead the horses as well as attend to all the parcels. Of these, there were soon a great number, for the ladies began at a cloth merchant's, buying lengths of velvet and brocade, went to another shop for embroidery silks, needles, and hairpins, another for soaps and perfumes, another for ribbons. . . . At noon, they bought bread, cheese, and fruit pasties, and picnicked in one of the squares. Then, leaving the boys and the horses and the packages behind, they headed for the West Gate and the docks.

By day, the streets and the shops outside the gate and along the wharf were crowded and noisy. Yet an air of decay pervaded the district, quite out of keeping with the hustle and bustle of business. Seagulls wheeled and dived, scavenging among the piles of refuse which lined the streets, the houses were all untenanted, and even the shops and warehouses suffered for want of repair.

The first such shop they entered was dark, crowded, and airless. After only a few minutes inside, the Queen complained that she could scarcely breath, swooned, and might have fallen had Ceilyn not been there to catch her.

He led her outside again, finding a place for her to sit among the boxes and bales stacked in the street, and the girls all gathered around, chafing her wrists and waving their handkerchiefs in her face. Gradually, Sidonwy's color returned.

"I shall be quite well, now that I can breathe again," she reassured them. "Go back in and continue your shopping. No, don't worry about me. Take all the time that you need. I shall just rest here until I feel recovered, then Ceilyn and I will take a little walk down by the water. Really, that is all that I need."

After much persuasion, the girls returned to the shop. And once they were gone, the Queen's recovery was little short of remarkable. She was on her feet in an instant, adjusted her veil so that her face and her dark hair were entirely concealed, accepted Ceilyn's arm, and set off at a brisk pace, forcing Ceilyn to lengthen his stride in order to keep up with her.

"I am sorry," said Sidonwy, as Ceilyn helped her to negotiate a difficult passage among the boxes and the bales, the puddles and the garbage. "I regret the deception as much as you do. I particularly regret that you should be placed in so awkward a position."

Ceilyn shook his head. "Don't think of that. If you must have dangerous secrets, I would far rather you shared them with me than confided in anyone else."

They walked a little farther. With every step they took, the seedy state of the neighborhood grew more pronounced, the odor of fish and garbage more pervasive, the houses and warehouses dirtier and more decayed. Loose shutters creaked in the breeze; bits of straw, blown down from the roofs during the winter storms, still littered the street.

"You know why I maintain this secret correspondence with my brother," the Queen said. "You know that Cadifor, lacking continued reassurance, would soon conclude that I had abandoned him altogether, and taking matters into his own hands would almost certainly make his present situation immeasurably worse. For all that, you are most uncomfortably placed between the oath of service you have sworn to me, and your fealty to the King."

"The day that I was knighted," said Ceilyn, "the King appointed me to the position of Knight Equerry in your household, and he specifically charged me with your safety. *Serve and protect the Queen as you would serve and protect me.* Those were his very words. He did not assign me to spy on you, or make me accountable for your behavior. Had he done so, I would have refused the post; were he to do so now, I would have no choice but to resign.

"It would be different," he added, "if I believed that anything you did threatened either the King's safety or his honor. As for your own honor and safety—if you *will* imperil them—I'd rather be on hand to avert any trouble that may develop."

The Queen came to a sudden halt, outside a tall, narrow house with a battered front door and a general air of faded grandeur. "I know this place," she said incredulously. "I remember when all the houses on this street were built—not so many years ago. Why were they abandoned?"

"No one cares to live outside the town walls anymore, not even the thieves and beggars," said Ceilyn, as they continued on their way. "Even the homeless move inside the town at night, and sleep in the gutters rather than use these houses."

They stopped again, this time outside a deserted warehouse. "This is the place," the Queen whispered, studying a faded sign above the door. They went inside, into a dim entry hall, then up a creaking flight of stairs. A little light filtered in through a shutterless window. At the door at the top of the stairs, Sidonwy knocked and spoke a single, identifying word. The door opened and the Queen slipped through.

Ceilyn stationed himself by the door, folding his arms and

propping himself up against the wall. He did not mean to eavesdrop—it was just that the door remained slightly ajar, and his hearing was so acute.

First, there was a crackling of parchment, as though someone unsealed a letter; followed, a moment later, by the Queen's low exclamation of distress. Ceilyn tensed, ready to burst through the door if she called for his assistance.

Instead, he heard her whisper urgently, "King of Rhianedd—what madness is this? The people would never support him. Yet though it were an empty gesture, it is one that will infuriate my Lord. You must send word at once and tell Cadifor how strongly I oppose this *wicked* foolishness."

"As you wish," murmured a second voice, too low for Ceilyn to recognize it, though the accent was unmistakable.

"Tell me this," said Sidonwy, her voice rising in her excitement, "has he confided in Lord Dyffryn? Does my uncle know of this?"

"He will know by this time," replied the other voice. "He was still at Glynn Hyddwyn when I left."

Now Ceilyn could hear the Queen's agitated footsteps as she paced the unsteady floorboards. "He will lend his objections to mine, I know. There will be no coronation at Glynn Hyddwyn while Dyffryn is there. But tell me of Llochafor—no, why do I ask? Llochafor supports Cadifor, I am sure. Ah, if only I had pen and ink now, that I might write to both my brothers immediately—but that must wait until our next meeting."

"There is a ship sailing north in the morning, and the Captain is to carry my report," said the messenger. "What would you have me say?"

"Assure my brothers that I do all that I can for them here. It is little, I know, but I cannot and will not do anything at all if by their own actions they place themselves beyond the King's forgiveness. For good reason, Cynwas opposed this dream of Cadifor's in the past; with better reason would he punish such overbearing ambition now!

"As for this letter," she said, "destroy it. Yes, burn it while I watch. We must be certain that nothing remains."

As the acrid scent of burning parchment filled the air, Sidonwy remembered to lower her voice to a whisper: "I shall have a letter and a token for you at our next meeting.''

A moment later, the door opened and the Queen appeared, looking pale and shaken, gratefully accepting the support of Ceilyn's arm. "I suppose that you overheard," she said, as they descended the creaking stair.

"A little," said Ceilyn miserably. "Enough."

"Please, Cousin," she begged him, "say nothing of this to anyone. My uncle and I may yet avert disaster. If it becomes evident that we cannot influence my brothers, then I will go to the King at once and reveal Cadifor's entire plan. I ask only that you remain silent for a few weeks' time."

"So long as the King's honor and safety are not endangered—that is what I promised you," said Ceilyn. "Can you swear to me, now, that neither one is in peril?"

"This plan of Cadifor's, you know something of the circumstances. . . . You must see how hopeless it all is. An empty gesture of defiance, lacking my support and Lord Dyffryn's. Are the King's honor and safety any less to me than they are to you? But I love my brothers, too, and would not see them ruin themselves. And they are not bad men—only willfully blind.

"Indeed, it may be that Cadifor has conceived this plan only to frighten me, hoping that I will renew my efforts to plead his case before the King. Yes," she said, taking comfort from her own words. "It is certain to be a bluff."

Ceilyn knew how like Cadifor it would be to make empty threats, merely to punish his sister for not pursuing his interests as actively as he might wish. And yet . . .

"As you love me, Ceilyn, you will trust me to do what is best," said Sidonwy. "I know that I have not always acted wisely in the past, but I will not be governed by impulse now. And I ask you not to act impulsively either. Only wait until further events make the best course clear to us."

It was an agonizingly difficult decision that she forced him to make, and what that decision would cost him later, the hours spent in prayer, fasting, and painful self-examination, Sidonwy would never know. Ceilyn knew what duty dictated: that he go to the King, whether he believed there was any substance to Cadifor's threats or not. But if he did go to the King and tell him what he knew, there was no telling what action Cynwas might take—action he might regret later—and the risk that the Queen would be implicated in the conspiracy and suffer along with her brothers was simply too great.

By the time that they reached the shop where he and Sidonwy had left the others, Ceilyn had chosen to follow his heart rather than his conscience. Rightly or wrongly, he knew that Sidonwy's well-being meant more to him than the King's—and if that was treason, if that meant forswearing himself . . . well, then, it seemed that he was a traitor and a man without honor.

"Very well," he whispered in her ear. "I will say nothing of this to anyone. At least for the time being."

"But blood," said the Raven, "carelessly shed, cries out for more blood and will not be silenced.

"As God is my witness," said the Raven, "I can think of no voice so terrible as the voice of the blood of the slaughtered innocent."

From The Black Book of Tregalen

13.

Of Blood and Seawater

"What comes next?" Calchas asked his mother, that night after supper.

"What should come next?" yawned Diaspad, arranging herself in her silver chair. She studied the game of chess set out on a little table before her. "All proceeds just as I had hoped it would—or very nearly. Do they meet except in public? Does he speak of forgiveness and reconciliation as he used to do? Does he not come, night after night, to sup with us privately, abandoning not only the Queen but also those he once called his friends?"

"Oh, he comes," said Calchas, listlessly moving an ivory playing piece, "but I can't say that he enjoys himself as much as he used to do. It takes more than elaborate pranks and live frogs in pies to amuse Cynwas, these days. As for his friends, the Marshall and the Lord Constable, it's they who haven't the time for private suppers."

Diaspad shrugged. "I ask them as a matter of courtesy, to please my brother. It is nothing to me whether they come or not. Ysgafn is a hard-headed fool," she added, "and he has hated me since the day I was born.

"And the Earl Marshall?"

"Manogan fab Menai—the man I knew—is dead," said Diaspad. "I do not trouble myself with the actions or motives of dead men."

Behind her back, the bedchamber door opened and closed. "There goes Prescelli," Derry observed, from his place by the fire. "Sneaking off to meet Iaen Og, no doubt, and most of her work undone. I wonder that you tolerate it."

There was a muffled shriek, followed by sounds of a vigorous struggle just outside the door. "Do you really?" The Princess selected a pawn and moved it. "But you see, I feel sorry for any woman foolish enough to pin her hopes of happiness on a man like Iaen fab Iaen."

"What she really means," said Calchas, in a bored tone, "is that some misdeeds just naturally carry their own punishment with them."

"Now see what you have done!" exclaimed Prescelli, vainly attempting to smooth the creases out of her dress. "You've spoiled my new gown and frightened me half out of my wits. Whatever possessed you to leap out at me that way?"

"I thought you would laugh," Iaen replied sheepishly. "I thought you would be pleased to see me. You ask me," he added, a trifle petulantly, "nothing I do seems to please you anymore. No, and you never seem to have any time—"

"*I'm* not the one who disappeared right after dinner," Prescelli pointed out. "Where were you all afternoon? I waited for hours."

"Oh . . . that." Iaen shuffled his feet like a rustic. "I had to go down to Treledig and just happened to meet an old friend. The most extraordinary thing—"

"Yes, I would like to hear about it, but not just now," Prescelli interrupted him again.

"No, really," she added soothingly, as the storm clouds began to gather. "You know that I love to hear about everything you do, Sweetheart. But we have so little time together. . . . Must we waste it all talking?"

"No, no . . . of course not," said Iaen, taking her gingerly in his arms. "I don't know why I am so damnably touchy. I swear to God, Prescelli, I never felt like this before. And I haven't had a decent night's sleep in weeks."

At this, Prescelli experienced a genuine pang of remorse. If Iaen did not know what had gotten into him, she certainly did.

Because Diaspad's silken girdle had worked. . . . Well, it had worked just like a charm, wiping all thought of the absent Seelie from Iaen's mind and throwing him into a perfect frenzy of passionate adoration for her sister. Unfortunately, Iaen was not the sort of man to whom romantic posturing and high-flown sentiments came naturally; the rapture had soon faded, embarrassment and bewilderment had set in, and the influence of the love charm, acting on his not-very-powerful intellect, had rendered Iaen sulky, suspicious, and demanding. Moreover, it was plain that living in a constant state of unnaturally heightened emotion did not agree with him. His eyes were rimmed with red, his hair had lost its curl, and the fine brown mustache (of which he had once been inordinately proud) drooped disconsolately.

But I will make it up to him, Prescelli vowed to herself. *I will find a way to make it all come right . . . for both our sakes. Because I have paid too high a price, and I am likely to go on paying it, not to make the most of every day, every hour we have left.*

Indeed, it was only the poignant realization that their time together was so limited that lent any real passion to their lovemaking.

Later, much later, after they found a private spot for some hasty lovemaking, when Prescelli lay exhausted and still oddly dissatisfied in his arms, Iaen told her about his trip into town. ". . . and there he was—a real surprise, I can tell you. . . . Years since I saw him. Not since I left Glynn Hyddwyn. . . . Pages together and then squires. A clever sort of fellow, though too poor to maintain himself as a knight. And perfectly devoted to Rhiannon, though I never understood. . . . Some sort of cousin of ours, but I don't precisely remember—"

"One of Cadifor's squires? Here?" Prescelli was suddenly very interested. Iaen's cousin Rhiannon also happened to be Cadifor fab Duach's wife.

"Not here. Down in Treledig," Iaen explained drowsily. "Oh, I see what you mean. A long way from home. I thought so at the time."

"And what was he doing here—so very far from home? Did you ask him? Did he say?"

"I don't really know." Iaen yawned, rolled over, and started to snore, but Prescelli prodded him in the side and asked her question again.

"What? Well, I didn't like to ask, if you see what I mean," Iaen mumbled. "If Cadifor sent him off . . ."

"Did he *say* that Cadifor and Rhiannon sent him off?" Prescelli asked.

"Did he—but it's obvious, isn't it?" Iaen said groggily. "Why else would he leave a good post like that?"

"If he did leave it," said Prescelli. "If he didn't come south on Cadifor's private business."

"If he . . . But that's not possible, surely." Her lover struggled to keep up with her. "Cadifor was banished. What private business could he possibly have in Treledig?"

"What indeed?" said Prescelli softly, as she mulled over this tantalizing piece of information and wondered what she might buy with it.

The first Sunday in May was a warm, bright day, and the Queen conceived a sudden desire to hear Mass celebrated down in Treledig. "St.-Ismael's-Down-by-the-Sea . . . a charming little church that I used to attend often, when I was young and summered at Caer Cadwy," she said. "Ceilyn shall join me on this pilgrimage, and little Gwenlliant and Nefyn, too. Surely that will be enough to satisfy convention."

So down the four of them went to St. Ismael's, where they heard Mass and took Communion. Afterward, they walked along the sandy shore, when the two children removed their shoes and their hose and waded in the foaming water. And when the children were completely absorbed in some game of their own invention, the Queen and Ceilyn slipped away and walked back toward the town.

"You are not happy about this," said Sidonwy, as they threaded their way through the bales and empty crates stacked up along the docks.

"How can I be happy when you place yourself in such grave danger?" Ceilyn replied wearily. "If the King were ever to discover . . . But you know all that already. We've discussed this a hundred times in the past fortnight."

This time, the Queen went into the abandoned building alone.

She stayed only a few minutes, and when she emerged, she and Ceilyn returned immediately to the beach to collect the two children.

They climbed the long staircase back to the castle, and cut across the outermost courtyard, heading for the Gamelyon Gate. As they passed the kennel, Ceilyn thought he spotted a tiny figure in grey entering the enclosure which housed the King's wolfhounds. When the Queen dismissed him a short while later, Ceilyn went down to the kennel, hoping to find Teleri still there.

Cynwas's favorite bitch lay panting in the straw. Both her forepaws were neatly bandaged, and Teleri was just trimming the rough grey hair on one flank, where the flesh had been torn away and blood still seeped from a nasty wound.

"She has bled so much, I don't think we need fear a dirty wound," said Teleri, by way of greeting.

Ceilyn knelt in the straw beside her. "What, in God's name, happened to her?"

"The King's pages took her out walking this morning, and she spotted . . . something . . . in the bushes and broke her leash trying to get at it. The boys brought the body back with them, but no one has ever seen anything like it."

She began to wrap a strip of clean linen around the wolfhound's slender midsection. "Some sort of hybrid, I think. Rather like a black squirrel, but it had terrible teeth and fought back fiercely."

Ceilyn frowned. "One of Gandwy's abominations, so far south?"

"It wasn't very large," said Teleri. "And Failinis killed the thing without any help from the boys."

But she knew, as he did, that Failinis was no ordinary hound. Like all the dogs in the King's kennel, the bitch was descended from the fierce red-eared hounds that the Princes Maelgwyn and Manogan brought with them from Tir Gwyngelli some twenty years before.

Fairy dogs, the common-folk had instantly dubbed them, for the farmers and herders of Camboglanna still believed in the Sidhe and the Sluagh, in pookhas and yell-hounds and the Cwn Annwyn, and many of them were even convinced that the Lord of Gwyngelli, holding court in fabulous underground halls lined with gold, was no mortal man, but the King of the Fairies himself. As for the youthful Prince Manogan, with his ferocious red stallion and his swift tireless hounds, and his habit of riding hell-bent through the southern countryside at an hour when all sensible men were locked up safe indoors, little wonder if some folk identified him with Gwern fab Mabon, the leader of the fairy Wild Hunt—a circumstance which the urbane Manogan of recent years found vastly amusing.

But whether or not the hounds from Gwyngelli sprang from supernatural stock, they and the descendents who followed after them had proven themselves to be the swiftest and cleverest and most relentless hounds in all of Celydonn.

Ceilyn was still wondering what it was that Failinis had surprised in the bushes, when Teleri broke into his thoughts, saying breathlessly, and quite unexpectedly: "The man is dead."

All the color had drained from her face and she stared intently ahead of her at someone or something on the far side of the yard. Ceilyn looked where she looked, but saw nothing out of the ordinary: only a squire over by the stable grooming his master's horse, two serving women drawing water from the well, and Calchas and Morc, just emerging from the South Tower.

"The man—what man? How did he die?"

Teleri shook her head. "I thought you might know him." She trembled violently, and looked as though she were about to be sick. "A tall, fair man. Calchas killed him. . . . There was blood everywhere . . . and when Calchas tried to wash his hands in the sea, the waves turned crimson. But the blood is still there—can't you see it, Ceilyn?—his hands all red with blood."

"I don't see anything," said Ceilyn. "Are you certain that someone *has* died—or might this be a presentiment of things to come?

"Oh no," said Teleri. "The man is dead. Long past hurting or helping. And the thing that he died to defend . . . that is in the hands of his enemies. But Calchas overlooked the ring."

"What ring?" Ceilyn questioned her patiently. "Was it valuable? A pledge of some sort?"

"I don't know," said Teleri, apparently as puzzled as he was. "But dangerous, more dangerous than the other, in its way. If Calchas or his mother recognized the ring . . ."

But there she stopped. And, though Ceilyn questioned her at

length and in detail, her account of the murder only grew more confused with each retelling.

In the anteroom outside his mother's bedchamber, Calchas hesitated, wiping his clammy hands on the skirt of his crimson surcote. "If you don't think that she will like it," said Morc, "why tell her everything that happened?"

"You must be mad," said Calchas, pushing open the door.

They found the Princess dressing for supper, standing breathless and motionless while Brangwengwen stood on a stool and laced her into a tight silken gown. "Well?" Diaspad said, as soon as she was able to breathe again. "You were gone long enough. Dare I hope that you discovered something to our purpose?"

Calchas perched uneasily on a corner of her bed. "Oh yes, it was a successful outing on the whole. And you were absolutely right: Her sudden urge to make a sentimental pilgrimage to St. Ismael's was all a sham. I don't know how you do it."

"But then," Diaspad said sweetly, "you've never been to St. Ismael's, have you? The dreariest little church, and Sidonwy and I used to attend Mass there only because the old woman assigned to govern us was related to one of the monks. But you—you were about to tell me whether or not she met with Cadifor's messenger."

"So I was," agreed Calchas, desperately trying to put off the moment of truth for as long as possible. "So I was. Well, she did meet the man. You were right about that, too. Thanks to Prescelli's information."

"Thanks to Prescelli," the Princess admitted graciously. "But you were about to say . . . ?"

"Yes, of course," said Calchas. "I was about to say that the Queen met the fellow in a sort of warehouse, while Ceilyn mac Cuel kept watch outside. That being so, Morc and I decided to wait until she had completed her business and gone on her way, and then we went inside, just in time to surprise Cadifor's man."

"And were you able to detain him for questioning?" Diaspad asked, clasping a jeweled belt around her hips. The dwarf climbed down from her stool and arranged the heavy folds of Diaspad's skirt.

"Well," said Calchas again. He took a deep breath. "Well . . . we did run into some . . . unforeseen difficulties."

His mother adjusted her neckline, displaying a fine pair of smooth white shoulders. "Oh? You allowed him to escape?"

"No. Oh no. We just—" Calchas gasped for air. "He resisted, naturally, and I had to—had to kill him."

The Princess was very quiet. "You had to kill him," she said at last. "The two of you pitted against the one man, and yet you couldn't restrain him without killing him. A man of more than ordinary strength, I take it?"

Calchas flinched. "Not exceptionally strong, no. But he put up a tremendous struggle, and I . . . I accidentally . . ."

Diaspad extended a silk-clad arm; Brangwengwen began to fasten the long line of gold buttons marching from wrist to elbow. "Accidentally . . . what?"

"Cut his throat," said Calchas, in a small voice.

A hiss of indrawn breath and a sudden swift movement by the Princess; Calchas cringed, but it was on the face of the little hunchback that three long scarlet scratches appeared.

Calchas reached into his shirt. "I brought you this," he said, gingerly handing his mother a piece of blood-stained parchment, then sliding off the bed and placing himself well out of reach of those raking claws.

Diaspad took the letter, read it three times, then tossed it aside. "There is nothing in this that could be of the slightest use to me. No names, no specifics. Why, she has even disguised her writing. She wisely follows her own advice and practices discretion for once in her life. And any woman in Celydonn might write such a letter to a reckless brother, cautioning him against treason, reminding him of his oath to his overlord."

"But we saw Sidonwy go in there to meet the man," said Calchas.

"Oh yes, you saw her, but how do you propose to prove that? Without proof, it's simply a case of your word and Morc's against the word of the Queen and the Celcynnon boy."

"And you think that he would lie for her?" Calchas asked weakly.

"Do you imagine, with her life hanging in the balance, that he would not?"

"Well, then," said Calchas brightening, "if he says that we lie, Morc can just challenge him to—"

"Oh no!" said Morc. "Not me. Not Ceilyn mac Cuel."

"Oh, for the love of God!" exclaimed Calchas. "You don't really believe that God would trouble himself to strike you dead, just for challenging the saintly Ceilyn? Besides," he added coaxingly, "this time *you* would be telling the truth. God would be on *your* side."

"It would need divine intervention before I could best Ceilyn mac Cuel," growled Morc. "I would be a bigger fool than everyone already takes me for, if I challenged Ceilyn to a trial-by-combat. Much you would care if I died . . . but where would that leave you?"

Calchas looked to his mother. "Morc is right," she said. "He's not as dull as he looks, you know. False witness against the Queen is a serious offense, even for one of your tender years. And Morc—let us be charitable—Morc possesses a certain brute strength, but no one has ever been impressed by his skill at arms. If he doesn't feel competent to take on young Ceilyn, I'm inclined to trust his judgment. Do you really wish to hazard your liberty, perhaps your very life, on a contest between them? No, I thought not."

She prodded the letter with a slippered toe. Calchas stooped to retrieve it. "But perhaps something can be salvaged here. Now that I come to think of it, the man can be identified. By Iaen Og, and perhaps by others. Of course, there is no way to establish that he is still in Cadifor's employ, but the body and the letter will serve to rouse my brother's suspicions, once we have returned the letter and arranged an 'accidental' discovery of them both."

Calchas shivered at the prospect of returning to the scene of his crime, particularly with night coming on. "Must I really go back there?"

The Princess considered. "Better, perhaps, if you don't. You've caused enough damage already, altering the balance with such injudicious bloodshed. What happens next is anyone's guess."

She opened her jewel box, selected several rings, and began slipping them onto her fingers. "I will return the letter myself, after supper. You need do nothing but send Bron after the horses. Tell him to wait for me down by the beach, and I will come to him as soon as it is dark."

. . . and there was, at that same time and living in that same village, a witch who could take upon herself the shape of a slender black cat. She fed on small birds and baby field mice, robbing the nests with great secrecy and cunning, hunting by night, and returning to her own bed and her own shape before the dawn. But her husband chanced to wake early one morning, and finding the woman asleep beside him with the fur and the feathers still on her lips, was filled with misgiving. And he began to wonder just what sort of woman this was, he had taken for his wife.

From a fragmentary account of The Life of St. Teilo

14.

A Game of Cat and Mouse

The night was clear; the moon was dark. On the sands below Brynn Caer Cadwy, Bron waited with the horses. The dwarf's own shaggy piebald pony slept, standing with crooked legs spraddled wide, and huge misshapen head hanging down. But the big black stallion shivered and fought the bit, refusing to be quiet.

Up above, in the western ruins, the sally gate swung slowly open, rusty hinges grating in protest. Derry mac Forgoll put his head through the opening. Raising his lantern high, he surveyed the treacherous path twisting down the face of the cliff. "Before God! I can see why no one ever comes this way. It would take a cat to scale or descend that path safely."

"A cat . . . or an Aderyn Islander," Diaspad's melodic voice answered him out of the depths of a dark, enveloping cloak. She took the lantern and passed through the gate.

Derry watched her descend the cliff. Soon, the lantern was no more than a tiny yellow spark moving in the darkness below. When Diaspad signaled her safe arrival on the beach, Derry lit a second lantern, closed the gate but did not secure it, and picked his way back through the rubble toward the stairs and the inhabited part of the castle.

There was movement among the stones at the base of a shattered tower, and Teleri emerged from hiding. She pushed the gate open a crack and slipped through.

A cat or an Aderyn Islander, the Princess had said. . . . And Teleri, like Diaspad, had spent her earliest years on that rugged little island. Her descent, by touch, was slow but sure.

A narrow causeway, starting at the foot of the path, led out to a little boathouse where a number of small boats were tied up. As Teleri stepped out onto the causeway, she stopped a moment to test the air.

She tasted something unwholesome on the breeze, a metallic taste like blood mingled with salt water. And the waves slapping on the rocks farther out seemed to strike with unusual violence. Teleri had a sudden uneasy sense of things dying beneath the water, fish and crabs and shellfish, the bay and everything in it poisoned because Calchas had tried to wash away his guilt in seawater.

It was a bad night to go out in a boat, a worse night to go out on the water alone. But the spark that was Diaspad's lantern was rapidly receding in the distance, following the curve of the bay, and Teleri knew there was no way to catch up with her but to follow by sea.

In the private apartments of the Queen, it was the same dreary scene that had been enacted in those rooms every night for weeks. As the pages cleared away the silver plates, after the evening meal, Fand brought out her harp, and two other girls began listlessly to practice an intricate new dance. Without the King and the gentlemen of his household present, no one had much heart for dancing, but the young ladies continued to go through the motions, more for the Queen's sake than for any pleasure they took in the exercise.

Over and over again, Finola and Megwen went through the same difficult passage, each time growing more dissatisfied with their own performance. "It's simply impossible," said Finola, coming to a dead stop.

Fand played a few more notes, then stopped, too. Finola glared at Ceilyn, who stood beside the Queen's chair watching the dance with a look of indescribable pain on his face. "Perhaps you can tell us what we are doing wrong?"

"I would have to show you," Ceilyn replied, wondering why, since none of them liked him, the young ladies invariably looked to him to correct their mistakes.

"Then come at once and do so," said Finola, extending her hand with an imperious gesture.

Ceilyn obligingly demonstrated the step, then led Finola through the dance another time. Little Gwenlliant clapped her hands to see the difficult steps so deftly performed, and even Sidonwy, who had hitherto watched the proceedings with little enthusiasm, began to look interested.

"You must teach me this dance," she said, rising eagerly from her chair and offering him her hand.

"With pleasure," he replied, bending to kiss her fingers—then froze in the act and stared at her hand as if struck by a sudden paralysis. A plain gold band that the Queen usually wore on the third finger of her right hand was missing.

"Is something wrong?" she asked, alarmed by his sudden change of color.

"Nothing," said Ceilyn, recovering himself, and leading her out to the middle of the floor. But as they assumed their positions, he asked (very low, so that the others could not overhear him): "Your ring—where is it?"

"I gave it to Cadifor's man, as a token for my brother," whispered Sidonwy. "Surely you remember? No, of course you don't. You were waiting down below."

The lilting melody began again. Ceilyn went through the entire dance without a misstep, though all the time Teleri's words were echoing in his mind: *"The man is dead . . . long past hurting or helping. But Calchas overlooked the ring."*

When the music ceased, he began to make his excuses. "If you'll pardon me . . . something I ought to have attended to earlier . . . I can't think how I came to forget."

"It can wait until morning, surely?" said Sidonwy.

"I fear that it can't," Ceilyn said regretfully, for he knew how tedious it was for the ladies, night after night, dancing with each other or the little boys. Then an inspiration struck him. "I'll send up Fflergant and Tryffin if you like. I daresay they both know the new steps."

The girls all brightened, and even the Queen smiled. And they were all so excited at the prospect of company that no one thought to wonder what business it was that Ceilyn found so pressing at that hour of the night.

Teleri tied up her little skiff at a pier just below the town, then scrambled up a short ladder to the planked walkway above. Torchlight from the walls of the town reflected off the water and cast a golden glow over the wharf and the shops, but the Princess Diaspad was nowhere to be seen.

Keeping close to the buildings, where the shadows were deepest, Teleri searched all down one street and then another, without success. Then, turning down a third street, she spotted two horses tied up outside a ramshackle old building. A flicker of lantern light moved at the far end of the lane.

Teleri dodged behind a pile of empty wooden boxes, peered cautiously around one corner. The light moved in her direction, and she was able to make out two cloaked figures, one of them small and misshapen. As Teleri watched in growing puzzlement, the taller of the two figures stopped outside a shop, took the lantern and held it high, studied the sign, and tried the door. Then, apparently dissatisfied, the two moved on to another building.

Something soft brushed up against Teleri's legs. Stifling the cry of surprise that rose to her lips, the girl looked down to see what had touched her. A pair of luminous green eyes gazed back at her.

Teleri flattened herself up against the piled boxes, hardly daring to move or breathe. There was no guessing what sort of creature she had encountered outside the walls of the town at night. Another hybrid, like the thing Failinis had killed in the bushes? Or worse, something intentionally malignant . . .? Yet Teleri was equally afraid of what might happen should any movement of hers attract the Princess's attention.

Gathering her courage, Teleri took several sideways steps, willing the thing to stay put. But the green eyes followed after her, and a solid little body bumped up against her legs, more forcefully than before. Growing desperate, Teleri bent down and shoved the thing firmly away. The beast hissed and struck her hand with sharp, punishing claws.

Curiously relieved, Teleri knelt down on the cobblestones. This was not the first time that a clumsy movement or an uninvited touch had earned her that same stinging rebuke—she was not likely to mistake either the reproof or the imperious beast who administered it.

It could only be Glastyn's cat, the big grey tabby who lived in the Wizard's Tower, the aloof creature who stayed on year after year simply because the tower provided her with such excellent hunting. Though what she was doing here, so far from home—and why, after that first repulse, she became so friendly—Teleri could not guess.

For the tabby was rubbing up against her legs, purring as she had never purred before. Then, satisfied that she had gained Teleri's whole attention, the cat strolled out into the middle of the street, sat down, and waited expectantly.

When Teleri did not follow, the tabby bristled with annoyance, stood up again, took another step, glanced back over her shoulder, and waited as before. This time, there was no mistaking the invitation.

The habit of obedience was strong in Teleri. The girl whose life for the past three years had been governed by unseen influences could not ignore so clear and imperative a summons as this. And the cat, after all, was Glastyn's cat. Teleri only waited until the Princess and the dwarf were occupied studying another building, then she followed the tabby, all curiosity about Diaspad's mysterious errand forgotten.

The cat led Teleri along a narrow alley to another street, where she stopped outside a dilapidated half-timber structure. The door hung loose on broken hinges, and the interior was as dark as a tomb.

Teleri pulled flint and steel out of one pocket, the stub of a candle out of the other. Fire blossomed in the darkness, revealing a tiny anteroom, a window with a broken shutter, and the body of a man sprawled out upon the floor. Teleri bent down to take a closer look.

The man's clothes were tattered and gory from a dozen vicious wounds, and a long ugly gash at his throat, severing the windpipe and the tendons, had allowed his head to roll back at an unnatural angle. Teleri sat down abruptly, breathing deeply, while the world grew darker around the edges and the sea roared in her ears.

Blood and death were old acquaintances of hers. She was a physician, and had learned at an early age to bind up bleeding limbs, attend the dying, and lay out the dead with perfect detachment. But this—this brutally slain man, the evidence of his desperate struggle, the miasma of panic, rage, and sudden death which lingered about the corpse—hit her with all the violence of a physical blow.

A long time passed before she was able to collect her thoughts. When she did, she remembered her own muddled prophecy: *". . . the ring, more dangerous than the other . . . If Calchas or his mother recognized it . . ."*

When a quick search of the dead man's purse revealed nothing of value, she put her candle down on the floor and forced herself to put a hand inside the dead man's doublet. There was pain, pain so excruciating that her stomach lurched and every nerve in her body screamed in protest. She snatched the hand away as though she had been scalded, nursed it against her chest until the agony faded.

All her life, she had heard tales of wizards and witches whose empathy for the terror and suffering of others became so exquisitely sensitive that they could no longer function as healers—indeed, could scarcely function at all. Had she, somehow, become so sensitized? Or was this merely a passing weakness, one that could be mastered?

Again, she slipped her hand inside his doublet. The sensation, though dreadful, was just bearable. Her questing fingertips searched through layers of wool and linen until they encountered a leather wallet.

The pouch was empty. Teleri let it fall to the floor. Now came a worse test. She forced herself to pick up his hands, one by one, and remove the leather gauntlets. The touch of his flesh brought pain, nausea, and terror even worse than before, but a circle of gold gleamed on the littlest finger of his left hand. Teleri pulled the ring off, thrust the slender band onto one of her own fingers, and forced herself to bear that, too.

Behind her, the door creaked open and a chill draft swept across the threshold. Teleri scrambled to her feet, and turned to meet Diaspad's cool, malicious gaze.

"So," the Princess said softly. "Glastyn's brat. The little grey mouse that nobody ever sees." She stepped over the threshold, and Teleri, concealing the hand with the ring in the folds of her skirt, took an involuntary step backward.

Diaspad reached inside her cloak and drew out a square of blood-stained parchment. "Were you looking for this? Do you know what it contains? Now, what made you think you could interfere in my affairs with impunity? Perhaps you thought I hadn't noticed you, skulking in the shadows in my brother's house. But I have seen you, indeed I have, though I scarcely considered you worth my trouble."

One slender white hand reached out to touch Teleri's fine light hair, and the girl had a fleeting impression of black fur and sheathed claws. "Better for you, my dear, had I continued to think so."

Teleri flinched away from that hand, took a sideways step toward the door, afraid to take her eyes off the Princess for even an instant.

Diaspad smiled. "Yes, I think you had better run along now. If you run very swiftly, just as swiftly as you can, you might reach Caer Cadwy before anything unpleasant catches up with you."

The words had scarcely passed her lips when the candle flickered wildly and died, extinguished by a draft neither of them felt. An instant later, the letter in Diaspad's hand flared into flame, lighting the room briefly, then crumbling into ash.

Teleri stifled a scream. Something huge and warm and hairy pressed up against her—and it was not Glastyn's cat, unless the tabby had suddenly grown to monstrous proportions. The breath of the beast was hot on her face.

She felt her way to the door. In the darkness behind her, Diaspad's voice rose high in panic. "Bron, is that you?" Teleri did not linger to hear the answer. She slipped past the door and out into the street, where she ran straight into a nightmare.

The glare of torchlight nearly blinded her, the press of so many bodies in that narrow street nearly suffocated her. Bewildered, Teleri looked around her. An angry mob had gathered outside the warehouse and more men carrying torches came pouring out of all the houses and shops along the street, swelling their ranks.

"Witch!" shouted someone. And: "Catch her!" roared the crowd. The hue and cry resounded on all sides, and hands reached out to clutch and pull her down. Teleri took to her heels and the entire mob followed in hot pursuit.

At the crossing of two streets, someone stepped out and caught her by the arm. She screamed, kicked, and fought frantically to be free.

"This way," said a voice in her ear, and recognizing it she ceased to struggle. "Come with me."

Miraculously, the crowd parted. Ceilyn pulled her down a dark alley, over a low wall, and finally through a door. There, they stopped and listened breathlessly in the dark.

After several minutes of this, Ceilyn whispered, "Perhaps you will tell me what it is we are hiding from?"

"The mob," said Teleri, her voice muffled because her face was pressed against his shoulder. "The witch-hunt. Surely you saw them? Surely you heard them?"

"There was nothing," said Ceilyn. "I saw no one, heard no one. Only you, running down the lane as though a thousand devils were after you."

"But they were there," Teleri protested. "So many people and such a noise . . . you must have seen them. They were right behind me."

Then, softly, as the truth sank in: "There was no one there. The streets and shops are deserted at this hour. The Princess simply took the image out of my mind and made my fears seem real."

They stood there a little longer. Pleased and shaken by his own reaction to the clinging softness in his arms, Ceilyn pulled Teleri closer still, buried his face in her hair. It smelled of sea-salt and bitter-sweet herbs. Experimentally, he dropped a kiss on the top of her head, and waited for her to react.

She continued to cling to him, more like a child seeking comfort than a woman in the arms of her lover, but he was encouraged to brush his lips across the tip of her ear, and then, when she still did not react, to venture a soft kiss on her cheek. He felt her stiffen, then lose substance in his arms.

"What is this place?" she asked.

"A stable at one time or another, by the smell of it," he said, drawing away in turn. He felt cheated, as if something long promised had been inexplicably denied. Something *had* been promised, he told himself, during those magical moments in the enchanted garden, and he could not understand why that promise should be withdrawn now.

"Ceilyn?" she said, growing a little panicky because she could not find him in the dark.

He was beside her in an instant, taking her hand and guiding her. "Sorry," he said, not sounding sorry at all, "I forgot that you couldn't see in this dim light."

"But there is no light at all," she protested.

"Even I can't see where there is no light at all. Look up," he said, and she obeyed. Parts of the roof were missing. Between the ragged piles of thatch, pieces of starry sky could be seen: tiny, distant pinpricks of light.

"There is a kind of a bench built into the wall behind you," he said, turning her around, guiding her hand until she found the rough wooden plank and sat down on it.

"I wish," she said, "that I hadn't lost my candle."

"No matter," he said, producing a candle stub of his own and lighting it.

"I suppose," he went on, sitting down beside her, "that we both came for the same thing: the Queen's ring. Do you have it?"

"You knew, then?" Teleri displayed the finger with the ring on it. "You knew that the ring belonged to her?"

"Not when you first told me about it. I didn't learn about the ring until later."

"But you knew about the letter?" Teleri persisted. "And the messenger—he came from Cadifor fab Duach, didn't he?"

"I knew there was a letter. But you never said anything about that. Only that a man had lost something. And I knew about the messenger, yes, but I had never actually seen the fellow. A tall, fair man, you said—but that meant nothing to me.

"How did you come to recognize him?" he asked. "You didn't know him before, when you saw . . . whatever it was you saw in the kennel."

"I knew him when I found the body. Because I had seen him before . . . oh, years ago . . . when he was just a boy and came here one summer in Rhiannon's train. So it wasn't difficult, with the ring and the letter, to guess who sent him here, or for what purpose. I don't know why I remembered him," she added. "I so often forget things."

"Your memory is selective, that is certain," said Ceilyn dryly. "But why did you come here? How did you find the place?"

"I came by sea," she said. "I began by following the Princess, but she had some difficulty locating the house where the body lay. Perhaps Calchas did not remember precisely where it was. But I was . . . guided . . . and arrived there first. And you?"

"Tegillus and I came down the long way. As I had no idea that the rest of you were on your way, I was in no particular hurry.

"Strange . . ." he added. "After that incident this morning, I expected to find nameless monsters lurking behind every bush, waiting in every doorway. But there was nothing. Still, you had best ride back with me. Tegillus can easily carry us both, and you can come back for your boat in the morning."

The chestnut gelding awaited them in another stable, closer to the town gate. "Do you feel safe back there?" Ceilyn asked, as Teleri climbed up behind him.

"Yes," she said. "I've never been up on anything so big before, but I learned to ride almost before I learned to walk."

On the ride back to Caer Cadwy, she told Ceilyn how she had discovered the body and how the Princess Diaspad had arrived to confront her.

"But why did she burn the letter?" Ceilyn asked, acutely conscious of Teleri's arms around his waist, irritated because she, so obviously, felt nothing at all.

"I don't think that she did burn the letter . . . not intentionally. Perhaps she only meant to relight the candle." Teleri did not tell him of that other presence she had felt in the warehouse. And perhaps, after all, it was not worth mentioning, only the product of her own imagination, like Diaspad's phantom witch-hunt.

They rode in silence for a time, each wrapped up in his or her own thoughts. "And yet . . ." Teleri said, as Tegillus began the long climb to the Main Gate, "as dreadful a thing as it was, I can't help thinking that the death of Cadifor's man may prove to be the Queen's salvation."

"I don't know what you mean," said Ceilyn, over his shoulder. "I don't see how the Queen can possibly benefit."

"Even witches like the Princess and Calchas have to obey the rules of magic—or else suffer the consequences," Teleri explained. "Really, that is why Wizardry is 'safe' and Witchcraft so dangerous. Because the Wizard, acquiring his power through study and meditation, acts with full knowledge of the consequences, while the Warlock, coming into his power naturally, and usually untutored, too often acts in ignorance."

Ceilyn frowned, wondering if this lesson was somehow intended for his benefit.

"Consider this," she said. "There is power in earth and stone, water, wind, and fire. There is a greater power animating every living thing. And anyone who works magic—white or black—must tread very carefully anytime that he or she becomes involved in matters of life and death.

"I told you, Calchas still has blood on his hands—it's not so easily washed away as you might think. That blood will have to be paid for, one way or another, or it will demand its own price. And anything which harms or hinders Calchas and his mother just now must work to the Queen's advantage."

Ceilyn turned that over in his mind. There was a certain logic in what she said, but it all sounded disturbingly amoral.

"I suppose what you are really trying to say," he said, "is that Calchas, in murdering Cadifor's messenger, committed a sin so black, a crime so outrageous, that retribution cannot be long in coming."

"Yes," Teleri agreed with a sigh, "that is what I am trying to say."

"I see," said the giant, "that you have performed every task. You have traveled far and seen much, and learned the secrets of earth, sea, and sky. Yet there is one secret remaining which you do not know."

"I have done all that you bade me," said the youth, "and your daughter is rightfully mine. It is not right for you to ask of me any more than you have."

"Alas," said Mael-Duir, "it is just as you say. You may take my daughter from me and I am powerless to prevent you. But stay awhile and listen, for there is something you should know.

"My daughter," said the giant, "has no heart in her body with which to love you."

From The Black Book of Tregalen

15.

Poisoned Sugarplums

The next morning, Ceilyn requested a private audience with the Queen. Sidonwy received him in her little chapel in the Mermaid Tower, a place of flowers and candlelight and polished wood, that always put Ceilyn in mind of his mother's private chapel, back at Caer Celcynnon. And it seemed to him, as he inhaled the sweet perfume of the flowers and the wholesome scent of beeswax, that it was a great pity to mar the peace of that holy place with so ugly a tale as he had to tell. Nevertheless, he told the Queen everything he knew about the letter, the ring, and Cadifor's messenger, omitting none of the details.

"So," said Sidonwy, very pale by candlelight. "My folly has resulted in this: A man lies dead—a young man, like yourself, full of courage and great promise, as devoted to my brother and his lady as you are to me—dead now, because I would not heed your warnings."

"But I never anticipated anything like that," Ceilyn protested. "My concern was all for you. But Cadifor's messenger knew what risk he was taking acting as go-between—and your brother knew it, too. Whatever their motives were, you acted only to protect those you love."

"I might have protected them better, had I acted more wisely," replied Sidonwy, absently slipping the ring onto her finger. "As it was, we have only just escaped ruin. If the messenger had allowed himself to be taken, if he had revealed my brother's folly, and mine . . ."

"But Cadifor chose his messenger well, a man he knew would guard his secrets with his life," said Ceilyn. "And perhaps some good may come of this. If Cadifor were allowed to believe that his messages were intercepted, that the King knows what he is planning to do, then surely your brother will think better of his scheme and abandon it altogether."

"I might have prevented all this," the Queen insisted. She began to move restlessly around the chapel, picking up things—a prayer book, a gilded candlestick—and putting them down again. "Had I thought less of my pride, had I been more diligent at pleading their cause to the King, he might have recalled my brothers long since, long before they grew so desperate and began plotting mischief."

"But how could you have influenced the King on your brothers' behalf, when Cynwas refused to even speak to you?"

"God knows how easily that might have been remedied," said the Queen, "had I gone to the King anytime this spring, and begged his forgiveness. But say that I am wrong, say that he would have hardened his heart against me, who never did so before . . . was it not still worth the attempt?"

"But you had done nothing to apologize for," Ceilyn insisted loyally. "You were not at fault."

"Perhaps I was and perhaps I was not," said Sidonwy. "But that does not excuse my larger culpability. And it is no use saying that Cynwas was as much to blame as I. He must bear the blame for his actions and I for mine."

She stopped beside the altar. Light shining through a stained-glass window painted the white altar cloth: scarlet, blue, purple, and gold, like a page in an illuminated Bible. "As Queen, I had no right to allow a private grievance of mine foster political dissension.

"I only hope," she added softly, "that it is not too late to undo some of the harm I have done."

"This might be an auspicious time," said Ceilyn, "to seek a reconciliation with the King."

For Teleri had predicted—had she not?—that the messenger's death might bring about some favorable result. Perhaps it was already taking effect, by shocking the Queen into reconsidering her past actions.

"Whether it be auspicious or not," said Sidonwy, "that is what I shall do—and before this day is over. But Ceilyn," she said, signaling him to kneel, removing another ring and pressing it into the palm of his hand, "I have not thanked you for your part in last night's events."

"I did nothing, really," said Ceilyn. "It was all Teleri's doing."

"Yet you have served me with loyalty and discretion. Yes, and given me good advice, too, though I was not wise enough to heed it. But as for your little friend . . . there is something I must ask you, and I hope you will not mind, for I think only of your welfare."

She took his hand in hers and went on gently, "But what are your intentions toward that child? You are constantly in her company, they say, display a degree of attachment you have never shown any young woman before. Just what do you intend?"

"Intend? I have no intentions—honorable or otherwise," he said, with perfect sincerity, though he flushed just as painfully as if he had been planning something truly reprehensible. He was still unwilling to define the feelings Teleri inspired in him, much less form any fixed intention. Yet, if his own emotions remained a mystery to him, her emotions—or lack of them—he believed he understood perfectly.

"That is just as well," said the Queen. "I do not wish to sound heartless, but surely you see that any real attachment would not do at all."

"Yes," said Ceilyn. "I know all that. And you need not fear that I will do anything to disappoint my family or you."

He had learned a little about Teleri's background: that she was not, after all, another of Glastyn's foundlings discovered under mysterious circumstances, but was distantly related to Cadwr of Aderyn, who employed her father as his seneschal, that her mother was dead. He did not know much, but it was enough. As the world reckoned these things, she was far beneath him. Such was the hypocrisy of that world he lived in that he might seduce a girl like Teleri, even live with her, unmarried, openly, and everyone would look the other way—but if he did the honorable thing, if he made her his wife, he would scandalize his peers. Yet that was nothing, birth, rank, and the conventions of his class were as nothing, beside the real barrier between them.

Something was lacking in Teleri herself. Were Ceilyn to conceive a passion for little Gwenlliant, were he to fall head-over-heels with a baby in the cradle, he stood a better chance of winning her heart—for the baby, though she take years to accomplish it, must eventually grow older, while Teleri, in all probability, never would. She had been approximately twelve the first time that Ceilyn had ever laid eyes on her, and it was obvious to him now that the intervening years had not aged her so much as a day. Whatever confusion he had ever experienced, born of the disparity between Teleri's chronological and apparent ages, that one brief embrace they had shared down by the docks had finally resolved it.

How and why Teleri had become what she was, Ceilyn did not know. He suspected that something was missing, that something had gone terribly wrong. Some spell of her own, perhaps, ineptly performed. Or (more likely) some contrivance of Glastyn's.

Oh yes, he could picture it all quite clearly: the old wizard—like that covetous giant in the fairy tale who hid his daughter's heart away lest some man capable of winning it come along—extracting some vital part from Teleri and putting it away for safekeeping during his prolonged absence.

And that being the case, what chance had Ceilyn to do anything foolish or romantic?

The Queen proved as good as her word. That very afternoon, she knelt at the King's feet, pleading for his forgiveness. "I have been proud, willful, and disobedient. A poor wife and an unfit consort. But if you can forgive me—"

"My dearest lady," said Cynwas, raising her up at once, for he was genuinely moved by her appeal. "My dearest love. Please say no more. Of course I forgive you. And this was not necessary. A word . . . a look . . . a smile . . . and I would have been at your feet long since."

As easily as that she accomplished it: banishing all the pain and bitterness of the past months with a few words—the same words that, spoken at the beginning, might have spared them both much suffering. But Sidonwy said nothing about her clandestine correspondence with her brother.

Thereafter, the King and Queen were constantly together, as giddy and mutually absorbed in their newfound bliss as any young lovers. An entire month passed, May blossomed into June, without a single royal quarrel to titillate the court gossips.

And such a June it was! A month of long, languorous days and short, sultry nights, a June of roses blooming wild in the ruins and overrunning all the gardens at Caer Cadwy. No one could remember a June of so many roses: pale as alabaster, ivory-tinted, honey-colored shading into old gold; shell-pink, lavender, and maiden's blush; damask, cinnabar, and port wine, opening their deep crimson hearts to fill the air with a heady perfume.

But all this beauty was wasted on Calchas. If the roses were thorny, he was thornier still. "Six months we have been here," he said to his mother, "and I stand no closer to the throne now than I did at the beginning. And now that the King and Queen have patched up their quarrel, now that he's decided to lift his ban on Cadifor and Llochafor—well, it seems to me as though all our efforts are brought to nothing!"

Calchas and the Princess were picnicking down in the meadow below the castle, and the half-eaten picnic was melting and growing rancid on a linen cloth spread out between them. The afternoon air was as hot and heavy as smoke, bees hummed lazily in the clover, and Pergrin the giant droned a dreary soprano accompaniment. Somewhere between sleeping and waking, the Princess lay beneath a scarlet canopy, on a pile of furs and cushions, while the tireless Brangwengwen waved a black ostrich fan overhead.

"For my part," said the Princess drowsily, "I am looking forward to Cadifor's visit. And Llochafor, too, of course. It has been years since we met."

Calchas eyed her suspiciously. "You're up to something, but I don't know what. This sudden desire to see Cadifor and Llochafor, and this equally sudden desire to visit your cousins up in Draighen. You've been very strange and mysterious ever since that night down by the docks. What happened to you there? What are you afraid of?"

Diaspad stiffened; the vivid green eyes flew open. "Afraid? I—afraid? What makes you say that?"

"Yes, afraid," said Calchas, growing reckless. "There's that girl, for one thing—now that you've found her out, now that you know she's been meddling, you do nothing to stop it."

"I warned her. Believe me, I gave her a real fright." Diaspad lay back again and closed her eyes. "I don't anticipate any more trouble from that source."

"If you want to know what I think," said Calchas—not before he placed himself carefully out of her reach—"I think that it was she who gave you a fright, not the other way around."

"Afraid of that child?" Diaspad was wide awake now. "Of that chit? That weakling? The simple truth is: I am reluctant to tamper with anything that belongs to Glastyn."

"But Glastyn is dead—or the next thing to it!"

"I am sure we all hope so," said the Princess. "Indeed, I was convinced of it once. But now I am not so certain. I received a warning that night . . . a warning, or perhaps a challenge." She sat up, began picking at the tepid remains of the picnic. "Whatever it was, it was very much in Glastyn's style of doing things. I am *not* afraid, but I have always found it wise to be cautious where that old man is concerned."

She started to dismember a tiny roasted fowl, rending it with her long, curved nails. "Up until now, we have made no provision against Glastyn's interference. Very well, that was a mistake, but one I shall not make in the future. So, naturally, we must revise our plans a bit."

"And?" Calchas wanted to know.

"And," said Diaspad, "I have decided to allow him to think that I have heeded his warning. I keep my hands off his little apprentice, and he believes that he has intimidated me."

"But he hasn't?" Calchas asked.

"Dear boy, of course not," Diaspad assured him. "In fact, I have decided to leave off these complicated indirect schemes and strike out against Cadifor fab Duach himself."

"Very well," said Calchas, pouring a goblet of warm wine. "But just suppose—now that everything hinges on Cadifor's return—just suppose he doesn't come back after all? He must know that you are here, must be aware that you mean to ruin him, if you can. Supposing he just stays away?"

''Whether he suspects a trap or not,'' said Diaspad, ''he won't be able to resist the bait that I offer him.''

Calchas set the goblet aside. ''And exactly what bait will you be offering him?''

''Why, the bones of his ancestors,'' said the Princess. ''The sacred relics of the Rhianeddi race.''

''The bones of the ancient kings of Rhianedd!'' Calchas gasped. ''But those have been missing a hundred and fifty years at least.''

''Yes, but you see,'' said Diaspad smugly, ''I think that I know who has them.''

''Truly?'' said Calchas, growing excited. ''And you really think that you can get them?''

''I think that I can,'' said Diaspad. ''This would not be the first time that I have successfully bargained with the Old Ones.''

''The Old Ones?'' Calchas's enthusiasm began to deflate. ''Glastyn's own people? Why would they deal with you, when—''

''That renegade! He was great among them once, it is true, but he betrayed them all, time and time again, serving a King who was never any king of theirs.'' Diaspad picked up the wine goblet, stirred the contents with her littlest finger. ''Even long ago, there were those who stood against him. His influence has steadily diminished, and few among them are loyal to him now.

''Nor have they,'' she added, ''any reason to love Cadifor. He has never lit any bonfires himself, it is true, but people have burned in Rhianedd, lacking his protection. That has scarcely endeared him to the pagan priesthood.''

Calchas frowned thoughtfully. ''Yes, but I can't see why they would be particularly eager to exert themselves on my behalf, either. Especially not that old fellow from Gwyngelli.''

''Oh well,'' said Diaspad, lying back among the pillows. ''A price will have to be paid, perhaps even a high one. But whatever that price is, we shall simply have to pay it.''

It seemed hardly the afternoon for vigorous exercise, yet up in the practice yard the clank of steel and the thud of metal on wooden shields continued for hour after hour, as Ceilyn subjected a group of squires to a grueling practice session.

''God save us!'' gasped one youth, collapsing on the ground beside some of his friends, while Garanwyn took his place in the melee: Ceilyn against the field. ''You would think he would realize that the rest of us are growing tired and stupid by now, even if he isn't. As though any of us has a chance of getting in a solid blow anyway—bloody left-handed Ceilyn mac Cuel!''

''A pity that life is so peaceful in these parts,'' said Kilraen. ''A chance to rip out somebody's guts in a real battle would do that lad a world of good!''

Gofan shook his head despairingly. ''I don't know what possesses Ceilyn. It used to be, he would take the time to tell us what we were doing wrong. It was never much fun, fighting Ceilyn, but it was an education. Now all he seems to care for is beating the rest of us nearly insensible.''

''He looks,'' said Derry, moving away from a window in the Princess Diaspad's bedchamber, ''like a man being devoured from the inside out.''

''Who?'' Prescelli looked up from her packing with a guilty start. ''Who looks like a man being devoured from the inside out?''

''Why, the virtuous Ceilyn, of course,'' said Derry, depositing himself in Diaspad's silver chair. ''Not quite so pleased about the royal reconciliation as one might have expected him to be. Perhaps not so pleased as *he* had expected to be. I would imagine that the Queen's unfortunate plight suited him rather well, actually, with all its opportunities for secret errands and minor heroics. So much more diverting than running her household, don't you think?''

''This state of marital bliss can't last forever,'' sniffed Prescelli, carelessly tossing several of the Princess's best gowns into the oak chest that stood open in the middle of the room. ''Not if the Princess has anything to say about it.''

''Ah,'' said Derry gleefully, ''but that is just the beauty of it—don't you see? When Sidonwy suffers, Ceilyn suffers right along with her, but when she prospers, then he is out in the cold, and feeling guilty as sin (if I know Ceilyn) for wishing everything back the way that it was.

''Come to think of it,'' he added, ''I did hear something as I passed by the boys' chapel last night. Likely it was Ceilyn, up to his old tricks.''

''Maybe,'' said Prescelli, who was not much interested in Ceilyn's problems or in his disgusting self-imposed penances. She changed the subject. ''I don't understand what it is the Princess thinks she is doing now. Why, she doesn't even know your brother Leam—so why should she go running off to Leth Scathach, just to see his children christened?''

Derry shrugged. "The ways of the Princess, as we well know, are often exceedingly mysterious. Suffice to say: She must have her reasons. And the christening of Leam's twins provides as good an excuse as any I can think of to hold a celebration.''

"Yes," said Prescelli, flinging two ivory combs and a hand mirror into the chest, "but I don't see why I am to be left behind. I would enjoy a little fun, too, you know.''

Derry grinned. "And here I thought you had an aversion to family celebrations. Why, there is a wedding taking place on Ynys Carreg this very minute that—''

"If everyone keeps talking about Seelie's wedding," Prescelli warned him, "I shall do something really dreadful.''

"That's a change of tune," smirked Derry. "It wasn't so long ago you told me that you couldn't be rid of Iaen Og soon enough. Or was that said merely to save your pride?''

"I *did* send him away," Prescelli insisted. "He begged to stay with me. . . . Yes, even after I took that lock of his hair and burned it. But nobody knows that. Everyone thinks that he simply tired of me and went home to Seelie. It is so humiliating! All the concealed smiles and pretended sympathy. And all for the sake of a lack-wit like Iaen fab Iaen!''

"I would be the last to dispute that," said Derry, examining the dish of sweetmeats which the Princess always kept by her chair. "But I must say, it took you a good long time to discover what the rest of us already knew.''

"Yes, it did," Prescelli admitted. "I guess I just fell in love with his face and never bothered to find out what went on behind it. But you have to admit that he was rather splendid to look at: those broad shoulders, that wavy hair, and that great curling mustache!'' She could not suppress a heart-felt sigh. "He and Seelie are well-matched after all. Both of them as beautiful as . . . as marzipan angels—and just about as intelligent!''

Derry laughed. "Marzipan. Yes, that's a good description of Iaen. Beautiful, but hardly exciting. And you—being a woman of sophisticated appetites—you will be looking for something . . . more highly spiced, shall we say?'' He gave her his most seductive smile. "Well, I'm not doing anything important, just at the moment."

"Thank you, no!" Prescelli slammed down the lid of the chest. "If Iaen Og is marzipan, you're just like one of those apricot comfits you like so well—only in your case, there is poison at the center."

"Ah," said Derry, more pleased than otherwise by the comparison. "But they do say that there are certain virtues in poisons. Arsenic, for instance, is said to be good for the skin and the hair and the fingernails.

"I've always wanted to ask Cadifor about that," he added thoughtfully, "for I have also heard it said that he is passionately fond of sugarplums laced with arsenic.

"But we were discussing your little problem," Derry suddenly remembered. "A terrible situation to find yourself in: seventeen years old and not a husband in sight, and not even a lover to keep you warm. You had better start casting your little spells soon, or you will be too old and crazy to know what to do with a man when you finally get one."

But Prescelli had finally endured as much of Derry's company as she could bear. "Someday," she said, "the Lady is going to tire of watching you slither after her, and she'll step on you, Derry mac Forgoll!" She stalked out of the room, slamming the door behind her.

Down three flights of stairs she sailed, past all the watching faces, the cruel mocking faces of the gargoyles and the satyrs and the zoomorphs, then out into the sunlight. She paused at the top of another set of stairs, just long enough to catch her breath.

"I'll show you. Yes, and the rest of them, too," she muttered, starting down the next flight. "Everyone who thinks that I can't keep a lover! But I have the Princess's love charm, and I can have any man I want." She tripped on the hem of her gown and stumbled down the last few steps, just as Ceilyn started up them.

"Before God, Prescelli!" he exclaimed, untangling himself after the collision. "Can't you watch where you are going?"

Prescelli picked herself up off the steps, speechless with rage. She would have boxed his ears soundly, if Ceilyn had not caught her by the wrists and pulled her into his arms.

"Oh, you would, would you?" he breathed, as she kicked at his shins and tried to claw his face. By now, they were both taking a perverse pleasure in the struggle.

Then their eyes met. Hunger . . . rage . . . frustration . . . a nature every bit as passionate, in its way, as her own. For Prescelli, the shock of recognition was devastating.

Oh God, she thought, *why didn't I see this before . . . or seeing, not understand*. For now, at last, she knew whose shadowed eyes had looked up at her out of the purloined chalice, recognized now and for all time the face of her one true love.

But Ceilyn, never guessing what passed through her mind, felt her grow limp in his arms, and was overwhelmed by remorse. "Prescelli . . . have I hurt you?"

"No," breathed Prescelli, still white with the shock. "You haven't hurt me . . . yet."

. . . and the Kings of Camboglanna, grown mightier than the rest, began to dream of Empire. They extended their rule from Celliwig in the west, to Walgan and Perfudd in the south and northeast, into parts of Draighen, and throughout the Lesser Isles . . . and still they were not satisfied.

They invaded the farther parts of Draighen, and took Cuan, Rhianedd, and Gorwynnion as well. Cynwal Mawr and his sons subdued the tribes of the Mochdreffi and set up a Lord of mixed blood to govern them. Then Cynwal proposed a treaty with the King of Tir Gwyngelli, and that Lord came down out of his hills and pledged his fealty.

And Cynwal was the first High King over All the Kings of Celydonn, and the first Emperor of the Isles; and his sons Cynfelyn and Cadwy ruled after him.

But as the High Kings waxed even greater in power and majesty, the other Kings and Princes diminished.

From a manuscript found at Dun Tragen, sometimes called The Book of Four Kings

16.

Encounter With a Dragon

Night crept over northern Camboglanna slowly at Midsummer. Like a predatory beast stalking her prey, darkness crawled in on her vast, starry underbelly, taking the last tardy light of day by surprise and tearing it into a thousand bloody tatters.

Long before that, however, the long line of wagons crossing the plain had stopped to set up camp. Diaspad's servants unhitched the sturdy horses that pulled the baggage carts and the Princess's big, painted caravan, pegged them out to graze, and erected an enormous scarlet pavilion and a number of smaller tents.

Meanwhile, a party of woodwoses and dwarfs heaped branches of rowan and apple in piles spaced at regular intervals around the campsite. They kindled the watchfires just as the sun disappeared below the horizon.

Outside the circle of golden firelight, the deepening twilight was full of ominous noises, but inside the circle Diaspad's people cooked and ate their suppers secure in the knowledge that Quickentree and Holy Apple would keep them safe.

Derry mac Forgoll retired early. Diaspad had not invited him to share her bed that evening, so he dug a comfortable little burrow among the parcels and bundles in the largest baggage cart, curled up, and immediately fell asleep.

He woke with a rude shock an hour or two later, to find Calchas perched on a box beside him, prodding him with a long stick. "Get up, you lazy toad. It's almost time to be going."

Derry sat up, rubbing the sleep from his eyes. "What time is it? Go where, in the name of God?"

"I suggest that you come along and see for yourself," said Calchas, adding portentously, "She's waiting for you."

Derry stretched his cramped muscles one last time, picked up his swordbelt, and climbed down from the wagon. "Where?" he asked, girding on his weapons. "Where are we going?"

"Over the hill, yonder," said Calchas, gesturing toward the northeast.

Derry peered out into the darkness, past the ruddy glow of the firelight. In the direction Calchas indicated, the plain looked perfectly flat, but Derry had been raised in country such as this, and he knew that the grasslands were not as flat as they appeared to be. A hundred paces from the camp, anything might be hiding.

"Out there?" he asked disbelievingly. "Outside the ring of watchfires? Do you know what night this is?"

"Of course I know what night this is," Calchas replied. "We would not be here, if it were any other night."

They found Bron, Morc, and Pergrin seated around the cookfire, the two big men chewing the last of their supper as blissfully as the carthorses cropping grass nearby. The Princess stood apart from the rest, swathed in a voluminous dark cloak, staring moodily into the flames. As Calchas and Derry approached, she turned a haggard white face in their direction.

"You've been a long time coming," she said icily.

Derry glanced over at the horses. "If you're in such a dreadful hurry, why has no one saddled the horses?"

Diaspad moved away from the fire. As she did so, her cloak fell open and Derry caught a fleeting glimpse of sleek red satin and sparkling jewels. "We won't need the horses. We don't have far to go."

Derry could hardly believe his ears. "Going out on foot? Just the six of us? On Midsummer's *Eve*?"

A tremor passed through Diaspad's body. "Derry," she said, in a voice that might have shattered crystal. "Derry, I am only going to say this once. You can come along with me, do exactly as I say, speak only when you are spoken to—or your career will be utterly ruined. In my household, at Caer Cadwy, any place in Celydonn you might choose to go. You've sworn to serve me, and serve me you shall or suffer the consequences." With a visible effort, she collected herself, smiled, and continued in her customary dulcet tones, "I hope I've made myself clear?"

"Yes," said Derry sullenly. "I guess you have."

"Good," said the Princess sweetly. She wrapped her cloak around her again and left the campsite. The others trailed after her, Derry tagging along at the rear.

Grass grew sparsely in that direction, amidst ragged clumps of heather and thistle. The ground was rocky and uneven underfoot. Now and again, something small that squeaked or rattled flew up out of the heather ahead of them or scurried past on tiny clawed feet. A pace or two behind them, someone or something a shade darker than the darkness followed them on enormous silent feet.

Ahead of him, Derry heard Calchas say: "I still don't understand precisely what you hope to accomplish tonight."

"Do you remember," the Princess asked, "a quarrel which took place between Cadifor and the King a year or two ago?"

"Cadifor had some fool notion about crowning himself King of Rhianedd, hadn't he?"

"Exactly," said Diaspad. "Once, this island was not one

kingdom but five: Camboglanna, Draighen, Rhianedd, Perfudd, and, of course, Gwyngelli. Under the kings of Rhianedd and Camboglanna, subject princes ruled in Gorwynnion, Walgan, and Celliwig, and the King of Draighen held nominal rule over the land of Cuan. But the tribes of the Mochdreffi owed allegiance to no man.

"You know our history," she continued, "you know how the High Kings rose, how the other kings and princes diminished, becoming mere vassal lords. All of them, that is, but one: the Lord and King of Tir Gwyngelli. His people were never conquered, his land never invaded, and his fealty, secured by treaty, is scarcely more than a formality. *Tir Gwyngelli,* the people still say: the Land of Gwyngelli. Not *degfed,* or tenth part, as the other nine portions are styled. And Cynwas is always 'the High King' or 'the Emperor'—a title which means next to nothing in Tir Gwyngelli. Maelgwyn is their King, and all their love and loyalty go to him.

"So Maelgwyn lives and rules just as his fathers did before him: a sort of sacred tribal king, honored by his Christian and pagan subjects alike. Naturally—if you know anything at all about the Queen's eldest brother—you can understand that it galls Cadifor to think that Maelgwyn rules as King, while he, whose ancestors once ruled Rhianedd in their own right, ranks no higher than the other great lords of the realm. He cannot see that Maelgwyn's title and the power that goes with it are Maelgwyn's own, and not in any sense a gift of the King of Celydonn."

"Well," said Calchas, "but *I* don't see—"

"My dear boy," said Diaspad, "you must see that Maelgwyn is going to continue as King of Tir Gwyngelli whether Cynwas acknowledges his title or not. Maelgwyn is quite secure in those rugged hills of his, surrounded by his fanatic and incorruptible Hillmen—and even the land, they say, fights for her rightful lord. But why *should* Cynwas challenge Maelgwyn . . . his great, his good, his generous friend? Maelgwyn is no threat to Cynwas. But the ambitious Cadifor, as King of Rhianedd, would present a considerable threat."

A slight strain began to tug at the back of Derry's legs and he realized that the land sloped downward now. After a time, the land began to rise again, and Derry became aware of something huge and angular blocking out the stars ahead of them.

At the top of the incline, everyone stopped to catch his breath, and the silent hunter, still padding along behind, drew closer. Derry could feel the hot breath raising the hairs on the back of his neck, but he understood the etiquette of these situations, and therefore knew better than to turn around and look. Derry knew that IT was there, and IT knew that he was there—so long as IT was willing to let the matter stand, Derry was willing to return the courtesy.

All evening, the moon had hidden behind a fraying veil of clouds; now the wind tore away her concealing vesture, flooding the plain with a nacreous light. Derry could not suppress a gasp of surprise. A double circle of rough-hewn dolmens lay in the exact center of the shallow valley below.

A few stones still stood straight and tall, but most had tilted or fallen over entirely. Yet even in their present disorder, Derry detected a certain symmetry.

"Leave your swords and your knives here," Diaspad commanded.

"Leave our—" Derry was aghast. "But how on earth are we supposed to protect you?"

"Derry," said the Princess very softly, "there is nothing down there from which you could possibly hope to defend me. And if we come bearing iron swords or knives, we will only antagonize those we have come here to meet."

"Oh God," breathed Derry. "Oh my God. Fairy Folk. You've brought us here to a fairy circle on Midsummer's Eve to treat with—"

"Men and women like ourselves," said the Princess. "But these are pagans, worshippers of the old gods and goddesses."

"Oh," said Derry, in a small voice. Among his people, as with the Gorwynnach and the Rhianeddi, the words "pagan" and "witch" were virtually synonymous. "This is their temple? They put the stones here?"

A hint of amusement crept into Diaspad's voice. "Dol Tal Carreg is far too old for that. Our ancestors found this place and others like it when first they migrated to these islands. No one knows who built these structures. But the Old Ones sometimes use them for their own purposes. And they would take it very ill," she added grimly, "were we to enter the circle below bearing cold iron."

Reluctantly, Derry took off his swordbelt and laid it on the grass, next to the weapons which Calchas and Morc had already discarded. Then he fished the dagger out of his sleeve and a small piece of steel he used for lighting fires out of his purse. To his relief, Derry saw that the dwarf and the giant were both armed with stout wooden cudgels, and these remained tucked into their belts. Scant protection against any of the things that walked in the night, Derry knew, but he was grateful for even that much.

They moved down the hill and circled around the ancient temple, the Princess still in the lead. On the eastern side of the henge, Diaspad seemed to find the entrance she sought, and passed through a precariously tilted trilithon into the outer circle. Something rustled in the brush directly behind him, and Derry hurried to catch up with her.

The Princess found a seat among the tumbled stones at the center of the temple; the rest took seats on the ground around her. Only Derry remained standing, shifting uneasily from one foot to another, glancing warily over his shoulder. "What now?"

"We wait," said the Princess. "You need not fear. These stones will ward us better than any walls could, better than any charm or incantation. But you may gather some firewood, if you like."

A few straggling bushes grew just outside the circle, but Derry was unwilling to venture even a few steps away from the others. Yet he was cold and he wanted that fire.

"Morc?" he whispered.

His brother groaned and rose ponderously to his feet. Together they gathered dry branches and piled them as the Princess instructed.

"But I still don't understand," Calchas said. "If Cynwas refuses to make him King of Rhianedd, why does Cadifor hazard his chance to rule *all* Celydonn someday against this impossible ambition?"

"Well, you see," said Diaspad, "Cadifor is not so many years younger than the King and may not outlive him. Even if Cynwas does name him as the heir, it would not be Cadifor but his son, Duach, who would enjoy the benefit. Oh, I don't doubt that Cadifor fancies himself as the father of a dynasty of kings, but he would much rather be a king himself. And his brother Llochafor, I should tell you, most particularly desires to be a prince.

"Whenever Sidonwy and her uncle, Lord Dyffryn, caution Cadifor against overweening ambition, that golden-eyed devil, Llochafor (playing some deep game of his own, I shouldn't doubt), is always on hand to encourage him in his folly.

"Yes, Derry, what is it now?" she asked impatiently, as Derry tugged at her sleeve and managed a pitiful little smile.

"How are we to light these? We left our steel up on the hill."

"Watch," said Diaspad, and ignited the wood with a touch and a murmured Word. As Derry had never before been privileged to watch her perform her magic, he was mightily impressed now. He sat down at her feet, touchingly confident that she could protect him from anything they might encounter here.

He edged a little closer, seeking reassurance, and the Princess leaned over and tenderly stroked his cheek. "You really are a pretty boy," she purred. "And charming, when you make the effort." She smiled, and the moonlight reflected off her tiny pointed teeth.

Derry wished that she had not done that. It put him in mind of certain nights—nights it was not good to remember—when he awoke in Diaspad's cavernous canopied bed to the sound of heavy breathing in his ear and the hideous sensation of a long, sinuous tail coiled around his bare leg. Of course it could only be one of the leopards, grown possessively affectionate, as cats sometimes will, but still . . .

"But where do the bones come into your plans?" Calchas asked. "And Lord Dyffryn. You have plans for Lord Dyffryn, I think?"

"Now that the Queen has succeeded in wheedling a pardon for her brothers, I do not want Dyffryn at Caer Cadwy making a nuisance of himself. I hope to make arrangements for Lord Dyffryn along with my other arrangements tonight."

She leaned forward toward the fire, and gold glinted under the hood which shadowed her face. "As for the bones: They would be immensely valuable to Cadifor. You see, he is not very popular in Rhianedd. Yet, lacking the King's consent, lacking the support of the Queen and Lord Dyffryn—both of whom, I should tell you, are well-beloved in Rhianedd and throughout the north—lacking all this, he might still hope to rally the Rhianeddi to his cause, *if* he possessed the bones.

"They are, as you know, sacred relics, believed to be the mortal remains of men of more than ordinary, even supernatural, stature. According to the ancient law, the King of Rhianedd was required to swear an oath on the bones, just prior to his coronation.

"But the last independent king presented the bones to Cynfelyn, and in so doing placed all his descendents under the power of the King of Celydonn. Each heir, when his time came, had to personally present himself to the High King in Camboglanna, in order to gain access to the bones, swear his oath, and claim his crown.

"When the High King began routinely to withhold his consent (and the bones, too, of course) there were no more kings in Rhianedd. Later, the bones disappeared during the dynastic wars, and never came to light again."

Derry was growing drowsy, sitting with cold stone at his back and firelight warming his face. As if from a great distance, he heard Calchas say: "Yes, I see. If the bones reappeared after all these years, all sorts of ideas about Rhianeddi independence might arise in the north. And what a hornet's nest someone could stir up then!"

"Indeed," said Diaspad. "Especially when Cadifor and his brother make their attempt to steal them."

Derry had just drifted off, with his head pillowed on Diaspad's knee, when a shrill piping and a sweet liquid ripple of harp strings awoke him.

The Old Ones appeared to materialize out of the very air, shining figures marching in from all directions, in robes of dazzling hue and richness. Many carried banners or standards, devices that, to Derry's sleep-drugged eyes, seemed to hold some deep, and somehow poignant, significance.

Morc hoisted Derry to his feet, and the Princess and the rest rose, too, turning first in this direction, then in that, bewildered by the wild, sweet music, and trying to see everything at once.

From the northeast came a tall, golden-haired man, robed all in purple like a prince, carrying in one hand a gilded staff surmounted by a fierce black raven. Moving as he did through a mass of seething bodies, the hesitation in his step seemed perfectly natural, but then the crowd parted, as if to make his passage easier, and Derry could see that the prince leaned heavily on his staff, and that the hand that held the staff was white about the knuckles. The man was lame, so badly crippled that every step he took must be an agony.

At his side, moving more lightly, yet still keeping pace with that painful, lurching gait, came a slender, bright-faced maiden whose every movement was so graceful and so joyous that her progress became a kind of dance. Gowned in silver and white, with gaily colored flowers wreathing her brow and cascading from her long pale hair, she carried in one hand a branch of blooming purple heather.

("Who?" breathed Derry, clutching Diaspad's arm.

("The Priest of Lludd—in bygone days, High Priest of the Rhianeddi," she answered. "And with him, one who represents Fiorwy, the Maiden.")

Out of the north marched two men crowned with oakleaves: one of them a strong man just past his prime, the other a pretty youth. Wild men, they might appear by their attire: hose and tunics of patched green and brown and yellow, like a dappling of sun and shadow in some forest glade, cloaks fashioned out of silky grey wolf pelts—yet majesty was in their faces, dignity in their bearing.

From the northwest, a handsome hard-faced woman in black and scarlet approached the inner circle, and a horde of cripples and lepers hobbled after her, keening miserably and struggling among themselves for an opportunity to touch her robes. But if she heard their piteous plaints, the grey-eyed Priestess of Donwy gave no sign.

In the wake of that clamoring throng, a red-haired man in sea-colored robes appeared, mounted on a milk-white stallion. Gold glittered in the stallion's frothy mane, gold upon his bridle, but as for his other trappings, all had been dyed with blue-azure.

("Vannen?" whispered Morc, and Derry nodded wordlessly, gazing on the hero of a hundred Draighenach nursery tales.)

From the southwest came two stately women in gowns as golden as ripe wheat, and behind them danced a merry crowd of children and yellow-striped tabby cats. The children giggled and jostled each other playfully, tripped over the purring tabbies, picked themselves up, and covered their mouths to stifle their laughter.

(This was all, Derry realized, somehow familiar. Thinking about it later, he would remember, with a jolt of recognition, the Princess's strange entrance at Caer Cadwy, six months before. But all that had been grotesque and gaudy and mocking then, was terrible and beautiful and heart-breaking now.)

Out of the south appeared two bent old women in shabby grey, escorting a tiny figure all but invisible under a tattered brown robe and a thick cobwebby veil which covered her head and shoulders. So small and delicate was she, under her rags, that Derry might have mistaken her for a child, were it not for her hands, which were wrinkled and spotted and knotted with age.

Derry felt the Princess stiffen under his clutching hands, and he followed her gaze to the southeastern portion of the circle, where a white-bearded old man had just arrived. Scarcely larger than the southern priestess, he came magnificently robed in gold and crimson, and he carried a golden dragon as his standard. A fierce, dark-eyed old man, who returned Diaspad's hostile gaze with an equally ferocious glare, though neither spoke a word.

To the very edge of the inner circle the Old Ones marched, and paused there, and waited, and the air seemed to quiver with their expectation. As no one had yet arrived from the west, their circle remained incomplete.

Then came a young boy all in green, bearing as his standard a simple branch of holly twined with oak. With his arrival, the music suddenly stopped.

The princely, golden-haired man stepped into the inner circle. "Who dares to intrude on our solemn rituals?"

The Princess lowered her hood, and Calchas and the giant helped her to remove her cloak. She had prepared carefully for this meeting, gowned and bejeweled and crowned as befits a king's daughter. And yet . . . as she stepped forward in her blood-red gown all sparkling with jewels, she did not look impressive but rather, small, defensive, and tawdry, as gaudy and defiant as ever Prescelli had appeared in one of Seelie's cast-off gowns.

"One who serves the Lady Celedon," said Diaspad. Her voice was steady but her hands, spread out before her in a gesture of peace and good-will, trembled violently.

A sharp crack of laughter exploded from the man in crimson, the bearer of the dragon standard. "Arrogance! You presume, Madam."

He addressed his companions indignantly. "This woman is not one of us. It is true she has served the Dark Mother, after a fashion, but when has she ever paid what is due to the Blessed Lady or to the Maiden?"

"I am a mother," said Diaspad. Her eyes turned, as if in entreaty, to the tall woman in black and scarlet, the stern-faced Priestess of Donwy. The priestess drew nearer, and Derry could see now that the grey eyes in that hard, cold face were softened by a boundless compassion. Though she seemed inclined to speak in Diaspad's favor, she remained sad and silent.

"Is not my beloved son here beside me?" insisted the Princess. "And I was young once . . . and loved many men."

"A fine mother!" scoffed the Dragon Priest, pointing a finger at Calchas. "Does she present this shifty-eyed, morally stunted, weak-hearted specimen as evidence of her tender motherly care? Oh yes, a fine mother!

"And as for love . . . this woman who teased and tormented, played one lover against another, until she drove Manogan fab Menai, that good man, to despair and bitterness—"

"I know you, Madawc," hissed the Princess, losing all control. "You who serve two masters! You who compromise yourself day by day, even as the great traitor himself—"

"Traitor, is it? Compromise? Fine words to hear from the Lady of Mochdreff!" Madawc retorted. "A race of traitors since the dawn of time! Black-hearted, sneaking—"

"Enough! Peace!" The man in purple held up his hand. "Your ancient quarrel does not concern us. Here, where all proclaim themselves united by a common bond."

"The Mochdreffi have no place among us. When have they ever paid homage to our gods? They worship *pigs* in Mochdreff," Madawc spat, "not gods!"

At this last, Calchas opened his mouth for an angry retort, but a hard brown hand placed over his mouth silenced him. "I wouldn't say it, young Lord," Bron whispered. "I wouldn't say it, were I you."

Many of those gathered around murmured their agreement, but the Priestess of Donwy finally yielded to Diaspad's unspoken plea. "It is true that votaries of the swine-cult have never joined our rituals. But this woman is not Mochdreffi-born or Mochdreffi-bred," she said, in a low, musical voice. "She is Draighenach by her mother, and of southern blood. She observes our rituals, has even, in the past, been admitted to our councils. Let us grant her the opportunity to tell us why she has come here now."

Again a general murmur of approval, though this time considerably subdued. All turned toward Madawc, as if soliciting his approval. He was not the mightiest or the most respected among them, but this was the festival of Midsummer, and no one desired to excite the Dragon's wrath.

The tiny priestess stepped into the ring of stones and took Madawc by the hand. "Indulge us, my brother and my husband," she said in a gentle voice. "What can it cost you, just to listen to her?"

(Even through her obscuring veil, Derry could see that she was much older than he had first supposed. Older than either of his grandmothers, certainly. Older than his surviving great-grandmother? He was inclined to think so, though she was far from feeble.)

Madawc shrugged his shoulders. "As you ask it, Lady, how can I deny it? Let her have her say, then, and be done with it!"

"I have come to strike a bargain with you." Diaspad addressed the old woman, but it was the man in purple who answered her: "A bargain? This hardly seems the time . . ." Then his eyes met those of the woman in scarlet and black, and he, too, shrugged. "But we have agreed to listen, at least."

Diaspad took a deep breath. "I ask . . . There are three things I have come to ask of you."

Again an explosion from the Dragon Priest. "Three! She comes begging not one boon but three! This woman's effrontery is apparently boundless!"

But Diaspad had gained an audience and refused to be deterred. "I want protections—safeguards against my enemy. I am loath to speak his name, here, where the very sound of it may give offense."

A protest rose from the fur-clad northerners, who apparently understood her very well. But the priest from Rhianedd silenced them. "Not unreasonable," he said.

"And I want the bones. The bones of the ancient kings of Rhianedd."

Another rude sound from Madawc. "One of our most revered symbols. One hardly dares to wonder what she will ask next."

"A little thing," said the Princess breathlessly. "A small thing to ask of such as you. I desire that Dyffryn fab Drwst be detained in Rhianedd indefinitely."

The lame man appeared to consider, for this matter concerned him more closely than it did any of the others. "How would you expect us to accomplish this?"

"I am indifferent as to the means," said Diaspad carelessly. "Strike him with disease or merely send nightmares to warn him away. Bring disaster down on those he loves, or kill him, if you must. So that he does not return to Caer Cadwy before my plans have born their fruit, I will be satisfied."

"And in return for all of this, what do you offer us?"

Diaspad hesitated. "I offer . . . I had hoped that you would name a price."

The southern priestess nodded approvingly. "Very wise, Princess. But we must take time to determine what to ask—or even if we desire to deal with you at all. A period of three weeks should suffice. Come again in three weeks' time, and some of us shall meet you here, to tell you what we have decided."

Diaspad frowned. "And in the meantime . . . how am I to know that you won't go directly to my enemies, selling information about my plans to those who could use it against me?"

"If you do not trust us, you were unwise to come here," said Madawc. "And you would be unwiser still to try our patience any further than you already have."

"Very well," said Diaspad reluctantly. "Very well. I shall go . . . for now. And I shall meet you here in three weeks' time."

. . . for the conjunction of these two (the Sun and the Moon) is like the union of Husband and Wife, who thus united in perfect intimacy produce offspring after their own kind.

"I am thy brother and thy husband," saith the Sun. "The Cup of Love and the Secret Fire will make us one."

"By our union," saith the Moon, "I receive thy nature as thou receiveth mine."

Take, therefore, the red man and the white woman and dissolve the bodies over white-hot ashes. . . .

From The Testimony of the Philosophers *(variously ascribed to Glastyn, Atlendor, and Moren Clydno)*

17.

Strange Bedfellows

Back at Caer Cadwy, the Midsummer Revels began at sunset with an illumination and dancing in the upper courtyards. A pageant followed, presented by a group of craftsmen from Treledig, then a bonfire and more dancing. At midnight, the King and Queen retired to a private chamber, there to partake of an intimate supper.

Squires and pages were still clearing away the last plates as a bell down in the monks' chapel tolled the call to morning prayers. Ceilyn sent the younger boys off to bed, and followed the others downstairs to supervise them as they cleaned and polished the silver. When the last plate and goblet were scrubbed, polished, and safely locked away, Ceilyn pocketed the key to the buttery and dismissed the last two boys.

He walked a long passageway through to the kitchens, found the kitchens empty, the ovens cold, and the fires in all the fireplaces dead or dying—which suited his mood admirably. On a table in one room, he discovered the remains of the squires' supper: a loaf of bread, some dirty dishes, and a flagon half full of spiced wine. Though he had fasted all day, Ceilyn ignored the bread. He poured a cup of wine, drew a bench closer to a fire, and poked half-heartedly at the pale coals.

The wine tasted bitter, had been left too long soaking up the oils and spices at the bottom of the flagon. But that suited Ceilyn, too. Life itself had a bitter flavor these days, the sour taste of envy and disappointment.

All those months, when the King and Queen were estranged, when Sidonwy was so wretchedly unhappy . . . had he not hoped then, and prayed then, for a reconciliation? Yet now that the thing had finally come about, he felt oddly dissatisfied. To make matters worse: Though the days of intrigue were past, one guilty secret remained. Sidonwy had never confessed to her clandestine correspondence with her brothers. Since she had not confessed and begged the King's pardon, neither could Ceilyn, and the burden of guilt he still carried on that account weighed more heavily with every passing day.

Even work, the old panacea for all that ailed him in mind and body, had failed him. He was unable to settle down to anything. And it all seemed so trivial. There had been something splendid in serving the Queen—even in such routine tasks as serving her meals, and supervising her pages, and shepherding her young ladies into town—so long as Sidonwy remained virtually friendless, but there was no dignity at all, so far as Ceilyn could see, in his present situation.

He swallowed the wine and poured another cup, sat down by the fire again. He was in love with Sidonwy, of course, had been absolutely devoted to her for years, and the last few months had brought them close—dangerously close. Yet was it love he felt for her? Did a feeling of possessiveness without any need to possess her physically, a fierce desire to protect a woman against all the rest of the world, qualify as love? And if he did love Sidonwy . . . what was it he felt for Teleri? Because he did want Teleri, wanted her so much it was a physical pain inside him—and what kind of a man felt that way about someone who did not want him at all?

"Is this a private celebration—or may I join you?" Prescelli had entered the room so silently that Ceilyn only became aware of her when she spoke.

He scowled at her, wondering what legitimate business could possibly bring her downstairs at this hour. And it seemed that everywhere he went, lately, Prescelli turned up, sooner or later.

"I'm afraid that I'm not very good company," he said. "And the wine has all gone sour."

Prescelli smiled and sat down beside him. "Oh, I wasn't looking for *good* company—or good wine. I've always been drawn to the other sort. I thought you knew that."

Ceilyn smiled mirthlessly, went over to the table, and poured another cup of wine. "Drinking all alone . . . not quite what one expects of the virtuous Ceilyn mac Cuel," said Prescelli, accepting the pewter goblet.

"There is a good deal you don't know about me," said Ceilyn. "Or the Princess Diaspad. Do you think she will be amused when you report this secret vice of mine?"

Prescelli took a sip of wine and grimaced. "Is that what you think—that the Princess asked me to spy on you while she is away? I am afraid that you flatter me. The position I hold in her household is . . . somewhat less exalted than that of an informer."

"Besides," she added, "what use has the Princess for spies, now that our royal Lord and Lady have resolved their differences? The King and Queen have no secrets from each other—or have they?"

"As you say," said Ceilyn, and took another swallow of wine. "Still, you have been following me, and I would like to know why."

Prescelli sighed. "You really are *amazingly* naive, aren't you?"

"That's God's own truth," said Ceilyn, and drained his cup again. "I'll not deny that. You can add it on to the tally of my faults."

Prescelli moved a little closer and the musky scent of her perfume completely surrounded him. "Until now, I never suspected that you had any faults at all."

"I never claimed to be infallible," said Ceilyn. "And I wish that other people would stop behaving as though I did. It's more tedious than you can possibly imagine."

"Oh, I think I can imagine quite easily," she said. In the dim glow of the dying coals her thin face and sharp features looked softer, rounder, decidedly more appealing—all but the dark, hungry eyes. "You and I have more in common than you might think. Everyone always imagines the worst possible motives for everything I do, just as they always allow you the benefit of the doubt. But what is the result? They dislike us both, just about equally."

"That's true," said Ceilyn, much struck by the aptness of the comparison. It astounded him that Prescelli, of all women, should prove to be so sympathetic, so understanding. And perhaps it was the effect of the wine, but he began to relax a little, to let down his guard. "I never thought of that before, but you're absolutely right. It doesn't matter if you are better or worse than the rest. Just that you are different, that's the great sin."

He eyed her with increasing interest. She really did look quite amazingly pretty, with her dark hair all tumbling down around her shoulders, and her gown of crushed peach-blush silk—like a rose just beginning to wilt, he thought. And if another woman had aroused this hunger he felt inside him, had engendered this intimate, aching need . . . did it necessarily follow that Prescelli— or any woman—could not satisfy him equally well?

He drew away from that thought, instantly ashamed. He rose, a little unsteadily, went over to the table, and refilled his cup. But perhaps Prescelli guessed something of what he was feeling.

"It must be dreadfully hard," she said, "to always be so dreadfully good. Don't you ever long to abandon the effort and do something utterly, outrageously wicked?"

"Constantly," said Ceilyn, bringing his cup of wine back to the bench. "That's why I never, never can." As soon as he said that, he regretted it. He had not meant to reveal so much.

Prescelli laughed softly. "Yes, I see. You think that you might like it rather too well. But really, I don't see what you could lose by indulging yourself just once. That reputation for perfection . . . you said, yourself, it was a tremendous burden. And others might like you better, for the display of a little human weakness."

"Perhaps they would," said Ceilyn. "Yes, perhaps they would. But they don't have to live with the consequences."

"Nor with the pain you are feeling now?" Prescelli suggested gently.

"No," Ceilyn admitted, just above a whisper. "Nor with the pain I am feeling now. That is all my own, I'm afraid."

"But you could share it." Prescelli moved a little closer. "You could share it with me."

Without thinking what he was doing, he slipped his arm around her waist. "Dear God . . ." he breathed, ". . . if I only could."

Half an hour later, they were upstairs in Diaspad's bedchamber, sitting on the edge of her big bed, Prescelli with the front of her gown unlaced, and Ceilyn stripped down to his shirt, hose, and breeches, as white as the linen, in a state bordering on panic: afraid that she would refuse him at the last moment, and of what he might do if she did, terrified that he might not be able to perform, or that he would do something completely wrong and look like a fool.

"You must have some idea how to proceed." Prescelli could not resist teasing him.

"I know how dogs and horses do it," he said miserably. "I've seen other men fumbling serving maids. But I have no idea what is expected here."

"Well, then, I'll just have to show you," said Prescelli. And she proceeded to demonstrate so expertly—not only what she wanted but what he wanted as well—that nature very soon took its course, and no further instruction was needed.

Ceilyn released a long shuddering sigh and finally subsided. He buried his face in Prescelli's long dark hair, reluctant to break their sweet, intimate contact, though all the passion was spent.

But then it occurred to him that she might find his weight difficult to bear. He rolled off of her and onto the sweat-soaked sheets. "Well," said Prescelli breathlessly. "That was . . . really quite good . . . for your first time."

"Was it?" His pleasure in that, and his incredulous relief, made her laugh.

And he looked so open and vulnerable, lying there naked beside her, his bright, nervous eyes for once exultant, and that impossible brown hair even more disheveled than usual—for the first time in her life, Prescelli felt a pang of pure, unselfish tenderness. "Oh yes," she said. "I'm terribly impressed."

"You're laughing at me," he accused her, his pleasure a little dimmed.

"I'm laughing," Prescelli admitted, "but this time, I expect, the joke is entirely at my expense."

It came to him then that he had said none of the things that a man ought to say in bed with a woman. Tentatively, he touched her face, searched his mind for something to say, some gift he could give her in exchange for what she had just given him. "It was good for me, too. Quite the best thing that ever happened to me. Better . . . than being knighted, even.

"You're laughing again," he said. "I don't see why."

Prescelli shook her head. "That's a lovely compliment. But I am afraid that I'm more accustomed to something more predictable . . . and less sincere. What you are supposed to do is tell me how beautiful I am, and how long you've been simply aching to take me to bed with you."

"But you are beautiful," Ceilyn said gallantly. "And I've always been . . . tremendously attracted to you."

"Truly?" She propped herself up on one elbow, studied his face with sudden intensity. "Have you really?"

Much to his own surprise, Ceilyn realized it was true. He had never really liked Prescelli, but neither had he been entirely indifferent to her. "You must know what a disturbing effect you used to have on me. All those teasing little games that you and the other girls played . . . Fand and Finola and their elaborate plots. But you—you had only to brush past me in the corridor, or surprise me looking at you. Surely you guessed how I felt."

"No," she said. "I never did. My goodness, how frustrating it was, and how exciting. Because you were always there like—like a thunderstorm about to happen. How much we all disliked you— and how we all might have adored you, given a little encouragement.

"Because you really are an exceptionally beautiful young man. Not a mark or a blemish on you anywhere," she marveled, placing a hand on his smooth, hairless chest, running it caressingly over his hard, flat belly. "Now, how did you contrive that? Most of the other men have scars to show for every hour they ever spent in harness."

The light in Ceilyn's face faded, and he began to suspect that he had just made a serious mistake. "They are careless," he said. "I don't allow myself to get hit, that's all."

Then, realizing how that must sound, he added, "I've been very lucky, of course. But I am fast, and stronger than I look."

"Yes, I had noticed that," said Prescelli. Her hand moved suggestively along his flank. "And other things.

"Don't look at me that way," she protested, suddenly terrified by something she read in his face. "Did I say something wrong?"

Almost instantly, he was ashamed of himself, sorry that he had frightened her. And after all, she could not have learned anything, really, not anything that Fergos or Gofan, or any of the other men with whom he had shared quarters over the years, had not already noticed.

"I'm sorry," he said. "I was thinking of something unpleasant. But nothing that need concern you."

For Derry, Leth Scathach proved to be an embarrassing disappointment. He had forgotten how uncivilized—how primitive, really—life in the north could be; and to be reminded—worse, to see it all exposed to the Princess Diaspad's scornful and amused eyes—was intensely humiliating.

Dun Dessi, Forgoll's principal residence, was a great drafty wooden hall, where the nobility and the peasantry (so it seemed to Derry, a half-dozen years more sophisticated now than he had been when he left Draighen) existed in just about equal squalor. Rats infested the place, the straw in all the beds was stale and mildewed, and the tapestries on the walls might have benefited from a thorough beating with a good broom.

As for his family: A more slovenly, rackety, and quarrelsome brood could scarcely be imagined. Derry was not a fastidious youth, to be sure; nevertheless, he found the studied shabbiness of his kinfolk decidedly offensive. He knew what wealth Forgoll's fertile and surprisingly well tended acres represented, so he knew there was no need for the Lord of Leth Scathach, his wife, his mistresses, and his eldest sons to deck themselves virtually in rags. Yet all of them seemed to enjoy their constant bickering, the continual plotting and scheming for Forgoll's favor and some small share of his hoarded gold, and even to take a perverse pride in their dirt, their rags, and their pretended poverty.

Despite all this, Derry continued to hope that the christening itself might provide some better diversion and represent his family to the Princess in a more favorable light. The naming of any child in these northern lands, and particularly of a noble babe, heir to vast tracts of land, was a momentous occasion, and for this double christening, Forgoll had invited all his cousins, second-cousins, and even more distant kinfolk. Derry therefore expected that his father would endeavor to impress them all.

Alas for Derry. Though Forgoll had followed tradition by opening his doors to the entire clan, he felt no obligation to exert himself any further. The christening was a thoroughly dismal affair. Both babies wailed throughout the ceremony, Leam bullied his poor little terrified scrap of a wife because the children were so ill-behaved, and the whole thing was crowned by a perfectly miserable feast that was meager, cold, and tasteless, offering no entertainment but a wretched wandering bard, who scraped away on a badly tuned harp for what seemed like hours.

By the time the day of departure finally dawned, Derry was more than eager to be on his way, and he took leave of his ancestral acres without a backward glance. But the discomforts of the long, dusty journey south soon blunted his enthusiasm for travel, and his spirits declined further as the night of the rendezvous at Dol Tal Carreg approached.

"I will hear no excuses, so don't bother to present them," said the Princess, when the fateful evening arrived. "You will come along with me, and behave yourself, too!" So Derry, with rare prudence, accepted the inevitable and kept quiet.

At the stone circle, three dark figures awaited them. Without their splendid robes, simply and soberly clad in grey or brown homespun, those three looked oddly diminished.

Donwy's handsome priestess spoke first. "It has been decided. If you are willing to pay our price, the bones will be delivered to you within the fortnight. It is for you to name the time and place."

Diaspad could not repress a smile of triumph. She had spent the last three weeks in an agony of apprehension, but now, meeting these three here, stripped of all the trappings which had awed her at their previous meeting, and finding them willing to negotiate, her confidence returned.

"I desire that the bones should come to light publicly—an accidental discovery it must seem to be. I do not wish to be present at the time, lest my part in this be suspected, but there must be others on hand to witness their discovery. I leave the details to you. But what of my other requests?"

"He whose interference you would guard against has little power to affect the course of events during the time between Beltane and Samhain." The priest from Rhianedd leaned on a short crutch like a lame beggar, and he wore a ragged bandage on his bad leg. "As he may be regarded as . . . manageable now, we are willing to guarantee that he will not trouble you for that period of time. As for Dyffryn fab Drwst, even as we speak, his young wife and infant daughter lie in bed, stricken by a mysterious malady."

"Both mother and daughter are in a delirium," added the grey-eyed priestess. "But their dreams are sweet, and their bodies free from pain. When they awake, their recovery will be swift. But Dyffryn believes them to be in peril of their lives, and does not leave their bedside."

"Well enough," said Diaspad carelessly. "But what price am I to pay for all these favors? That has not yet been named."

"Little enough," said the dark-eyed, hostile Madawc. "If it were mine to decide—"

"Yes, yes." The other priest interrupted him impatiently. "You have had your say, Madawc, and your wishes have been taken into consideration. That you know. But this is of some importance to us all. And we should be honest with this lady: It is not a small thing we would ask of her."

"Well," said Diaspad, her confidence a little dimmed. "I am listening."

"You know," said the lame man, "that every year at Samhain we give the great sacrifice. In recent years, we have been unable to offer the sacrifice in the appropriate manner at the appointed place. But this is the end of the twenty-seven-year cycle, and this is the year when the full sacrifice *must* be offered and all the attending rituals performed.

"The peace of the realm is in considerable peril as it is. But if Donwy should not be appeased . . .!"

"You know where the sacrifice was presented in ages past?" asked the priestess.

"Yes," said Diaspad. "I know the place. A dangerous spot to celebrate the ancient rites."

"Yes," agreed the tall priest. "And yet, situated as you are, you ought to be able to make the necessary arrangements and do what we dare not attempt."

Diaspad could hardly believe her good fortune. Oh yes, she had been confident at the beginning that she could manipulate these people—but that they should grant all that she asked, and ask so little in return, that she had never dared to hope. Very gladly would she offer the sacrifice and perform the rituals for them—and turn the power she gained in the process, if she could, to her own dark purposes.

"We know that there is some risk in this, even for you," the priest continued apologetically. "But all the rites must be properly observed and celebrated—without the consecration, of course, as there is no suitable candidate—and I must tell you . . ." (growing stern) ". . . that there is no other way in which you could possibly serve us."

Diaspad pretended to think it over. "Very well," she said at last. "It is risky, yes. But I am willing to undertake it."

"We have a bargain, then?" Donwy's priestess asked.

"Oh yes," said Diaspad, smiling her old, sweet, dangerous smile. "We have a bargain!"

"Like calls to like," said Glastyn. "The mind and the heart can easily be deceived, a mere resemblance will do for either of them. But blood and bone, muscle and sinew: These will always know their own."

18.

A Casket of Bones

"And what makes you so certain," said Calchas, "that those people aren't going to trick you? How will we know that the bones they give us are the real thing, and not just any old bones they happened to find lying around? And even if they are the real thing, how are we to prove that? We can hardly step forward and swear to their authenticity. If we say anything at all, Cadifor and Llochafor will sense a trap."

"Very true," said the Princess lazily. "But I think that Cadifor and his brother will be willing, even eager, to believe in them, simply because *I* pretend that I do not."

Diaspad and her party had arrived at Caer Cadwy the night before. Though it was nearly noon, Diaspad remained in bed, propped up by satin pillows in an untidy nest of feather mattresses and rumpled sleeping furs. Calchas prowled restlessly from one part of the room to another, in one of his tiresome questioning moods, but his mother had rested well and breakfasted well in her own bed, was drowsy and content, and therefore willing to humor him.

"As for how to identify the relics," she continued. "Just any old bones won't do. The ancient kings of Rhianedd (so legend informs us) were men of enormous stature. Not actually giants, like our Pergrin, but great, strapping, beautiful men . . . not unlike your young friends, Fflergant and Tryffin. But more than that, the real bones are marked by certain stigmata. Shattered skulls, broken ribs . . . that sort of thing. They were warriors, those old kings, and many of them died in battle—martyrs to the homeland, you might say, which is one reason why their bones came to be revered.

"And the bones have been described in detail. I don't recall their kind or number, but others will. Our friends the Old Ones would be forced to sort through a vast quantity of old bones in order to assemble a convincing counterfeit. But it's nothing to me whether or not the bones are genuine," she said. "A counterfeit will suit my purposes just as well, so long as Cynwas and Cadifor are both deceived. Indeed, I hope our friends *may* try to cheat me, for that would relieve me of any obligation I might otherwise owe them."

All this time, Calchas had continued to pace the floor. Every now and then, he narrowly avoided a collision with Prescelli, who bustled around the room unpacking the Princess's gowns. Such a changed Prescelli: respectful, dutiful, and industrious—the very picture of a guilty conscience hiding behind a demure manner.

"Well," said Calchas, "all very well and good. But supposing—" Diaspad cut him short with a motion of her hand.

Derry had been dispatched earlier to ferret out the latest news and acquaint the Princess with all that had happened at Caer Cadwy during her absence, and now he oozed in past the half-opened door, making an elaborate show of trying to catch Prescelli's eye.

"Prescelli, dear," said Diaspad, wrinkling her nose delicately, "do clear away these dishes for me. The smell of them makes me quite faint."

Without a word of protest, Prescelli gathered up the silver plates and left the room. "Well?" said the Princess to Derry. "What have you to tell me?"

Derry lounged across the room, deposited himself on the tygerskin rug by the fireplace. "They say that Cadifor and Llochafor have accepted the King's kind invitation, and are expected to arrive here at any time."

"Good," said Diaspad. "But what of that other rumor I heard last night? I gather from the amusing little pantomime we just witnessed that the story is true?"

"Incredible as it may seem, yes," said Derry. "Or perhaps not so incredible, if she used your love charm."

"I think not," said Diaspad. "The girdle was all very well for entrapping a simple-minded soul like Iaen Og, but I can't imagine a complex, stubborn young man like Ceilyn succumbing—not without a tremendous struggle. No, it is entirely possible that the attraction between them is genuine.''

"Then what," Derry asked, "do you intend to do about this grand passion? How do you plan to go about ending it?"

"End it?" said Diaspad. "But why should I want to end it? I am very pleased about this. Ceilyn mac Cuel could be of considerable use to me, just at this time.''

"Oh yes," Derry agreed. "I can see how he could be useful: Knight Equerry to the Queen, Sidonwy's fair-haired boy. But *would* he help you? Except for this one insignificant transgression, the man has always lived like a monk. And if you think that a toss with Prescelli is sufficient to corrupt him, you just don't know Ceilyn."

"Oh yes," said Diaspad. "I do know Ceilyn. Or, I've known men like him. For the Ceilyns of this world, there are no 'insignificant transgressions.' A virtuous young man like Ceilyn is driven by such devils as you and I, Derry, for all our wickedness, can scarcely imagine. Guilt, frustration, self-hatred . . . they can goad a man into anything. They have apparently driven him into Prescelli's arms, but that won't be the end of it—not if I have anything to say about it.

"Such an unhappy girl, our Prescelli," said Diaspad, with evident satisfaction. "If I am right, if he cares two pins for her, she will put him through Hell before she is finished. But you are quite right about one thing. A tumble or two won't suffice. Even Prescelli will need time—time to introduce Ceilyn to the very worst part of his own nature.''

"And you intend to see that she has that time . . . by some magical intervention, I take it?" said Derry.

"Yes, I do," said Diaspad. "Though something stronger than the silken girdle will be required.''

"It will have to be something in his food, I expect," volunteered Calchas, sitting down on the edge of the bed.

"No good," said Derry, propping his chin on the tyger's huge, wolflike head. "He only eats plain, simple food. It was a vow he made to his father: to avoid the corruptions of life at court by living a life of simple purity . . . or some such nonsense. Oh, he tests the

Queen's food and drink, from time to time, but never more than a taste. For himself, he avoids rich foods and spices, and won't touch anything that isn't served on wood, crockery, or pewter. So, unless your potion is tasteless, colorless, and odorless, Ceilyn will probably detect it.''

"A difficult young man, to be sure," mused the Princess, curling up among the pillows. "But a way will have to be found. This is too good an opportunity to be allowed to pass by."

It was a fine, hot day, and Garanwyn and his cousins Fflergant and Tryffin, after spending the morning in the stables grooming horses, discovered that they all three had the entire afternoon free. "But if we loiter around here," Garanwyn pointed out, "someone will find something useful for us to do. Why don't we go for a swim after dinner?"

"Too strenuous," said Fflergant, as he led the way upstairs to the dormitory and a change of clothes before the afternoon meal. "Or were you forgetting Tryffin?"

They both stopped and looked at Fflergant's brother. At eighteen, the last of his baby fat was hardening into solid muscle, but Tryffin was still growing. He approached every meal as though it were destined to be his last, and he was inclined to be as sluggish as a dragon after dinner.

"A ride, then," said Garanwyn. "Not too strenuous, I think?"

Tryffin considered the question solemnly. "I may summon up the energy," he decided.

With dinner served and their own share of the left-overs divided and devoured, the boys went immediately back down to the stables. They saddled and mounted their horses and headed for the Main Gate, but crossing the courtyard they met Fand.

"There you are," she said, glaring up at Garanwyn. "I hope that you know where to find her, for I certainly do not."

Garanwyn groaned. "Not again. You haven't allowed Gwenlliant to run off by herself again?"

"Well, really!" Fand exclaimed, growing pink with indignation. "I'm not your little sister's nursemaid!"

Garanwyn apologized. "I will be glad to help you look for her," he offered, climbing down out of the saddle.

"Well, after all, you might just as well go on with your ride," said Fand, somewhat mollified. "It may be that you are heading in the right direction. The Captain of the Guard tells me that some of the castle children went out the gate about an hour ago, and Gwenlliant may be with them."

"Let us hope not," said Garanwyn, swinging back into the saddle. He kicked his horse lightly and rode through the gate. But Fflergant and Tryffin lingered by the gatehouse, grinning down at Fand.

"Want to come along, then?" Fflergant suggested.

Fand glanced from him to his brother—from one pair of laughing dark eyes under a thatch of sun-bleached hair to another— threw prudence to the winds, and replied, "Why not?" She accepted the big brown hand that Fflergant offered her, and allowed him to hoist her up into the saddle with him.

They had traveled some distance down the dusty road beyond the gate, and had nearly overtaken Garanwyn, when they spotted a crowd of dirty children playing by the crumbling outer curtain wall. Garanwyn stopped and waited for the others to draw abreast.

"There she is," he said, pointing first to his sister, then to the party of stonemasons repairing the wall not a dozen paces from the spot where Gwenlliant and her lowborn companions played. "Playing with the servant's children, and associating with common laboring men as well!"

He dismounted and handed the reins up to Tryffin. But his sister, all unaware of his approach, gathered up her heavy skirt in one hand, and attempted to scramble atop a pile of stones. A shout from one of the workmen distracted her; she lost her footing and tumbled down, landing in the dirt, winded but unharmed.

Tryffin tethered his horse and Garanwyn's to a hedge, reached up to help Fand dismount. "Such a commotion," she said. "What do you suppose is happening?"

"It seems they have found something," said Fflergant, hitching his horse to another bush, craning his neck to see what it might be.

Meanwhile, Garanwyn had picked Gwenlliant up out of the dirt, straightened her dress, dusted her off, and hauled her with him, to get a better look at the stonemasons' discovery.

It was a large wooden chest with elaborate carvings, all clogged with dirt and moss. One of the workmen raised his pick to strike off the lock, but another man stopped him. "Have a care. This may be worth something. Pry off the hinges. . . . They're loose already."

The hinges came off easily and two men eagerly lifted the lid. Someone gasped, and "Bones" cried somebody else. Gwenlliant and the other little girls all shrieked and covered their faces with their hands.

"For the love of . . . It's only a box full of moldy old bones," said Garanwyn, prying one hand from Gwenlliant's face. "There now . . . do you see? Nothing that can possibly harm you."

Gwenlliant spread her fingers, took a tentative peek. "Yes, I see. Can we go now?" Then her hand dropped and her expression changed to one of bewildered delight. "Grandfather?" she asked tremulously.

To her brother's horrified amazement, she knelt down in the dirt beside the casket, and picked up one of the bones. "Grandfather?"

Garanwyn stood paralyzed by embarrassment. "Gwenlliant," he said weakly, "put the bone down. It's not a toy, for God's sweet sake."

The workmen muttered ominously and the other children grew owl-eyed, staring at Gwenlliant aghast. In another minute, Garanwyn knew, someone would speak the word he dreaded to hear.

But Fand and his kinsmen had finally arrived, and Tryffin, acting with his usual presence of mind, pushed through the crowd and scooped his little cousin up into his arms. "Come along, Sweetheart. There's no reason to be upset. Only a pile of old bones, it is, nothing to fear in that."

"But I'm not afraid," Gwenlliant insisted, laughing up at him. "It's my *grandfather*—don't you recognize him? I think you might, for he is your grandfather, too."

"Our great-grandfather, do you mean?" he asked softly. "But that can't be, Dear Heart. He's buried in Tir Gwyngelli."

"Not that grandfather," said Gwenlliant, offering the fragment of bone to one of the masons—who gingerly accepted it. "My grandfather's grandfather's grandfather, maybe. He was a king once, in Rhianedd."

A silent message passed between Tryffin and his brother. Fflergant nodded and knelt down by the casket to take a closer look at the bones. Tryffin put a hand on Gwenlliant's forehead, and proclaimed in a clear, carrying voice, "She's been running about in all this heat. No wonder if she's feverish and spouting obscene nonsense!"

Abruptly, he handed her over to Fand. "And what were you thinking to allow her out on a day like this?" he asked sternly. "Before God! She oughtn't to be here at all. Old bones and sick fancies brought on by the heat!"

Fand cringed under his rebuke and meekly accepted the child into her arms. "What are you waiting for?" chimed in Garanwyn. "Take her back home again, for the love of God."

The girl from Draighen began to recover herself. "I certainly will," she sniffed. "But this is the last time that I go riding with any of you!" She set Gwenlliant on her feet, and marched off in a huff, dragging the child behind her.

Fflergant concluded his examination of the bones. "Whatever we have here," he told the masons, "I think that someone ought to show it to the High King—and that immediately!"

He dusted himself off, then followed Tryffin and Garanwyn back to the place where they had left the horses. "There will be the Devil to pay when Fand speaks to the Queen," said Tryffin, gazing up the dusty road at Fand and Gwenlliant trudging back toward the castle. "Discourtesy to a lady—where were my wits when I needed them?"

"Where were mine?" said Garanwyn. "I couldn't think of anything to say. If you hadn't come along . . . Do you honestly think it was only the heat?"

"No," said Tryffin regretfully. "I don't think that. Oh, she was a little warm, as you might expect, but no more feverish than you or I. And I would swear she was as rational." He glanced at his brother. "You had a closer look at the bones. What do you think?"

"I did feel something. Impossible to describe it," said Fflergant. "Like spotting a familiar face in a crowd, or—no, more like recognizing someone you've not seen in a long time. What do you think? Do you think they have uncovered . . . what I think they have uncovered?"

Tryffin turned to Garanwyn. "You ought to know, better than either of us."

Garanwyn furrowed his brow. "I didn't really look at them; I was concentrating on Gwenlliant. But supposing they are the bones of the ancient kings of Rhianedd? What will we say? What can we tell people?''

"No need to say anything," said Tryffin. "If they are the bones of the kings, Cynwas and Sidonwy will know.''

"Yes, but how do we explain Gwenlliant . . . knowing?''

"Now that I come to think of it, there's every reason she should know," said Tryffin. "Wasn't she born in the Rhianedd Highlands? Didn't she spend the first six years of her life listening to your nursemaids tell stories of those old kings and their magical bones? It doesn't take any supernatural ability to recognize something you've heard about all of your life.''

"Do you think that was the way it really happened?'' Garanwyn asked eagerly. "That she just saw the bones and made the same guess any child in Rhianedd would? Do you think there was nothing more to it than that?''

Fflergant and Tryffin exchanged another glance. They did not think anything of the sort, but knew how desperately Garanwyn wanted to believe it.

"Ah well, who can say?'' said Tryffin.

The masons delegated a party of four to present the casket to the King: two sturdy fellows to carry the chest up the hill to the castle, two others to serve as a kind of rustic honor guard. The guards at the gate directed them to the archery range, where they found the King and the Earl Marshall.

The masons placed the casket at the King's feet, bowed awkwardly, and withdrew to a respectful distance. The King handed his longbow over to a page, and bent down to examine the chest more closely. At least half-Rhianeddi himself, Cynwas experienced a pleasant shock of familiarity as soon as he touched the lid, much as Fflergant had experienced earlier when handling the bones.

But Ceilyn mac Cuel—who had a Rhianeddi great-grandmother —as soon as he entered the yard, was assailed by emotions so poignant, at once so joyous and so heart-wrenching, that only with difficulty could he master himself and escort the Queen to the casket with *no* outward display of emotion.

He whispered a suggestion in Sidonwy's ear. She nodded, and

Ceilyn dispatched a page to summon Teleri. Having accomplished that much, he might have withdrawn to a safer distance, but the Queen detained him. So he was still standing there, stiff and self-conscious at Sidonwy's side, when Teleri arrived.

Astonished by this unexpected summons, Teleri was painfully embarrassed at finding herself the focus of so many curious eyes, but she knelt on the ground beside the casket and dutifully inspected the bones. They were old—no doubt about that—and a residue of power still lingered, as it might cling to an object which men have revered over a period of years. Beyond that, the excitement and anticipation she felt on every side—emanating from the King and Queen, Ceilyn, Gofan and his brother Nefyn, Tryffin and Fflergant, Garanwyn and Gwenlliant—told her all that she needed to know.

Like calls to like, Glastyn had taught her, and proof of his teaching was all around her. Though the centuries had reduced those proud warrior kings to cracked and splintered bone, though the years had also, generation by generation, bred or trained the old earth-born instincts out of their descendents, there remained *something* which, had the bones been further reduced to a handful of dust, would still have constituted a vital link between living flesh and blood and moldering bone. Though all these distant grandchildren might have experienced difficulty identifying the remains of their own, more recent, grandparents and great-grandparents, these, the sacred relics of the Rhianeddi race, these they knew.

But they had all learned to distrust or conceal whatever of the old gifts remained to them. So they all waited impatiently for Teleri to complete her examination and tell them something that they already knew.

"Well?" said the King, as Teleri placed the last bone back in the box and closed the lid. "Are these . . . what they appear to be?"

Teleri sat back on her heels. Without looking up, she answered softly. "The bones of the ancient kings of Rhianedd? Beyond all question, they are."

The King signaled to two of his personal guards. "Take the casket away. Put it . . . in the Treasury, I suppose."

The guards picked up the chest. Cynwas watched them, frowning, until they passed through the gate into the next yard.

"Surely, my dear Lord, you do not mean to dispose of them so casually?'' the Queen asked softly. ''Ought they not to be handled with a little more respect?''

''I do not know what I shall do with them,'' replied the King. ''I shall have to consider carefully.''

Meanwhile, Teleri stood up and waited patiently for someone to dismiss her. She felt unaccountably shy in Ceilyn's presence, unable to meet his eyes. So she stared at her feet, instead, more disconcerted by his steady gaze than by the curious scrutiny of the others. And because she wanted to hide from Ceilyn, more than anyone else, she did not even try to *imagine* herself elsewhere. He knew all her hiding places; she had nowhere to go.

And Ceilyn, for his part, remained at the Queen's side, uneasy and embarrassed, wondering how to interpret Teleri's shyness. She would know by now that he was sleeping with Prescelli— impossible to keep a secret like that in a place like Caer Cadwy— but he had never imagined that the news would move her, one way or the other. Yet there she stood, visible and vulnerable, shrinking from his gaze—as though she, and not he, had done something to be ashamed of—and he did not know what to make of that, at all.

Mercifully, the Queen soon sensed his embarrassment—or perhaps she recognized Teleri's distress. With a nod and a word of thanks, she gave the little sorceress leave to depart.

And in the Reign of Saturn, the Body, dying, releases the volatile spirit, which passes through the Eclipse, both of the Sun and the Moon, and through the Gate of Blackness (which some call Purgatory) where it remains in Utter Darkness for forty-two days.

For I tell you truly, there is no Generation without Corruption, and Death precedes Life as surely as Night the Day.

From The Testimony of the Philosophers

19.

In the Reign of Saturn

The warm weather continued through most of July: days of sticky heat alternating with warm, lashing rains and thunderstorms at night. All over the castle, the vegetation ran positively wild in the unnatural heat and damp, the ivy and the bramble rapidly overtaking the wild-rose, until the three of them threatened to engulf the whole pile. Grass sprouted between cobblestones, giving pathways and courtyards an untidy appearance, a feathery green moss crept up walls and staircases, and an army of massive tree roots attacked the outer walls, crumbling stone and crushing mortar into dust.

On the twenty-fifth of the month, on toward evening, the hot spell finally broke, and a peculiarly oppressive dampness crept in from the sea, completely enveloping the town and the overgrown castle. Down in Treledig, the streets were empty. Up at the castle, the inhabitants drifted through the halls as pale and listless as ghosts. Outside in the gardens there were ghosts of another sort: shapes of statues and bushes distorted by the fog, wisps of grey mist struggling to acquire form.

Ceilyn and Prescelli walked together in the Queen's garden. "For the love of God," Ceilyn said impatiently, "let's not begin again. I've said I'm sorry, if that is not enough—"

"Oh yes," she interrupted him tartly, "a few words and all is mended. I've never met a man who didn't believe that—so long as it was only a *woman* he had insulted. But your own quarrels are another matter—you don't pass those off so lightly."

Ceilyn sighed. "If it is satisfaction you want—"

"Listen," she said, clutching at his arm. "There is someone following us. I heard footsteps just now. Someone is spying on us."

"Why would anyone—?"

"There it is again," Prescelli insisted. "You heard it, too. I saw you turn your head."

"I heard something," he admitted. "But why should anyone spy on us? We've hardly made a secret of our affair, and the gossips have already exhausted speculation. Why would anyone lurk about in the damp and the dark, only to confirm something that everyone already knows?"

"I don't know," she said with a shiver, glancing over her shoulder apprehensively. "Perhaps I am imagining things. But I'm so tired of prying eyes.

"It's been worse since the Princess returned," she went on plaintively, their quarrel forgotten for the moment. "I do wish we could find someplace to be private together. We simply can't go on like this."

"I know," he said wearily. "If we could only find a place . . ." If they could only find a place to be alone and make love properly, if it could be the same way now that it had been in the beginning, perhaps they would not quarrel so often. "Summer affairs are supposed to be so easy," he said. "All moonlight and roses and making love in the gardens the whole night long. But nobody ever bothers to mention foggy nights, or thunderstorms, or tell you that the dew falls, even in July."

He put his arms around her, pulled her under his cloak—a protective gesture, not a passionate one, intending to warm her. But she came to him so eagerly, clung to him so fiercely, that desire soon kindled within him. And somewhere at the back of his mind a voice goaded him: *If someone is following us, if someone is watching, why shouldn't she see exactly what she came for?* He bent his head and kissed Prescelli savagely.

Somewhere in the darkness and the fog there was a tiny sound like a stifled gasp, followed by feet scurrying across the courtyard. Prescelli wrenched herself out of his arms. "There was someone spying on us. And I know who it was, even if you pretend otherwise!"

Teleri slammed the door shut behind her, threw the bolt into place. She ran across the room, hurled herself face down on the scarlet counterpane, and burst into tears.

Why do you lock the door? said a voice, almost in her ear. With a gasp, Teleri looked up. One of the stylized beasts carved in stone above the fireplace, a shaggy creature vaguely resembling a lion, was watching her intently.

Why do you lock the door? the voice asked again. *You can't lock it out now. It came in at the door seven months ago with Ceilyn mac Cuel.*

Teleri looked around her. "There is nothing there," she said aloud. She sat up, wiped the tears away, and regained a measure of composure. "Everything is exactly as it was."

Are you exactly as you were?

She thought of what she had just seen in the garden, felt her palms grow damp and her heart begin to beat painfully hard. A hot flush spread over her. "I am," she whispered. "I am exactly as I was."

But even as she spoke, she could feel the changes taking place inside of her, her own body betraying her, becoming something strange and terrible: the body of a woman, subject to urges and impulses, fashioned for purposes she did not dare to contemplate.

Change had come in at the door, and who was to blame if not Ceilyn?

"He said that he wanted to be my friend," she said. "I trusted him and this is what comes of it. He made it all *real*—growing up and growing old, falling in love and dying—he made it all real, and what am I to do now?" She buried her face in her hands and wept until she was exhausted.

Then, wearily, she rose from her bed and began to undress. She hung her shawl on a peg by the door, took off her little grey sandals, and slipped out of her gown. In her white shift she walked barefoot across the cold flagstone floor, over to the chest at the foot of her bed. She took out a crystal flask, containing a syrup of poppy and soporific herbs which had lulled her to sleep the last three nights.

And yet . . . is it so terrible a thing? asked the voice of the lion. *It is a great cycle: birth, procreation, death. Even the very metals mate, engendering offspring after their own kind.*

Teleri did not answer. She poured a little water into a wooden cup, uncorked the crystal flask. The lion spoke again, this time insinuatingly.

They say it is a pleasant thing, to mingle your flesh with that of another. Come, admit it. Aren't you the least bit curious? All the dark, mysterious, thrilling things that lovers do . . .

She lifted the flask, allowed three drops of the potion to fall into the water. "The whole idea is absurd. Whatever would I do with a lover?"

As soon as she said that, Teleri wished the words unsaid. The beast had tricked her into asking the question aloud.

Look, then, and see, the lion growled. An image formed on the face of the water before she could turn away, and Teleri had no choice but to look and to see.

A tiny cobwebby bedchamber, lit by the last rosy light of a summer evening. The two might just have entered, for Prescelli was laughing and kicking off her shoes, and Ceilyn stood with his back against the closed door, his arms folded across his chest. He laughed, too, but he was not at ease, his pose one of coiled, controlled tension.

Prescelli moved toward the bed, loosening her hair, shaking down her heavy tresses. Ceilyn crossed the room in three swift strides, and his arms went around her, roughly, possessively. For a moment, Prescelli permitted the embrace, arching her neck so that the dark hair fell away and his kisses fell on the tender nape. Then, suddenly, she twisted in his arms, as agile as a cat, and tried to push him away. Ceilyn caught her wrists and held them behind her, trying to subdue her with hard, biting kisses on her face and throat.

Though Prescelli continued to put up a token resistance, she returned his kisses just as eagerly.

Then there were two white bodies tangled together on the bed ... two mouths searching and finding one another ... Prescelli's arms twined around his neck ... Ceilyn's face looking down at her, no longer wary, but open, vulnerable, tender. ...

The crystal flask fell to the flagstone floor, shattering into a thousand fragments. Picking up the larger pieces, Teleri cut her feet on the smaller ones, staining her white nightdress in her efforts to stop the flow of blood.

Her dreams that night were troubled. She wandered through her castle of ice, but the walls had hardened and darkened into a hall of polished mirrors. In every mirror, Teleri saw Prescelli: shaking down her long dark hair, struggling in Ceilyn's embrace, naked and wanton beneath him.

But in the morning, waking to a throbbing head and an ache she did not know how to name, Teleri swept up the last of the glass, and resolved to put everything she had seen out of her mind forever.

Fand was not one to easily forgive an insult. For days after the incident in the meadow, she maintained a stony silence whenever Garanwyn and his cousins approached her. When she finally broke that silence, she spoke long and eloquently on the subject of unmannerly youths and uncouth striplings.

The three boys took Fand's rebuke with characteristic good nature and a becoming air of apology. Between them, they managed to make amends and convince Fand not to take her complaint to the Queen.

That little matter out of the way, Tryffin and Fflergant both heaved a profound sigh of relief. Their family's fortunes were definitely on the rise—Cadifor and Llochafor had been pardoned and recalled, Lord Dyffryn had also been pardoned—and it would not do for either of them to attract unfavorable attention now.

On the evening of the day that Sidonwy's brothers arrived at Caer Cadwy, Fflergant and Tryffin were asked to serve at a private banquet honoring the visitors from Rhianedd—a sure sign that they, too, had been restored to the King's favor. They arrived in the banquet hall, an hour before the feast, to find Ceilyn there ahead of them, inspecting the hands of two very nervous young pages.

Any meal supervised by Ceilyn was certain to run smoothly, but woe betide the unfortunate squire or page serving under Ceilyn's watchful eye who came to the table with dirty fingernails, who spilled the wine or spotted the linen, whose genuflection before the High Table lacked the proper grace and reverence, or who—most terrible of all—failed to respond instantly to one of Ceilyn's signals.

After Ceilyn finished his inspection and sent the pages downstairs to bring up the plates, he beckoned to Fflergant and Tryffin. "I swear to God," said Fflergant, under his breath, "if he asks to look at our hands . . .!"

This time, however, he spared them the indignity. He looked them over from top to toe, but he did not inspect their fingernails.

The King and Queen and their guests soon arrived, and the meal proceeded as smoothly as even Ceilyn could wish through the first and second removes. A polite exchange of news, a general expression of sympathy for Lord Dyffryn, detained in the north by family illness, a comment on the excellence of the food—conversation was confined to safe topics until the third course, when Cadifor fab Duach finally mentioned the bones.

"Naturally, I am most eager to see the relics," said Cadifor. "Is it true, as I have heard, that the casket has been relegated to the Treasury? Hardly a fit resting place, I should think, for the ancient kings of Rhianedd."

The King took a sip of wine from his jeweled goblet. "I have already discussed a proper Christian burial with my confessor, but Brother Dewi, I regret to say, was not encouraging. To bury our pagan ancestors in hallowed ground, he tells me, would be impossible."

"But some of our ancestors—Selyf and Selgi, in particular— were known to be devoted sons of the church," protested Llochafor. "Surely they, at least—"

At the other end of the table, the Princess Diaspad laughed softly. "What a great fuss over nothing. Pagan . . . Christian . . . the bones might be either, and no way to distinguish between them. Who knows for certain that they really are the bones of your illustrious ancestors?"

"I had thought," said Llochafor, "that the relics had been thoroughly examined and verified."

Diaspad shrugged. "Hardly that. A cursory examination by Glastyn's little girl, an indescribable sensation experienced by one or two people who handled them . . . hardly convincing proof. So if you are considering some grandiose sentimental gesture— building a tomb, erecting some monument—you would do better to save yourselves the trouble and expense."

"As to expense . . ." said Cadifor, eager to support any project which the Princess opposed, " . . . as to expense, I am willing to bear my share, in order to see the relics properly interred."

"But you forget," the King said testily, "that neither the expenses nor any responsibility for the bones is yours to assume. They are mine to dispose of, as I see fit."

It seemed that months of dreary exile in the north had finally taught Cadifor the value of diplomacy. "But naturally, Cousin, I do not dispute that," he replied, smiling urbanely. "If I seemed . . . But I only meant to assure you that you can call on me for any assistance you might need."

"A generous offer, to be sure," said Sidonwy, the peacemaker, and the King grunted a grudging acknowledgment.

But the Princess laughed merrily. "Really, you are all so very serious about this! If you follow my advice, you will put the bones back where the stonemasons found them, or simply dig a hole in the ground and toss them into it." Then, leaning closer to her brother, she whispered in his ear, "If you treat the bones too reverently, no one will doubt their authenticity—and perhaps that would suit Cadifor very well! But what of your own best interests?"

The King's grey eyes clouded with suspicion. "If Cadifor wishes to make use of the bones, then surely the treasure room is the best place to keep them," he replied.

"The Treasury, or someplace equally secure," the Princess agreed. Then she laughed again. "No, no, I take it back. A tomb would be the very thing! A tomb so cleverly constructed that the bones would be even safer there than in the treasure room. You would enjoy planning and building it, Cadifor and Llochafor could not complain that the relics were mishandled, and they would be forced to bear the entire expense. What a fine joke that would be!''

''Why not?'' said the King, laughing along with her. He raised his voice so that the others could hear. ''A tomb it shall be! A grand and glorious sepulchre of marble and granite, as befits the final resting place of kings. Like a shrine it shall be,'' he added mischievously. ''What do you say, Cousins? Are you willing to provide the gold for this monumental undertaking?''

Cadifor and Llochafor both hesitated, wondering what had passed between the King and his step-sister. Nor had they really intended to commit themselves to so ambitious and costly a project.

But Cadifor could hardly retract his offer now. ''If you would have it so, Lord,'' he said, in a voice devoid of all enthusiasm, ''how can *we* fail to be pleased?''

''Of all the bloody fools!'' Fflergant said to his brother an hour later. ''As though a child couldn't see that she was leading them into a trap, arranging everything to her own liking! But even if you and I had dared to open our mouths, there is not much chance that our dear cousins would have listened to *us*.''

The pages had all gone down to the kitchens carrying the dirty plates and platters, the guests had all dispersed, and Ceilyn was escorting the Queen to her rooms, so Fflergant felt entirely free to express himself.

''The truth is,'' said Tryffin, as he impudently took the seat that the King had just vacated, and cadged a piece of fruit from a golden bowl, ''if Cadifor and Llochafor weren't cousins of ours, I'd not really care what came of all this. Let the Princess and Cadifor ruin each other, if they can, I'd say then. There isn't much to choose between them, so far as I can see . . . though a Mochdreffi heir goes against the grain, there's no denying that.''

''True enough,'' Fflergant admitted gloomily, taking Diaspad's seat, pouring a goblet of wine for himself. ''But Sidonwy and her brothers are kin to us, and no denying that. A pity a fellow can't choose his own relations. And speaking of near relations . . . I wish I had been in Ceilyn's place tonight. I imagine he heard everything with those damnably sharp ears of his!''

"Oh aye." Tryffin took out his dagger, began to slice his pear into neat sections. "In a position to see and hear quite a bit these days, our cousin Ceilyn."

Fflergant grimaced. "This business of babbling secrets in bed—it goes both ways, I suppose. But bedding a woman for what she knows is hardly the act of an honorable man. As for selling Sidonwy's secrets, and Prescelli his reward—"

"—not a shrewd bargain on Ceilyn's part," Tryffin finished for him. He offered his brother a piece of the pear.

They ate in silence for a while. "The fact is," Fflergant said, after some thought, "it makes no sense at all. Ceilyn mac Cuel and a girl like Prescelli!"

"But then when you think of it," said Tryffin, "when has anything Ceilyn ever did make good sense?"

"It makes no *sense*, Ceilyn," said the Queen, as they climbed the winding stair to her rooms in the Mermaid Tower. "I try to understand, but I simply cannot. Tell me this: Can you possibly imagine yourself in love with the girl?"

"No," said Ceilyn wearily, for they had been through this before. "I do not imagine myself in love with her. There is something there, but it's certainly not love."

"Lust, then? Sheer animal lust . . . You would ruin your career, disappoint your family and friends, all for the sake of—"

"It isn't that either," said Ceilyn, wishing that she would lower her voice so that the pages and the young ladies would not hear everything she said. "Do you honestly believe that I wouldn't know where to go if all I wanted was a woman in my bed? But there is something between Prescelli and me, something more than . . . lust . . . and less than love, and I don't know how to name it."

The Queen heaved a sigh. "But what will your father say . . . to you . . . to me? I dread the day that word of this affair reaches Caer Celcynnon."

"I am sorry if this embarrasses you," he said, "but I don't see how you are to blame, or why my father should think so."

"Do you not? And has it not occurred to you that I might forbid you to see Prescelli ever again?" retorted Sidonwy.

"Do you forbid me to see her?" asked Ceilyn.

They paused on the landing a floor below the Queen's bedchamber. "No," she sighed. "Who knows better than I do, what comes of forbidding people to see one another? And if I force you to meet her secretly, I won't be able to trust you ever again.

"But really, Cousin," she went on, as they started up the last flight of stairs, "these impossible attachments! One expects a young man to sow some wild oats—indeed, I wish you had sown yours earlier, for then you might be ready now to fall in love and marry someone suitable.

"Although I must say," she added, "that I liked the other one much better, and I begin to regret that I ever said a word against her. At least she is young and—"

"She is a year older than Prescelli."

"—and innocent," the Queen continued, "and I suppose we might have made something of her. But Prescelli . . . that wicked, scheming, ungrateful girl! And the worst of it is, you know exactly what she is."

"Yes," said Ceilyn. "I know what she is, but I don't believe you do. The life she has led, the pain she has experienced—"

"I know what Prescelli's life has been," said Sidonwy. "I tried to help her, you know that I did. But I do believe that Prescelli was ruined beyond redemption long before you or I ever met her. And you deserve better, Ceilyn. Don't you know that?"

"No," said Ceilyn. "I can't say that I do."

When Ceilyn left the Queen that evening, he did not go directly to his own room. Instead, he took a torch and crossed the battlements to the Keep, where he climbed a flight of creaking stairs to the top floor. At the top of the stairs, he walked along a dusty corridor, ducking his head, now and again, to avoid the trailing cobwebs which hung from the low ceiling. Though he did not know it, he passed right by the room where Prescelli had once performed her spells in secret.

He stopped outside a locked door at the end of the corridor and sorted through the keys he carried. Unlocking the door, he passed through into the stuffy little chamber beyond. He placed his torch in a bracket by the door, and looked around him with a faint air of disgust.

It was a bare, ugly little room, and Prescelli's efforts to make it more comfortable had only partly succeeded. A motheaten cloak had been spread across the bed and some draggled furs piled at the foot. A battered breastplate was hung on the wall, to serve as a mirror when Prescelli did up her hair, and a comb and a few scattered hairpins were on the mantelpiece.

"*Hardly luxurious,*" Prescelli had sniffed, when Ceilyn first brought her there. "*I'm sure the straw in the mattress is damp, and I think I am going to sneeze.*"

"*If you don't like it, I'm sorry,*" said Ceilyn. "*It is the best that I can do. You said we needed a place to be alone together, a place with a bed we could use, and so I found one. But if you would rather not stay here—*"

"*It will serve well enough, I suppose,*" sighed Prescelli, gingerly seating herself on the edge of the bed. "*I've made love in worse places, anyway. Anyplace was good enough for Iaen, and as for Derry mac Forgoll . . .*"

"*Thank you, Prescelli,*" Ceilyn had replied ironically. "*It is kind of you to remind me that I'm not the first.*"

Prescelli had the grace to look ashamed of herself. "*I don't know why I always bring up the past,*" she admitted frankly. "*Perhaps I am afraid that you will, if I don't. But tell me—how did you get the key? What did you tell Dillus?*"

"*I didn't tell him anything. I just asked him for the keys to the rooms on the top floor and he handed them over without a question. I wish he had asked. It was as bad as a lie to let him believe that I had some legitimate business up here—and all the worse because he trusted me.*"

The memory was still an uncomfortable one. Ceilyn pulled off his boots and stretched out on the bed. An hour passed before the door opened and Prescelli walked in with a lighted candle in her hand. Her hair was disarranged and her eyes heavy-lidded.

"In God's name, where were you?" he demanded.

"She wanted me to stay and help her prepare for bed," Prescelli replied. She extinguished the candle and set it down on the mantelpiece, then sat down on the foot of the bed and began to remove her shoes and stockings.

Ceilyn sat up, reached out, and took her by the wrist. "The Princess never asks you to help her undress before bed. You told me that yourself."

Prescelli suffered his painful grip, unresisting. "She asked me tonight. She always finds extra tasks for me to do, when she knows that I'm tired or in a hurry. Please let me go. She made me brush her hair until my arm fairly ached.''

Her gaze fastened curiously on the iron bracelet encircling his wrist. ''You never take that ugly thing off. Whyever do you wear it?''

Ceilyn's hand dropped. He had been prepared to answer that question, sooner or later—at least, he had thought he was prepared. ''I wear it as a sort of penance.''

''A penance?'' Prescelli raised her eyebrows. ''But I thought you had put all that behind you. The sackcloth and the ashes.''

Ceilyn glared at her. ''Not all . . . not everything.''

''What a hypocrite you are,'' she said, beginning to unbutton her tight sleeves. ''Imposing penances on yourself and hearing Mass every day I shouldn't be surprised—and all the time, you're no better than the rest of us.''

''If I were a saint,'' he retorted, ''I would have no need for Mass or penances, now, would I?''

He lay back on the bed and watched her undress, because he knew how she hated that, how vulnerable it made her feel to strip before him. Sometimes it appalled him, the sadistic edge their relationship had taken on, but other times, like tonight when he was still smarting from her remarks about the iron bracelet, he took a perverse pleasure in evening the score.

Other things troubled him as well. The gown Prescelli wore tonight (a gift from the Princess, and it was not the only one) had none of the old flaunting shabbiness that characterized her older gowns. A gown of orange and crimson satin, cut in the fantastic Mochdreffian style: gaudy, to be sure, but certainly the most beautiful dress Prescelli had ever possessed. And Ceilyn could not help wondering why the Princess Diaspad had chosen this particular time to shower her handmaiden with expensive gifts.

Moreover, he knew that someone was laying traps for him: potions in his food and in the wash water the pages brought up to his room in the mornings—once, he had found an unspeakable bundle of filthy rags and feathers among the covers of his other bed. So far, he had not mentioned any of this to Prescelli, for though they angered him, such pitiful attempts to ensorcell him impressed Ceilyn not at all. He even found them oddly reassuring, for so long as Prescelli took the trouble to set snares for him, he knew beyond doubt that he was still his own man.

"But I don't really believe you wear that thing as a penance," Prescelli said suddenly. "No . . . I think it was given to you as a love token."

Ceilyn scowled ferociously. "What are you talking about? What gives you that idea?"

The gown slipped silkily off Prescelli's shoulders, lay like a pool of fresh blood at her feet. When she moved in Ceilyn's direction, he almost expected to see bloody footprints appear on the floor behind her.

She sat down again on the bed beside him, ran a finger over the signs cut into the iron bracelet. "I've seen these before, somewhere. They're magic, aren't they? *She* gave it to you as some sort of a pledge or a love token, didn't she?"

"I told you—it was never like that between us."

"Then why does she watch us?" Prescelli demanded. "Why does she spy on us?"

"She was watching us that one time," said Ceilyn. "It doesn't mean anything. She watches everyone. That is just what she does. And it's absolutely harmless: She's totally unmoved by everything she sees, never repeats anything she hears, and forgets it all sooner than you would think possible."

"You're very sure of that?" she said.

"Oh yes," said Ceilyn bleakly. "I'm very sure of that."

"Behold," said the wizard, "I will show you wonders." And there appeared before them a vision: a pageant of great kings and noble princes gorgeously robed and crowned with jeweled circlets, all moving together in a stately procession as if in time to some silent measure. And they saw women of great beauty, the mothers of future generations; heroes performing deeds of valor; mighty castles and great cities rising up and crumbling into dust, all in the space of a single heartbeat. These things Glastyn revealed to them, and many more besides, splendors and spectacles beyond the telling.

"Make Anwas your king, and all this shall come to pass," said Glastyn. "But if you choose another, I foresee years of bloodshed, a land ravaged, and the fall of many noble houses."

And the Lords of Celydonn marveled and whispered among themselves. "Surely the man who has shown us these things possesses the wisdom necessary to guide us. Let us do as he says, and make the boy our king."

But there were those among them who put no faith in shadows or visions, no matter how beguiling; these men kept their own council and left Dinas Moren unconvinced.

From The Great Book of St. Cybi

20.

An Insubstantial Pageant

In the days that followed the supper party, the King met often with his Rhianeddi kinsmen to discuss plans for the construction of the tomb. The Princess Diaspad made an uninvited fourth party—and proved remarkably vociferous for one who still maintained that she had no interest in the project at all. Sketches were made and almost immediately discarded, the relative merits of Draighenach marble versus the native stone endlessly debated, estimates of gold and manpower constantly revised. In the end, the entire plan, from the design of the sepulchre to the number of men engaged to construct it, differed radically from anything anyone had envisioned at the beginning.

Since the church remained adamant, a vault in any of the castle's private or public chapels was out of the question. But someone proposed a certain walled garden located between the splendid chapel dedicated to St. March and the Scriptorium, adjacent to Sidonwy's heraldic garden, and everyone eventually agreed that this offered an excellent spot to build the tomb.

Early plans revolved around a subterranean chamber, to be surmounted by an enormous marble slab, but later plans extended the walls of the vault upward, raising the marble capstone a full two feet above the level of the ground. As a final touch, Cynwas designed four decorative bronze plaques, to ornament the exterior walls.

Work began the second week in August. A party of laborers from Treledig marked out a section of turf in the center of the garden, and began to dig. These initial preparations naturally drew a crowd of curious onlookers, but a few hours spent watching the tedious business of digging a deep hole and tossing out the dirt satisfied most folk. The crowd gradually dispersed.

Late on the second day, after the workmen had all gone home, Diaspad arrived in the garden. She regarded the excavation with evident satisfaction. "Six feet deep, but it will be less when the floor is in," she said to Derry. "You and Morc should have little difficulty in passing the casket up to us."

"No difficulty at all," said Derry, "once we're inside. But I still don't see how we are to move that bloody great slab the King has set his heart on, once they have lowered it into place."

Diaspad stroked his cheek affectionately. "No, of course you don't. But you needn't worry about that. It isn't for your intelligence that I keep you on."

She smiled sweetly. "This begins well, and the omens are good. I think the time has come to send for the Celcynnon boy."

She received him in the kitchen garden, a pleasant meeting place shaded by appletrees and vine-covered arbors, more orchard and apiary than vegetable garden. The Princess sat on a marble bench by a carp pond, dangling one white hand in the cool green water, while Calchas and Derry sprawled in the high grass at her feet. Prescelli sat nearby, shelling a lapful of last year's walnuts.

The Princess had neglected to inform Prescelli that Ceilyn was expected. When he appeared at the garden gate, the girl started to her feet with a strangled protest, only to subside again under Diaspad's reproving stare.

Then Diaspad's frown became a cordial smile. "How kind of you to come. No need to stand on ceremony here. . . . Come, sit down beside me, where it is shady and cool."

Now, Ceilyn had only answered her summons as a matter of common courtesy, and fully intended to take his leave just as soon as he could withdraw gracefully. So he joined her on the bench, but did not look comfortable about doing so.

The Princess laughed melodiously. "Dear me! Is this your idea of gallantry? Come a little closer and try not to look so formidable. Yes, that's right. . . . Now give me your hand. My goodness, you're very like your father!"

"Thank you," said Ceilyn, though he doubted she intended a compliment. It was all that he could do to keep from snatching his hand away, for something in her touch made his skin crawl and the hairs at the back of his neck stand up.

"Oh yes," said the Princess. "Quite a remarkable resemblance. The hair, the eyes, even the posture . . . though now that I look more closely, I can see your mother, too."

Ceilyn refused to be disarmed. "Perhaps you will tell me just why I was invited here?"

Diaspad's smile lost a little of its warmth. "Ah yes, you're a busy young man, aren't you? Most commendable. I've had my eye on you for quite some time. And I found you . . . well worth my attention."

"You surprise me," Ceilyn said uneasily. "Most people find me rather dull. I can't think what I have done to merit your attention."

The Princess laughed again. "Indeed, it is true, you do lead a circumscribed life here. But that is exactly why you interest me. For though you lead an ordinary life, you are, yourself, an extraordinary young man."

Ceilyn looked suspiciously at Prescelli, but the girl shook her head, all innocent confusion.

"Yes, quite extraordinary," the Princess went on. "Extraordinary talents, extraordinary vision. Such a pity, to see a young man like you denied the opportunities he so richly deserves."

Ceilyn began to relax. Surely, he thought, if she knew anything against him, she would have said so by now.

"Look," said the Princess, gesturing toward the pond, and Ceilyn, taken by surprise, obediently turned his eyes in the direction she indicated. The water was dark and weedy in the shallows, reflected leaf-green and sky-blue toward the center of the pond. But gradually, these reflections changed, until he thought he could perceive the tiny images of men and women apparently engaged in some titanic struggle.

"This was Ynys Celydonn fifty years ago," Diaspad said softly. "The land in chaos, the green fields we know today all sere and wasted." Slowly, the picture shifted: A king was crowned, a child christened, a band of men in shining armor rode out across the barren landscape, bringing with them the first tender green of spring. Ceilyn thought that he knew some of those men: a grey-eyed youth wearing a circlet of gold upon his burnished locks; a big, dark-eyed boy who rode laughing into battle; a stocky man in a bearskin cloak, and his companion, fiery-haired, brandishing a gleaming blade.

"Cynwas," murmured the Princess. "Manogan—as I remember him best. Ysgafn and Scilti. And other men known to you: Branach and Dianach, Maelgwyn of Gwyngelli, Gofynnion, Dillus, and Rhodri. And men you never knew, because they died heroic deaths before you were born. The goal these men strove to accomplish, a unified Celydonn, took thirty years to establish, and the peace they won for us lasted twenty years—a lifetime, it must seem to you."

She looked up, and the insubstantial pageant faded. "Alas, that peace deteriorates. Outlaws grow more daring, rebellion and Black Magic ferment in the north, dissatisfaction breeds, even here in the south. But Cynwas and his knights, grown lazy and spoiled, are unwilling to bestir themselves. They play at heroism in bloodless tournaments instead of real battles, and dwell on past glories."

"And who can blame them?" she added hastily, as Ceilyn's fixed stare became indignant. It was one thing to think these things for himself, quite another to hear them spoken out loud by her.

''They have earned their rest, a peaceful and comfortable old age. Yet they have also become greedy, and jealously guard their reputations by standing in the way of promising young men like yourself, denying you the opportunity to match or surpass their deeds.

''Nevertheless,'' she went on persuasively, ''there *are* opportunities—if a man be determined to find them, and ready to take them when they appear—and a bright boy like you, Ceilyn mac Cuel, could go very far, given a little influence in the right places.''

The garden was very still, save for the cooing of doves up in the branching appletrees, the crack of one of Prescelli's walnuts. Ceilyn's eyes were dazzled by the vision he had seen upon the bright water. Slowly, the Princess came back into focus. He had seen her there, too, among those heroic scenes of the past, offering a rose to the youthful, joyous Manogan. For a moment, a younger, softer image covered the hard, passionate face he knew.

''And you are offering to exert your influences on my behalf? In return for . . . what?''

''Oh no,'' said Diaspad coyly. ''I'll have your vow of silence first. I will tell you this much: The Queen shall not be harmed. Ah, that surprises you? But I would never ask you to betray the Queen, or do anything to compromise your oath of fealty to the King.''

''Don't listen to her,'' Prescelli protested urgently. ''This is how she trapped me. If you do what she says even once, she will never let you go.''

But Ceilyn ignored her, all his attention on the Princess. ''Cadifor and Llochafor, then, if not the King and Queen. Surely I have a right to know, before I promise you anything, who I am to sacrifice on the altar of ambition.''

She considered for a moment. ''Oh, very well . . . why should I not admit what you have already guessed? I require certain information about Cadifor and his brother, their movements and their habits. I believe you might be able to obtain that information. No breaking of oaths there, I believe? No friendships violated?''

''No,'' said Ceilyn. ''No oaths broken, no friendships violated. But to betray my own flesh and blood—surely for that I should demand a high price. And how do I know, once I have provided you with the information you seek, that you will keep faith with me?''

"Look around you," said the Princess. "Surely you can see that I look after those who serve me. Prescelli may complain of me, but you can see for yourself that she now has all the pretty things she could only dream about before. As for Morc and Derry—would either of them wear the spurs and baldric of a Knight of the Order of the Lion of St. March, were it not for my influence? And if I could do so much for the two of them, what could I not do for a promising youth like you? Lord Constable . . . Earl Marshall . . . It wouldn't take much to convince either Ysgafn or Manogan to resign. Have you never imagined what you might do, given either post? Of course you have. . . . I see it in your eyes."

Ceilyn did not answer her. Mistaking his hesitation, she said, "Perhaps you have no faith in such grandiose promises, perhaps you believe you can do just as well without my patronage. But there are other things I could offer. The little girl with the grey eyes, I've seen you look at her. Everyone knows that you want her. I have potions, love charms . . . ."

Ceilyn suddenly smiled; it was not a pleasant smile. "Yes, I know that you do."

"You have noticed my little traps and evaded them, have you?" Diaspad sounded amused. "I thought that you had. But you've been on your guard. No such problem is likely to arise with your innocent little friend. I have the means to render her absolutely obedient to your will."

"You think that is what I want?" Ceilyn asked. "A toy . . . a plaything, with no will of her own?"

The Princess shrugged. "Isn't that what most men want in a woman? Isn't that what your precious chivalry is all about: an adventurous life full of peril and possibility, and a compliant woman the ultimate prize?"

"To be won," said Ceilyn quietly, "not gained by trickery or witchcraft."

"Tell me the difference . . . from the woman's point of view," the Princess challenged him.

Ceilyn shook his head. "I can't, of course. But I can't accept what you are offering me, either. And as for your kind offer of patronage, I'll have to decline that, too. Because you are entirely wrong: I never wanted to be a great man, only a good one—though it's true I always believed that extraordinary measures might be necessary, in my case, to achieve that ordinary goal.''

Diaspad's already bloodless face grew paler still, the nearly transparent skin seemed to stretch tightly over her prominent bones. No trace remained of the younger, beautiful Diaspad now; he saw only a dissipated, overpainted woman slipping helplessly toward an embittered old age. ''You are refusing my offer?''

''I am refusing your offer,'' said Ceilyn. He rose to his feet, bowed gracefully, turned on his heel, and marched out of the garden.

''Holy Mother of God! He has a nerve, hasn't he?'' Calchas sat bolt upright in his indignation. ''He never even waited for you to dismiss him.''

''Oh no, he doesn't lack for nerve,'' said Prescelli, rising to her feet so suddenly that the walnuts all fell out of her lap and rolled through the grass in all directions. ''Or for integrity.''

''Don't permit yourself any foolish notions about following his example,'' snapped the Princess. ''I may have acted prematurely and lost him, but I still have you, my girl, and don't you forget it! And your delight in this is somewhat misplaced. He'll have little use for you, after today, you may be sure of that!''

Prescelli's mouth began to tremble. ''Why should he be angry with me? I tried to warn him, not entrap him.''

Diaspad smiled nastily, glad of someone on whom to vent her rage and frustration. ''He's undergone a revulsion of feeling. His recent associations will appear to him in a new light. In refusing me, Ceilyn has regained some of his self-respect—and what use has any self-respecting man for a cheap little trollop like you?

''But if you doubt my word,'' she said airily, ''you have my leave to ask him. Yes, run along now and ask your precious Ceilyn whether you've now become an embarrassment to him.''

''I will,'' Prescelli said defiantly. ''Yes, I will, then, and prove you wrong.'' But she hesitated, wringing her hands in an agony of apprehension, afraid to put it to the test.

And when she finally gathered her courage and turned to run after him, Diaspad's mocking laughter followed her all the way to the gate.

She overtook him on the steps in the shadow of the Keep, in nearly the same spot where they had come together so violently and memorably before. She caught up with him, breathless and speechless because she had run all the way across the inner courtyard, and stopped him with a touch on the arm.

"Well?" he asked impatiently. "What do you want?"

Prescelli drew back in surprise. She had seen Ceilyn angry and suspicious, cold and malicious, but he was seldom intentionally rude. "But I didn't know," she protested. "I had no idea she would try to involve you in her schemes."

"If you didn't," he said, "then you and I were the only ones. Everyone else knew, and tried to warn me, but I refused to listen. And now that she really has tried to subvert me, now that I have offended her by refusing, she will use every tool she has to draw me in against my will. And you are one of her tools, Prescelli, you can't deny that."

"But I would never—" Prescelli began, only to be gently but firmly interrupted.

"Perhaps you think you wouldn't, but you would. And it's bad enough, what I have done so far, pretending I could play with fire and I would be the only one burned. But it would be twice as bad, now that I know the danger, if I didn't put an end to it all here and now.

"I am sorry," he added, more gently still. "I don't blame you for any of this. But you said so yourself: Once she has you, you're hers forever. And even if—for once in your life—you showed a little moral courage, stood up to her and refused to do what she told you to do, still, she could use you to entrap or manipulate me through some trickery you never suspected."

As he spoke, Prescelli went from white to red and back to white again. "What you are really saying," she said, in a low, furious voice, "is that you are afraid—and not above sacrificing me to save your own skin!"

"I don't think so," he said. "I can't say for certain that I wouldn't do the same if I were the only one at risk—but it happens that I'm not the intended victim in these infamous plots of hers. She wants Cadifor and Llochafor—perhaps even the Queen, though she says otherwise."

"But don't you owe *me* anything, after all there has been between us?" she cried. "More than you owe Cadifor and Llochafor. Or did it mean . . . so very little?"

"It meant . . . I don't precisely know what it meant, but it was not a little thing, no," he said. "And if I believed—if I truly believed—that I held your happiness in my hands . . . but the truth is that we aren't any good for each other, and you know it as well as I do. It was sweet in the beginning—my God, it was sweet!—but it grows uglier with every passing day.

"And I never deceived you," he added. "I never pretended to love you."

"No," she said bitterly. "You never pretended to love me. It might have been kinder if you had. But I knew from the beginning who it was you loved."

"Then you knew more than I did—more than I know even now," he replied. "But if you weren't first in my heart, neither was I first in yours. I knew that you still cared for Iaen Og."

"Iaen Og?" Prescelli laughed disbelievingly. "That great lumbering fool! Do you think I ever spared a thought for Iaen fab Iaen after I learned to care for you?"

"Perhaps I was mistaken, then," he said. "If I was, if you did care for me more than I ever imagined . . . why, then, I'm very sorry, but that still doesn't change—"

"Don't be," she interrupted him. "Don't be sorry for me. You're quite right—it had continued too long. I was growing bored, if you really want to know."

"Then we agree," said Ceilyn. "I don't carry any hard feelings, and I hope that you don't either."

But that was more than Prescelli was willing to allow, even for the sake of her dignity. "Oh no," she hissed. "Oh no, it's not going to be so easy as that! You come into my life like an act of God, take what you want, then imagine that you're finished with me—but this isn't the end of it, not at all.

"You're going to be really sorry, before this is over," she said, "and not for *my* sake, Ceilyn mac Cuel!"

"Tell me," said the lad, "where your daughter's heart may be found. If I must journey as far as the Highlands of Hell, that I will do in order to obtain it."

"It is well that you should say so," said Mael-Duir, "for only a hero of great courage will ever win my daughter's heart. Though you have traveled far and seen much, there is nothing you have learned that will avail you now.

"As God is my witness," said the giant, "your adventures are only now beginning."

From The Black Book of Tregalen

21.

Where the Waves Meet the Shore

"You did what was right," the Queen told Ceilyn, as they danced together in the Hall, that evening after supper.

"I wish that I could be certain of that," Ceilyn replied ruefully. "God knows, I never thought myself the sort of man to seduce a woman and then abandon her. . . ."

"And I am certain that you are not," said Sidonwy. "If anyone was seduced . . .!" The figures of the dance took her away, then brought her back again. "But truly, Ceilyn, I never doubted that you would make the right decision in the end."

"But you ought to have doubted," said Ceilyn. "I gave you reason enough. And the Princess Diaspad . . . I practically invited her to make use of me."

"And yet, when she offered you everything that you ever wanted, you refused her. And you may be very certain," Sidonwy added, placing her hand in his, "if she had believed you might be approached in any other way—through anger, or revenge, or pity—that she would have done so without hesitation. No, you eluded the best snare that she could set for you, and justified my faith in you.''

But Ceilyn was still not satisfied that he had done all that he might to foil the Princess's schemes. ''Ought I to go to the King? Ought I to tell him all that I know?''

The Queen shook her head. ''What could you tell him that hasn't been said before . . . by Cadifor . . . by myself? He only laughs my fears away, tells me that I should not allow my brothers to influence me, my brothers who are so quick to imagine malice where none is intended.

''And that, as you know, is uncomfortably near the truth,'' she added, with a sigh. ''Cadifor, especially, sees assassins behind every bush, poison in every cup that he is offered. Yet that does not mean that all his enemies are imaginary, or that Diaspad does not mean to ruin him.''

She lowered her voice, lest the other couples overhear her. ''I wish that I had confessed everything. About the letters and the ring, and the death of Cadifor's messenger. Surely, then, my Lord would have recognized her for the ruthless woman she is. But I was afraid to tell him all, and so I let the opportunity pass, and now it is too late. Thus am I punished for my cowardice!''

''I was wrong to refuse her outright,'' said Ceilyn gloomily. ''If I had pretended to be willing to do what she asked, she might have told me more.''

''But unless you had sworn yourself to silence, she would have told you nothing. We cannot even be certain that what you did learn reveals her true intentions. I may be the real victim, and my brother perfectly safe.''

''I might have sworn her oath—why not?'' said Ceilyn, determined to indict himself for something. ''What would it have mattered if I swore a false oath, with so many other sins on my conscience?''

''It is fortunate that you did *not* swear her oath,'' the Queen said warmly. ''Had you done so, she might have found the means to hold you to it. A false oath can be dangerous, in more ways than you may think.''

The dance ended, she took his arm, and allowed him to escort her back to her seat on the dais. ''But as for these other sins of yours,'' she said, with a sympathetic look, ''the sooner you have gone to confession, been absolved, and done your penance, the better you will feel.''

Ceilyn frowned. "I don't think that I can do that.''

"Don't be foolish,'' she said firmly. "Don't continue to punish yourself; there is no need. And don't be presumptuous, either. Worse sins than yours are forgiven every day. God won't abandon you; neither should you abandon yourself.''

"But that is just it,'' said Ceilyn. "I feel as though God *has* abandoned me. All these weeks, I've been filled with anger and I've done . . . The things I have felt and thought and done don't bear repeating. And nothing happened—not to stop me or to punish me. I truly believed there would be a sign. I was hoping for a sign, an excuse to stop, but there was nothing.''

"Nothing?'' said the Queen, pausing at the foot of the dais. "How can you say so? God did send you a sign—though not one you might easily recognize. The Princess offered you a choice, forced you to choose, before it was too late, between sin and salvation. In doing so, she became the unwitting instrument of your salvation. If that did not come about through divine intervention, if that is not as near a miracle as we are likely to see in such times as these—proof positive that God works in mysterious ways . . .!''

She pushed him gently in the direction of the door. "Go find Brother Dewi, and make your confession. Make your peace with God, Ceilyn, and then make peace with yourself.''

Teleri stared helplessly at the book lying on the worn tabletop in front of her. This was a volume that had always opened for her in the past, one she had spent many hours studying. But this morning, no matter how many times she repeated the names, the book remained tightly sealed. She took a deep breath and tried again:

"I conjure you with the names of the Three Mighty Princes,

> Cynfelyn   the Emperor
> Selgi   of the Iron Crown
> Sceolan   Flamingbeard.''

But it was no use. The book, obstinately, remained shut. Teleri looked around the room, at all the other volumes: scattered across the table, piled on the floor, lining all the shelves. She had tried, in the last few days, to open every one of them, all the books she had studied before and all the books she had yet to read, and not one of them opened at her command. Even the nonmagical books, the histories and genealogies, the books of "household" recipes, for candles and wines, inks, incense, and dyes—volumes which usually responded to a touch and a simple command—each and every one refused her.

She felt the old, stifling fear rise up inside her: fear of change, fear of aging, fear of life and death. Had she changed so much, since that night of rude awakening, that the books and the spells that sealed them no longer recognized her? But if that were so—why had she no sense of that herself, no inner awareness of a step irrevocably taken?

Instead, she felt a kind of restlessness, a feeling of unfinished business, some important task left undone. "But what?" she asked the mummified crocodile, the skull nailed up over the door. "What must I do?"

The crocodile made no answer; the skull remained mute. She knew there had to be an answer somewhere. But if not in Glastyn's books, not anywhere in the laboratory or the garden—where?

The day was fair and bright, and a stiff breeze blowing in across the bay set all the banners and pennons flying. Down in the lower courtyard, the Queen and members of her household were just returning from an afternoon ride.

Ceilyn dismounted first, handed Tegillus over to a waiting groom, and reached up to assist the Queen. "You look much better today," she said, as he set her on the ground. He was as pale as ever, but the haggard, haunted look around the eyes had gone. "Did you take my advice? Did you see Brother Dewi?"

"I did," said Ceilyn, as they crossed the yard and passed through the Gamelyon Gate. "And you were right—I only punished myself, staying away from the church when I wanted so much to go. I thought I had stopped tormenting myself for not being so nearly perfect as I would like to be, but I had only found a new way to make myself miserable. Will I never learn moderation?"

"Not overnight, I think," said Sidonwy, with a smile. She stripped off her green leather gloves. "As you followed my last piece of advice, I am minded to present you with another. Pay a visit to the Wizard's Tower, Ceilyn, you've been too long away.''

"Visit Teleri?" Ceilyn asked. "But surely you told me I would be unwise to form any serious attachment.''

"Yes, but you see . . . my advice is not *always* good. And I think I would rather see you happy than well-married. Also, Cousin, you have made a powerful enemy—one who is my enemy as well. As your attachment to me is well-known, it occurs to me now that it might be used against us both.

"Hitherto," she went on, "we have been fortunate. Because you were so much younger than I, because everyone believed that you preferred to lead a celibate life, we have been spared unkind speculation. Now, however—"

"—now that I have so foolishly and conspicuously lost my virginity," Ceilyn finished for her, "I'm no longer a fit companion for you.''

"I don't say that," she protested. "Only that things have changed and we must be discreet where once we were careless. But it could not last forever, you know. Even that difference in our ages, which once seemed vast, grows less significant with every passing year. I am only a dozen years older than you, Ceilyn . . . and you are no longer a boy.''

"Yes," said Ceilyn, under his breath, "that had occurred to me, also.''

"Well, then, you see," the Queen went on, as they began to climb the stairs to the next courtyard, "that you would be wise to cultivate other friendships—not only to spare us from gossip but for your own sake as well.

"But don't you want to see her?" she asked, when Ceilyn remained silent.

"I want to see her," said Ceilyn. "In fact, I've already tried. I knocked at her door this morning, looked in Glastyn's garden. But I have a feeling she is avoiding me.

"Little wonder if she is," he added. "I was insufferably arrogant: choosing her for my Lady, assuming she had no choice in the matter. And then when I realized she was different, not to be won in the usual way, I didn't want to see her anymore.''

They started up another set of stairs. "If she is avoiding me," said Ceilyn, "I don't stand much chance of finding her. She is adept at concealing herself. And except for the garden and the tower, I wouldn't know where to begin to look."

They walked along the battlements atop the southern wall. Every now and again, between two buildings, Ceilyn caught a fleeting glimpse of the sea, the blue-grey waters of the Bay of Camboglanna. A fragment of conversation hovered on the edge of his memory.

"Where do you go when you disappear? Where do you go when you want to hide?"

"Down by the sea," she said. *"Sometimes . . . I imagine myself down by the sea."*

"Or maybe I do," Ceilyn said softly. "Maybe I do, after all."

The sun was a hot white glare on the blue-grey water and silver sand, but the salty breeze was cool. The tide rose, and little wavelets rushed in, around and over the craggy rocks that dotted the beach, wetting Teleri's feet and the hem of her dress.

She searched among the rocks, dug in the wet sand, filling her basket with her gleanings: mosses and seaweeds for their medicinal properties, oddly shaped pieces of driftwood and fragments of whalebone, ivory, and shell to be used as charms and talismans. When she first heard her name, the wind had thinned it out almost beyond recognition.

The second time that Ceilyn called to her, she looked up. Even so, it took her a moment to spot him, for the muted hues of his riding clothes blended with the greys and browns of the rocks. When she did see him, she stopped where she stood, up to her ankles in seawater, with a panicky notion that she might still be able to disappear—though he had already spotted her, and the sun was at her back.

He walked out to meet her, there where the waves met the shore, and relieved her of her basket and her sandals. They stared at each other uneasily, for neither one knew what to say.

Ceilyn finally broke the long awkward silence. "You have been avoiding me, I think."

"I would have said it was the other way around," she suggested softly. There was some quality, some depth of emotion, in her voice that he had never heard there before, and she seemed altogether different today: more substantial and ordinary. Her long braided hair, silvery in some lights, was just a commonplace dark blonde, the color of damp sand, and the mist-colored eyes were an ordinary grey.

He looked down at her, seeing her—really seeing her—for the first time: a rather plain girl in an old grey gown and a scrap of faded blue tartan, stripped of all the glamour he was wont to bestow on her, bereft, even, of her own innocent camouflage. In that moment, all his illusions about her vanished, and in their place stood a real person, capable of love and sorrow, pain and joy, and a whole range of emotions in between.

"You have changed," he said. "Or I have."

"I have been changing for a long time," she said. "We were both of us slow to notice."

Another silence followed, until Ceilyn said, "My feet are getting wet. . . . Would you mind very much?"

And Teleri looked down to see the sea soaking into his high leather boots and her own skirts growing all heavy and sodden.

She walked with him back to the last remaining stretch of beach, even allowed him to lend her a hand clambering over the rocks and the bits of broken shell piled up at the base of the cliffs. He pulled her down to sit beside him on a smooth shelf of stone, and handed over her sandals. "Those pebbles are sharp. Take care you don't cut your feet."

Wondering what he could possibly have said to throw her into such confusion, he politely averted his eyes while she dusted off her feet and laced up the little grey sandals. His gaze wandered seaward.

A chain of tiny islands guarded the mouth of the inlet, islands inhabited by raucous white seabirds and little brown seals who liked to sun themselves on the rocks.

"Selkies . . ." he said softly, reminiscently. "We have legends of the seal-folk up in Gorwynnion. Skinchangers they are, not shape-shifters like me. They say that the women are very beautiful, and that sometimes a fisherman will catch one and marry her. But she never stays with him for long. . . . She always returns to the sea in the end."

"There are tales told on Ynys Aderyn," said Teleri. "Of pirates and selkie-maids, or rover women who take selkie lovers, when their men are away at sea. Elffin of Aderyn claimed selkie blood.

They say, too, that the young man the Princess Goewin loved was a selkie, driven to shore by a great storm. If those stories are true, then you and I both have a touch of selkie blood.''

He looked at her, sitting demurely beside him now, with her feet tucked under her skirts. ''You never told me,'' he said, ''much about your family, or how Glastyn came to choose you for his apprentice.''

''There is little to tell,'' she said. ''My mother died soon after I was born. I don't know much about her, except that she was little and light, and very young when she died. 'That child, Afon'—that is how they used to speak of her. I liked to pretend she was still alive. Not as a mother to hold and care for me—I knew next to nothing about mothers—but as a little girl for me to play with.

''And though I met him nearly every day, I scarcely knew my father. He is the Seneschal at Castell Aderyn, quite devoted to his ledgers and accounts. . . . He used to look right through me, as though I wasn't there. There may have been a woman to take care of me when I was a baby, but I remember nothing about her. You might say that Cadwr of Aderyn raised me, if anyone did. A gruff old man with a fine, piratical swagger and a kind heart, but he knew very little about raising little girls.''

''And Glastyn?'' Ceilyn asked.

''Glastyn was always in and out of Castell Aderyn. He came to see Cadwr and use the library. It's a famous collection at Castell Aderyn—fifty or sixty volumes at least. I used to see him often, walking the battlements deep in thought, or striding along the beach with his green and scarlet robes flapping. But I . . . I was running wild on the island.

''I played on the beach, climbed the cliffs in search of birds' nests, ran with the wild ponies, learned to ride bareback . . . then Cadwr decided that I ought to be taught to read and write. After that,'' she concluded, ''I discovered the library, and Glastyn discovered me.''

Ceilyn tried to think what it must have been like, passing from the care of one fearsome old man to that of another, living a life devoid of all the usual ties of affection: not mother or father or sister or brother. He found that he could not. He had always thought his own life a lonely one, but he flinched before the thought of her solitude, her isolation.

"You see," she said, "it's difficult for me to even think about . . . caring for another person. Because I never did before, not in any of the usual ways. I am changing, whether I want to or not, but even so, there is no guarantee that I will ever be capable of the—the kind of affection you might like me to feel."

He scooped up a handful of sand, watched it trickle slowly through his fingers. He felt a sorrowful kinship with those Gorwynnach fishermen. What was the use of reaching for something you could never hope to hold?

"I know that," he said.

"But if you would like to try again, just to be friends," she ventured. "I think I could be a better friend to you now than I might have been in the past. If you could be content with that . . ."

"I could be content with that," he said, taking her hand in his. "I can't promise not to hope for more someday, but if friendship is what you offer me now, I can be content with that."

. . . and in this manner, Our Mercury acquires the force of the things above and things below.

Know, then, that the two natures, united at last, alter each other reciprocally, the Body incorporating the Spirit, and the Spirit transmuting the Body, whereupon the Matter assumes another nature or set of properties, a new color, a new form, a new virtue, which it never possessed before.

From The Mirror of the Ancients

22.

Michaelmas

August melted into September, and everything continued to grow at an amazing rate. Below Brynn Caer Cadwy, beyond the castle's embattled outer defenses, the oats and the barley lost all sense of proportion. On every patch of uncultivated ground, the fennel, broom, and wild mustard stood forest high, and the hawthorn hedges dividing the fields had become vast, impenetrable thickets.

Yet the days grew shorter, the roses in the ruins dropped their petals one by one, and mornings and evenings there was a tang of autumn in the air.

For Teleri, this was a busy time. Each morning, she went down to the stable, saddled Kelpie, her sturdy grey pony, and rode out into the fields, gathering September's bounty: oakgalls and black-thorn bark, damsons and elderberries, rushes, hazelnuts, chestnuts, and wild mushrooms.

On Market Days, she rode into Treledig to trade for the things she could not make or grow or gather for herself: skins and tallow; needles, thread, and good grey woolen; charcoal for the athanor in the laboratory.

The skins, she scraped and cured for parchment. The oakgalls and bark provided her with ink. Of the rushes and tallow she made rushlights and candles. And besides wines and medicines to be made, and a new winter cloak, all her clothes had to be let down and let out, and the room at the top of the Wizard's Tower—no longer Glastyn's laboratory, but Teleri's—really cried out for a thorough cleaning.

This latter project took up several evenings, as Teleri turned the laboratory upside down and inside out, dusting and scrubbing and sweeping. She emptied all the unlabeled bottles of medicine that had resided at the back of the shelves and cabinets for years, and rearranged all the books and paraphernalia according to her own ideas of convenience. No longer content to live from day to day, expecting Glastyn to return at any minute and take charge of things, she was ready to take charge herself.

And when she went back to the books, she soon discovered that every single volume in the tower was willing to unseal at her bidding. Thereafter, she could choose her own course of study for the first time.

And study she did, often late into the night, sometimes forgetting to eat or sleep. Fortunately, Ceilyn was a frequent visitor to the laboratory that September, arriving of an evening, after the King and Queen had supped, and bringing his own supper with him to be shared.

On those nights, they sat by her fire, cracking nuts and eating bread with honey or rowan-berry jelly, feasting on crabapples, pears, and cold roast fowl, drinking sloe, or damson, or marshflower wine, in a comfortable, companionable silence.

Down in the ornamental garden behind the Chapel of St. March, work on the tomb continued at a steady pace. Though laborers from Treledig and the surrounding countryside had been employed to dig the hole, masons and other craftsmen from as far afield as Golchi and St. Maddiew began arriving at the end of August, to set up a camp in the lower courtyard and begin work on the vault. They expected to complete the sepulchre in time for a Michaelmas interment.

To the masons' encampment, one evening in the middle of September, came a solitary stranger: a slender young man in a green cloak and the golden spurs of a knight, who demanded to speak to the Master Mason. Two journeymen escorted him to their master's tent, and the stranger spent the better part of the evening drinking wine with the mason. The journeymen and apprentices, all curious to discover if another commission was about to be offered, found a series of excuses to intrude on them—all in vain, for the visitor fell silent whenever they entered, and he kept his hood up and sat with his face in the shadows the whole time. Finally growing tired of so many interruptions, the Master Mason banished his underlings from the premises before they could learn anything.

The next afternoon, two apprentices, sent into town for supplies, spotted the Master Mason (normally a frugal man) freely spending a purse full of gold, and overheard him talking to a tradesman about a tomb, "a great monument, promising virtual immortality," which he would soon be building somewhere in the north.

Yet for all the speculation which these two incidents provoked, no one would have remembered them in the excitement which soon followed, had they not been linked to a third: The Master Mason went off on some nameless errand, just two days before Michaelmas, an errand from which he never returned.

"I wonder," said Derry, stifling a yawn and laying his cards face down on the table in front of him, "just what one ought to wear to an affair such as the Grand Interment? Something very fine, I should imagine." He glanced over at Prescelli, who sat opposite, frowning at the cards in her own hand. "What will you be wearing—if one might ask?"

Prescelli threw down her cards. They had been playing for purely imaginary sums all evening, and she saw no reason to play out a hand she could not possibly win.

"The Grand Interment, indeed! And what are the ancient kings of Rhianedd to me, pray tell—or to you, for that matter? Let the King dispose of them as he likes. Let him build memorials and chant prayers over all his ancestors, if it pleases him to do so—but why should I trouble myself to be there?"

"Oh well," said Derry, gathering up the cards. "You never

know. The ceremony may have its amusing aspects, and everyone will be there."

"I won't be," said Prescelli. "Nor will the Princess."

Derry lowered his voice, so as not to be overheard by Calchas, who sat on the rug by the fire, cutting little figures out of paper and throwing them into the flames. "She says she won't be there, she says she isn't interested, but you know the Princess . . . she'll be there."

He shuffled the cards, took three off the top of the deck, and placed them in front of Prescelli, then dealt three more for himself. He turned over the next card, examined it briefly, and glanced across at Prescelli. "Remind you of anyone you know?"

The card depicted a belligerent-looking youth bearing a knotted cudgel. Spiky leaves, evidently intended for holly, wreathed the young man's head and sprouted from his club. Prescelli shook her head.

"Do you want to know what I think?" Derry asked.

"No," said Prescelli.

But Derry told her anyway. "I think that you don't want to attend the ceremony because you know that Ceilyn will be there, dancing attendance on the Queen. I think that you've fallen in love again, and with the last man in Celydonn likely to love you in return."

"That's all you know about it," Prescelli retorted. "He did care for me. And he would have learned to care more, if the Princess hadn't . . . Well, anyway, whatever I felt for Ceilyn before, I hate him now!"

Yet she still wore a bracelet he had given her, and a string of carnelian beads. And a certain nosegay of meadowflowers (an unimaginative gift, and she had told him so at the time . . . yet nobody until Ceilyn had ever given her flowers) was carefully dried and tenderly preserved, and hidden in her clothes chest among her shifts and stockings. Despite all that, she could still say that she hated Ceilyn and never suspect that she lied.

She shoved the card back in Derry's direction, pushed back her chair, and stood up. "I'll make him sorry he treated me so shabbily!"

Derry followed her into the next room. "Contemplating revenge?

A pity you won't be able to put your little schemes into effect."

"What do you mean?" Prescelli asked irritably.

Derry was momentarily abashed. "I forgot you weren't supposed to know about that." Then he shrugged. "Oh well, what's the harm? I can't tell you the whole of it, but just rest contented. By the day after tomorrow, the next day at the latest, Ceilyn will be up to his ears in trouble. I'm afraid that he'll no longer be available for whatever it is you are planning, but I daresay you'll enjoy watching him squirm."

The twenty-ninth of September finally arrived and the tomb stood ready for the ceremony of interment. Long before dawn the masons were up and working by torchlight, assembling the apparatus that would lower the coverstone into place. By noon, when the King, the Queen, and the other spectators arrived, every gear and pulley functioned smoothly.

While two sturdy guardsmen lowered the casket into the vault, Brother Dewi began a lengthy prayer and blessing, naming those two most Christian princes, Selyf and Selgi. It was assumed that the pagan bones mixed in with the Christian would neither benefit nor suffer from a prayer so specifically directed. As the monk pronounced the final "Amen" and stepped back, there was an audible stir of anticipation among the spectators.

While everyone held his or her breath, the machine creaked into action, lifting the marble slab into the air and spinning in place until the stone hung suspended over the gaping hole, then it slowly lowered the slab until it came to rest squarely atop the sepulchre. A sigh passed through the crowd.

From a vantage point atop the Keep, the Princess watched it all. Afterward, she turned to Calchas and smiled. "Something of an anticlimax, I am afraid. I wonder what they were all expecting?"

"Some sort of manifestation, like in the old days?" Calchas suggested. "One of Glastyn's little touches, I should imagine."

"Yes," said Diaspad, sounding strangely disappointed. "I must confess, I almost expected something of the sort myself. The old man never could resist a spectacle—I wonder what he would have made of this one?"

*   *   *

The hour was sometime between Compline and midnight, when Ceilyn climbed the dark stairs to his bedchamber. As he approached the second floor of the tower, a familiar musky perfume surrounded him, and he detected a tiny rustle of movement on the landing above.

"Prescelli?"

She stepped into a circle of torchlight. "Come with me," she hissed. "It's terribly important."

Ceilyn shook his head. The hour was late and he was in no mood for melodramatics. "For the love of God, Pres—"

"*Please,*" she insisted. "I daren't be seen with you tonight, and Derry's room—"

"—which he rarely visits. Oh, very well." Taking her by the arm he propelled her through the nearest doorway, which happened to lead into the boys' chapel. He closed the door behind him, folded his arms across his chest, and stood glaring at her.

"I knew it would be like this," she sighed. "I don't know why I bothered to come."

"Neither do I," Ceilyn reminded her. "But perhaps you will enlighten me, before we are very much older."

Prescelli wrapped her cloak around her, sat down on a narrow bench. "You are in terrible danger. The Princess—"

"—has vowed revenge. I knew that already—it stands to reason. But she's not the only one. If memory serves—"

"Oh, do be silent and listen to me," Prescelli pleaded. "I've not come here to threaten, but to warn you."

Ceilyn sat down on the bench beside her. "Very well. I'm listening."

"I don't know much, only what Derry let slip," said Prescelli. "But he said you would soon be in serious trouble, thanks to the Princess Diaspad."

"And that isn't exactly what you want?" he asked.

Prescelli shook her head. "Not exactly what I want. There would be no satisfaction in watching the Princess hurt you, because I hate her . . . well, rather more than I hate you."

Ceilyn thought that over. "That might be true," he decided at last. "That much I can believe."

Prescelli heaved a sigh of relief. "As I said: I don't know

much . . . but I can make a few guesses. She is more interested in the tomb than she pretends to be, and knew about the bones even before they arrived here.''

"Good God," he said. "Are you certain of that?"

"Absolutely certain. She spoke of them the morning *before* they were discovered. And she seems to believe they will give her some sort of power over Cadifor and Llochafor. But they are your ancestors, too, those old kings—and I know that she means to ruin you along with the Queen's brothers.''

Ceilyn sat thinking that over. "Oh, don't you *see*," Prescelli exclaimed impatiently. "Whatever she is planning, tonight is the night. Calchas has been terribly excited all day long, and the Princess, too, though she tries to hide it. And it must be tonight . . . with the bones finally in the tomb. I'd not put Necromancy past her, nor worse things either, and they are not even buried in their native soil.''

"Oh yes," said Ceilyn. "I can see all that, and other things begin to make sense, too. But I'm wondering what I ought to do with all this newfound knowledge of mine. Or did you come prepared with a suggestion or two of your own?"

"Do?" said Prescelli. "What could you possibly hope to do? You have no idea what she actually intends, and a fine fool you would look carrying this story to the King or to the Queen's brothers. All you can do is remove yourself from the danger. You ought to go away, go down to Treledig for the night. You should be safe enough there.''

Ceilyn continued to eye her suspiciously. "And how do I know that isn't exactly what she wants me to do? That she didn't send you here to 'warn' me and keep me out of her way, while Cadifor and Llochafor go down to ruin in my absence?"

"You have my word," said Prescelli earnestly. "I know that isn't worth much, but I'll swear on or by anything you name: She didn't send me here and doesn't know that I came."

He slipped his hand under her chin, turned her face toward him. "Supposing I believe you really mean that. How am I to know that Derry didn't let something slip intentionally? How do I know the Princess isn't counting on you to do exactly what you have just done?"

"How could she know what I would do—when I didn't know it myself? I agonized over this for hours—my pride against your safety. She couldn't know what I would finally decide."

"Still," he said, "I can't just run off and try to save my own skin, without even trying to help Cadifor and Llochafor. Just what, precisely, do you take me for?"

"For a chivalrous idiot," she said, rising to her feet, blinking back tears. "I should have known you would leap at the opportunity to indulge in some perfectly pointless heroics."

She started for the door, but Ceilyn put out a hand to stop her. "I thank you for the warning, in any case. I do believe you thought you were helping me, and I am grateful."

"Don't be grateful," she said. "Nothing has changed. I only want to save you for my own revenge."

"I can't believe that," he said. "Oh, I don't flatter myself that I still retain any hold on your affections, but I know that you aren't like the others: the Princess, and Calchas, and Derry. I can't guess what hold she has over you, but surely if you left her . . . if you went home to Ynys Carreg and made a fresh start—"

"That's all you know about it," she said bitterly. "You made a fresh start, but I never can. You've no idea what it would be like, back on Ynys Carreg.

"I never intend to do such dreadful things," she went on, as Ceilyn wiped away her tears with the ragged edge of her cloak. "The lies and the thefts and all the rest of it. But I get angry and discouraged, and things . . . just *happen*. You wouldn't understand—your people always taught you to do the right thing. But nobody ever cared enough about me to take the trouble to teach me anything."

"I care," said Ceilyn, pulling her into his arms, burying his face in her hair. "I do care what happens to you, Prescelli."

She drew away, looked up at him hopefully. "Then marry me, and take me away from here."

"I can't do that," he said brokenly. "You know that I can't."

"Then don't marry me," she said, "and just take me away."

"I'm sorry," he said, more firmly than before, "but I can't do that either. Where could we go? What would we do, except make ourselves and each other utterly miserable?"

Prescelli gave him an angry shove. "If you really cared for me . . . if you cared enough." Her eyes, which had been softened by tears just a moment ago, were hard and contemptuous now. "But all you can spare for me is pity—and I am tired of second best. You can save your compassion for someone else, because I don't want it."

. . . as for the hour of Midnight (being not only the darkest hour of the night, but also the threshold of a new day, and the time when the Three Worlds draw nigh) there is no doubt that it is a perilous time for men to be abroad, for witches and warlocks, restless spirits, creatures of the night, and men of ill-will are all active at that Unholy hour.

From Moren Clydno's Book of Secrets

23.

Meetings at Midnight

Ceilyn opened his bedchamber door, stepped into the room, and softly closed the door behind him. He waited a moment while his eyes adjusted to the dark. The beds, all except for his own, were occupied, the occupants, by the sound of their breathing, all fast asleep. Ceilyn sat down on the edge of his bed and unbuckled his spurs.

Moving silently, he walked around to the foot of the bed and opened his clothes chest. Discarding the bright silks and velvets he had donned after supper, he put on a linen shirt and green wool tunic, and his plainest and darkest cloak. Then he picked up his swordbelt and girded it on.

In the corridor, he paused a moment outside the room assigned to Morc and Derry. Detecting no movement on the other side of the door, he proceeded down to the end of the passage and descended two flights of stairs as noiselessly as possible.

The courtyard was flooded with moonlight, the moon, riding low in the east, almost full. A poor night for clandestine activities, he thought, but the garden where the tomb was located lay in the shadow of the Keep. It would be much darker there.

He crossed the yard, entered the Oriel Tower, and climbed a

flight of stairs to the next level. Crossing the innermost courtyard, he realized that he was not alone. Someone followed him, keeping pace but making every effort to remain unseen in the shadows around the edges of the yard. Ceilyn continued as before, looking neither to left nor right, pretending not to notice that secretive presence. But he was alert for any sound or movement that might indicate a threat.

He entered the Queen's heraldic garden, and walked down an avenue bordered by white marble statues on one side and fantastic topiary sculptures on the other. He felt that other draw near. He whirled around, and seized on someone small and soft who squeaked like a mouse when he grabbed her by the arm and dragged her into the moonlight.

"I should have known better than to trust—I beg your pardon! I was expecting . . ." He loosened his grip and Teleri slipped out of his grasp. "Why didn't you tell me it was you?"

"I wasn't sneaking after you," she said, rubbing her arm. "I meant to speak, but I didn't want to attract attention by calling out, and you were walking so fast, I couldn't get close."

"I'm sorry," said Ceilyn again. "But aren't you . . . I know you keep late hours, but isn't this a bit late for you to be out?"

"These last three nights, I've been so certain that something was about to happen," she said, "that I've spent most of each night standing watch by the tomb."

"You had a premonition? You foresaw some trouble down at the sepulchre? You should have told me," he said reproachfully. "I would have kept you company."

"It was just a feeling I had," she said. "I didn't see why you should be bothered."

Somewhere on the wall above them, a muffled voice called out, and there was a dull thud, like a body falling. "Hark to that," Ceilyn whispered. "It sounds like the guard is in trouble up there."

They ran toward the nearest set of stairs, but drew up short in the shadow of a topiary griffon, at the sight of two men descending the stairs. Both wore long cloaks fastened at the throat with silver brooches, but the hoods had been thrown back, revealing the dark, wavy hair and aristocratic features of Sidonwy's two brothers.

"Llochafor and Cadifor," whispered Teleri.

Ceilyn nodded. "And heading for the tomb, unless I miss my

guess. I sense a trap." He moved toward the stairs, intending to hail the two men and warn them, but something in the way that Cadifor walked alerted him. He melted back into the concealing shadows, pulling Teleri along with him. "Wait. . . . There is something wrong here."

The two men reached the foot of the stairs and set out across the garden, passing within inches of Teleri and Ceilyn.

"What is it? Why didn't you speak to them?" Teleri asked, as soon as they were out of earshot.

"I don't believe that was Cadifor," said Ceilyn. "And I *know* it wasn't Llochafor. That was Derry Ruadh mac Forgoll—I'd stake my life on it."

"Derry? But he looked exactly like Llochafor!" Teleri exclaimed softly.

"Holy Mother of God! Of course it was Derry. Who else stinks like a dockside trol—too much cheap perfume and not enough soap and water. It was Derry, no doubt about that. And the other one, the clumsy one, that will be his brother, Morc. I have an idea," said Ceilyn, "of what they intend to do."

Together, they moved in the direction Morc and Derry had taken, down a long boxwood alley and past the Chapel of St. March. But this time, it was Teleri who reached out to detain Ceilyn.

"I wonder. . . . If that really was Morc and Derry we just saw, then where are the real Cadifor and Llochafor?"

"Safe in bed, at this hour—where else? I daresay the Princess took steps to insure that," said Ceilyn. "If all this means what I think it means, there is no reason to suppose they aren't perfectly safe, at least for now."

"Or is there?" he asked, as Teleri continued to hang back. "This presentiment of yours, or whatever it was—did it warn you of any physical danger?"

"I was just thinking about the man that Calchas and Morc killed," she said. "The Princess had every reason to want him taken alive, but Calchas cut his throat anyway. One of us ought to go and see if Llochafor and Cadifor really are safe in their beds—or if another unfortunate accident is about to occur."

Ceilyn thought that over. "Very well, you go and see. I will continue to follow Derry and Morc."

"You take the more dangerous task for yourself," she protested.

"We don't know that," he said, though that was certainly his intention. "But if any harm has already befallen Cadifor and his brother, I would be of little use to them.

"And you needn't worry about me," he added. "As soon as I discover exactly what is happening, I will summon what help I can."

A small cold hand touched his briefly. "Be careful," she whispered, by way of parting.

As soon as she left him, Ceilyn moved stealthily in the direction of the Mermaid Tower and the gate to the garden of the tomb. Ahead of him, he heard sounds of a brief scuffle, followed by another dull thud. Throwing caution aside, he raced toward the tower, arriving outside the Queen's apartments just in time to see Derry and Morc drag a limp body into a little boxwood maze. Ceilyn dodged behind a hedge, and remained hidden while the two men disposed of the body and then passed through the gate into the next garden.

Ceilyn came out of hiding, knelt beside the body. As he had expected, it was the guard who watched nightly outside Sidonwy's rooms. Not dead but unconscious, with a rapidly swelling purple lump on the side of his head. If he was not suffering from concussion, he would be awake and able to describe his assailants by morning.

Probably, the guard on the wall had suffered the same treatment. Ceilyn could think of no reason for Derry and Morc to parade around the castle wearing Llochafor's and Cadifor's faces, unless they intended to leave witnesses.

He left the unconscious guardsman lying on the ground, and moved toward the gate. But then he caught the sound of rapid footsteps, this time coming from the direction of the Keep. He ducked back into the maze, just in time to avoid being seen by two cloaked figures who passed within a yard of him and disappeared beyond the garden gate.

In their tiny bedchamber three stories above, Fand and Finola hastily dressed for a midnight assignation.

"I can scarcely believe you are really going to do this," said plump, red-headed Megwen, as she sat up in bed and enviously watched her two roommates brush and braid their long dark hair. "Only think of the scandal if anyone finds out."

"No one will hear of this," Fand answered firmly, though her hands, as she braided her hair, were far from steady. "And Fflergant begged so prettily for a few minutes alone with me, how could I refuse him? It's really too bad—the way the King took it into his head last spring that Fflergant was the most terrible womanizer. Now that it looks like he is finally about to be knighted, the poor boy hardly dares to be seen even talking to a female."

Megwen laughed. "This won't help him much, if it gets out. To say nothing of *your* reputation. Such a persuasive young man he is, too. Mind you don't let him talk you into anything worse."

"You needn't worry about me," Fand said haughtily, as she slipped into her best brocaded red velvet gown. "I know my own worth, and I'll not settle for less." Indeed, Fand was an intensely practical girl, determined to make a brilliant marriage, and she was not about to go to bed with Fflergant—or any man—until after he placed a wedding ring on her finger.

She picked up her cloak and fastened it on. "Are you ready?" she asked her sister.

Finola nodded and reached for her cloak.

"Well, then," said Fand, "I suppose we ought to be on our way."

Teleri tapped hesitantly on Cadifor fab Duach's door. Minutes passed and no one answered, so she knocked again, much harder than before.

Still no answer, though someone ought to be within. Growing frantic, she pounded with both hands on the unyielding oak, rattled the handle, and pushed against the door with all her strength. But the door was locked, and still no one on the other side answered.

Something must be terribly amiss, she knew, but how was she to get inside and discover what that was? If only Glastyn were here, she thought, a locked door would present no problem.

She leaned against the door, remembering how the old wizard had taken her through the castle, stopping at every door to teach her the inner workings of the locks, and demonstrate how each might be opened by sheer effort of will. She supposed that this door and lock had been learned with all the rest, but she had no recollection of either.

A door of sturdy oak, held in place by wrought-iron hinges, built low and narrow for defense . . . How could she remember this one door among so many doors exactly like it? But when she turned and placed her hand experimentally on the handle, it seemed as if Glastyn's warm, parchment-dry hand covered hers for an instant, and a clear memory of the inner construction of the lock came into her mind at once.

After that, it took surprisingly little effort of mind and will to move the tumblers and open the lock. When she tried the handle again, the door opened readily.

The anteroom on the other side was cold and dark. She slid her hand over the wall, searching for the torch she knew must be there. Finding a torch, she reached into her pocket, searching for her flint and steel.

But then it occurred to her: What need had she for flint and steel, when she was a Wizard and able to summon fire with a simple command?

Encouraged by her success with the lock, Teleri placed the fingers of her free hand on the flammable end of the torch and whispered the name of fire into the darkness. Only at the last possible instant did she remember to snatch her hand away, narrowly avoiding a serious burn when the flax and resin burst into flame—a dangerous blunder that shook her new-won confidence.

Teleri glanced around the antechamber. Two boys and two manservants lay sound asleep on narrow pallets—too soundly asleep, as Teleri discovered, for no one awoke or even responded, not even when she held her torch directly over their faces.

She opened another door and passed into the next room, raising her torch high to illuminate the inner bedchamber. The big bed, all hung with crimson velvet, was empty. But over by a cold fireplace, Cadifor and his brother slumped in two high-backed chairs, apparently as deeply asleep as Cadifor's attendants. Between the two chairs stood a low table, on which someone had arranged a chessboard and silver playing pieces, two jeweled goblets, and a flagon.

Teleri placed the torch in a bracket above the fireplace, bent over

Cadifor, and listened to his breathing. Light and irregular. She leaned closer and sniffed his breath, detecting wine and spices and something else. She recognized the drug at once: a potent but slow-to-act soporific.

The wine cups and the flagon were empty; the two men had evidently consumed all the wine before succumbing to the drug. And when they awoke in the morning, with their minds all muddled by the drug, when they were asked to account for their actions on the night before—how could they ever hope to prove that they and the servants had all spent the entire night in an unnatural slumber? Even were she, Teleri, to come forward and back them up, who would believe her?

She knew that another witness was needed, someone able to identify the drug as she had done, but more credible than herself. Someone whose word carried weight with the King. That someone could only be Brother Gildas, the Royal Physician.

Teleri weighed her choices. She knew that the surest way to foil Diaspad's plot lay open to her. Indeed, if Ceilyn failed at his end, everything would depend on what she did here. But Gildas, like the other monks, lived in a tiny cell in the outer walls, and to go there, rouse the physician, and bring him back would take time. Meanwhile, Ceilyn might be in deadly danger—in danger, and in need of Teleri's help.

She continued to hesitate, agonizingly aware that she wasted precious seconds, knowing also that any decision she made might prove disastrous. But the decision, though painful, was not really difficult. She had already committed herself back there in the garden, and that choice made, only one logical course lay open to her.

She left Cadifor's bedchamber and headed for the lower levels and Gildas, hoping fervently that the decision she had just made was not one she would regret for the rest of her life.

"Poison," he cried, "O perfidious poison!" and fell to writhing upon the floor.

They all watched him, more in wonder than in fear, for many had eaten from the same plate, and only he had suffered.

From The Book of the White Cockerel

24.

Skulduggery

In the garden of the tomb, in the shadow of the Keep, the Princess and Calchas found Morc and Derry waiting for them. "Calchas—the light," said Diaspad, and Calchas uncovered a lantern he had carried under his cloak. A golden ball of candlelight materialized in the darkness.

"God of Heaven!" Calchas gasped, nearly dropping the lantern as he got his first glimpse of Morc's and Derry's new faces. "As God is my witness, a remarkable likeness!"

Derry smirked and struck a dramatic attitude. The effect was chilling, but not in the way he intended, producing a ghastly distortion of Llochafor's usually rigid features.

Diaspad took the lantern and held it up, the better to view her handiwork. "You made certain that both guards observed you closely?"

"Oh yes," Derry assured her. "The fellow outside the Queen's door even addressed us by name—as he thought. And there were no accidents this time: Both men will live to tell a tale in the morning."

"Excellent," said the Princess, lowering the lantern and turning back toward the tomb. "Let us hope that your friend the mason was worthy of his hire."

Derry knelt down beside the tomb. "I told him just what you told me. Two hands' breadth from the left, on the southern face. Look here: The bricks are laid so close together, you can hardly see a crack between them, and you'd never notice the lack of mortar unless you were looking for it.''

The unmortared bricks came out easily. Behind them, where the space between the inner and outer walls of the vault ought to have been filled with rocks and packed earth, there were only pebbles, twigs, and straw. Derry stepped aside, allowing Morc to dig a passage through the rubble and knock loose the blocks that formed the inner wall.

Calchas stood apart from the rest, his mind dwelling uneasily on the bones buried in the vault below. As his mother had forbidden him to be present when the bones were publicly examined, the boy could only guess what the casket actually contained. So much had been made of the Rhianeddi relics, by now, that his vivid imagination had conjured up something indescribably gruesome. When Morc finally broke through to the inner vault, Calchas turned away, convinced that he could detect a breath of corruption issuing from the tomb.

Hidden behind a piece of heroic statuary, Ceilyn watched the Princess and her henchmen break into the tomb. He had managed to slip past the gate and follow Diaspad and Calchas down the broad staircase into the garden, without being detected, and then, while the others stayed grouped together around the tomb, he had moved swiftly from one place of concealment to another, until he reached his present vantage point.

Though Calchas and Diaspad kept the hoods of their cloaks drawn so close over their faces that it was impossible to make out their features, he recognized them by their voices. By now, Ceilyn had seen and heard enough, and would have been on his way to summon help and surprise the tomb-robbers in the act, were it not for one small problem.

That problem was Calchas, who continued to stand some distance from the sepulchre, on the edge of the circle of lantern light, staring moodily into the darkness. In order to reach the stairs again, Ceilyn had to cross a large expanse of open ground and then ascend the staircase directly in Calchas's line of vision. Ceilyn did not think that Calchas, with his ordinary eyes, could see in the dark as far as the steps, but he could not be certain.

Ceilyn considered the other two possibilities: a door below the Chapel of St. March, and another door opening into the Scriptorium. But the former would be locked at this hour, and to go through the Scriptorium and from there search for help would entail a long walk around on the walls. Ceilyn did not want to take his eyes off the Princess for the time that might take.

All he could do was wait, hoping that Calchas would eventually give him an opportunity to reach the stairs, or that he could follow the Princess and her cohorts out of the garden, raising the alarm at his first opportunity.

While Ceilyn watched, Derry and Morc disappeared into the gap in the side of the tomb. A thump and a muffled curse announced their arrival on the floor of the vault. In another minute, one end of the casket appeared in the gap. Diaspad grasped the handle and pulled the rest of the box through. Then she opened the casket and examined the contents.

"These are undoubtedly the real thing. It would seem that our friends the Old Ones kept faith after all."

Calchas stole a brief look at the inside of the casket. He was relieved to discover that the bones were so ordinary. And they were very old. No taint of fleshy corruption, no stink of the charnel house rose up to offend his nostrils. It was almost disappointing.

Derry slithered back into view, followed a moment later by Morc. "We must hurry now," the Princess admonished them. "The guard will be changing soon." Yet she could not resist reaching into the casket and picking up one of the bones.

"How curious," she said. "The bones are warm to the touch."

"And what does that mean?" Calchas asked uneasily.

Diaspad took a moment to consider. "It may mean that one of *us* has an unexpected affinity for the bones," she said slowly. "Or it may mean—and this I think more likely—that we are not alone here in the garden."

In his hiding place behind the statue, Ceilyn silently cursed his luck and drew his sword out of the scabbard. A metallic hiss a few yards away warned him that Morc and Derry did the same.

"Look to the gate, Calchas," said the Princess. "We don't want our visitor slipping away." She straightened up, and tested the air with all her senses.

"Over there," said Diaspad, in a voice that set all three blades humming. "You'll find him over there, behind that statue."

* * *

In the Queen's garden, Tryffin fab Maelgwyn grew tired of waiting. "Likely she has changed her mind," he said to his brother. "I thought Fand had better sense than to keep her promise—even if you don't."

"Don't worry about Fand," Fflergant said confidently. "She'll come, and Finola, too. I depend on you to keep Finola—" Just then, the door at the base of the tower opened, and two graceful figures stepped through.

Fflergant's triumphant grin was quickly replaced by an expression of melting gratitude. "Dear heart, I knew I could depend on you."

Fand's delicate dark eyebrows came together in a frown. "I don't know why I agreed to come here. This is no better than madness."

"But such sweet madness," Fflergant said winningly. Slipping an arm around her slender waist, he planted a chaste kiss on one smooth white cheek.

Meanwhile, Tryffin took Finola by the hand and led her into the boxwood maze. "And just what does Tryffin imagine he is doing?" Fand demanded suspiciously. "We consented to meet you here, it's true, but if you think—" At that precise moment, Finola let loose a bloodcurdling scream.

Fand stiffened. "If your brother—" she began. But just then Finola reappeared and cast herself panting into her sister's arms.

"There is a *body* in there."

A moment later, Tryffin appeared, dragging the limp body of a guard into the moonlight. Fand's glance would have withered a less substantial man than Fflergant. "You told me that you were going to *bribe* this man."

"But I . . . You don't think that we . . ." Fflergant gasped. "Why, we never even saw this man. We just assumed that you ladies had convinced him to take a little walk."

"However this happened," said Tryffin, going down on one knee to examine the unconscious guard, "I think that you ladies had best go back to bed and leave everything else to us."

"But what do you intend to do?" asked Fand.

"See that this man has proper care, to begin with. But this isn't the kind of thing that can be hushed up, you know. By morning, the whole story will be all over the castle. And you certainly don't want your names circulating with it."

"Oh yes, I see," Fand said tartly. "You're willing to take the whole blame onto yourselves, just for the sake of our fair fame. Very gallant, I'm sure, but I can just see myself allowing you to do it!"

"Nothing you could say or do would make things any better for us," Tryffin pointed out. "And this man isn't dead. Chances are good he will be able to tell who actually attacked him." Tryffin rose to his feet in one fluid movement. "But even if Fflergant and I are blamed, the worst that can happen is that Cynwas would send us back home to Castell Maelduin."

"Well . . ." said Fand uncertainly. It was true that the King was hardly likely to visit any severe punishment on the sons of his powerful ally simply because he believed they had, in an excess of youthful high spirits, knocked one of his guardsmen over the head. "Oh, very well."

As soon as the ladies left them, Fflergant turned to his brother. "How do we manage to stumble into these things? Not much chance now, I fear, that either of us will wear a green baldric this side of the grave."

"Listen," said Tryffin. The unmistakable clash of steel on steel issued from the next garden.

"Christ Almighty!" breathed Fflergant. "What is happening here tonight?"

Tryffin knelt on the ground, divested the guard of his weapons. "Maybe an opportunity to play the part of heroes—instead of scapegoats," he said, tossing the sword to Fflergant, keeping a long knife for himself.

But when they reached the garden gate, it slammed shut in their faces and the massive wooden bar on the other side fell heavily into place.

Ceilyn came out from behind the statue fighting. He hurled the dark cloak at Derry, enveloping him head and shoulders, and launched himself at Morc, almost overbearing the big man with the fury of his onslaught.

This was no time for a chivalrous exchange of blows. Morc cried out in anguish as a knee drove into his groin, and the hilt of a broadsword smashed into his collarbone with shattering force. As Ceilyn jumped aside, Morc toppled.

By the time that Derry fought free of the cloak, Ceilyn crouched out of sight in the bushes. Nursing a set of bleeding knuckles, he planned his next move. Morc, he could hear moaning and retching, probably the victim of a broken collarbone, and Calchas and Derry, singly or together, did not worry him. But Diaspad was another matter entirely—there was no knowing what dark arts she might employ against him while the others kept him occupied.

He heard her soft, suggestive voice moving his way. "You might as well surrender at once," she said sweetly. "We have you outnumbered." But if she intended her words to conjure up phantoms to frighten him, Ceilyn was immune.

She came closer, and Ceilyn crouched lower, grinding his teeth in frustration. Something stuck at attacking an unarmed woman, no matter how dangerous she might be in other ways. He allowed her to pass right by him, heading in the direction of the Scriptorium, cutting off one means of escape.

He could smell Derry, heard him moving his way, thrashing about in the bushes. On hands and knees, Ceilyn circled around him, hoping to gain the advantage of surprise and finish Derry off before Calchas or the Princess arrived to interfere.

They met in a dark alley between two hedges, where Ceilyn relied on his superior night vision to increase his advantage. But a twig snapped underfoot, betraying his approach, and Ceilyn's attack came a fraction of an instant too slow. Derry parried the blow easily, and a fierce struggle ensued.

A sound behind Ceilyn warned him of Calchas's approach. As the boy darted into the fray, Ceilyn side-stepped and swung his sword up to block—almost too slow again.

And after that it was circle and retreat, retreat and circle, in a desperate attempt to keep one opponent or the other from getting at his back and taking him from behind. The clatter of steel rang in his ears. It seemed to Ceilyn that all his movements were slow and heavy, as though he fought underwater or in heavy armor. To make matters worse, the fingers of his left hand grew cold and numb, and the icy numbness continued to move up his arm, until he was forced to fight right-handed.

Circle and retreat, block and parry. Ceilyn's breath came painfully now. It made no sense . . . he should not tire so soon . . . yet his movements were so slow and clumsy it was only a matter of time before Calchas or Derry got past his guard.

Circle and retreat, strike high and swing low to block the next blow. Then Derry's sword took him in the side, just below the ribs, and the impact doubled him over.

There was a searing pain and a warm gush of blood, and Ceilyn heard Derry's exultant cry: "That will finish you, you Rhianeddi bastard!"

But those were the last things he knew or heard, because the ground suddenly hurled itself at his head, and everything went dark.

A short or a long time later, a distant voice penetrated that darkness, saying something he could not quite understand in a soft southern lilt. Gradually, the voice began to make some kind of sense. "Will you look at that—God—he's been bleeding like a pig!"

Light appeared behind Ceilyn's eyelids. Struggling to open them, he saw nothing at first but a formless paleness that hovered over him, only slowly taking on recognizable features: Tryffin fab Maelgwyn and, behind him, holding a three-branched candlestick, his brother Fflergant.

Ceilyn tried to sit up and managed to prop himself up on one elbow. But his side seemed to rip open, forcing him to lie back, gasping in pain.

"For the love of God, don't try to move," Tryffin advised.

"It's only a scratch, I'll be up in another minute," Ceilyn insisted weakly. He put a hand to his side, attempting to conceal the extent of the damage.

Tryffin sat back on his heels. "It looks like considerably more than a scratch to me."

"No, really," Ceilyn insisted, making another effort and sitting up. "It looks worse than it is. . . . These things often do."

He looked around him. "The others . . . where are they? You didn't let them get away?"

"We came down the little stair at the back of the chapel and broke the lock on the door. No doubt a hero like yourself could have opened it with a single blow, but we took longer. By the time we arrived, the garden was empty," said Fflergant. "Or so it seemed, until we found you. The gate's still barred, so whoever it was did this to you, they must have left by way of the Scriptorium. They could be anywhere in the entire castle by now, but if you will just tell us who it is we ought to be chasing after, we're willing to give it a try.''

"As you say.'' Ceilyn winced. ''They could be anywhere. In their own rooms . . . pretending they never left.'' He felt blood oozing between the fingers of his right hand, but the left remained numb and lifeless. He stared at his torn and bloody knuckles, tried to remember how that had happened. He had a dim memory of Morc looming over him, and a glitter of silver at the big man's throat.

"But who?'' Fflergant was saying—his voice sounded a long way off. ''You've neglected to tell us who. And what, in God's name, happened here?''

Ceilyn set his teeth, tried to get to his feet but failed. ''A woman, a boy, and two men. When I arrived . . . they were robbing the tomb. I couldn't see any faces—not to recognize them—but I knew their voices: the Princess and Calchas, Morc and his brother Derry. For the love of God,'' he added wearily, ''someone has to run and fetch the guards. And the King ought to be informed as well.''

"Yes, of course,'' said Tryffin. ''And a doctor for you and that poor fellow upstairs, if he's not come around yet.''

"No!'' said Ceilyn. ''Not on my account. I told you there was no need. And no need either, now that I come to think of it, to tell anyone you saw me here.''

Fflergant and Tryffin looked at him disbelievingly. ''I can't swear to the identity of the tomb-robbers,'' Ceilyn explained. ''And it's better if the Princess doesn't know I was here. Something Derry said leads me to hope that I wasn't recognized in the dark.'' But Derry would know that the man he had injured ought to be dead by now.

"That's not a request!'' Ceilyn added sharply. ''You are not to say a word to anyone.''

Tryffin and Fflergant exchanged a puzzled glance. They were on slippery ground, and knew it. If Ceilyn had come here on some business that Cynwas or Sidonwy wanted to remain a secret, they most certainly ought to do as he told them. Yet the circumstances were so odd and suspicious. . . .

"I don't think," said Fflergant cautiously, "that we are obliged to obey you. Ordinarily, yes . . . and you needn't tell us you have the authority to make things damnably unpleasant for us if we don't. But how are we to know, this time, that you aren't in this with the Princess—you and your lady-love, Prescelli?"

The pain in Ceilyn's side had subsided, but his injured hand was slowly coming throbbingly back to life. "If you know so much about my private affairs," he said acidly, "you also know that particular bit of folly is behind me now."

"I'm afraid," said Tryffin, "that that's not enough."

Ceilyn removed his hand from his side, discovering, to his relief, that the bleeding had stopped. "Will my oath satisfy you? That I am the Queen's man in word and deed, that I came here for her sake and for the sake of those near to her, and that nothing I have done tonight is against the King's interests, or your interests, or those of your family?"

The brothers exchanged another glance. "What will you swear by?" Fflergant asked.

Ceilyn could not think of an oath that would satisfy them. "You say . . . you decide."

"Swear by your own name, by your mother's, and your grandfather's," said Tryffin. "May the blood in your own veins turn against you, if you lie to us tonight. Not forgetting, as you swear your oath, that Fflergant, in receiving it, does so as Crown Prince of Tir Gwyngelli."

"Yes," said Fflergant, much impressed by the sound of this. "Swear me that oath."

Ceilyn took a deep breath and began: "I, Ceilyn Conyn Isfan mac Cuel mac Cadellin mac Cei . . ." But he was forced to stop, partway through. ". . . I don't know all your names." Fflergant supplied them, and Ceilyn went on to the end.

"You'll be on your way now," he said, as Fflergant and Tryffin rose to their feet.

"You're quite certain there's no need for a physician?" Fflergant asked.

"If I need one," said Ceilyn, "I know where to find one."

But once they left him, and he staggered to his feet, his side split open again. And the pain was so fierce, and the flow of blood so copious, it occurred to him that he might really die, this time. He could bleed to death like any other man, long before he reached the Wizard's Tower and Teleri.

She found him, lying cold and unconscious on the broad steps leading down to the garden of the tomb. The moon was high, but even allowing for the effect of moonlight, he looked more dead than alive. There was a great gaping wound in his side and sure to be internal damage as well, and a prodigious loss of blood, his clothes and the ground beneath him all sticky with it.

He groaned and opened his eyes. "Don't try to move," she cautioned him. "Wait until the bleeding stops. You've lost too much blood already."

"Not going to stop," he muttered. "Shapeshifter power's little use now. . . . Morc's brooch . . . silver brooch."

Because his transformations were not governed by the moon, it had never occurred to her before that silver might be poison to him.

"Help me away from here," he whispered urgently. "Before anyone . . ."

"Not yet," she said. "Let me bandage this first, and then I will find someone to carry you in."

"No," he gasped. "You don't understand. No one must know. Derry knows . . . I ought to be dead."

He tried to pull himself up the last few steps, but Teleri gently pushed him down, held him by the shoulders so that he could not move. "Ceilyn," she said firmly, "if you don't do as I say, you'll *be* dead, and that will be an end of it."

"Better that way," he insisted, "than burned for a warlock. Damn it . . . help me up!"

She slid an arm under his shoulders and helped him to sit. It hardly seemed possible that he could stand or that she could lift him, but somehow they accomplished it between them. He leaned heavily on her shoulder for support. Though he was not a big man, she was so tiny herself that she could scarcely bear his weight.

"Sorry," he mumbled in her ear. "I can't . . ."

"Don't worry," she said breathlessly. "I have you. I won't let you fall." But the warm blood spilled out of his side and over the arm and hand that supported him.

Their progress up the last few steps and across the yard was painfully slow. But she thought to herself: If I can open locks without a key, call fire out of darkness, surely I can do this.'' And somehow she found the strength.

She brought him, half dragging, half carrying, to her doorstep, and then into her bedchamber, where he slipped out of her arms and fell unconscious on the bed. She removed his swordbelt, took the knife from its leather sheath, and cut away his shirt and tunic.

She spent a long time sewing him up, during which time he remained mercifully unconscious. But he revived while she bandaged him, wrapping strips of white linen around his torso. ''It's deep, isn't it?'' he whispered.

Teleri nodded, securing the last bandage. ''Have you any idea how long you lay there bleeding?''

''Not long, I think. It did stop . . . before . . . then it began again, when I climbed the stairs. You have stopped it?''

''I think so,'' she said softly.

''But?'' he asked.

''But Ceilyn, if you are bleeding inside, or if you take a fever in the wound . . .''

''Yes, I understand. Ironic, isn't it? Who could have predicted I would ever be in danger of *bleeding* to death?''

She examined the cuts on the back of his hand. ''You never told me that silver was poison to you. I suppose I should have suspected. But how do you avoid touching it? It's everywhere at court.''

''No harm just touching it. But I break out in a rash if I wear . . . or handle it too much. And I get sick at my stomach if I drink more than a sip of wine . . . from a silver cup. Everyone believes that I eat off wood and pewter . . . because of a promise I made my father,'' he said weakly. ''I never lied. I did vow to live simply, you know.'' He closed his eyes.

''Ceilyn,'' she said softly. ''Ceilyn . . . would you like me to send for a priest?''

His eyes opened again. ''No,'' he said, surprisingly vehement. ''No priest. If I don't die, he'd be bound to wonder how I recovered. And I have . . . to be on my feet and apparently unharmed as soon as possible. I don't think that Derry or the others recognized me, but when nobody turns up dead, if they hear that I was hurt . . . Derry and Prescelli know enough about me between them . . . if they put the pieces together, and tell the Princess . . . she's bound to find a way to prove it against me.''

She opened the chest at the foot of the bed and took out a tiny flask. She uncorked the bottle and slipped an arm under his shoulders. "Drink this. It's syrup of poppy, mostly. It may ease the pain."

He nodded, obediently took a sip of the potion. Slowly, the pain drained out of his face. He closed his eyes and drifted off to sleep. She sat beside him for a long time, watching the rise and fall of his breathing.

She looked at him—not past or around him as she had been doing for some months now. She knew him better than she knew anyone, better than old Cadwr of Aderyn, better even than Glastyn. But she wondered if, before tonight, she could have accurately described him. Brown hair with just a hint of auburn in it, hazel eyes, fair complexion—she knew his coloring, but had never before noticed the way his hair curled, or the shape of his mouth and hands, the lean hardness of his body.

As she watched him move restlessly beneath the red coverlet, she could not help wondering if other women—women who were interested in those things—found him attractive. She remembered seeing Ceilyn and Prescelli together in the garden, and later . . . and she almost found herself wondering, as she had then, what it would be like. . . .

But by morning, Ceilyn might be dead. Never to hold or kiss any woman again, never to laugh or frown or torment himself with his own imperfections, never to be there at the laboratory door or the garden gate when Teleri looked up from her books or her gardening.

She looked at her hands. They were stained with his blood, and dried blood was caked all the way down the side of her gown. She stripped off her kirtle, poured water into the basin on the table by her bed. When she reached up to brush a stray lock of hair out of her face, she found Ceilyn's dried blood there, too.

She unbraided her hair and washed it in the basin. Then she put on a clean gown and sat down by her hearth and lit a fire. How long she slept there, with her head pillowed on her knees, she did not know, but her hair was dry when she heard Ceilyn moan and thrash about on the bed. In an instant, she was beside him.

"Teleri?" he whispered.

"I'm here."

"I thought . . . I thought I must be dreaming. I was dreaming for a moment there.'' He studied her face, the look of real tenderness he had never seen there before, the tears glistening in her eyes. He reached up with his good hand, and wrapped one strand of silvery fair hair around his fingers. ''I used to dream about you, you know. You fascinated me . . . when I first came to Caer Cadwy. You reminded me of a little bird, a little seabird, a grey-winged gull, always fluttering away when something startled you, or . . . ill-mannered boys like me stared at you. I watched you in those days . . . and I thought—''

''You thought that I was casting a spell on you,'' she finished for him.

''Yes . . . at first. Until it occurred to me that you were much more frightened of me than I was of you.'' He let the soft hair slide through his fingers, marveling at the texture. ''I would have spoken to you then, but you know, I never had a way with wild things.''

''I wish that you had spoken to me,'' she said. ''I was too accustomed to being alone, in those days, to know that I was lonely. But now . . . I think I needed a friend.''

He smiled sleepily. ''Yes, we do need each other, don't we? Because we are so much alike . . . and so different.''

''For both those reasons. For all the things that we share, and for all the things that we can teach each other,'' she said, taking his hand in hers.

''I do need you, Ceilyn,'' she added fiercely. ''If you need a reason to fight to live, think of that. I don't know what would become of me now, if you left me like this.''

''Not much chance of that,'' he said. ''I've waited too long, wanted you too much. You and I have a good many pleasant things to teach each other in the days ahead, and I intend to stay around for a long time.'' He drifted off, this time into a sweet, painless sleep.

And by morning, his breathing was faint but regular, his heartbeat strong. When she looked at the place on the back of his hand where the skin had been scraped away, there was no sign of injury, not even a scar. She knew then that the healing process had truly begun, and that Ceilyn would live to keep all his promises.